Dream Thief

DREAM THIEF

Stephen R. Lawhead

CROSSWAY BOOKS ● WESTCHESTER, ILLINOIS
A DIVISION OF GOOD NEWS PUBLISHERS

For Harold

The center of every man's existence is a dream.

G. K. Chesterton

Part I

GOTHAM

CHAPTER ONE

THE MAN is sleeping. The huddled mass of nerves and sinews rests easily on the bed; outwardly there is no movement. Inwardly, the brain hums with random activity. A maintenance force continually monitors the man's internal activity by way of a vast trunkline of nerves.

At rest the network is dark. Momentary sparks of electrical impulses shunt their messages to and fro along the axons. At the outer fringes, the individual beads of light link up and begin their journey up the spinal column like midnight trains heading for the city. Eventually they arrive and send their impulses off into the tangled circuitry of the brain where each flash, briefly noted, dies out. Except for these momentary pinpoint flares, the system is dark and quiet.

Gradually, the sparks increase their activity; more messages are coming in, flooding the circuits. The lines begin to hum, glowing with energy. Impulses of light speed to their destination deep with the labyrinth, illuminating their passage. Soon the darkened webwork is alive with light—arcing, tingling, pulsing, throbbing with electricity. The man is waking.

The dreams had been at Spence again. He could feel their lingering presence like a dimly remembered whisper. They were unsettling in a vague sort of way. Nothing he could put a finger on—haunting. There was a word that seemed to fit. He felt haunted.

Now, nine weeks into the project, he was not so sure he wanted to finish. That was a strange thought. For almost three years he had worked for nothing else but the chance to test his theories in the most highly respected advancement center: the orbiting space lab GM. It had taken him a year to write the grant proposal alone. And he was here; against considerable odds his project had been chosen. To back out now would be professional suicide.

Spence raised his head carefully from his pillow. He removed the scanning cap—a thin, plastic helmet lined with neural sensors—and placed it on its hook over the couch. He wondered how the night's scan had gone, but realized he was feeling less and less interested than before. When he had started the project, his first thought was to run to the control room to see his scan as soon as he awoke. Now he seldom bothered, although he still occasionally wondered. He shrugged and stumbled into the tiny sanibooth to begin his morning routine.

He emerged from his quarters and hurried off to the commissary without stopping by the control room. *I'll check in later,* he thought, not really caring if he did. He headed down the axial and joined the flow of traffic. The space station, even one the immense size of GM—or Gotham as it was called by those who considered it home—was beginning to wear on him. He glanced around at his colleagues, and at the well-scrubbed faces of the student cadets, and knew that he was in the presence of the brightest minds on any planet. But he watched as the cadets followed one another dumbly into Von Braun Hall and thought, *There must be something more.* Knowledge was supposed to set one free, wasn't it? Spence did not feel very free.

He suddenly felt an urge to lose himself among the eager students, and so allowed himself to be pushed into the lecture hall. When the line stopped moving he flopped into a cushioned chair. The overhead lights dimmed and the automatic transcriber poked its hood up from the seat directly in front of him. He absent-mindedly flicked a switch at the arm of his chair which sent the hood sliding back into its receptacle. Unlike everyone else around him, Spence had no intention of taking notes.

He swiveled his head to his left and was shocked to find himself sitting next to a skeleton. The skeleton's sunken eyes blinked brightly back at him and the thin skin of its face tightened in a grimace. On anyone else it would have been a hearty grin.

"My name is Hocking," said the apparition.

"I'm Reston." Spence's mouth was dry and he licked his lips, trying not to stare.

Hocking's body was painfully thin. Bones jutted out at sharp angles, and his head wobbled uncertainly on his too-slender neck. *Why isn't the man in a hospital bed somewhere?* wondered Spence. He looked too weak to endure even sitting through the lecture.

Hocking rested in the hi-tech comfort of a pneumochair; his body, which could not have weighed more than eighty pounds, sank into the supporting cushions. He looked like a mummy in a sarcophagus. A thin tangle of wires made its way out of the base of Hocking's skull and disappeared into the headplate of the chair. *Obviously mind-controlled,* Spence considered; the chair probably monitored its occupant's vital signs as well.

"What level are you?" Spence heard his voice asking. It was an automatic question, one that opened every conversation between Gotham's inhabitants.

"A-level. Sector 1." Hocking blinked. Spence was immediately impressed. He had never heard of anyone reaching that designation. To most people it was merely a theoretical possibility. "How about you?" Hocking nodded slightly in his direction. Spence hesitated. Ordinarily he would have been proud to share his designation, but it was embarrassing to him now.

"Oh, I'm C-level," he said, and let it go at that. Spence knew that most of his countrymen never progressed beyond the lower sectors of E-level. Even those allowed aboard advancement centers were mostly D-level—although none were ever below Sector 2.

Spence realized he was staring again. Hocking shifted his weight awkwardly in the chair. It was clear that he suffered from some neuro-muscular ailment—he had no muscle control at all, or at least very little. "I'm sorry," Spence said at last. "It's just that I've never met an A-level before. You must be very proud of yourself." He knew it sounded foolish, but the words were already out.

"It has its advantages," Hocking replied. He flashed his grimace again. "*I've* not met many Cs."

It was impossible for Spence to determine if the skeleton was joking or not. True, Cs were a rarity, and Bs were almost nonexistent, but on Gotham there were plenty of both. Before he had time to wonder further, Hocking spoke again.

"What is your specialty, Reston?"

"I sleep," said Spence sarcastically.

"And do you dream?"

Spence prickled at the notion that this spectre might know something about his special problem. He also noticed that Hocking's voice came not from his throat but from a source at either side of his head. The chair amplified his voice as he spoke. This colored Hocking's speech with an eerie cast, as it overlapped his natural voice somewhat and gave Spence the impression that Hocking was speaking a duet with himself. Hocking noticed his glance, and his voice automatically lowered a tone. Hocking had only to think and some need was accomplished. Having never actually seen one of the rare and expensive bio-robotic devices, Spence wondered what else the chair could do.

The lecture began and ended much as lectures do. Spence remembered nothing of it, except the feeling all through that the person sitting next to him was watching him, appraising him, sizing him up for some unknown purpose. Spence squirmed in his seat uncomfortably.

When at last the lecture was over, he stood up, turning to tell Hocking that he would see him again. On an orbiting university, no matter how huge, one always ran into the same people. But as he turned, he realized Hocking was already gone. He thought he glimpsed the back of the white ovoid chair in the flood that moved out the doors of the lecture hall, but he was not sure.

Spence wandered along to the commissary nearby. One was conveniently located on every level of the station since scientists hated to be more than a few steps away from their coffee. He fell into the short line and picked up one of the blue circular trays and a matching plastic mug.

He slid into a booth at the far side of the dining area and dosed his hot black liquid with a liberal amount of sweetener. His mind drifted back to the day he left Earth. He could still see his father beaming at him through the tears and he smelled the soft citrus scent of oranges in the air. They were sitting at a table beneath an orange tree in the courtyard of the visitor's center at the GM ground base.

"Just relax and don't tense up," his father was saying. "You won't black out that way. Don't forget to . . ."

"I won't forget. I don't have to *fly* the shuttle, you know. Besides, it isn't like it used to be."

"I wish your mother could see you . . . She would be so proud."

"I know, Dad. I know."

"Do you think you could write now and then? I know I don't know much about what you're doing—your research and all—but I like to know how you are. You're all I've got now . . ."

"The effect of long-term space travel on human brain functions and sleep patterns. I'm part of the LTST project. I told you. I'll be fine—it's a small city up there. And you have Kate. She's here."

"You and Kate. That's all."

"I'll try to write, but you know how I am."

"Just a line or two now and then so I'll know how you are."

A loudspeaker hidden in the branches of the tree crackled out, "GM shuttle Colossus now ready for boarding. Passengers, please take your places in the boarding area."

The two men looked at each other. It was then Spence saw his father cry. "Hey, I'll miss you, too, Dad," he said, his voice flat and unnatural. "I'll be back in ten months and I'll tell you all about it."

"Good-bye, son," his father sniffed. Twin tracks of moisture glistened on his face. They hugged each other awkwardly, and Spence walked away.

Spence still saw the tears and his father standing in his shirt sleeves under the orange tree, looking old and shaken and alone.

An unbroken horizon of gently rolling hills stretched out as far as Spence could see. They were soft hills of early spring; the air held a raw chill under gray overcast skies. Silhouetted in the distance, Spence could see people moving among the hills with heavy burdens. He walked closer for a better look.

The people were old—men and women working together, peasants dressed in tatters. They wore no shoes, though some of them had wrapped rags stuffed with straw around their feet to keep out the cold. In their long bony hands the peasants held wattle baskets filled with stones. Those with full baskets were walking stoically toward a dirt road, single file, with their burdens on their shoulders. The baskets were obviously heavy; some of the peasants strained under the weight.

Spence was overcome with pity for these unfortunate people. He turned to those working around him, pulling stones from the soil. The stones were white as mushrooms, and big as loaves of bread. Spence bent down to help a struggling old woman lift her heavy load. He pleaded with her to rest, but his words were unheeded. The woman neither looked at him nor made any sign that she had heard him.

He ran from one to another trying to help them, but always with the same result—no one seemed to notice him in any way.

Spence sat down, brooding over his ineffectiveness. He noticed the air was deathly silent, and when he looked up all the peasants were gone. They had left the field and were moving along the road. He was all alone. Suddenly, he felt a tremble in the earth and at his feet a white stone slowly surfaced from beneath the ground. As he looked around other stones erupted from the soil like miniature volcanoes. Spence became frightened and began running across the field to catch up with the last of the retreating figures.

When he caught up with the peasants they were standing atop the high bank of a river, its dark, muddy water swirling below. The workers were dumping the rocks into the water. He rushed up, breathless, just in time to see the last few peasants empty their baskets. To his horror, he saw that the baskets contained not stones now, but heads. He stepped closer as the last heads tumbled into the water. In grim fascination he recognized Hocking, and Tickler, and then with a shock he saw his own.

"Are you dreaming, Spencer?"
"Yes."
"Is it the *same* dream? The same as before?"
"It is. But it's over now."
"You may sleep a little longer and then awaken when you hear the tone."

A high-pitched electronic tone awakened Spence from a deep sleep. He spun around in the chair and glanced at the digiton above the console. He had been asleep only twenty minutes. Tickler was still nowhere in sight. He rubbed his face with his hands and wondered idly where his assistant managed to hide whenever he needed him. He rose from the chair and stretched.

Soon Tickler came bustling into the room. He was all apologies. "I am sorry to have kept you waiting, Dr. Reston. Have you been here long?"

"Oh, about an hour, I guess . . ." Spence yawned.

"I was, uh, detained." Tickler's sharp features gleamed with a slight perspiration. It was clear that he was worked up over something. Spence decided it was too late to start another session that day.

"I think we'll try it again tonight. I won't need you 'til then. I suppose you have something to do elsewhere?"

Tickler looked at him, his head cocked to one side as if examining some new variety of mushroom spore. "I suppose." He scratched his chin. "Yes, no problem. Tonight, then."

Spence handed him a sheaf of folded printouts which he required to be deciphered and charted in a thick logbook—a purely meaningless task, since the same computer that spit out the information could chart it as well. But Spence preferred the personal touch.

"Thanks," he said without meaning it. Tickler took the printouts to an adjacent room and set to work. Spence watched the back of his head as he weaved over the printouts and then left the lab.

Spence made his way down to Central Park—the vast circular expanse of tropical plants and trees grown to help recycle the carbon dioxide of Gotham's fifteen thousand inhabitants. The park formed a living green belt around the entire station and provided a natural setting for relaxation and recreation. The place was usually crowded, though quiet, with people seeking refuge from the tyranny of duralum-and-plastic interiors. He had nothing else in mind other than to lose himself among the ferns and shrubbery and let the day go.

His first thought upon reaching the garden level was that he had discovered a fine time to come—the section was virtually empty. He saw only a few strolling couples and a handful of administrative types sitting on benches. He took a deep breath. The atmosphere was warm and moist, reeking of soil and roots, vegetation and water: artificially controlled, he knew, but he could not help thinking that this was exactly as it would be back on Earth.

He walked aimlessly along the narrow winding paths looking for a private spot to stretch out and meditate upon the state of his being, to think about the dreams and try to get a hold on himself. He was not afraid of "going mental"—a term they used to describe a person cracking under space fatigue—although that was something everyone eventually had to face; he knew that wasn't it. But he also knew he was not feeling right and that bothered him. Something on the dim edges of his consciousness was gnawing away at the fibers of his mind. If he could figure out what it was, expose it, then he would be able to deal with it. Presently he came upon a secluded spot. He stood for a moment deciding whether to stay or look further. With a shrug he parted the ferns and stepped into the semi-darkness of the quiet glade.

He sat down on the grass and tipped his head back on his shoulders. High above him the sunlight slanted in through the immense chevrons of the solar shields. He saw the graceful arc of the space station slide away until it bent out of sight. One could tramp the six kilometer circumference of Gotham at the garden level and achieve the illusion of hiking an endless trail.

Ordinarily the green and quiet soothed Spence's troubled mind, but not today. He lay back and tried to close his eyes, but they would not remain closed. He shifted position several times in an effort to get comfortable. Nothing he did seemed to make any difference. He felt ill at ease and jittery—as if someone very close by was watching him.

As he thought about those unseen eyes on him, he grew more certain that he *was* being watched. He got up and left the shaded nook, glancing all around to see if he could catch a glimpse of his spy.

He struck along the path once more and, seeing no one, became more uneasy. He told himself that he was acting silly, that he was becoming a prime candidate for that room with the rubber wallpaper. As he scolded himself he quickened his pace so that by the time he reached the garden level concourse he was almost running. He glanced quickly over his shoulder to see if he was being followed; for some reason he half-expected Hocking's egg-shaped chair to come bobbing into view from behind a shrub.

Still looking over his shoulder he dashed through the entrance and tumbled full-force into a body entering the garden. The unlucky bystander was thrown to the floor and lay sprawling at his feet while Spence stood blinking, not quite comprehending what had just happened.

"Sorry!" he burst out finally, as if prodded by electric shock. The green-and-white rumpled jumpsuit of a cadet flailed its arms in an effort to rise. Spence latched onto a swinging arm and hoisted the suit to its feet. Only then did he glimpse the bewildered face which scanned him with quick, apprehensive eyes. "I'm Dr. Reston. BioPsych. Are you hurt?" he volunteered.

"No, sir. I didn't see you coming. It was my fault."

"No, I'm sorry. Really. I thought . . ." he turned and looked over his shoulder again. "I thought someone might be following me."

"Don't see anybody," the cadet said, peering past Spence into the garden. There was nothing to be seen except the green curtain of vegetation, unbroken but for the careless splashes of white and yellow flowers blooming at random throughout the garden. "I'm Kurt. And I'm BioPsych, first year. I thought I'd met most of the faculty in my department."

"Well, I'm not an instructor. I'm research."

"Oh," Kurt said absently. "Well, I've got to get back to work." The cadet started off. "Glad to meet you, Dr. Reston. See you around."

On the overgrown donut of the space station the cadets always said, "See you around." Spence appreciated the pun.

CHAPTER TWO

THE UNBROKEN horizon of gently rolling hills stretched out as far as Spence could see. The same horizon, the same hills as in previous dreams. In the distance he saw people moving among the hills with heavy burdens. Closer, he recognized these as the peasants who labored in rags to rid the arid hills of stones, which they tumbled into their rough twig baskets with their skinny hands. All was familiar, painfully so, to Spence who had lived the dream often.

He watched as the barefoot peasants shifted the weight of the baskets upon their bony shoulders and shuffled single file along the road. Others around him still strained to lift the stones, white as mushrooms and big as loaves of bread, from the soil. He knew he was powerless to help them in any way; his words and actions were ignored. He was invisible to them.

Spence again sat down, brooding over his ineffectiveness. Again the air was deathly silent; the peasants were gone. He felt the earth tremble at his feet as a round, white stone surfaced from beneath the ground. He looked around him and other stones were erupting from the soil like miniature volcanoes.

When he stood he found himself once again atop the high bank of a river. The dark, muddy water swirled in rolling eddies below. The last peasant dumped his basket into the water and Spence heard a voice call his name. He turned and saw a dozen huge, black birds wheeling in the air. He followed them and realized he was standing on an immense plain which stretched limitless into the distance. Rising in front of him on that flat, grass-covered plain stood an ancient, crumbling castle.

He lifted his foot, the landscape blurred, and then he stood within the courtyard of the castle before a scarred wooden door which he tried and found open. An empty marble corridor of stairs spiraled down away from him. He followed it. Deeper it wound, eventually arriving at the entrance to a small chamber, dimly lit.

Spence rubbed his eyes and stepped forward into the room. The light of the room seemed to emanate from a single source—an incredibly large egg floating in the center of the chamber. He watched, horrified, as the egg began bobbing slightly and rose up higher into the air. As it rose it revolved and he then saw what he feared—the egg was the back of Hocking's chair. But it was upside down. As it slowly revolved, he saw Hocking sitting serenely in his chair, laughing. The chair floated closer. Hocking threw him a toothy grimace and became a leering, malevolent death's-head.

Spence turned and fled; the egg-chair-death's-head pursued him. He raced for the door at the end of the corridor and burst through to discover an inky black night scattered with a thousand stars. Over his shoulder Earth, a serene blue globe, rose in the sky as he stumbled bleeding across a rocky, alien landscape. . . .

Spence watched the shuttle pull away from the huge arcing flank of the space station. He stood on a small observation platform overlooking the staging area watching the routine arrival of supplies and the departure of personnel going down, or rather back, to Earth on furlough. He wished he was going with them.

He had never felt more like giving up than he did right now. His life had settled into a dull aching throb between depression and loneliness. He did not know which was worse: the black haze through which he seemed to view life around him, or the sharp pangs which arrowed through his chest whenever he immersed himself in the stream of people moving along the trafficways and realized that he did not really know a single other soul.

But underlying both of these unpleasant realities was, he knew, the very thing which he dreaded most: the dreams.

Since that afternoon in Central Park nearly two weeks before, he had begun to feel those invisible eyes on him every waking moment. He fancied they watched him while he slept. He felt his sanity slowly slipping away.

He gazed up through the giant observation bubble into the velvet black void of space burning with a billion pinpoint flares of nameless stars. He was gazing at the rim of the Milky Way but remained oblivious to the sight. "What am I going to do?" he whispered aloud to himself.

He turned away as the shuttle's white bulk dropped slowly from view below him. There was a whir as the docking net was withdrawn and a faint whispered hiss as the inner airlocks equalized. Spence yawned and thought again, for the billionth time, how tired he was. He had not closed his eyes to speak of in the last three days—quick cat-naps, a few minutes here and there was all.

He had been avoiding sleep like a youngster avoids the dentist when the tooth throbs and pain numbs the jaw. He hoped that by some miracle the pain, the dreams, would just go away. At the same time, he knew that hope was futile.

He would have to have some real sleep soon if he was to remain even partially upright and coherent. He had the odd apprehension that he was turning into a zombie, one of those pathetic creatures of myth destined to roam the twilight regions neither completely dead nor fully alive. No thoughts, no feelings. Just an ambulatory carcass directed by some demon will beyond itself.

But the idea of sleep had become repugnant to him. Becoming a zombie was less frightening than the thought of the nightmare which waited for him to drift into blissful peace before enfolding him in its awful insanity.

Spence shook his head to clear it; he was beginning to ramble. He looked around and realized that his unattended steps had brought him to Broadway.

Turning to the left he started to make his way back to the Bio-Psych section and the sleep lab, to his own quarters—there again to wrestle with the question, "to sleep, or not to sleep"—but something caught his eye and he stopped and looked again. All he saw was a brightly illuminated sign, the same as any other which identified the trafficways of Gotham. Spence stood staring at the sign for several sec-onds before he realized what had arrested his flagging attention. The words OFFICE OF THE DIRECTOR and the red arrow pointing the opposite way seemed to hold a special fascination for him in his be-fuddled state.

Without thinking about it, or making a decision at all, he discov-ered his feet moving him mechanically along toward the director's of-fice. And, without surprise, he knew why he was going there. Perhaps subconsciously he had intended to request a psych leave for some time. Now, in his sleep-deprived condition his body was taking him where he had wanted to go all along but had not dared, for lack of nerve.

Spence moved blindly along, somehow managing to avoid the others hurrying to and fro along the trafficway. Twice he caught strange looks from passersby, but their glances of questioning concern failed to register. It was as if he had withdrawn to an inner mental cell and only peered out curiously from behind the bars. The reactions of others meant nothing to him.

After much turning, and several level changes—Spence was oblivious to it all—he arrived at AdSec. As he stood contemplating the partition which separated him from the receptionist inside he came to himself.

"I can't go in there like this," he muttered. He spun around, spied a convenience station, and took himself inside. He peered into the mirror as he leaned over the duralum basin and marveled at the sight he presented. Red-rimmed eyes burned out of a pallid, expressionless face; unwashed hair started from his head as if afright; deep lines drew a pliant mouth into a frowning scowl.

It was the very visual representation of how he felt: the outer man imitating the inner.

Spence shook his head in disbelief and filled the basin with cold water. He let the water run until it threatened to overflow and then plunged his hands in, scooped up a double handful and splashed it on his face.

The sting of the water cleared his senses somewhat and he felt better at once. He repeated the procedure several times and then made an attempt to flatten his hair. He dried his hands at a nearby blower and then stepped from the vestibule once more into the trafficway.

With some hesitation he pushed the access plate and the translucent partition slid open slightly. He stepped woodenly in and forced a grin at the tight-lipped receptionist who greeted him with the flash of a professional smile and the standard, "Good afternoon. Whom do you wish to see, please?"

"I'm—I've come to see the director," said Spence as he looked around for his office among the several which opened off of the central reception area. He saw it and started toward it.

"I'm sorry," called the receptionist, "do you have an appointment?"

"Yes," Spence lied, and kept on going. He approached the door, pushed the access plate, and walked in.

He was not expecting anything in particular, but the room which opened before him startled him with its size and regal appointments. Compared to his own crabbed cube of a room, and all the other totally space-efficient quarters, chambers, and labs he had been in on the station, this one was palatial in its utter disregard for constraint.

He could not help gawking as he stared at the beautiful expanse of open space which met his eyes. The room was a huge octagonal chamber with a high curving dome above a broad area, part of which was given to a sort of loft which was reached by a spiraled rank of broad steps. The princely spaciousness of the quarters was further enhanced by a huge observation bubble which formed part of a convex wall over the loft. The effect to an observer like Spence was one of entering a great hall with a window opening onto the universe beyond.

His feet were sunk into several centimeters of thick, buff-colored carpet. Green plants of several types and miniature flowering trees splashed color against pale slate-gray walls and tawny furnishings. Notably absent was any hint of aluminum or other metallic surfaces. It was an office such as one would find in one of the great bastions of corporate power back on Earth, but rarely on a space station. Rank, thought Spence, did indeed have its privileges.

"Yes?" said a voice close by. Spence jerked around quickly, immediately embarrassed.

"I'm sorry. I didn't see you when I came in."

The bright, china blue eyes which met his sparkled. "That's all right. I'm often overlooked."

"No, I didn't mean . . ." He broke off. The young lady, several years his junior, was laughing at him. He colored at that, feeling ridiculous and completely out of place. He did not know what to say and for a few moments stared unabashedly at the girl sitting casually at a low desk just inside the entrance to the mammoth office.

She wore a jumpsuit like everyone else on GM, but hers was a light powder-blue—definitely not regulation. Her long blonde hair hung down in loose ringlets, swept back from her temples and secured somehow at the back of her head to fall in curls along her slender, well-formed neck.

"Was there something?" she asked. The smile this time was accompanied by just the barest hint of a flutter of her long, dark lashes.

"Oh, yes." Spence brought himself forcibly back to his mission. "I have come to see the director."

"Why, may I ask?"

Spence started. How impertinent. "I'd rather discuss that with the director himself, thank you," he said stuffily, and hoped it had put her back in her proper place. The nerve.

"Certainly," she smiled again. "Only if I knew what it was about it might help you to get in to see him sooner, that's all."

"I had hoped to be able to see him at once."

"I'm afraid not."

"But it's very important. I must see him today. I won't take but a few minutes of his time. Couldn't you just tell him it's private and urgent?"

"No."

Again that impertinence. Spence, in his exhaustion, felt a hot current of anger rising to his head. He willed himself to remain calm. "May I wait?" he asked, nodding to a chair set in among a grove of miniature palms.

"If you like," said the girl coolly, and as Spence moved to take his seat she added, "Only it will most likely be a rather long wait. He . . ."

"I don't mind," interrupted Spence firmly. He plopped himself down in the soft fabric cushions of the chair with a demonstration of defiant resolve.

The young woman went back to her work without another glance at him. For a while he ignored her and busied himself with studying the dimensions of the director's official lair. Tiring of that he moved his attention by degrees to the woman at the desk opposite him. She had begun entering data into a terminal at the side of her desk. He marveled at her quickness and dexterity. That was obviously why she had been hired for the job of assistant to the director, observed Spence; it was not for her tact.

As he watched, he formed several other opinions about her. She was, he determined, of the giddy sort, given to supressed giggles and flouncy sentiments. Undoubtedly frivolous. Very likely not a brain in her head. At the barest hint of anything intellectual she would probably flutter her eyelashes and simper, "I'm afraid that's too deep for little ol' me."

She was pretty, there was no denying that. But, Spence told himself, it was a superficial beauty which had no lasting quality. For someone unparticular, she would make a suitable mate. But for one like himself she would never do. Never in a billion chronemes.

It did not occur to Spence that he had just painted her with exactly the same unflattering strokes he painted nearly every other woman. That, for him, was easier than just admitting that he had no time for women, that romance would interfere with his research and career, that he was afraid of women because he did not trust himself to be faithful to both an intimate relationship with another human being and to his work.

He had a certain right to be afraid; he had seen too many gifted men burdened by cares for a wife and family succumb to second-rate research centers and teaching jobs. The young Dr. Reston intended to fly as high as he could, and no woman was going to hold him down.

The young lady squirmed under his unrelenting gaze. She tilted her head and peered back at him. Their eyes met and Spence looked quickly away. But soon he was staring at her again. She smiled and then laughed as she turned to confront him.

"Is this your way of getting a girl's attention?"

"Excuse me?" He was unprepared.

"Staring. Is there something you want?"

"Was I staring? I'm sorry. I didn't mean . . . Look, I only want to see the director. When will he be available?"

The girl glanced at her watch and said, "Oh, next week some time. Maybe Thursday."

"What?" Spence leaped from his seat and bounded over to the desk. "I thought you said I could wait!"

"You may wait as long as you like, but he won't be back until next Thursday."

"You said . . ." Spence sputtered. His hands clenched themselves in angry fists at his side.

"I said it would likely be a rather long wait. You interrupted me before I could finish."

"Is this the way you treat everyone on important business?"

She flashed him a defiant smirk. "No, only those who waltz in demanding to see the director without an appointment."

She had him; he was defeated and disgraced. It was true, he had behaved like an idiot. A wave of cool shame instantly quenched the anger just as the flames threatened to touch off his temper.

The young secretary smiled at him again and he did not feel so bad. "So, we're even," she said. "Now, would you like to start again at the beginning?"

Spence only nodded.

"Fine. Is this personal business or official?"

"Well, personal."

"See? That wasn't hard. I'll put you down for an appointment Friday morning first thing. His assistant will call you."

"You mean you're not his assistant? I thought—"

"You thought I was, I know. No, I'm only filling in while they are away. Mr. Wermeyer is his assistant."

Now Spence felt doubly the fool. He wished only to be allowed to melt into the carpet and slink away. "Thank you," he muttered and backed away slowly. The partition slid closed, terminating the episode in the director's office. He sighed and made his way back to his quarters more hopelessly tired than ever.

CHAPTER THREE

THE OLD head came up slowly. Lizardlike. The large oval yellow eyes gazed outward from under half-closed lids. Yellowed skin, the color and texture of ancient parchment, stretched tautly over a smooth, flat skull and hung in folds around the sagging neck. Not a hair remained in the scalp; not a whisker, not an eyelash.

A thin, slightly rounded band stretched across the smooth brow.

This circlet pulsed with a purplish light of its own, throbbing as waves of energy flashed and dimmed.

Hocking could see him as if wreathed in smoke—clearly in the center of his field of vision, but shimmering and indistinct on the periphery. The face regarded him with a steady glare, the expression beyond contempt or malice though traces of both were there, beyond weariness or simple age. Cold. Reptilian. It was an expression utterly alien to any assignable human emotion.

In a lesser being the face and its mysterious scowl would have created at least a sense of dread, if not outright fear, but Hocking was used to it.

"Ortu." He said the name softly, distinctly. "We are ready to proceed with the final experiment. I have found a subject especially receptive to the stimulus." Hocking licked his lips and waited for a reply.

For a moment he doubted whether the image before him had heard, but he knew it had. The reply would come in time.

"Proceed, then, as I have instructed." The words were spoken evenly, but with an unusual coloring—the faintest suggestion of a foreign accent, but indecipherable.

"I thought you would be pleased, Ortu. We can begin at last." Hocking's upper lip twitched enthusiastically. "At long last . . ."

"Pleased? For what reason should I be pleased? Oh, there are so many." There was no mistaking the venom in the voice. "Pleased that it has taken so long? That even my inexhaustible patience has been tried time and time again to no result? That my plans should rest on the feeble efforts of a creature too stupid to comprehend the smallest fraction of the work?" The circlet on his forehead flashed brightly.

Hocking endured the sarcasm bravely. "I have been particularly careful in my choice of a subject this time. He is a sleep scientist named Reston, and he's quite malleable. We will not be disappointed again, I assure you."

"Very well, begin at once." Ortu closed his eyes and his ancient head sank once more.

"It shall be done." Hocking, too, closed his eyes and when he opened them again the glimmering image had vanished. He sat in his chair in the center of his darkened quarters. The whisper of a smile flitted across his skeletal features. Now, at last, all was ready. The final test could begin.

Spence stepped from his sanibooth actually whistling. He felt better than he had in weeks. Rested, alert and happy. He had slept the whole night long the sleep of the dead. And not one dream had intruded upon his slumber—at least not the dreams he had learned to fear of late:

those without color, without form, which seemed born of some alien, sterile intelligence, which came into his mind and left him shaking and drained, but without memory.

Whatever had been bothering him was now gone, or so he hoped. Perhaps it had only been the strain of adapting to the confines of the station. GM was the largest of the orbiting advancement centers; it was also the highest. Actually, it was the world's first self-sustaining space colony, maintaining an orbit three hundred and twenty thousand kilometers above the earth around a point astrophysicists called libration five. That distance, or rather the *thought* of that distance, sometimes had a strange effect on newcomers. Some experienced symptoms of claustrophobia; others became nervous and irritable and had difficulty sleeping, or had bad dreams. Often these problems were not immediately apparent; they developed slowly over the first weeks and months of the rookie jumpyear and had very little in common wth the allied problem of space fatigue, which only seasoned veterans—those in their fifth or sixth jumpyear—seemed to contract. That was something else entirely.

So Spence, feeling very pleased with himself that he had weathered the worst and had come through, rubbed his body with a hot, moist towel to remove the fine blue powder of the personal sanitizer and then tossed the towel into the laundry port. He dressed in a fresh blue and gold jumpsuit and made his way into the lab to reweave the dangling threads of his project.

He slipped into the lab quietly and found Dr. Tickler hunched over a worktable with an array of electronic gear and testing equipment spread out around him.

"Good morning," said Spence amiably. There was no real day or night, but the Gothamites maintained the illusion, and the station flipped slowly over on its axis on a twelve-hour cycle to help in the deception.

"Oh, there you are! Yes, good morning." Tickler bent his head around to observe Spence closely. He wore a magnifying hood which made his eyes bug out absurdly, like two glassy doorknobs splotched with paint.

"Anything serious?"

"One of the scanners is fritzing. Nothing serious. I thought I would take the opportunity to set it in order."

Spence detected a slight rebuff in Tickler's clipped tone. Then he remembered he had missed the work assignment he made for last night.

"I'm sorry. I—I wasn't feeling very well yesterday." That was true enough. "I fell asleep. I should have let you know."

"And the days before that?" Tickler tilted his head forward and raised the hood to look at him sharply. Before Spence could think of a suitable reply, his assistant shrugged and said, "It makes no difference to me, Dr. Reston. I can always get another assignment—not with so prestigious a colleague, perhaps, but one where my services will be taken seriously.

"You, on the other hand, I suspect, would find it somewhat difficult to secure an assistant at this late date. You would be forced to postpone your project, would you not?"

Spence nodded mutely.

"Yes, I thought so. Well, the choice is yours, but I will put up with no more of this. I respect your work, Dr. Reston, and I will have mine so respected. Now"—he smiled a stiff little smile devoid of any warmth —"now that we understand one another I am sure there will be no further problems."

"You are correct," returned Spence woodenly. He felt like a schoolboy who had been tardy once too often and now had been properly scolded. That was bad enough, but he hated being reminded that he was only on GM by way of a generous grant and could not chart his own course beyond the narrowly defined limits of the grant. He had no money of his own, at least not the kind needed to pay for a berth aboard even the smallest space lab, let alone GM. By sheer brainpower alone he was here; that and the goodwill of the GM Advancement Board.

"I can assure you that there will be no further misunderstandings. Now, we will begin where we should have last evening."

As they worked together, readying the lab for the next battery of experiments, the happy inner glow rekindled Spence's spirits. He did feel better than he had in weeks. And, after all, it could have been worse for him: Tickler could have requested reassignment. That would have really bolixed up the works and made him look bad before the Board.

In the end he came around to feeling fairly grateful to Tickler for the reprimand. He had it coming, maybe even needed it to settle his mind on his work once more. And he felt a little sorry for Tickler—an older man, himself a C-level Ph.D., reduced to playing lab assistant and watching younger men advance in his place. One had to feel sorry.

As he passed by the control booth with its huge reading board he caught a glimpse of himself in the reflection of the half-silvered window. He saw a young man leaving his twenties, lean, slightly above average in height, straight of limb and steady of hand. Large dark eyes looked out from under a brown thatch of hair which, no matter how it was combed, always appeared rebellious. The face showed a quick intelligence and by the thrust of a firm jaw a decisive resolve almost bordering on stubbornness. It was a face which did not easily show emotion, but one which was saved from being completely cold and aloof by a full, sensitive mouth perched above a deeply-cleft chin.

The shift wore away and by the end of it he was ready to begin the next round of sleep experiments. He celebrated the return of his will to work by treating himself to an hour in Gotham's arcade playing *Rat Race,* his favorite hologame. It was one of the latest generation of holo-games featuring a biofeedback variable that homed in on the player's mental and emotional reflexes. In his present good spirits Spence racked up half-a-million points before the rats caught him and he turned the game over to a group of impatient cadets. He left the noisy arcade and was soon strolling idly along his favorite path among the great green ferns of Central Park.

He had stopped to steep himself in the damp, earthy atmosphere of the place—eyes closed, face tilted upward to receive shield-reflected sunlight, drawing great gulps of air deep into his lungs—when he heard a rustle behind him. Reluctantly he turned to allow the other to pass, and as he opened his eyes discovered himself blinking into two liquid orbs of china blue fringed with long dark lashes.

"*You!*" Spence jumped back involuntarily.

The disarming intruder laughed and replied gaily, "I thought it was you; I see I was right. I never forget a face."

"You startled me. I didn't mean to shout at you."

"You are forgiven. I've been following you. You certainly wander around an awful lot. I almost lost you several times."

"You were following *me?*"

"How else was I going to apologize? I happened to see you in the concourse—I always come down to the park, every day."

"Apologize?" Spence kicked himself for babbling like an imbecile. "For what?" he added.

"For my shocking behavior yesterday. I'm sorry, really. I had no right to treat you that way. Very unprofessional of me."

"Oh, that's all right," he muttered.

The young lady chattered on. "It's just that it was close to the end of the shift and I was getting a little giddy. I do that when I get tired. And anyway, Daddy has been gone so long I'm afraid I've kind of let the decorum of his office disintegrate."

"Daddy?" Another inner kick.

"Oh, there I go again. I'm always getting ahead of myself some-how."

"You mean your father is the director of GM?"

"Yes—the colony, not the corporation."

"Then you're his daughter . . ." *Buffoon! What are you saying?*

"That's right," she laughed. "It makes it nice that way."

"You work for him? I mean . . ."

"No, not really. I was just helping out because both he and his assistant are gone. I didn't have anything else to do. They've been gone all week setting up some sort of field trip or something."

"That sounds interesting." Spence was dying for something half-intelligent to say. At least he had passed imbecile and was now merely moronic.

"Does it? I suppose so, to a scientist, I mean. I have no desire to go tramping around on Mars or anywhere else. I didn't even like the jump up here very much."

Spence had heard about such "field trips," as she called them; at least once a session various cadets would be chosen to take a trip to one of the extra-terrestrial bases to see firsthand the work going on there. Mars was without doubt the deluxe trip. Anyone who made that one would add an appreciable amount of prestige to his credentials.

"When is the—ah, field trip supposed to take place? I hope you don't mind my asking. Would you like to walk for a while? My name is Spencer. Spence."

"I know. I looked it up in your file, Dr. Reston." To his look of mild surprise she added, "Oh, it wasn't hard. I told you I never forget a face. And I remembered the bar code on your jumpsuit."

"Right." They began to walk slowly among the ferns and leafy trees. Now, however, Spence was aware of a new scent among the musky odors of the tropical garden. A fresh clean scent: lemons, he decided.

"I'm Ari. It's short for Ariadne, only if you ever call me that I'll never speak to you again."

For an instant Spence considered that would be an extremely unfortunate event, but then realized he hardly knew the girl at all. "Hmmm." He screwed up his face into a contemplative scowl. "Ariadne—that's Greek mythology. She was the daughter of King Minos of Crete. She gave her lover Theseus a ball of twine which he used to escape the labyrinth of the minotaur."

"Very good!" She laughed and clapped her hands. "Not one person in a thousand remembers that."

"Oh, I regard myself something of a classicist," remarked Spence with a mock-serious air. "Ari. It's a nice name. I like it."

"I like yours, too." They stopped walking. As Spence turned to look at her he could feel his nerve evaporating. "Well, it's been nice talking to you," she said. "I do have to go now. Maybe we'll run into each other again sometime." She hesitated. "Bye."

She turned quickly and ducked under a large frond and Spence watched her dart away like a deer, her long blonde hair flagging behind as she disappeared among the green shadows. He stood perplexed by the strange mix of emotions which assailed him. He was sorry to see her go; and yet he told himself that he could not feel that way, that he had never seen her before yesterday, that she was just like every other girl he had ever met. Still, a vague sense of loss settled on him as he continued to walk the garden paths.

CHAPTER FOUR

SPENCE STUMBLED bruised and bleeding across a rocky, alien landscape. Over his shoulder Earth, a beautiful, serene blue globe, rose full in the black, formless sky. He winced with pain as needlelike shards of tiny cinders sliced the soles of his bare feet and scraped the flesh away from his knees and the palms of his hands when he fell. He felt a cool wetness on his cheek and lifted a hand to his face.

Tears. He was crying.

Then he was standing on the top of a low mountain overlooking a lush green valley. Around him a gentle breeze played among tiny yellow flowers, shifting their sunny heads playfully with each gust. The air bore a sweetly pungent scent and seemed to vibrate with a faintly audible tinkling sound which reminded him of bells.

In the valley below, small white houses, each surrounded by its own neat acreage, dotted the slopes in an orderly fashion. He could see the minute figures of people going about their daily chores, moving in and out of the little houses. An atmosphere of unfathomable peace and wholeness enfolded the valley like a golden mist and Spence was crying —heartbroken because he did not belong in that valley, among those people who lived in such simple splendor.

The air grew cold around him. The fragile yellow flowers shriveled at his feet. The tears froze on his face. He heard the empty howl of frigid winds roaring down as if from incredible heights. He looked down in despair and watched the verdant valley wither and turn brown. The whitened wisps of dried grass and leaves flurried about him in the savagely gusting wind.

He shivered and wrapped his arms tightly across his chest to keep warm. He glanced down at his feet and saw that he stood upon hard, bare earth. He saw something sparkle and beheld a small pile of diamonds glittering in the icy glare of a harsh, violent moon. They were his tears—frozen where they had fallen. The earth would not receive them.

Spence was awake long before he opened his eyes. He simply lay and allowed the waves of feeling to wash over him, filling the cavernous emptiness inside his chest with fiercely contending emotions. He felt like a leaf tossed in a tempest, a rag blown before the glowering storm. He lay with his eyes clamped shut and tried to make sense of it all.

At last the storm subsided and he wearily opened his eyes and got up, placing the scanner cap on its hook. He sat for a moment on the edge of the couch experiencing a mild light-headedness which he had not noticed before. The moment passed and he stood up slowly, and in doing so his hand brushed his headrest. He stared at it as if he had never seen it before. The light sky blue of the pillow's case bore two darker stains side by side. He touched them lightly, knowing what they were. The pillow was damp with his tears.

". . . And I can't help feeling that it was a mistake to use myself as a subject in the research, that's all." Spence was speaking quietly, but with some conviction to Dr. Lloyd, head of the BioPsych department of Gotham. He had sought out Dr. Lloyd as a sympathetic ear.

"But I disagree, Dr. Reston. I was on the academic board that evaluated your grant proposal. I voted for it; I think it is quite sound, and if I may say so, quite insightful. How else can a scientist fully evaluate subjective data without himself experiencing the phenomena which produce the data? Your work with tyrosine hydroxylase interaction with catecholamines is little short of revolutionary. I think you have touched upon a very viable research model, and one which, if successful, could pioneer the way for some very prime developments in sleep science. Your research is key to the LTST project as a whole. Speaking as a colleague, I'd like to see you continue. I think that is imperative."

Spence was not hearing what he had hoped to hear. Dr. Lloyd, with great enthusiasm, was defending Spence's own proposal against him.

"Perhaps there would be a way to restructure the project, maybe—"

Dr. Lloyd smiled benignly and shook his head from side to side slowly. "You haven't given it a proper chance. Why not see where it will take you."

"I could interpose another subject into the same design—I wouldn't have to . . ."

"No, no. I can understand your anxiety. But you have already done so much. How do you know that you are not even now evincing some of the signs of LTST yourself? Eh? Have you thought of that?"

"But—"

"Dr. Reston, believe me, I admire your work. I would hate to see anything augur ill for the progress you've already made. Your career is in its ascendancy. You will go far. But as a friend I must warn you. Don't tinker with your design now. It would not look good to the Board. You would not wish to appear, shall we say, undecided? Wishy-washy?

"I am afraid the Board would take a dim view of any changes at this late date. And, as a member of the Board, I would have to agree."

"I suppose you're right, Dr. Lloyd. Thank you for your time." Spence rose reluctantly to his feet and his colleague led him to the door with his hand on Spence's shoulder.

"Any time, Dr. Reston. Please feel free to stop by any time. That's what I'm here for." Lloyd chuckled, delighted that he could be of help to the legendary young Dr. Reston. "Go back to your work. I should tell you we're all watching your progress with the greatest interest."

"Thank you. Good-bye, sir."

"Don't mention it. Good-bye. Come by any time."

Spence had met with a brick wall of his own making. He had not considered it before, but it made sense that GM would want him as much as he had first wanted them. His presence would lend to the overall prestige of the Center, and now that they had him they were not going to let anything happen to him that would lessen his value as a contributor. They were not about to let anything stand in the way of Dr. Reston's glorious success, not even Dr. Reston himself.

He walked gloomily back to the lab, feeling trapped. What was happening to him? Was he losing his sanity? Was this how it started?

The dreams were back, and they were beginning to exert more and more control over his sleep state. He awoke in the morning drained and unrested, his emotions on the ragged edge. The dreams themselves he could not remember. They were shadowy forms which moved barely beyond the edges of consciousness.

Was Lloyd right? Was he undergoing the strain associated with long-term space travel? If so, how was that possible? He had not been on GM long enough. Was there some mechanism which acted to somehow speed up his own experience—the encephamine injections, perhaps? Or was there some other explanation?

Only one thing was certain: the dreams had returned to haunt him.

Perhaps he should do as Dr. Lloyd suggested, simply follow where his mind would take him. Spence shrank from the thought. There was something in him that rebelled at that suggestion. Irrationally rebelled, it seemed, because it was solidly logical advice. Yet something within Spence—his spirit, his conscience, that tiny inner voice—screamed a warning at the thought of abandoning his reason to the design of the project. Even if it was his own project.

Spence sought to quell this inner mutiny as he walked back to the lab. There was no reason not to continue as planned—no scientifically objective reason.

He entered the lab with the faint whisper of the sliding partition. The lights were off and Tickler was gone. The lab was quiet. He stepped in and the door slid closed behind him, leaving him in complete darkness and silence.

He turned to fumble in the blackness for the access plate in order to switch on a lighting panel overhead. As he wheeled around, the faintest trace of a glimmer caught his eye. He stopped and turned back slowly.

In the darkness of the empty lab he perceived a strange luminescence, a sort of halo, barely visible, hanging in the air in the center of the lab. He closed his eyes and opened them again and the slight greenish glow remained. As Spence watched, the radiant spot seemed to coalesce, to focus and grow brighter by degrees, and he moved toward the glow as if drawn by a heavy magnetic force.

The halo was quite visible now; it even threw off a gentle reflection all around. Spence walked slowly around it, his muscles tensed like a cat ready to spring. It was like nothing he had ever seen. Whichever way he moved, the shimmering halo showed always the same face to him: a luminescent wreath of pale green light shining with a gleaming radiance which shifted and danced under his gaze. The center of the halo remained unaffected by the light. Through it he could see the dim outlines of objects on the other side of the room.

Spence edged cautiously closer, sideways like a crab. He attempted to look away, but his curiosity, or some greater force, held his attention firmly. He could not resist.

Now he was standing very close to the glowing presence in the center of the lab. So close that he could feel a tingling sensation on his hands and face, a tiny prickling of the flesh as if with extreme cold. He raised one hand toward the aura and saw it surrounded by the greenish cast.

Gradually he noticed a movement within the halo—a very transparent shimmer of deepest blue, almost beyond human vision. The radiance intensified and cast out beams which glittered gold and silver as they fluoresced within the green aura of the halo.

Although he stood rooted firmly in his place, he experienced the unnerving sensation of traveling very rapidly into the halo, as if he were being sucked into a swirling vortex of cold blue fire. With this sensation came a quickening of his physical senses. His heart began beating rapidly, his breathing labored, sweat beaded up on his forehead and neck.

He was feeling very weak and dizzy, teetering on the brink of consciousness, when he felt a unique sensation: the flesh at the base of his neck began creeping upward in tiny pinpricks over his scalp. For one brief instant he wondered what that could mean. What could it be? The answer hit him like a shock: every hair on his head was standing on end.

Spence opened his mouth to cry out, but no sound came. He was held in the steely grip of a terror he could not name, a fear which came swimming at him from the darkened corners of the room—of his mind. He could not move or scream or look away. Only endure.

Some small part of his mind withdrew from the horror which now twisted his features. It watched with dread fascination as the green aura flared brilliantly and the whirling blue lightning slowed and began to take shape. To his rational inner eye it appeared that a scene was taking place behind a filmy curtain of light, but the movements were too indistinct and too remote to be understood.

Gradually he became aware of a sound which perhaps had been there all along, but had gone unnoticed. It was the thin, needlelike tinkling of tiny bells. This he heard not with his ears, but inside his head and on the surface of his skin. And hearing it now, in this way, turned his blood to ice water in his veins. For up to this moment it was a sound heard only in his dreams.

With an effort he raised his hands and clamped them over his ears and screamed with every fiber of will left in him. Then he toppled insensible to the floor.

CHAPTER FIVE

"HERE HE IS." The flashlight beam played over the slumped figure on the floor. "Passed out."

"I'll get the lights," said a second, slightly higher pitched voice.

"No, leave them off. He might wake up," replied the first.

"What shall we do with him? We can't just leave him on the floor . . ."

"Why not? We can come back later."

"He might remember."

"Right. Let's put him in the sleep lab."

"Good idea. Hook up the scanner, too. That way he won't be sure. Even if he remembers he won't be sure."

"I'll take his feet. Careful, don't wake him up."

To Spence it seemed as if his mind returned like a rock dropped into a lake. He felt his awareness returning, falling slowly through the void of darkness, while he himself waited floating to receive it.

The floating sensation continued for some time. When he tried to move his head he was overcome by a powerful dizziness and the feeling that he was falling in slow motion into a vast, bottomless pit.

So he lay motionless and tried to collect the fragments of his thoughts—what was left of them. He remembered talking to Dr. Lloyd and then returning to the lab. That was all—only darkness after that. And yet there must be something more. For here he was, if his guess was correct, in the sleep lab lying on the scanner's cav couch. How he had gotten there he could not say.

From the control room he heard the soft chime of the session clock. Then Tickler's voice sounded over the speaker, drifting down from above like snow. "The session is terminated, Dr. Reston. Shall I bring up the lights?"

"Yes," he heard himself say, "bring up the lights."

The overhead panels began to glow, faintly at first but steadily until he could make out the ordinary cylindrical dimensions of the room. He sat up slowly as the last waves of dizziness rolled over him. He gripped the sides of the cav couch and started awkwardly to his feet, aware that Tickler was watching him closely from the control booth.

He felt a tug and realized that he was wearing the scanning cap. He slipped it off and tossed it back onto the couch in the depression his head had made, and then moved slowly, as in a dream, toward the booth.

"Good scan this session, doctor," Tickler said happily.

"Bring it to me after breakfast." Spence shook his head groggily.

"Anything wrong?"

"No. I, uh, didn't sleep very well, that's all."

"You remember, of course, that you have scheduled to interview cadets for the assistantships today."

"Tickler, do we really need an assistant? I mean, the project is just myself and you. It isn't as if we were in HiEn—those guys want thirty people for every experiment."

"Each department is required to take a cadet."

"Well, couldn't Simmons take an extra one? I don't really see where we need to . . ."

"BioPsych is a small department, yes," Tickler sniffed. "But it will hardly expand if those of us in a position to encourage the interest of bright young minds fail to take full advantage of the assistantship program."

Spence hated Tickler's testimonials; so to prevent further aggravation he replied as evenly as he knew how, "You are right, of course. In fact, I think it would be a good idea for *you* to interview the cadets yourself."

"Me? But, Dr. Reston, I—"

"I don't see why not. You have a good feel for that sort of thing. I will, however, want to approve your choice. When you've found the right candidate for the job, bring him to me."

Spence ducked quickly out of the control booth, bringing an end to the matter. He stepped into the corridor and began threading his way to the commissary. Once free from Tickler's annoying presence his mind returned to the mysterious problem of his blackout.

In the jumble of the crowded cafeteria he found seclusion to properly mull it over in his mind. Noise, considered Spence, was just as good an insulator as perfect quiet. Maybe better. With a proper level of random sound the mind turned naturally inward, completely shutting out the rest of the world.

The clash and clatter of trays and utensils and the din of voices and the unrelenting drone of insipid background music which filled the busy commissary raised the noise factor to the perfect volume for contemplation. With his tray of scrambled eggs, grapefruit, and coffee he made his way to an empty table in the corner past others dining on an assortment of foods. He saw spaghetti, roast beef, tomato cups, chicken salad, pancakes, omelettes, and hot dogs—breakfast, lunch and dinner served simultaneously to accommodate the schedules of various shifts. The sight of roast beef and gravy sitting next to scrambled eggs and toast always threw him; it did not look right somehow.

Spence chewed thoughtfully and at the end of his meal was no closer to an answer than before. The missing hours were simply gone. Ten hours—maybe twelve—could not be accounted for. Not by his own memory, at any rate. He gulped the last of his tepid coffee and determined to check the scan in the lab—the scan tape would show a moment-by-moment account of his mental whereabouts on its four red wavy lines.

He entered the lab with the sigh of the partition and saw that Tickler had gone. He went to the control booth and found the spool where Tickler had left it, duly cataloged and ready for filing after his inspection.

Spence snapped the seal and unrolled the strip to the beginning, watching the yards and yards of wavy lines unravel through his fingers. At the start of the tape he saw the date and time notation: EST

5/15/42 10:17 GM. The scan continued for nine-and-a-quarter hours without interruption. Each peak and valley, every blip of an alpha spark or beta flash was duly recorded. He saw the even, rhythmic progress of his night's sleep. His presence was accounted for.

But what about *before* the scan? Where had he been? What had he done? Why couldn't he remember?

Spence rolled up the tape and resealed the spool. He had to get out of the lab and think—or not think. He decided on Central Park.

The humidity increased noticeably as he approached the concourse entrance to the park. It was only when he smelled the slightly musty fragrance of the garden's atmosphere that he realized how flat was the carefully controlled and filtered air of the rest of the center.

He stepped down onto the turf and threw a hand up to protect his eyes from the dazzling brightness which engulfed him instantly. The solar shields, those immense louvered slats which could be opened or closed to regulate the amount of light allowed in upon the garden, were open wide in an approximation of high noon. Spence stood blinking for some moments until his eyes became used to the brilliant light, then struck along one of the many meandering pathways. He followed the path toward the center of the garden and the greensward, hoping to find an empty bench in one of the secluded nooks formed by the trees and hedges which were landscaped to provide privacy.

A quick survey of the perimeter showed that all the benches were taken, mostly by young women soaking up the sun's beneficial rays. He had just about completed the circuit when he stopped in front of the last bench. It, too, was occupied. He was about to turn away when he realized he knew the owner of the upturned face and closed eyes.

"Mind if I sit down?" he asked. The blue eyes fluttered open and a hand rose to shade them.

"Oh, Dr. Reston—Spence, I mean. Please, do sit down. I'm taking up far more than my fair share of space."

He sat down at the extreme end of the bench and looked at the young lady, realizing that he had nothing at all to say to her. He smiled. She smiled back.

Idiot! Spence shrieked to himself. *Say something!* The smile lingered, evaporating at the edges.

"Did you have a successful meeting?" Ari saved him by starting the conversation.

"Meeting?" *Oh, no!* he thought, *I'm babbling again!*

"You've forgotten already? You had a meeting with my father—or was that some other Dr. Reston?"

"Is he back then?"

"You mean Mr. Wermeyer hasn't called you yet? I could say something to him, if you like. Daddy's been busy since he got back, but you should have been called. I'll see what I can do; I have a certain amount of pull, you know."

"No, I wouldn't think of asking you. I'll wait my turn."

"Maybe it *was* another Dr. Reston, then. The one I had in mind was quite insistent. Very urgent—matter of life and death."

"Apparently the crisis has passed—I had time to cool off. Thanks for the offer, though. I still do want to see him."

"Well, you may be in luck if you care to wait for a little while. My father's coming down to get me when his meeting's over. We're going to lunch together. You could talk to him then."

"I wouldn't intrude—""

"Don't be silly. I don't mind. Anyway, I wouldn't have offered if I still didn't feel a little guilty about treating you so disgracefully."

"I've forgotten all about it. Believe me."

"You're nice." She smiled again, and Spence felt the warmth of it touch his face like the rays of the sun.

And in that moment, without either one of them thinking very much about it, without desiring it at all, they became friends. It was a natural thing for Ari; she had many friends, and made friends easily. For Spence, though, it was quite a different thing. He did not make friends easily—especially with women. He didn't know how to talk to them and never felt comfortable around them. So it was with a shock that he realized some time later that he had spent over an hour talking with Ari without for a moment feeling ill at ease.

And it was with a pang of genuine regret that Spence saw the portly, though dignified, form of the GM director approaching from across the lawn.

"Oh, Daddy!" shouted Ari, jumping up. Spence stood as well. "Daddy, you'll remember Dr. Reston—"

"Yes, indeed!" The man called "Daddy" held out a wide, firm hand which Spence took in his own and received vigorous shaking.

"It is good to see you again, Director Zanderson." The last time Spence had seen the director had been at a reception for the new grant winners a few days prior to making the jump.

"I am always pleased to see one of our brightest new colleagues. In fact, I believe you have your first review coming up, do you not? Yes, I believe so. I saw it on my calendar. How do you like it here, Dr. Reston? You're finding it all you hoped it would be?"

"Yes, and much more," Spence said truthfully.

"Daddy, I've asked Spence to join us for lunch. I know how you love a new audience." Ari put her arm around her father, who looked amused.

"Daughter, the decorum of my office!" She kissed him on the cheek. "What will Dr. Reston think? Tell me, did you ever see such an impertinent young lady?"

Spence was saved from having to answer by Ari who announced, "I'm starving. Let's go to lunch this instant, or you will both have to carry my limp and languishing body through the garden to the commissary. How would that suit your precious decorum?"

"Dr. Reston, I regret my daughter's shocking manners." His eyes twinkled at the sight of her. "But I reiterate her invitation. Would you join us?"

There seemed to be no graceful way out, so he said, "I'd be delighted."

CHAPTER SIX

THEY WERE walking back to their respective places: Spence to his lab, the director to his office, and Ari to the cultural arts center. It had been one of the most enjoyable lunches Spence could remember. They had eaten not in the commissary, as he expected, but in one of Gotham's four excellent restaurants, the *Belles Esprit,* a very commendable copy of a French café.

Spence had not previously visited any of the restaurants and was surprised and pleased to find them quite different from the commissaries. He was less surprised to find that, like exclusive restaurants on Earth, they were quite expensive. The commissaries were free; the restaurants were not.

They had dined on hearts of palm and artichoke vinaigrette and quiche lorraine. And Spence had come away feeling soothed and refreshed—as much by the company as by the food and atmosphere. The Zandersons, father and daughter, proved themselves very convivial hosts. They had so drawn him out that he talked a great deal more about himself than he ever did as a rule, but he had enjoyed it. And more than once during the meal he had looked up to discover Ari's bright blue eyes watching him with a curious expression.

Now they were nearing the junction tube where he would leave them to go back to the lab. For one who had inwardly shuddered at the luncheon invitation he was honestly sorry to see their short time together end.

"I hope you'll consider my offer," Director Zanderson was saying. "I think you'd find the experience rewarding. It would even help in your research, I dare say. A smart young man like yourself—I imagine you could devise a few experiments that would make the trip quite worthwhile."

Spence was only half listening to the director's proposition. "I'm afraid that with my review coming up . . ." he started to object.

"Oh, that's just a formality," grinned the director. "Besides, should you decide to lead one of the research teams on the trip the review could be postponed, or perhaps waived altogether. Terraforming is the future —very exciting business. I wish I could go back myself; but . . . duties, you know."

He looked a little awkwardly at the director. Ari noticed his discomfort and came to his aid. "Oh, Daddy. Terraforming is *your* great mania, it isn't everyone's. Quit badgering him about it. I'm sure Spencer has better things to do than to go roaming about on a dusty old rock. I know I do."

The director clucked his tongue. "Such a worrisome girl. Well, I won't press you for an answer, Dr. Reston. But I hope you'll think it over. The Martian experience *is* truly fantastic."

"I will think it over. And thank you both for a most enjoyable lunch. It was really very nice."

"I'm glad you could join us. I always like to get better acquainted with my colleagues. Well, good-bye."

"Good afternoon," said Ari. They turned and strolled arm-in-arm off along the main axial. Spence watched them go and then started back along the tube to the lab.

Tickler was waiting for him when he returned. The fussy assistant appeared miffed about something; he gave Spence a series of sideways glances which Spence figured were supposed to represent disapproval. Spence happily ignored the vague reproofs—after all, he had just eaten lunch with the director. There was nothing which could even remotely threaten his self-esteem at that moment.

"Well, Tickler, how are we coming along this afternoon? Are we ready for tonight's session? I plan to increase the electroencephamine quotient by another five percent. I would like to test the scanner before we run the experiment."

"I haven't forgotten," Tickler said. He nodded toward the control room and Spence saw that they had a visitor. "Perhaps you will remember assigning me to secure our new assistant."

"So soon? You certainly didn't waste a minute. Very well, let's meet him." He motioned to the cadet who sat watching them through the control window. The young man got up and came to stand beside Tickler.

Spence offered his hand to the short young assistant. "I see that you have already met Dr. Tickler. If I know him he's probably put you to work already. I'm Dr. Reston."

"Yes—we've already met," replied the stranger as they shook hands. Spence looked at him a little closer; though the cadet seemed familiar, he could not place him.

"I'm sorry . . ."

"I don't expect you'd remember," said the cadet. "I bumped into you in the garden concourse one day a week or so ago."

"Kurt, wasn't it?" He did remember the incident.

"That's right. Kurt Millen. First year. D-level; sector 1."

"Well, very good to have you aboard. I hope we can make this an interesting assignment for you."

"I take it you approve of my choice?" asked Tickler. Spence did not see the queer smirk which accompanied the question or he might have had second thoughts.

Instead he said, "Yes, yes. I think Kurt will do just fine. He can begin by helping you ready the scanner test while I prepare the encephamine."

The shift proceeded uninterrupted, and as he worked Spence thought again of his talk with Ari and embarrassed himself with the warm feelings which accompanied those thoughts. *There is something about that girl,* he told himself. *Be careful,* his cautious inner voice replied.

The golden mist had vanished in the empty howl of frigid winds roaring down from untold heights. The lush, green valley withered and turned brown. The whitened wisps of dried grass and the petals of tiny yellow flowers flurried around him in the savagely gusting wind.

He shivered and wrapped his arms tightly across his chest in an effort to keep warm. He stared down at his feet and saw that he stood upon hard, barren ground. Around him he saw the sparkling glint of diamonds glittering in the icy glare of a harsh, violent moon.

They were his tears—frozen where they had fallen. The hard earth would not receive them.

Spence turned and lurched away, and he was instantly standing on a vast open plain under a great windswept sky where thin clouds raced overhead to disappear beyond the horizon. As he watched he was overcome by the urge to follow those feathery clouds, to see where they went.

He began to run, lifting his feet and leaning ahead. But his legs did not obey properly. Each step dragged more slowly than the last, as if his strength were being mysteriously sapped away. Soon his legs had grown too heavy to move. He felt himself sinking into the arid soil, sucked down as by quicksand.

He struggled to move as the dry red sand rose above his knees, but his weight pulled him down and down by centimeters. He screamed and his voice rang hollow in his ears. He looked around and saw that he was trapped in a great glass bubble and the sand continued to rise.

Now it seemed to be falling out of the sky, burying him alive. He felt the gritty sting and heard the dry, bristling hiss as it pelted down on him. It filled his hair and eyes. He looked up and saw the glass bubble narrow far above him and sand pouring through a tiny opening to come trickling down. As the sand rose to his chest he pushed it away with his arms, but it fell relentlessly and soon he was deeper than before.

He screamed again and heard the ring of silence, knowing that his cries could not be heard beyond the glass. As the sand closed over his head he realized that he was trapped in an hourglass, and the sand had just run out.

Spence awoke with a gasp and sat bolt upright on the couch. The sleep chamber was perfectly dark—a black, velvety darkness which pressed in on him with an oppressive weight. He could feel it enfolding him, covering him, smothering him.

He wanted to get up, to run away and escape the awful presence of the dream. But an unseen force held him in his place. He lay back down slowly and as he did so he saw something in the heavy darkness which made his breath catch in his throat.

Directly above him, midway between the couch and where he judged the chamber ceiling to be, a very faint greenish glow hovered, shimmering in the dark. He sank back into the cav couch and watched as the glow intensified and took the shape of a luminous wreath with tiny tendrils of light radiating out from it. The center of the wreath was dim and unformed, but he sensed that something dark and mysterious boiled within the radiant halo.

There was a familiarity about the glowing green halo which puzzled him. He felt as if he had seen or experienced it before somewhere— but where? He could not remember. Still, the sense of recognition persisted, and with it mounting fear.

His body began to tremble.

In the center of the halo the dim outlines of amorphous shapes could be seen weaving themselves of blue light. Subtle and indistinct, they flared and subsided; shifting, roiling, synapsing inside the green aura. The transparent blue fibrils sparked silver flashes that glittered when they touched the green halo.

The thing seemed to tug at him, drawing him up and into it. He had the sensation of falling. He reached out a trembling hand to ward off the fall. Fear arced through him like a high-voltage shock. His heart seized in his chest, clamped tightly in an unseen fist. Blood drummed in his ears.

The swirling inner eye of the shining wreath distilled into a translucent core, a round, glimmering mass made up of tiny pinpoint flecks of pure light. The ovoid shape spun slowly on its axis. Spence dug his fingernails into the fabric of the couch as his flesh began prickling to the thin, needlelike tinkling of a sound felt rather than heard. The sound of his dreams.

Spence fought a wave of nausea rising in him. Sweat beaded on his forehead and upper lip. He struggled weakly to look away, but the force of the shining thing held him fast. His mouth opened in a silent scream of terror; his tongue cleaved to the roof of his mouth.

Still the shimmering mass rotated slowly and Spence sank even further into the depths of the nightmare. He watched it—turning, turning, refining itself, pulling together, creating itself out of atoms of light. With eyes wide and horror-filled Spence at last recognized the solidifying shape. It was a face. And a face he knew too well to feel anything but the utmost dread and repulsion.

Staring out at him from the blazing halo were the skeletal features of Hocking.

CHAPTER SEVEN

"HELLO, DAD. Listen, thanks for coming down to the center . . ." The image on the screen peered back at him apprehensively. "Can you see me okay? Fine. I said, 'Thanks for coming down to the base.' I know it isn't easy for you."

"Are you all right, Spencer? When they said you wanted to talk to me I was afraid something had happened to you. I hurried over as fast as I could. The lady here said you were ill."

"Not ill—I had an accident. A *minor* accident. I fell down and hit my head, that's all. But when I went in for an aspirin they popped me into the med bay." Spence had stuck with his story about falling down and saw no reason to change it now. He did not want to worry his father any more than he already had.

"You're sure you're all right?" The face in the vidphone screen did not look reassured.

"Of course I'm all right; it was nothing. But since they wanted to keep me in here for a few hours I thought I'd have them patch in a signal to the base for me. You get to do that when you're sick."

"Oh," was all his father said.

"Anyway, I haven't been able to write or anything so I thought it might be fun if we could phone each other—almost as good as being there."

"Is your work going all right?"

"Fine, Dad. Everything's fine. Listen, I wanted to tell you that I won't be able to call you again for a while. I'm going to be pretty busy. I may be going out with one of the research teams on a field assignment."

"How long would that last, Spencer? You wouldn't be gone too long?"

"No, not too long," Spence lied. "A couple months, that's all. I'll vidphone you when I get back." He could see that his father did not understand what he was talking about. He looked worn and worried, and was apparently struggling to accept the fact that his son would be away longer than anticipated. Spence wished he had not called; his breaking-the-news-gently strategy was not working. "How have you been, Dad? Is Kate taking care of you?"

"Kate is very busy with the boys. She has her hands full, you know. I don't like to bother her."

"The boys are in fourth form, Dad. They're in school all day. You won't bother her. Call her if you need anything. Will you do that?"

"I suppose so," Mr. Reston said doubtfully.

"Listen, I have to go now. I can leave here in a few minutes. I only wanted to tell you not to worry about me if you don't hear from me for a while. I'll be working, that's all." He hated to tell his father like this, but there was no way of telling him directly. He would not have understood.

In all of Spence's growing-up years his parents had never understood. They did not comprehend his work, nor could they follow his explanations when he tried to describe it to them. He was simply too far beyond them. He had eventually given up trying to make them understand; he stopped trying to bridge the gap.

The image on the vidphone screen licked its lips nervously and leaned into the picture. "You'll call when you get back?"

"Yes, it's the first thing I'll do."

"I miss you, Spencer."

"I miss you, too, Dad. Good-bye."

"Good-bye, son. Take care of yourself." The screen went blank.

Spence sat staring at the blank flickering screen for several moments, then pushed the unit away. It retracted back into a nook in a panel beside the bed. He looked up just in time to see his physician approaching.

"Feeling better, Dr. Reston?" The medic came to stand at the head of his bed. He entered a code on the data screen above the bed and read Spence's chart.

"Feeling fine, Dr. Williams. With a good word from you I'll be on my way," said Spence as cheerfully as he could. "I'm taking up too much of your time."

"Not at all. We're having a special this week. Free tune-ups for all first-time customers. You're a lucky guy."

"Thanks, but if it's all the same to you, I'll take you up on that some other time." He made a move to get up, but a troubled look from the doctor stopped him. "What's the matter?"

"I was hoping you would tell *me*."

"I—I don't understand. Have you found something?"

"No, you're perfectly healthy as far as we can determine. But I think we should have a talk."

Spence had a sinking feeling. "There *is* something wrong."

"I think so, yes." The doctor drew up a stool and sat down beside Spence, who chewed his lip nervously. "Not physically," continued Williams, "that is, at least not in any of the areas we have checked out."

He gazed at his patient intently and Spence got the idea he was being measured for his tensile strength, like a spring being stretched to see how much it could take before snapping. He waited for the tension to break.

"Spence . . ." The doctor started, then hesitated.

Bad sign, thought Spence. *Whenever they use your first name it means trouble.*

"Do you have any idea why you're here?" The calm physician's eyes watched him carefully, his face a mask of impassive interest which gave away nothing.

"Yes," Spence laughed. "I tripped over a stool in the lab. I bumped my head, that's all."

"You weren't in your lab, Spence."

Spence had had another blackout—that much he knew. He thought his story about bumping his head had been accepted without question. He cringed at the thought of—what? His memory was blank, and that scared him more than anything.

"No?" Spence asked, more timidly than he would have liked. "Where was I, then?"

"You were in the cargo bay air lock."

"Impossible! Who told you that?"

"The workers who found you. They brought you in. And I see no reason to doubt their story; it's on videotape. All air locks are monitored for security."

Spence was dumbfounded. He could not believe what he was hearing.

"There's something else."

He didn't like the doctor's tone of voice. "What's that?"

"The air lock was depressurizing. You were bleeding off air preparatory to opening the outer doors."

"That's absurd! Why would I do a thing like that?"

"I don't know, but I'd like to find out." The doctor pulled a thin metallic object out of his pocket and began fingering it.

"Look, if you think I wandered into an air lock and then depressurized it on purpose . . . you're crazy. That would be suicide!"

The doctor shrugged. "Sometimes people can't take it. They want so badly to get out they don't wait for a shuttle. You were lucky. A cadet saw you heading for the air lock and reported it to the crew chief. There were some workmen in pressure suits nearby. Another few seconds and you'd have been . . . beyond repair."

"No. I'm not buying it. I'll have to see the tapes before I believe it."

"That can be arranged, of course. But I was hoping you'd level with me. If there is something bothering you I could help."

"You don't understand. I don't know what you're talking about. I tripped and bumped my head. *That is all!*"

"That's *all* you remember? Nothing else? No unusual feelings lately, nothing uncomfortable? Other blackouts, perhaps?"

Spence winced at the word "blackouts." Did the doctor know something more? "No, there is nothing else."

The physician sighed heavily.

"What are you going to do now? I mean, what will happen to me?"

"Nothing. You're free to go."

"But—you won't . . . I mean, have to . . ."

"Report this? No, I don't think so. You don't seem to me to be in any immediate danger. You are stable, in other words."

"Thanks," Spence said darkly. "Then I can go?"

"Yes, but I hope you will remember that my door is open—if you think of anything else, or want to talk about it further."

"I'll remember."

Spence swung himself down from the high bed and followed Dr. Williams out of the room. In the small reception office he turned aside and pressed the access plate. As the partition slid open he turned to nod to the physician who still watched him closely.

"Thank you, Dr. Williams. Good-bye."

"One other thing, Dr. Reston." With a sideways glance the medic stepped close and whispered, "You don't have any enemies . . . do you?"

CHAPTER EIGHT

"IT WAS a stupid, foolish thing to do! What were you thinking of? You imbeciles! Do you think this is some kind of game? We're not dealing with peasants this time, gentlemen. Reston is a very intelligent, sensitive man. Another mistake like the last one and he will smell the rat. Oh yes, he will. Reston is smart, and he is strong-willed. We must handle him very carefully." Hocking glared at the two quaking before him.

"Maybe it would be better to get someone else," suggested the younger of the two men.

"Are you questioning my decision? Do you doubt me? Look at me, you two!" Hocking's eyes started from his skull and veins stood out on his forehead. His lips drew back in a savage sneer.

"It was only a suggestion," muttered the offender. "Anyway, you said he wouldn't remember a thing."

"Shut up!" Hocking's chair rose in the air with a faint whir of its internal mechanism. It swiveled away momentarily and when he turned again to face his henchmen his features had relaxed somewhat.

"Do either of you have any idea how close we are to our goal? We are on the very threshold of a new epoch in human history. Think of it, gentlemen! The wealth of the universe will soon be ours—and that is only the beginning. Our power will be limitless. All mankind will bow before us. We'll be gods, gentlemen. We will control the minds of the entire human race." Hocking's voice was a whisper. His eyes shone like hard, black beads as the chair inched closer.

A sudden flash arced across the gap from Hocking's chair to his assistants and a tremendous cracking sound filled the room. Hocking opened his mouth and laughed as his helpers lay writhing on the floor beneath him. "Just a taste of the agony awaiting those who disappoint me. Do not disappoint me again, gentlemen.

"Now, then. Pick yourselves up off the floor and listen to me. We have work to do."

He had just reached the main access tube and was still pondering Dr. Williams's question about possible enemies when he heard a voice behind him.

"They let you go, Spence?"

He turned to see Ari hurrying up behind him. "It was nothing."

"It must have been *something*—you're blushing, Dr. Reston."

He felt the crimson flush rise to his cheeks. "How did you find out about it?" He tried to sound unconcerned.

"The director gets a list of all sick bay admissions. I saw your name on the list. I wanted to see how you were."

"You came to see me?"

"Yes, but they said you had already been dismissed. I must have missed you by only a few seconds. Are you sure you're all right?"

"I'm fine. Really. Just a little tired. If you'll excuse me . . ." He turned to leave, but Ari fell into step beside him, linking her arm in his. Spence felt his skin tingle under her touch.

"I'm on my way to my quarters. I'll walk with you." She smiled her sunny smile at him. "You don't mind, do you, Spencer?"

"No, not at all." They walked off together arm in arm.

Spence imagined that everyone they passed stopped to gawk at them. He tried to shrug off the feeling that this was anything but an innocent promenade, a guy walking a girl to her door. But to his shrunken sense of social etiquette, the occasion loomed much larger.

They made their way along the tube to a main axial and then toward the AdSec cluster where Ari and her father had their quarters. She kept up a running monologue the whole way, relieving Spence of the obligation to provide anything more than a perfunctory nod or grunt.

He paid little attention to what she said, wondering instead how he might gracefully excuse himself and make his getaway. He told himself he had more important things to do than escort aggressive young women around the space station. He wanted to free himself to think about what was happening to him.

"Well, here we are," said Ari. They stood before a buff-colored panel. "Would you like to come in? I'll make some tea."

"Tea?" Well, I don't think . . ."

"Please, do. I'd like it very much if you would." She had already punched her access code into the digits of the glowing plate and the panel slid open. She kept her hold on his arm and tugged him gently inside.

He stepped hesitantly through the portal and looked around. The Zandersons' quarters were quite plush; much more luxurious than his own spartan accommodations.

"It's shocking, I know. But it can't be helped, I'm afraid." She followed his gaze around the large, spacious rooms. "The director does live well—too well, perhaps."

"Oh, I don't know," said Spence. "It's a tough job. He needs a place like this to unwind. You can't do that in a cubbyhole."

"Still, I feel guilty sometimes. Look at this—carpet on the floors yet! It must have cost a fortune to lug that up here. And leather furniture!"

"I like it. It's beautiful."

"Sure, it's beautiful. Go ahead and take a seat. I won't be a minute."

Spence settled himself into the soft leather cushions at one end of a long handsome couch. He rubbed his hand absently over the dark, polished grain of the leather and wondered how long it had been since he had felt anything so fine, so natural.

Next to him on a low teak table sat a star globe with an Earth the size of a grapefruit surrounded by a transparent shell upon which were painted the major stars of the galaxy. It was an exquisite antique.

Next to the globe was a picture in a walnut frame. A striking, dark-haired woman smiled out from the picture and Spence realized at once where Ari had come by her good looks. But there was an unsettling quality about the picture. The woman's eyes were not focused on the camera. They held a distant, aloof look—almost a vacant stare. Though the woman smiled warmly, her smile did not light up those cold, empty eyes. It was as if two separate pictures had been somehow overlapped. Two very different moods had been captured in that single photographic moment, and the effect was chilling.

Ari returned and saw him studying the picture. She placed the tray of tea things on the table, and began to pour.

"Your mother?" he asked, still looking at the photograph.

"Yes," said Ari. She did not look up.

"I don't think I've ever met her. Is she here?"

"No, she's not—"

"Prefers the Earth beneath her feet, is that it?"

"Mother . . ." Ari started, and then hesitated. She glanced at Spence and then looked away. "Mother isn't with us anymore."

"I'm sorry . . . I didn't know." He raised his mug to his lips and sipped. "Ow!"

"Oh, careful! It's hot. I should have warned you. Did you burn yourself?"

"I'll live."

An uneasy silence settled over the room. Spence shifted nervously in his seat.

"I wanted to come up here in the worst way," said Ari after a while. "I thought it would be an adventure."

"Disappointed?"

"A little."

"I know what you mean—it's like an enormous office building, only you can never go outside."

"You're right. If not for the garden, I don't know what I'd do. Well, I'd go berserk; I know I would."

"You could leave any time you wanted, couldn't you? Why do you stay?"

"Daddy. He needs me. Besides, this being my first jump, I could never let it be said that the director's daughter couldn't even endure one tour of duty."

"You'll get used to it. Everyone does."

"Not everyone. I've already seen several who haven't. It's a frightening thing."

Spence found the conversation had wandered too close to a topic he did not wish to explore. He changed the subject. "Good tea."

"Thank you." She bent her head and sipped from her steaming mug. He watched the delicate curve of her neck and the way the light reflecting off the table filled the hollow of her throat. Her blonde curls swung down as she drank and she tossed them back with an easy, practiced flip. Their eyes met. Spence looked away.

"I should be going. I have to get back to work. I sat around in sick bay a little longer than I should have, I think."

"Very well, but you must promise to come again. Soon."

"I will." He rose to his feet and headed for the door.

Ari followed him and said as the panel slid open, "Spence, I almost forgot. We're having a function here tomorrow evening—I mean, second shift. You're invited."

"I am? Since when?"

"Since right now. I'm inviting you. It's just a few of the faculty and research people. Daddy thinks it's a good idea for the two groups to mix. You'll fit right in."

"I don't know. I'll think about it." He stepped through the portal.

"Please come. I'll expect you—" The sliding panel cut her short and Spence headed back to the lab.

He thrust his hands deep into the side pockets of his jumpsuit and ambled along with his head down. Soon he was lost in thought over his inexplicable behavior in the cargo bay. Assuming that the physician was right—and there was no reason to doubt him—what had he been doing down there? Why couldn't he remember?

I'm cracking up. I am losing my mind.

CHAPTER NINE

"ARE YOU relaxed, Spencer?"

"Yes."

"I am going to give you a new suggestion. Are you ready?"

"Yes."

"I want you to think about the color blue. Do you understand? Think of all the things that are blue and that suggest the color blue to you. The color blue, Spencer. Blue."

The wind had risen out of the east and Spence turned his face into it. It blew cold and the sky above glowered down in a fierce blue-black rage. Close by he heard the chop of water as waves dashed themselves against rocks in the shallows. He turned to the sound and saw the ocean stretching out to the horizon, blue under the dark blue clouds.

He looked into the clear blue water and saw small silver-blue fish darting by in schools, speeding like tiny rockets away into deeper space. Suddenly Spence was with them. He felt himself sinking into the water as around him the fish flashed through the blue half-light of their frigid world. He could see their silver sides zig-zagging off into the murky distance. He could see their large, round eyes staring at him as they fled.

Down and down he sank. Slowly—like a coin spinning over and over to rest finally upon the silt at the ocean's bottom. He felt the ocean floor rise up beneath his feet, and as he touched down he realized he was not in the water at all. He raised his eyes and saw that he had dropped into an enormous cavern whose high vaulted roof arched away into blue shadows.

Curiously formed projections sprouted from the floor and dangled from the ceiling. These were translucent and faintly luminous, glowing with a cool greenish-blue inner light. He walked a few hesitant steps among them as among the timbers of a silent forest, his footsteps echoing back to him from the dark depths of the cave.

He became aware of another sound which seemed to come humming up from beneath the floor, through his feet and into his bones, a grinding sound which grew louder as he descended deeper into the tunnel.

Spence walked among the glowing stalagmites following the sound. Soon he heard a rhythmic thrumming as if the Earth were churning, grinding the great stone roots of the mountains to dust. The sound grew until it filled the cavern; he walked on as if drawn to its source. His stomach vibrated with the rumble and he smelled a sharp, bitter scent in the dank air of the cave.

Far ahead he saw a pulsing blue light illuminating a far wall of the cave. He felt something gritty on his lips. He raised a hand to his face and saw that it was covered with a fine blue powder. The grit fell down upon him in a gentle rain, drifting like fine snow, covering his clothing and hair.

Then he was standing on the brink of a vast chasm which split the cavern floor. The rumble had grown to thunder, deafening him as raking light flashed blue lightning around him. The gritty powder rose like smoke from a pit as he gazed into the chasm.

Something was moving in the churning depths of the hole—as if some enormous beast were thrashing out its life in agony. In the darkness he made out a roiling black mass heaving and subsiding, groaning and shuddering amidst the roar.

Now jagged flashes of blue lightning tore through the darkness, illuminating the pit. Clinging to the rocks he lowered himself to peer over the edge deep into the chaos below. In the piercing glare of the lightning bolts he saw strange shapes tumbling and tumbling, grinding against one another, crushing each other and sending up an endless cloud of powdery blue grit like a velvet mist.

Another flash peeled away the darkness and he saw clearly into the tumbling mass below. Some of the shapes were elongated and curved, others round and bulky as boulders, still others long and thin. In that instant he realized what it was that filled the huge stone caldron: bones. The gigantic bones of prehistoric monsters whirled below him in perpetual motion—a disjointed *danse macabre*.

In that instant of recognition he felt his grip on the rocks give way and he fell. He twisted in the air and his hands clawed for a scrabbling hold on the smooth rock face, but it was too late. He plunged screaming into the grinding, churning dance of the bones.

Spence came to himself sitting upright on the couch. The trailing echo of his scream still rang in the darkened chamber like a fading memory. But the dream had vanished like a vapor. It was gone and he could remember nothing but the terror that had awakened him.

Presently the lights began to come up faintly. He guessed that Tickler stood behind the glass and heard the scream.

"Tickler," he called.

"Yes, sir?" His assistant's voice grated metallically through the overhead speakers.

"Did I scream just now?"

"I'm sorry?"

"Did you hear anything unusual—a scream, a yell? Anything like that?"

"When, Dr. Reston?"

"Just now. When I woke up."

"No, sir. The alarm went off in the control booth, so I turned on the lights. That is the procedure."

"You're quite right. Thank you." His heart was still beating rapidly. He could feel the tension in his shoulders and neck. His hands still clutched the sides of the cav couch in a death grip. He felt certain the scream had been real, that it was not merely part of his dream.

But why would Tickler lie about a thing like that? Perhaps he had not been in the booth when Spence screamed, or perhaps he was covering up the fact that he had himself dozed off at his post. Possibly. But it was not like Tickler.

Spence rose and stretched and made his way into the control room. Tickler was just winding the scan onto a spool. Spence watched him finish and place a seal on the loose end.

"Will that be all for now?" Tickler asked.

"Yes; you may go. I won't be needing anything further this shift, but tell Kurt when he comes in that I'd like the log posted and I'd like to see the averages for the last three sessions."

"The averages?"

"Yes. Just as soon as he gets them finished."

"But we have never—"

"Don't argue, Tickler. Please, just do as I say. I know it's a little extra work. But that's what we have an assistant for, isn't it?"

"Very well, I'll tell him."

Tickler turned brusquely and went out. *I wonder what's eating him this time?* With Tickler it was always something.

Spence brushed the thought from his mind and left the control booth, crossed the lab, and entered his quarters. Despite the night's sleep he did not feel at all rested. He felt as though he had run several miles or climbed a sheer rock cliff. His muscles were tense and knotty and he could smell that he had sweated through his underclothes.

He thought to sanitize and change, but then had a better idea: the exerdome. Why not? He could use the exercise. Maybe he would find a threesome who needed a fourth for a game of pidg.

As he donned his silvered mylar exersuit it occurred to him that perhaps his problems stemmed from stress and overwork. He had exercised little since coming to Gotham; except for his occasional rambles through the garden and a swim now and then, he had indulged in no physically strenuous activity. A fast game of pidg or a few laps around the dome would loosen him up and relax him.

He took a main axial to the low-grav central tower of the city. Nearly weightless, he sprang four meters from the corridor to the lift and stepped onto a disc, pulling up the handgrips as it engaged the belt. Up he rose to the dome. He could hear laughter and shouts pinging down the metal tube from above. It reminded him of going swimming as a boy and hearing the sounds of happy frolic ringing from the pool a long way off.

When the lift gate opened he stepped off onto the spongy surface of the dome—or rather bounced off with the first step, for he was now completely weightless. He spun awkwardly for a moment before remembering to pull in his arms and legs to regain control. He brought his knees up to his chest and, when he floated near enough to the curved surface once again, thrust his legs down. He arrowed off the side of the dome and flew straightway toward the center. High above him a net stretched across the observation portion of the dome to keep errant human missles from colliding with the tempered glass.

Beyond the netting he could see a bright mist of stars hanging in their inky void. Lower, he could see the upside-down crescent of the moon and the smaller blue thumbnail slice of the Earth. Spence flew into the netting, tucked his head down and landed on his back. He pulled himself across the net to a near wall.

Above him a group of cadets performed an intricate display of aerial acrobatics—doing flips and somersaults across the center of the dome. Around the perimeter several joggers sped along the track; another group ran perpendicular to the first. A couple of fluffy pidg birds floated down near the lift platform. No one seemed interested in getting up a game, so Spence swam to the edge of the net and walked up the great bulging sphere of the dome to the red stripe designated as the track.

The track's surface bore a slightly irregular, bumpy grain which gave a runner that little extra bit of traction needed to get moving in zero gravity. Spence carefully set his feet on the track and then started walking smoothly, with exaggerated care; one false step and he would go spinning off toward the center of the dome. But he maintained his concentration and increased the pace, feeling the illusion of weight return to him. Actually it was only momentum he felt, and which held him to the track. Soon he was running easily around the inner wall of the dome.

He caught the other joggers on the track and fell into pace with them. In the rhythm of running his muscles relaxed and the tension flowed from him. Automatically his body took over and his mind turned once again to the enigma of his dreams.

That he dreamed was certain. His REM line on the scan showed plainly what he knew instinctively, and if he required further proof the emotional residue—that silt left behind when the angry waters had raced on—was real enough. Not to remember a dream was normal enough; one remembered only the tiniest fraction of one's dreams over a lifetime. They simply flitted by in the night—spun out of the stuff of the subconscious and reabsorbed into the fabric of the psyche upon waking.

But blackouts were *not* normal. Spence felt as if whole chunks of his life were missing. There were gaps in his memory which he could not cross, dark curtains behind which he could not see. That scared him.

More than the nightmares, more than the cargo bay incident, he feared the helplessness, the utter defenselessness of not knowing what was happening to him. The carefully reasoned and researched framework of his life teetered precariously, threatening to topple completely, and he did not know what to do about it.

He lowered his head and spurted past the others. His lungs burned and sweat stung his eyes, but he continued running faster and faster as if to escape the fear which came swimming out of the darkness of the star-spangled night beyond the netting. Closing his eyes he thrust the fear from him as if it were a solid object he could throw aside.

After his run Spence lay motionless in the center of the dome, turning slowly on his own axis like a minor planet. The warm glow of exertion throbbed through his limbs. He had reached that blissful state of exhaustion where body and spirit were reconciled one to the other and the universe hummed with peace.

He listened to the play of others and watched through half-closed lids as the red line of the track circled him aimlessly. It was, he thought, a tribute to the supreme egotism of the mind that he seemed completely stationary while the entire space city of Gotham revolved around him. Around and around it went, spinning in its own lazy orbit—now the black mirror of the observation bubble, now the red line of the track.

The red line of the track. Something about that seemed important. Spence jerked his head up and sent himself floundering away at an obtuse angle. In the same instant it came to him: the red line of the track was the red line of his sleep scan. He had meant to check it, but had forgotten, or the thought had been driven from his mind by the circumstances of his latest blackout.

Suddenly it seemed more important than ever. He dove for the nearest wall and then propelled himself toward the lift platform. He raced back to the lab with his heart pounding and the certainty drumming in his brain that he was very close to finding an answer to the riddle of his dreams.

CHAPTER TEN

SPENCE SNAPPED the seal and unrolled the strip to the beginning, watching meters and meters of paper tape unwind through his fingers. At the start of the tape he saw the date and time notation: EST 5/15/42 10:17 GM The scan continued for nine and three-quarter hours without interruption. Each peak and every valley, every blip of an alpha spark or beta flash was duly recorded. He saw the minute fluctuations in cerebral blood flow; the rise and fall of body temperature, heart rate and thyroid activity; the intermittent REM flutters. He saw, in short, the even, rhythmic progress of his night's sleep. His every moment was accounted for. Undeniably so—he held the evidence in his own hands.

But it was not enough. He turned to the cabinet where all the spools were kept. There were dozens of them, each one containing the polysomnographic information of one night's sleep session. He lifted the row containing the scans of the last week. He checked each one. They were all there, labeled and sealed correctly.

He checked the week before that and the next one, too. All was in order. Tickler was as precise as he was stuffy. Spence knew that if he looked at every spool over the last ten weeks he would find them in order. Still, a small gray shadow of doubt clung to his mind.

He turned once more to the scan he had unrolled—the one from the night of his first blackout three days ago. He pulled the tape through his hands and examined it closely. It was no different from all the others.

He spied the yellow plastic cover of the log book on the corner of the console and pulled it to him. On top of the log book lay a piece of green graph paper on which was plotted the averages Spence had requested for the last three sessions. Kurt must have come in and finished it while he was out. He glanced at the graph of the averages and then opened the log book and traced up the columns to the session of the fifteenth. He found no irregularities in any of the figures or information.

He closed the book with the sinking feeling that all was in order and only he was out of sync.

He threw the book down on the console and leaned back with his hands clasped behind his head. If an answer existed to his problems it would have to exist in some form in the hard data before him. Somewhere in the miles of tape, or in the figures in the book, the key to the locked room of his mind could be found. Of that he was certain. His faith in the scientific method stood on solid, unshakeable rock.

On a whim he swiveled to the data screen at one end of the console. The wafer-thin, half-silvered glass shone smooth as polished stone. "MIRA," said Spence, "Spence Reston here. Ready for command."

A mellifluous female voice said, "Ready, Dr. Reston."

Spence uttered the simple command: "Compare entries for PSG Seven Series LTST five-fifteen to five-eighteen for similarities. Display only, please."

He laced his fingers behind his head and leaned back in his chair. Instantly the wafer screen flashed to life and the results began filling the screen. It seemed there were many similarities between one night's scan and the next in terms of basic numerical components. All of the information gathered during a scanning session was translated into numbers for purposes of data storage and retrieval. They were all alike in many ways, and yet all different.

The command was too broad. That much he could see, but he did not know how to narrow the question because he did not know precisely what he was looking for. He crossed his arms over his chest and frowned at the screen. Just what did he hope to find?

After several minutes of hard thought he stood and began pacing the cramped confines of the booth. *Compare and contrast,* he thought. *That's where you start on a fishing expedition of this type. Compare and contrast.*

He had already compared and that had not shown him anything out of the ordinary. Perhaps contrasting the same information would produce something. He turned to the screen and said, "Contrast PSG LTST entries for five-fifteen to five-eighteen. Display only, please."

The numbers vanished and in their place the screen began printing: Zero contrast within normal range of variability ± 3%.

In other words, dead end.

Spence glanced at the digiton above the console. In a few minutes Tickler would arrive to begin the session. He did not want Tickler to find him here like this playing detective. A silly thought he knew—*I have a perfect right to examine the data of my own experiment, for goodness sakes*—but he preferred that Tickler should know nothing about his inquiry.

Judging he had time for two more stabs in the dark, he said, "Compare PSG LTST Seven Series entries five-fifteen to five-eighteen for similarities of less than one percent variability. Display only, please." He nodded with satisfaction; by decreasing the percentage of variability he had narrowed the question significantly.

In moments MIRA came back with its findings. The message read: Zero comparison. Spence frowned again. There were apparently no great similarities or differences in any of the scans—beyond the normal range of his individual sleep pattern.

With a sigh he kicked back his chair. This kind of blind fumbling was useless. Unless he knew what he hoped to discover, no amount of random searching would help. "Thank you, MIRA. That is all for . . ."

He stopped in mid-sentence. It occured to him that he had not compared all of the scans, only those from the fifteenth to the eighteenth—the two dates encompassing his blackouts.

"MIRA, compare *all* PSG LTST Seven Series entries. Display entries with similarities of less than one percent variability.

There was a slight hesitation; the wafer screen went blank. He imagined he could hear the chips crackling with speeding electrons as MIRA wracked her magnetic memory.

Spence sat on the edge of his chair and watched the clock tick away the seconds. Any moment Tickler would come walking in. *Hurry!* Spence muttered. *Hurry!*

Then the words appeared. He read the message as it came up: PSG LTST Seven Series entries with less than 1% variability = 3/20 and 5/15.

Jackpot! Spence jumped out of his chair and stared at the screen in disbelief. There it was; an anomaly too large to exist, its very presence an impossibility. If he had discovered it any other way he would have chalked it up to a computer glitch. But he had a strong suspicion that it was no glitch. He had uncovered a vital bit of information—stumbled blindly over it, more like—but there, spelled out in fluorescent orange, was the evidence.

He picked up the yellow log book and paged through to the entry of 3/20. He pulled the sheet and placed it next to the entry of 5/15. They were not at all similar. Each entry in Tickler's neat, precise hand was slightly different—not enough to vary a great deal, but enough for Spence to see that they were both unique.

Apparently, MIRA had glitched after all. There was no similarity between the two scans.

Spence heard the swoosh of the panel opening and Tickler's quick footsteps entering the lab. He said, "That is all, MIRA. Thank you."

"Good evening, Dr. Reston."

"Good evening, Tickler." Spence turned and forced what he hoped was a casual smile.

"Are we ready to begin our session?" Tickler's small, weasel eyes glanced from Spence to the wafer screen above the terminal.

"Oh, I meant to tell you about that. I am canceling the session this evening." Spence surprised himself with that announcement.

"I don't understand, sir. I've prepared everything—we're all ready. If you—"

"Never mind. It can wait. I have something else for you to do tonight. You and Kurt, that is. I want you to run averages for the last two weeks. I think a curve may emerge that we may want to explore. That should take you most of the session, I think."

"But—pardon my asking—what are *you* going to do?"

Spence could see that Tickler was upset. The inflexible little man did not bend easily to the unexpected.

"I'm going to a function at the director's suite. I imagine it will be rather late when I get back; so when you finish you can go. I will expect to see you tomorrow first shift." Spence turned to leave. Tickler's jaw pumped the air in silence. "Yes? Was there something else?"

Tickler shook his head. He had recovered himself. "No, I imagine we can handle it from here," he snapped.

"Good night, then," said Spence, stepping from the booth. He smiled a devious smile to himself as he crossed the lab to his quarters. A quick change and he would still make the party in plenty of time.

CHAPTER ELEVEN

SPENCE DONNED a clean, informal, nonregulation jumpsuit and struck off for the director's quarters. He was pleased with himself for remembering the party at the last second—it was perfect. He wanted to get away from the lab and out of Tickler's presence to think about his discovery. What exactly, if anything, did it mean?

At the time it had seemed electrifyingly significant. Now, as he hurried along the crowded trafficways of Gotham flowing with the changing shifts, his startling revelation seemed a little on the trivial side. There were at least a dozen different ways of accounting for the match up of the two entries. Spence ticked them off one by one as he dodged and elbowed his way to the Zandersons'.

By the time he arrived at the buff-colored portal he had convinced himself that his discovery lacked any real bones. It would never stand up. There had to be more, something else that would tell him what this bare shred of fact meant. What that something was he had no idea.

"Spencer! I'm so glad to see you. Come in!" Ari beamed at him over the threshold as the panel slid open. Spence shook himself out of his reverie and returned her smile.

"I hope I'm not too late." She drew him into the room which was humming with the conversation of the guests. Several turned to regard the newcomer with frank, disapproving glances; most ignored his entrance.

"I think some of your guests are sorry I bothered to show up at all."

"Nonsense, silly. You just haven't been properly introduced. Come along. Daddy will want to do the honors."

Ari steered him into the gathering and around conversational cliques to where her father held forth at a buffet, urging tiny sandwiches on doubtful patrons. He was surrounded by women—the wives of faculty and fellows, decided Spence—who tittered politely at his jokes while they picked among the delicacies offered on the board.

"Daddy, look who's here." Ari took her father's arm and expertly wheeled him around to face Spence.

"Dr. Reston! Good of you to come."

"Kind of you to invite me."

"Here, get yourself a plate and dig in. The rumaki is delicious."

"Thank you, maybe a little later, I—"

"Daddy, I told Spencer that you would introduce him to some of the others. Won't you, please?"

"Oh, of course. I'd be delighted to. Look—there's Olmstead Packer, head of High Energy. Come along. Who's that with him? Another new face, I believe." Director Zanderson piloted them both forcefully ahead through the standing clusters of socializers. Spence bobbed along in his wake. Out of the corner of his eye he saw Ari disappear into a knot of partygoers with a plate of hors d'oeuvres. He abandoned himself to his immediate fate.

"Tell me, Dr. Reston, have you thought any further about the research trip?"

"Why, yes. I've considered it—"

"I'm not pressing, not pressing. Oh, here we are. Gentlemen!" The director broke in on the two men, clapping a hand on a shoulder of each. "I'd like you to meet Dr. Reston, BioPsych."

Before any further introductions could take place, the man previously identified as Packer thrust out a hand and said, "Glad to meet you. I'm Olmstead Packer and this is my colleague Adjani Rajwandhi."

"I'll leave you gentlemen to become better acquainted. Don't forget to go by the buffet, now. Don't be bashful." The director left Spence in the care of his new acquaintances and plunged back into the swirl.

Olmstead Packer laughed heartily and said, "There goes a dynamo! A roly-poly dynamo. Why, if we could harness that energy—just think!"

"These HiEn bookworms!" remarked Rajwandhi. "They cannot stand to see anything without an outlet in it. They think all the world is a power grid."

"Not true, Adjani. Not true at all. The *universe* is one big reactor, and we're all subatomic particles bounding around in our random orbits." Packer smiled broadly.

Spence took to the big, red-bearded cherub immediately. With his kinky red hair that looked like rusty steel wool and his droopy-lidded brown eyes he appeared an almost comic figure always on the verge of laughing out loud.

Adjani, on the other hand, was a slight mongoose of a man who looked at the world through keen eyes, bright and hard as black diamonds. He had about him an air of mystery which Spence found intriguing and slightly exotic.

"Dr. Rajwandhi is a fellow of my department—" began Packer.

"But not of your discipline!" interrupted Adjani.

"No—sadly not of our discipline."

"What project are you attached to, Dr. Rajwandhi?" asked Spence politely.

"To my colleagues I am just Adjani, please. I am currently assigned to the plasma project. This is under Dr. Packer's supervision."

"You flatter me, Adjani," roared Packer, his teeth flashing white from out of the auburn tangle of his beard. He said to Spence, "Adjani here is under no one's supervision. The man has not yet been born who can keep up with him, and he does not know how to take direction."

"Can I help it if God granted me full measure of what other men possess only in part?"

'You'll get no argument from me, snake charmer. I'll sing your praises from here to Jupiter and back." Turning once more to Spence he explained, "Adjani is our Spark Plug—and the best in the business."

Spence looked at the slim Adjani with new respect. A Spark Plug, as they were called, was a member of an elite group of men and women so gifted as to be completely expert in numerous fields of study—as many as five or six. Whereas most scientists and theoricians were specialists, training their professional vision to ever narrower bands of the scientific spectrum, those like Adjani—and there were very few of them —worked in reverse, enlarging the scope of their knowledge wider and wider. In effect, they were specialists in everything: physics, chemistry, astronomy, biology, metallurgy, psychology, and all the rest.

Most often they were employed as systematicians—men who could view the overall course of a project and draw valuable information from other areas of study and bring it to bear upon a particular problem. They acted as catalysts of creativity—spark plugs—providing those quick, dynamic bursts of creative insight for projects that had grown too complex to rely on the accidental cross-pollinization of ideas from other disciplines.

They were the "connection men," making much needed connections between the problem at hand and useful data from areas unrelated to the project which nevertheless offered possible insight or solutions to stubborn problems. And connection men were in great demand. Science had long ago realized that it could no longer afford to wait for chance to match up and germinate the ideas from which scientific breakthroughs were born. The system, if it was to remain healthy and viable, needed help; the scientific method needed the boost that geniuses like Adjani could give.

So Spence was duly impressed. He had never met a spark plug; there were not many of them, and the discipline was still too new to have penetrated into all branches of study. Mostly, connection men were snapped up by the bigger and more lavishly funded programs like high energy or laser physics.

"I'm glad to know you, Adjani," said Spence, and he meant it.

Olmstead Packer fixed on Spence with keen interest. "Tell us about yourself."

"Me? I . . . ah . . ." Spence could not think of a thing to say. "I'm new here. This is my first jumpyear."

"I thought so. This is Adjani's first jump, too. I had one devil of a time trying to get him up here. Cal Tech had their claws in him and didn't want to let him go. *You're* not from Cal Tech, are you?"

"No—NYU. Why do you ask?"

"Oh, it just seems that I remember a Dr. Reston from Cal Tech— but it couldn't be . . . Why, that was years ago, now that I think of it."

"It's not an uncommon name." Spence could not bring himself to admit that Packer was talking about his father. Dr. Reston—the professor Spence had never known; he did not want to discuss his father's breakdown.

"Did you attend Cal Tech?" asked Spence.

"Stanford," replied Packer proudly. "Though most of my time was spent at JPL. You are engaged in the LTST sleep study, correct?"

"Why, yes—"

"Fascinating work," said Packer.

"And vital," said Adjani. "If we are ever to probe beyond our solar system we must understand the delicate psychological balance between sleep and mental well-being. Can the sleep state be prolonged indefinitely? Is it a function of certain chemical interactions within the brain? Can individual sleep patterns be molded to the changing demands of space flight? Very interesting. Very important questions you are working on, Dr. Reston."

"My friends call me Spence." Now it was Spence's turn to be flattered. Adjani, true to his calling, seemed to know intimately the nature of his work.

"Tell me, Spence, do you think we'll be able to put our crews to sleep for, say, a year or two on a trip between stars?"

"That's a tough one." Spence puffed out his cheeks and let the air whistle through his teeth. "It is not entirely out of the question. Though I admit right now it looks like a long shot. This is still virgin territory we're exploring, you understand. Our expectations are likely to run beyond our abilities for some time to come."

"You are a pioneer, Spence. And a cautious one. That is good." Adjani smiled at him. "Packer asked the question with ulterior motives, I surmise."

"Oh, how so?" Spence raised his eyebrows and regarded Packer with mock suspicion.

"See! What did I tell you? He's a quick one all right. Yes, I admit it. I had something in mind and I thought I might get a little comfort from your answer."

"Olmstead is leading the research trip this year since he's taking sixteen of his third-year students with him. He dreads the flight."

"It isn't the flight I mind. It's my third trip to Mars and I get so *bored*. Five weeks is a long time to occupy oneself aboard a bucket—I wouldn't mind a long nap."

"It would not *take* five weeks if you and your HiEn theorists would stop theorizing and perfect the plasma drive," jibed Adjani.

The big physicist pulled a hurt face and shook his head wearily. "See, Spence? See what I have to put up with? Now it's *my* fault that we have no plasma drive. Just between you and me, Dr. Reston, I think Adjani is a saboteur sent from Cal Tech to disrupt our experiments. *They* would like to be first to patent the plasma-ion drive."

"I've been thinking about coming along on the research trip myself. Director Zanderson has asked me."

"Then you must come, by all means," said Adjani.

"Not so fast. Do you play pidg?" Packer fixed him with a hard look.

"After a fashion, yes. I've not had a great deal of zero-G experience. But I like the game."

"Fine. That settles it. You must come and you must be on our team. The faculty and students always have a pidg tournament during the Mars cruise. It has become something of a tradition, and an object of intense competition. The only trouble is, not many of the faculty indulge in the sport."

"They lose consistently," remarked Adjani.

"I really haven't made up my mind. I have so much to do here . . ."

"If Zanderson has suggested you go, I would think seriously about it. He does not extend the invitation to everyone. You are fortunate to have it come so soon."

They talked a long time, though to Spence it seemed only seconds, when Olmstead Packer's wife came to pry her husband loose to mix with some of her friends. Adjani excused himself as well and vanished into the press around the buffet. Spence felt naked and obvious, having no one to talk to. The camaraderie he had experienced with the two men evaporated all too quickly.

"I thought I'd never get you back," said a voice behind him.

He turned to see Ari standing there. She seemed always to be popping up unexpectedly. "I'm drifting—save me," he said.

"It didn't look to me like you needed saving. It looked like you were having a good time."

"No, I mean now."

She smiled shyly and said, "I'll save you. Would you like something to eat? Daddy will be most disappointed if you don't at least try the mousse."

"I'd love to try it."

Ari led the way to the buffet and Spence followed gladly. He had begun to feel that above all else he did not want to be lonely anymore.

CHAPTER TWELVE

THE BUFFET looked as if it had been attacked by sharks.

"Daddy's pride and joy—look at it now," lamented Ari. She handed Spence a plate and took one herself. "Oh, well, we might as well join in the plunder. Let's dig in."

They inched their way along the table laden with platters and serving dishes containing a varied and exotic fare: shrimp on ice, salmon aspic, sweet and sour meatballs, souffles of several kinds, quiches, a great cheddar wheel, cold roast beef and ham, baby lobster tails, relishes and pickles, brandied pears, deviled crabs, avacados stuffed with chicken and tuna salad, petits fours, cakes, and many other delicacies, some of which Spence did not readily recognize.

Not that it made a difference whether he recognized any particular dish. Ari adroitly ushered them through the snarl of elbows and reaching hands and filled both plates while Spence tagged after her trying not to spill anything.

"Oh, no," sighed Ari as they arrived at a great empty bowl; the cut glass vessel appeared to have been recovered from a mud wallow. "Just as I feared. The mousse is gone. Too bad. But I think I know where there may be some more. Follow me."

They edged through the crowd and dodged diners who stood on the periphery holding their plates to their mouths. She led him away from the confusion of the gathering, through a dim passageway, and into a room which had been transformed into a makeshift kitchen; it looked more like the staging area for a major battle. Several employees of Gotham's food service worked over platters, valiantly attempting to reconstruct beauty from the spoils on the plates before them, replacing wilted lettuce and replenishing depleted items. They worked deftly and quickly, shouldered their trays and faced once more into the fray.

"We should have come here first," murmured Ari. "It's quieter. Here's the mousse, or what's left of it." She picked up a spoon and shook a healthy dollop onto his already overflowing plate.

"It will take me a week to eat all this."

"Nonsense. I've seen you eat. Remember?"

He looked around for a place to sit. There were no chairs in the room at all.

"Shall we join the others?" asked Ari.

"I would rather face lions."

She raised an eyebrow. "That was the right answer. I know a place that may not have been discovered. Come along."

They ducked out through a side door and across the hallway into a small vestibule. He gathered the room was a sort of private sitting room. Bookshelves lined the walls on three sides; on the fourth there was a large abstract green painting above a low couch. A table in front of the couch bore the telltale traces of diners who had eaten and departed, leaving behind the litter of their repast.

"Daddy calls this his reading room. He says it's cozier than his library or office. Most often he just comes in here to nap."

They sat down on the couch and fell to eating at once. Spence sampled a bite of each of the items on his plate in turn before devouring them one at a time.

"It's very good," he mumbled around a mouthful.

"Only the best for our guests."

He regarded her with a look of genuine gratitude. "Thanks for inviting me. I don't usually—" He stopped. "I'm glad I came."

She looked down at her plate. "I'm glad you came, too. I guess I didn't think you would."

"To tell you the truth, I didn't either."

"What changed your mind?"

"I don't know. Maybe I'm just a pushover for chocolate mousse."

"Then we'll have to serve it more often," she said gaily. "But you're not eating yours."

He glanced down at his plate. It had become a muddied palette of confused colors and textures. He put it down on the table in front of him. "I don't like mousse," he admitted.

She laughed then, and to Spence it seemed as if the room suddenly brightened. "Silly, then why did you let me give it to you?"

"I don't know. You seemed to be enjoying yourself."

Ari blushed slightly and lowered her head. "Well, I am." She seemed to become flustered then and said no more.

Silence reclaimed the room and laid a gulf between them. It grew until neither one wanted to cross it. The atmosphere became sticky.

"Ari, I'm not too good at this sort of thing." Spence was surprised to hear his own voice bleating uncertainly into the vacuum.

"You don't have to say anything," said Ari. She raised her blue eyes to his. "I understand."

"It's just that I . . ." Words failed him.

"Please, it isn't important." She smiled at him and cocked her head to one side. "I think we should rejoin the party. Daddy will wonder what happened to me."

"You're right." Spence stood slowly. Ari remained seated, and he looked down on her and then offered his hand and helped her to her feet.

"Thanks," he said softly.

They crossed the room and Ari turned, putting on her jaunty demeanor again, once more the vivacious hostess. "We'll be lucky if they don't eat the tablecloth as well," she said as they passed the buffet.

"Well, next time I get hungry for mousse, I know where to come," said Spence.

She turned to him and placed her hand on his arm. "I hope you won't wait that long." Before he could answer she whirled away into the crowd and was gone.

Spence walked back to his quarters alone in a mood of fluttery anticipation, almost wonder. He had forgotten his anxiety of only hours before; in fact, he had forgotten a great many things. What had taken possession of him now left no room for those darker thoughts. Though he had no name for what he felt—having never felt it before—he knew it to be in no small way connected with the person of Ariadne Zanderson.

The warmth of the feeling surprised and confused him. It was wholly beyond his rational ability to describe. It seemed to defy objective analysis, leaving him fumbling for an explanation like a man groping for a light switch in a dark room. That the elusive feeling might be love did not occur to him.

He punched in his code and the panel whispered back, admitting him into the darkened lab. Neither Tickler nor Kurt were to be seen; he guessed they had finished and gone long ago. That suited him. He did not care to think about the project, Tickler, or the scans. All he wanted was to throw off his jumpsuit and flop into bed—which he did, after leaving an alarm call with MIRA.

Spence peered into the depths of a vast chasm as the rumble of underground thunder shook the rocks he clung to fearfully. His inward parts trembled to the awesome roar. Below him, whirling in the seething darkness, he could see strange shapes churning and grinding, sending up a fine blue powder like a velvet mist.

Great jagged flashes of blue lightning rent the air and peeled away the darkness of the pit. He looked down and saw clearly into the tumbling mass below. In the fleeting illumination of the lightning he saw the groaning, shuddering, grinding contents of the pit: bones. The enormous skeletal remains of gigantic prehistoric creatures, thrashing in perpetual motion.

A bolt of lightning raked the rock on which he perched and he felt his hands torn away as he fell backward into the chasm. He twisted in the air, his fingers clawing empty space for a hold on the rock. It was too late.

Spence plunged screaming into the whirling dance of the bones.

Down and down he spun, turning and turning. The fine blue grit ascending on the warm updrafts stung his eyes and filled his nose and mouth, choking him. He squirmed and gasped as black mists closed around him.

The sound of the terrible rumbling thunder gradually died away. He dropped like a stone through formless space. He felt nothing and heard nothing—only the beating of his own heart and the thump of his blood as it pounded in his ears. He felt as if he would fall forever. He told himself the notion was absurd.

Perhaps, thought Spence, *I am not falling at all.* But what else could it be? All at once a new terror seized his mind: he was shrinking. Instantly he could feel himself becoming smaller—dwindling by fine degrees, becoming ever smaller. Though he had no point of reference by which to gauge himself, he felt that by now he must be very tiny. And still the shrinking continued.

This is the way it will end, thought Spence. The universe imploding on itself, racing back into its flash of creation, compressing its atoms back into that single elemental spark from which all matter was born. And he was part of it; he was one with it. Now and forever.

There was no waking this time. Spence was fully conscious of his surroundings, and was aware, too, that he had been conscious for some time. There simply was no dividing line he could point to and say, "Here I was asleep, and here awake." The shadowy line between waking and dreaming had been erased. It no longer existed. In Spence's mind dream and reality had merged.

Before him hung the shimmering iridescent halo of blue light with its tendrils glowing faintly as they waved in the darkness of his quarters. The luminous tendrils seemed to be reaching out for him, pulling him up into the green shining halo. He felt the rising, pulling, falling sensation and knew that he had felt it before in just this way.

He knew that he had experienced all this before—the shining wreath, the glistening tendrils, the shapeless mass moving darkly in the center—he knew it, but there was no memory of it. There was simply a knowing.

He watched in grim fascination as the swirling inner eye of the halo condensed into a glimmering mass of light. He felt a pressure in his chest; his lungs burned and he realized he had been holding his breath. His heart flung itself against his ribs and he could smell the fear rising from him as the reek from the fur of a wet animal. But the thing held him firmly in his place.

The terror seemed merely a physical response. He noted it with scientific curiosity, as one might note the progress of water boiling in a beaker and turning into steam, or chart the stages of a well-known chemical reaction. The horror he felt belonged to another part of him, and that part no longer connected with his mind.

A sound like needles clinking or glass slivers breaking against one another rose in volume. He noted the sound and marked how it seemed to tingle on the surface of his skin. He gazed more deeply into the green halo and saw the forms within weaving themselves into vaguely human shapes. These ghostly features then hardened into the recognizable form of a face—the thin, wasted face of Hocking.

Spence blinked back dully at the leering apparition. His mouth was dry; he could not speak or cry out. The will to do so had left him.

Hocking began speaking to him, saying, "You are becoming accustomed to the stimulus, Spencer. That is good. You are making remarkable progress. Soon we will begin a few simple commands. But one thing is needed yet before you are ready. We must establish a permanent mental link through which my thought impulses can travel to you. Heretofore, I have been sending suggestions to you through your dreams. When our minds are linked, however, I shall be able to do so in your waking state as well."

Hocking smiled his skeletal smile and Spence, held in his place, stared impassively ahead.

"This will not harm you," soothed Hocking. "Relax. Close your eyes. Empty your mind of all thought. Think only of the color blue. Concentrate on the color blue, Spencer. Think of nothing else."

Spence obeyed the image's commands. He closed his eyes and filled his mindscreen with an intense, vibrant shade of blue. He relaxed his clenched fists and slumped; his head hung forward and his chin rested on his chest.

"In a moment I will tell to open your eyes and look at me. But not before I tell you—do you understand? Concentrate. Do exactly as I say . . . concentrate . . ."

Spence felt his consciousness slipping away. It was as if his soul—all of that which he called Spence and recognized as himself—began flowing from him, poured out like liquid from a bottle. The sensation sent a quiver up his spine and through his limbs. Once more the high-pitched tinkling sound increased, boring through the top of his head and into his skull.

Dizziness overcame him, and with it a tough little kernel of resistance formed somewhere deep within. But the powerful forces working on him threatened to steal even that away.

No! thought Spence. *I cannot let this happen!* Those words echoing inside his brain lacked force. All strength had gone out of him.

No!, he cried again. *Stop it! Stop it!* He did not know whether he spoke the words aloud or whether he merely thought them. It did not matter. He held to the hard kernel of resistence, fighting to hang on to that last tiny shred of himself. He found that as he struggled to grasp it, a remnant of his will returned.

"Relax. Do not fight it. Relax, Spencer. This will not hurt you." Hocking's voice sounded inside him. Hocking was there *inside* him!

The hideous realization broke upon his shriveled awareness.

"I will not!" shouted Spence, snapping his head up. He opened his eyes and saw the shimmering green halo with Hocking's dreadful face glaring down on him. But he saw something else that shocked him back to his senses.

The quavering fibrils around the edge of the halo were stretched taut and extending toward him, touching him. He knew that if he did not break that contact at once he would cease to exist. Spence Reston would become a hollow shell inhabited by Hocking's mind and controlled by Hocking's will. He could not let that happen.

Already he felt Hocking's presence seeping into him. He screamed and threw himself onto the floor, forcing his leaden extremities to move. But the tendrils did not release their hold, remained attached to his forehead.

Shaking with the effort, his muscles turning to jelly and his strength flowing away like water, he dragged himself across the floor to the sanibooth. Hand over hand he pulled himself to his feet.

"Sit down, Spencer. Relax. We are nearly finished. Relax. Concentrate . . ." Hocking's voice chanted inside his head. "Relax . . . relax . . . relax . . ."

He punched the access plate, and the door of the booth slid open. He teetered on the threshold.

"Relax, Spencer. Sit down."

Spence heard a crack and felt his cheek sliding down the stall's smooth wall. The booth seemed to tilt upside down and he slid to the floor, half in and half out. His head struck the sensor plate in the floor and he heard the whir of the mechanism as the gentle rain of powder began descending upon him like fine snow. The quiet drone of the mechanism was the last thing he heard.

CHAPTER THIRTEEN

ARI SAT in a white molded plastic chair next to Spence's bed. The nurses had just finished washing the last of the blue sanitizing powder from his hair. One side of his face bore the red poached look of a sunburn. He appeared to have suffered nothing worse than falling asleep on the beach at high noon.

The patient's breathing came slow and regular—the doctor had said that the worst was over. There would be some slight inflammation and pain due to the inhalation of the chemical, but nothing more serious. The physician indicated that it was a wonder Spence had not suffocated in the powder. His skin would be sensitive for a week or so and it would probably peel. Spence was fortunate, remarked Dr. Williams, that he had not fallen face up into the booth. He could have been blinded by the ultraviolet light. All in all, he had escaped unharmed.

"Did he tell you about his first 'accident,' Miss Zanderson?" Dr. Williams had asked.

"No—he mentioned a bump on the head, I believe. He seemed fine. I never dreamed . . ."

"Oh, it's serious all right. Our young friend is manifesting definite self-destructive tendencies. He was found in the cargo bay with the lock open. He nearly died. I wouldn't tell you this, you understand, but he seems not to have any close friends—except you, of course."

Ari frowned and bit her lip. "What can I do, doctor?"

The medic shook his head slowly. "Only watch him. Get him to talk about what causes these attacks, if you can. We'll wait and see. It'll be better in the long run if he volunteers the information on his own. If we pry too hard, try to force him to tell us, it could drive the cause deeper.

"Of course, if the bottom drops out we'll intervene. I would rather it never came to that. And so would he, I'm sure. As with a lot of men in his position, one incident like that on his record and he would be ruined professionally."

Ari had listened to Dr. Williams intently, and her features reflected the turmoil of her emotions. She looked so forlorn when he finished speaking that he felt compelled to comfort her and discount his dire predictions. "Forgive me for speaking frankly," Dr. Williams said apologetically. "I tend to function on a 'worst case' basis. I may have overdramatized things a bit. He'll be all right. Your Dr. Reston is a strong-willed chap. He'll snap out of it, I daresay."

Ari thanked the doctor then and he had gone away, leaving her to wait beside the bed. She occupied her time puzzling over the physician's parting words: *Your* Dr. Reston. Was it really so obvious then? she wondered.

After a while a nurse brought in a cup of coffee for her and stayed to chat a little. There were no other patients in that particular wing at present, so Ari was free to stay as long as she wished. "You can even stretch out on one of the other beds if you like," the nurse suggested.

"I'm not tired, and I don't mind waiting. Thank you for the coffee, though."

The nurse left again, dimming the lights and immersing the rigidly efficient and scrupulously spotless hospital room into cool, soothing shadow. Ari heard the door sigh shut and, folding her hands in her lap and bowing her head, began to pray.

The golden crown of her bowed head was the first thing Spence saw when he woke up.

"I seem always to be waking up here." His voice was a hoarse whisper. His lungs burned and his throat felt as if it had been stripped raw.

Her head came up smiling. "It's because you fall asleep in such funny places."

"You heard about that, huh?"

She nodded her head, regarding him with eyes which seemed a deeper shade of blue, darkening out of sympathy for him. "You could have told me yourself," she said.

Spence shrugged. "There wasn't much to tell."

"How do you feel?"

"Okay."

"You *sound* terrible."

"Thanks." Spence was suddenly convulsed by a fit of coughing. The flames in his lungs leapt up and he felt as if his throat was on fire.

Ari stood quickly and grabbed a plastic cup of ice water from the tray beside his bed. "Here, sip some of this." She held the cup for him and guided the straw to his mouth. "Better?"

"Much." They looked at one another without speaking for a moment, then Spence turned his head away.

"Was it that bad this time?" His voice sounded small and faraway.

Ari sat down on the edge of his bed. She placed a hand on his arm. "Don't you remember?"

"I don't remember anything."

She placed a cool hand on the side of his face and turned his head toward her. "It's all right, Spence. It's going to be all right."

In the soft light falling from recessed panels overhead Ari was transformed in his eyes into a ministering angel who had come to succor him in his hour of need. Her fair hair shone with a soft luster and her eyes glimmered with calm assurance. Her lips curved upward in a smile and the shadows caressed the gentle curve of her smooth cheek.

He lifted a hand to her face and gazed into her eyes. She took the hand in hers and kissed it gently. Spence felt revived. He squeezed her hand and pulled it to him.

"How long will I be here this time?" he asked at length.

"The doctor said at least twenty-four hours, but it's up to you, really. How do you feel?"

"Tired."

"I'll leave you to get some rest." She stood up from the bed and placed his hand back on his chest, giving it a gentle squeeze.

"No. I didn't mean—"

"Shh. Don't worry. I'll come back. Get some sleep now." She smiled again as she turned to leave. "You had me worried—for a moment I thought it was the mousse."

"I didn't eat it, remember?" He smiled faintly.

"Good night, Spencer."

He closed his eyes and drifted off into deep, untroubled sleep.

* * *

"He resisted the attempted mindlink," said Hocking flatly. He did not like admitting failure, especially to Ortu. Often the repercussions were unpleasant.

Ortu's yellow eyes narrowed as he glared coldly out of the shimmering halo. "So?"

"He is a strong-willed subject, Ortu. I don't know where he found the strength to resist. It did not seem possible that this time he could withstand."

"There seem to be a great many things you do not know, and far too many impossibilities. It does not suit me at all. I am displeased with you, Hocking." The metallic band on his brow pulsed more quickly.

Hocking fought to keep his voice under control. "A minor setback. A small delay. We are nearly there. Next time—"

"Next time!" The wizened countenance suddenly contorted in a snarl of venomous rage. The thin-lipped mouth gaped open, revealing a row of sharp, even brown teeth. The yellow eyes flashed fire, and the gleaming circlet quivered. "Next time! You speak to me of next time? I, Ortu, say what is to be. Or have you forgotten?"

Hocking drew back into his chair as if it were a shell he could hide in. His fingers jerked spasmodically on the tray before him.

"I have not forgotten. How am I ever to forget?" There was an icy tinge of hate in the underling's voice.

Ortu's eyes narrowed once more. "I made you what you are. I can unmake you. You came to me a pathetic mass of misshapen flesh. I saved you, fed your intellect, increased the power of your mind. Do not now pretend that you are sorry. It is too late for that, crippled one. Much too late."

"I meant nothing by it, Ortu. I ask your forgiveness for my error." Hocking swallowed hard and looked steadily into the glowing blue wreath of light. His answer seemed to appease his unpredictable mentor. Ortu drew back and his twisted features went slack, becoming once more blank and remote as if he were carved of cold stone.

"What would you have me do?" asked Hocking. His breath came easier.

"We are in dangerous territory at present. One more projection could break him and he would be ruined for our purposes. It could kill him. Either outcome would be unfortunate. It would mean starting over yet again. I do not wish to begin again. Besides, his ability to resist interests me. We will continue."

"As you wish, Ortu. I will allow him time to regain his strength and then increase the frequency of the dream suggestions. That should sufficiently wear down his mental defenses.

"Dr. Reston is, after all, a very adept subject. We have a great wealth of dreamstate images from him already. I will have no trouble altering the content of his dreams to suit our purposes."

"The next projection must not fail," warned Ortu. The hollow, empty voice was devoid of anger or malice. The utterance chilled Hocking to the marrow.

"It will not."

The halo dimmed and began to fade away. Hocking watched until nothing was left but a faint glow in the air. Then that, too, disappeared. The egg-shaped chair spun silently around and whisked out of the empty chamber.

"I have been too easy on him," muttered Hocking. "I have let him escape. But no more. I will break him like a twig. He will acknowledge me. Reston will crawl to *me!*"

CHAPTER FOURTEEN

"You are looking chipper this morning!"

Spence turned as Ari entered the room. She was dressed in a fresh green tunicked jumpsuit with a high collar. Her hair spilled over her shoulders in flaxen curls. She appeared the picture of health and good will.

"I am. I'm leaving."

"When?"

"Right now—or just as soon as the nurse comes back with my clothes."

She cocked her head to one side. "Are you sure you're up to it?"

"Of course. I only slipped in the shower. I'm fine. Besides, if I stay here much longer, I'll starve. The food is like . . . don't ask."

"You still sound like a frog. Your poor throat—"

"Dr. Williams says it will clear up in a day or two. The chemical isn't harmful, but it doesn't do to inhale it in quantity, that's all. He says if I can stay out of the rain I won't catch pneumonia. There's no reason to keep me here."

"Can you breathe all right? Does it hurt?"

"Not too much. What's all this? Don't you want me to get out?"

"Certainly I do. But I don't want you to have a relapse."

"Relapse?"

"You know—another spell or whatever."

Spence stared at the ceiling for a few moments before speaking again. And when he did, the bantering tone had gone out of his voice.

"Ari, what do you think has been happening to me?"

"I don't know. Honestly."

"What has Dr. Williams told you?"

"Nothing. He's as puzzled by all this as anybody."

He considered this. "Listen to me, Ari, I—" He was interrupted by the arrival of the nurse with his clothing.

"Here we are. Good as new, Mr. Reston." Everyone was *Mister* to the nursing staff—that was the only way they could distinguish the medical doctors from all the other varieties abounding on Gotham. She laid the neatly folded gold and blue bundle of his jumpsuit at the foot of his bed.

"I'll wait outside while you change, Spence," said Ari. She left with the nurse.

When he emerged from the sick bay ward he looked fit and rested and better than Ari had seen him. She wondered if she had been over-concerned; surely Spence knew what was best. He turned his head when he saw her and she saw the "sun-burned" portion of his face. No, she was right to be worried. He needed looking after.

Dr. Williams stepped up to dismiss his patient as Spence met Ari at the portal. "I hope you'll think about what I said, Dr. Reston. My offer still stands."

"I'll think about it. But I don't think I'll change my mind."

The physician shook his head. "It's up to you. I'm always available."

"I appreciate that."

The panel slid open. Spence and Ari stepped through. "Good-bye, doctor. I'll try to stay out of trouble for at least a week."

"Please! I need my beds for sick people." The sliding door cut him off.

"Well, where to?" asked Ari. "How about lunch? I'll buy."

"Yes, to lunch. But *I'll* buy. I have a favor to ask you."

"All right. Where shall we go?"

"*Belles Esprit* is okay with me. Okay with you?"

"My, it must be some favor. But I'm game. Let's go."

They made their way along the trafficways of Gotham to the so-called leisure level, taking several lifts and a shunt tube to their destination. When they arrived in the plaza there was a line of people waiting to be seated in the restaurant.

"Ah, perfect timing," said Spence. "That's the trouble with a good beanery. Word gets out and the tourists take over. Want to go someplace else?"

"It's worth the wait. Let's stay."

The line moved slowly and the two filled the time talking about mundane items of Gotham news. Spence did not mention again his reason for the rendezvous, but Ari let him work up to it in his own way.

At last they were ushered to a small table and sat facing one another over a stiff, white tablecloth. Spence hardly glanced at the menu and put it aside. Ari decided he was getting ready to tell her what he had begun to explain in sick bay.

"Ari—" The waiter, attired in a black suit with white shirt and tie and looking very continental, appeared to take their order.

"What would you like, Monsieur?" Even the French accent was commendable. Spence decided that the waiters for the various restaurants were recruited for their acting ability as much as for their efficiency. They seemed to be the flower of their flock, and far better than any Spence had had the fortune to run into on Earth. Perhaps they were in fact French waiters after all.

"We will have the artichokes vinaigrette to start. And the sole."

"New peas or cauliflower, Monsieur?"

"New peas. And I think I would like a nice Beaujolais."

"Shall I bring a bottle, sir?"

"A half bottle will be fine, thank you."

It was only after the waiter had gone that he realized he had not consulted his guest for her order. "I'm sorry. I'm afraid I neglected to ask you what you wanted."

She laughed. "Don't be embarrassed. You read my mind."

"I do this so seldom, I'm afraid I'm out of practice."

"And don't apologize. There's nothing to apologize for."

"Just the same, next time I'll let you do all the talking."

"I'm not complaining, Spencer. A girl would be a fool to scorn a free meal."

The waiter returned with the wine. He showed Spence the bottle and Spence pretended to read the label. He then deftly uncorked it and splashed a swallow into Spence's glass and handed it to him, laying the cork at his hand. Spence took the cork and sniffed it, not knowing what he was smelling for, then took a sip of the wine. It was smooth and good, warming the palate with a vibrant charm.

"That's very good," he said. The waiter poured their glasses half full and then left.

The glasses stood before them, casting faint crimson shadows on the white cloth. Spence did not lift a hand toward his glass, so Ari folded her hands on the table and waited.

"I want to tell you something—it's about what has been happening."

"You don't have to say anything."

"I want to—I want you to know." He raised his eyes from the white expanse of the tablecloth to meet hers.

"All right, I'm listening," she said gently.

"Ari, I don't know what's happening to me. Not really." He looked at her and for a moment she saw how frightened he was. He shook his head and the fear receded, pushed back behind its barrier once more. "But I don't think it's me. At least not entirely."

"Oh?"

"I know what Dr. Williams thinks. And I have a fair idea what he must have told you. But he's forgetting that I am trained in psychology, too. I know the symptoms and the causes.

"I don't think I fit the profile. I mean, I'm hardly manic-depressive, and I'm not schizophrenic. At least, I don't think I am."

The waiter returned to lay the glistening green-gray artichokes before them. He unrolled the napkins and placed them on their laps, arranged their silver, and then vanished.

Spence continued as if the waiter had never been there. "At this point, I realize I would have a very rough time proving my sanity."

"Nobody thinks you're insane."

"Dr. Williams might dispute that."

"Nonsense. He's concerned, and I am too. You have to admit, though, we haven't a lot to go on."

"Granted. These past few weeks, however, I have doubted my sanity. I could feel it slipping away and there was nothing I could do to stop it. It was like I was being drained, bit by bit, only I didn't realize it at first. I tried to tell myself that it was overwork, pressure, new surroundings. But I don't think so anymore."

He sampled some of the artichoke. Ari, who had been nibbling all along, laid down her fork. "I don't think I'm getting all of this, Spence. Perhaps you'd better start at the beginning."

"You're right." He nodded and took a few more bites of his food. "I can't remember the beginning. There are a lot of things I can't remember. Whole chunks of my memory are missing.

"But it was some time after I came here, though not long after. A couple weeks, that's all. It started with the dreams."

"Dreams?"

"Don't ask me what they're about, because I don't know. Sometimes I am almost on the verge of remembering—I can almost see a picture in my mind. A word or a sound will trigger it, but then it's gone. Everything goes blank.

"But I can tell you this: they are strange, frightening dreams. I wake up in a cold sweat, trembling. Once or twice I believe I have screamed. I know I have cried in my sleep.

"There is no pattern to it that I can see. Sometimes it happens during a session—the experiments, you know—and sometimes when I'm asleep in my own quarters. But the emotional impact stays with me for a while, lingering over me like a ghostly presence, haunting me."

"That's horrible!"

"It gets worse."

"Your order, sir." The waiter materialized out of nowhere to place several steaming dishes before them. "Enjoy your meal, Monsieur, Mademoiselle."

"Uh-oh," said Spence. "Something's wrong."

"What is it?" said Ari, afraid that some new horror had descended upon Spence.

"Red wine with sole. How gauche." He pulled a wry grin. "Ari, you are dining with a gauche person."

She laughed and the sound was a bubbling of music. "Down with convention! I don't care. Besides, you know what they say."

"What do they say?"

"Foolish consistency is the hobgoblin of little minds."

"Is it?"

"Well, Emerson thought so. He said it."

They both laughed then and Ari saw the lines of strain ease from around his eyes and mouth. He let go; the ice had been broken. He had trusted her with his secret; now he would confide in her. She, too, relaxed, discovering she had been sitting on the edge of her chair since they were seated.

"Cheers!" said Spence, lifting his glass and clinking it against hers. He took a sip of wine and then dug into his food with the haste of a hungry man. They ate in silence until he pushed back his plate with a motion of finality. He had reached a decision.

He launched back into his confession willingly. The words spilled out in a torrent; the floodgates had opened. Ari sat spellbound as she listened.

"The blackouts began a week ago—five days, to be exact. Nothing in my family history would indicate a condition such as this. No epilepsy, catalepsy, or anything of that sort. It's completely original with me, whatever it is.

"What takes place during the blackouts, I have no idea. Neither do I know how long they last precisely. I estimate anywhere from six to ten hours, working backward from the time I can last remember until I wake up again. Obviously I am fairly active during these episodes, judging from the fact that I seem to be able to get myself into varying degrees of difficulty." He raised a hand to the red side of his face.

"These self-destructive acts, as Dr. Williams calls them, are well known in psychological literature—especially in association with blackouts or amnesia. It is not unusual for a blackout to result from the trauma of a very destructive or threatening act. In other words, the mind blocks the memory of the episode because it is simply too painful to remember.

"In my case, however, I believe it is just the other way around. I can't prove anything one way or the other, but something inside tells me I'm right in the assumption. I thought about it all last night as I lay in sick bay. It's just a gut hunch, but right now it's the best I've got."

"I'm not sure I understand."

"What I'm trying to say, I guess, is that in my case the blackouts come first and trigger the self-destructive acts. Only I don't think the point is to destroy myself."

"What is the point?"

"To escape. Flight is one of the oldest animal reflexes. It's basic, universal. Even the most timid creature will flee into an unknown danger in order to escape a known one."

"But, Spence," Ari gasped, "who or what would want to harm you?"

"I don't know—yet. But I mean to find out." He glanced at Ari's worried face; she was chewing her lower lip and scowling furiously. "I know how fantastic this all sounds. You must think I'm a raving madman. Why invent invisible enemies? Why concoct outrageous theories when the same facts can be explained more simply with known principles? I've asked myself those questions a thousand times in the last twenty-four hours. But there's something inside me that won't let me accept the other alternative. And right now that's all I have."

Ari leaned across the table and placed her hands on his. She looked him full in the face and said, "I believe you, Spencer."

"You do?"

"Yes, I do. For one thing, no one could talk the way you do—so objectively, so logically—who was suffering the kind of mental distress you describe. So I believe you."

"I didn't think it would be that easy. I mean, there's every reason to lock me away before I hurt myself or someone else. But . . . you don't think I'm going crazy?"

"No, I don't. Whatever it is that's causing these—these seizures, it must be something outside yourself."

"That's it, Ari. You've said it. Something outside of me. I've felt it hovering over me. A presence . . . I can't describe what it's like."

"How can it be, though?"

Spence clenched his fist. "I don't know. I scarcely believe it's possible. But that's the feeling I get sometimes."

"Did you enjoy your meal, sir?" the waiter asked. How long he had been standing there Spence wasn't sure. He was surprised to see the table cleared of the dishes; he had been so wrapped up in his story he had not noticed them being taken away.

"The meal was fine, thank you."

"Very good, sir. I will bring your check."

"Thank you, Spence. It was a lovely meal."

"If somewhat gruesome."

"No, I mean it. I can't say I enjoyed the conversation—knowing what you have been through. But I've enjoyed being with you."

The waiter brought the check on a silver tray and placed it before Spence, handing him a silver fountain pen at the same time. He signed his name and personal accounting code.

"Thank you very much, Monsieur. Join us again very soon. Adieu." The waiter turned and snapped his fingers and a white-coated young man appeared with a silver coffeepot and filled their china cups. He placed between them a tiny silver bowl which contained four delicate pink rosebud mints.

Spence sipped his coffee thoughtfully. Ari could see him weighing his next words carefully.

"Ari, I've told you all this because I want to ask a favor of you."

"Go ahead."

"It's a small thing, but it's important to me. You'll probably think it's silly."

"No, I won't. Not after all you've told me today. I don't think any of this is silly. I think it's extremely serious."

"Well, your father asked me to join the research trip to the terra-forming project on Mars."

"I remember. I was there when he asked you."

"Right. The thing is, I've decided to take up his offer. I'm going to go on the trip. Only no one can know. That's where you come in. I want you to fix it for me so that all the necessary arrangements are made without anyone beyond your father and his staff knowing about it. Can you do that?"

"I think so; I can try. But, Spence, do you think that's wise? You'll be away a long time—anything could happen. You could have blackouts again, and out there no one would be able to take care of you, no medical facilities."

"I have to get away, don't you see? The blackouts started here, and if I stay they'll continue. They may happen out there, too, I realize that. But I have to take that risk."

Ari was not convinced. She frowned. "I don't like it—it's too dangerous. Why don't you stay here and arrange to have someone monitor your activities—your assistant maybe. Or, let Dr. Williams check you over. That would be the sane thing to do."

"The *sane* thing?" he snapped.

"Sorry. Unfortunate choice of words. But you know what I mean. He offered to let you come in for a complete physical and psychological. And he'd keep it off the record."

"He told you about that? What else did he tell you? What have you two got cooked up?"

"Nothing, Spence. I didn't mean anything—"

"What was the idea? Keep me talking until I convinced myself to check in as a psycho? Was that what you had in mind?"

The sudden shift in Spence's mood frightened Ari. She did not know what to do, so she said, "Listen, Spencer, I'll do as you say. I'll get your trip cleared and I'll arrange it so no one will know. But I want a favor from you. Let Dr. Williams look you over before you go. It couldn't hurt."

He leaned back in his chair and fought to regain control of his temper. He still glared at her, and the look on his face scared her. "I'll think about it," he snapped.

The next moment he was on his feet, jumping up so quickly that he sent his chair crashing to the floor. Heads turned as he stormed out of the restaurant, and diners at the tables all around stared at Ari and talked behind their hands. She colored under their scrutiny. The waiter leaped forward instantly and righted the chair.

"No trouble, Mademoiselle," he said and graciously helped her from her seat.

She hurried from the cafe, her cheeks burning scarlet.

CHAPTER FIFTEEN

By the time Spence reached the lab he was in a foul mood. Ari had betrayed him. He had trusted her, confided in her, only to find that she was working for Dr. Williams. The two of them ganging up on him he did not need, he argued. He did not need anybody.

In his present state he was ready to bite the heads off nails. The unlucky Tickler discovered this to his dismay when he met Spence at the portal as the panel slid open. "Where have you been, Dr. Reston? We've been worried about you."

"You have, huh?" Spence threw him a nasty look. "Not worried enough to check the sick bay."

"I was just on my way down there," said Tickler. He wrung his hands as if to wipe off something distasteful. "When you didn't show up for the session I . . . well, I didn't know what to do."

"Well, you can stop worrying. I'm all right. I just had a little accident, that's all."

"Your voice . . . your face. What happened?"

"Maybe I'll tell you about it someday. Right now I want to go over those averages I asked you to get for me."

Tickler spun completely around in a circle before heading off to the datafile at the opposite end of the lab. Spence smiled darkly; he had really upset the finicky Tickler this time.

He crossed the lab and went to his place in the booth. He flopped into his chair and took up the log book, fully intending to bleed off his anger with a few hours of furious work. But as soon as he settled himself in his chair the ComCen screen on the wall next to him began flashing and the beeper shrilled its tone code.

The tone stopped after one sequence and the flasher stopped too, leaving a red bar across the screen. Evidently the message was not of particular urgency; he felt at first inclined to ignore it, but instead he punched the display key on the panel beneath the screen.

He watched as it spelled out his name and ID number and the characters INOF-CLS-A-RDYRD. In computerspeak this meant that the message was of interoffice origin of the lowest grade and was ready to read by simply tapping the display key once more. Several of the higher grade levels required that a personal access code be entered before the message could be received, and some would not be displayed at all but would only be dispensed on paper through the ComCen printer lest anyone unauthorized accidentally view the screen when an important message was transmitted.

Spence tapped the display key and read the following:

Spence, Come see me when you get a chance.
I'd like to talk to you. Adjani.

This was an unexpected development; he was being invited to drop in on the genius just as if they were old friends. He was flattered in spite of himself and wondered what Adjani wanted to talk to him about. *Only one way to find out. Go see him.*

He rose just as Tickler entered the control booth. "Here are the averages, Dr. Reston," sniffed his assistant, waving a sheaf of printouts at him.

"Thanks, Tickler. I'll see to them later. Something's come up. I'll be back soon. Ready the presets for the next battery of experiments. We'll start those tonight. And Tickler, *please* be careful with the encephamine. Another spill like last time and you could put the whole station to sleep. Besides, the stuff is expensive!"

Spence ducked out leaving the miffed Tickler sputtering. He left the lab feeling much better than when he had entered it, and moved out onto the trafficway heading for the main axial. For some reason he received perverse pleasure in befuddling the stuffy Tickler. The realization gave him a momentary pang of guilt which he rejected without a second thought.

He paused on his way to view a directory. He had never been to the HiEn section before and knew only vaguely how to get there. He tapped HiEn into a ComCen screen below the directory and instantly received a route suggestion, and hurried along. He took Fifth Avenue where it branched off from the main, and then made for the Belt Line tube tram. That saved him from having to meander through the complex inner core of Gotham. He got out of the tube in the blue section and took the nearest lift up four levels to his destination.

Adjani's quarters were two cramped cubicles overflowing with electronic gear, magcarts, and bubbleplates. The rooms were barely larger than sanibooths and Spence could see they had been hastily partitioned off from one of the larger labs. In one cubicle was a bed and a chair, on which were stacked a multicolored tower of magcarts; in the other room was a desk and a data base with three wafer screens and keyboards.

"I am afraid one of us will have to sit on the bed," explained Adjani apologetically as he ushered Spence in. "My arrival has caused some hardship among the housekeepers, I believe. Olmstead was kind enough to divide his quarters with me until a more suitable arrangement can be found. Come in, come in, please."

"Thank you." Spence glanced around the cluttered interior. Every square centimeter of space, except for a tentative pathway through the rooms, was crammed with data in its various disguises—on paper, disc, tape and sealed cartridge. It reminded Spence of his own study cube back at the university years ago. "I will never complain about my miniature quarters again. Compared to these, mine are cavernous."

"I don't mind, really. I'm not here very much. Mostly I'm in one of the labs or hotrooms. They keep me pretty busy, you know. Personally, I'm beginning to think the only reason Packer wanted me here was so he wouldn't have to think anymore." The slim brown man paused, then added deviously, "I'm fixing him, though. I make him and his shuttle bums think *twice* as hard!"

He turned and threaded his way carefully into the adjoining cubicle. Spence followed lightly, careful not to start an avalanche. Adjani plopped the multicolored cartridges onto a knee-high stack of disc cartons and waved Spence to the chair. He curled up on the bed in lotus position. Spence wondered if his host was Hindu.

"Where are you from, Adjani?"

"San Francisco." He laughed at Spence's expression, rocking back and forth on the bed. "I know, everyone makes the same mistake. My people are from Nagaland. My father was from Imphal; my mother from Manipur. They met in London when my father was teaching at the Royal Academy. He is at Oxford now."

Adjani spoke with pride of his parents; Spence sensed they were close. Somewhat wistfully he found himself envying Adjani's relationship with his family—though he knew nothing at all about them—and regretting his own.

Adjani continued: "They waited eight years to bring me to the United States. We came under the Necessary Skills Program just after the war, and it cost my father over twelve thousand dollars to buy our entrance visas. I was eight years old when we came—I remember because I was in seventh form and everyone made fun of me for being so small."

"You were in seventh form when you were only eight?" Spence's eyes grew wide in disbelief.

"It was all they could do to keep me in printout paper," laughed Adjani.

"You stayed in California then?"

"Yes, for the most part. When I finished school we went back to India and I spent some time in my father's homeland—a very enlightening experience. Every son should have the chance to see his father as a young man. That's what I saw in Nagaland.

"Anyway, we could not go back to the United States because our visas had expired. Father went back to Great Britain. I would have joined him, I believe, but Cal Tech summoned me for their Think Tank."

"What about your visa?"

"The government waived the regulations. Olmstead arranged it, though he won't admit it. We had become friends at Stanford, and he was afraid that if he did not find me a job he would never see me again. Quite possibly it was true." Adjani spread his hands wide. "Now you know my whole life's story—but for one or two important details."

"It's an interesting story. I'm sure your parents are very proud of you."

Adjani shrugged. "Yes and no. They realize that I am what I am, but they do not deny they had greater plans for me."

The remark struck Spence as absurd. Adjani was possibly the highest man in his discipline. "What could be greater than what you're doing right now?"

"They had hoped I would become their *purohit*—the family priest."

"You are Hindu?" asked Spence, thinking his first impression had been correct.

"Oh, no!" laughed Adjani. "I use the word in a general sense. We are Christians. My family hoped I would be a minister, like my grandfather."

This admission made Adjani seem even more foreign and mysterious. For Spence, religion was merely a holdover from a superstitious age in man's history. No true scientist held to dogma.

"Does this surprise you, Spence?" Adjani's black eyes glittered intently as he leaned forward on his couch.

"A little, I guess. People don't take that stuff seriously anymore."

"Ah, that's where you're wrong. Religion is elemental to man's being. True religion ennobles; it never debases."

"I guess I haven't thought much about it one way or the other." Spence shifted uncomfortably in his seat.

"Don't worry." Adjani smiled broadly. "I did not invite you here to preach to you."

Spence relaxed and leaned back in his chair. "I was beginning to wonder. Why *did* you ask me here?"

"A selfish reason. I would like to know you better." Adjani clasped his hands beneath his chin and rested his elbows on his knees. He weighed his next words before saying them.

"And?"

"And—I do not wish to offend you—I thought you looked like someone who could use a friend."

Spence did not speak right away. The comment seemed charged with implications he could not fathom at once. His eyes became wary and his tone guarded. "That's very kind of you. I appreciate that," he said slowly. The suspicion in his voice leaked through.

Adjani pounced on it as if it were a snake. "Is that so unusual?"

"Why, no. Of course not. I have lots of friends." Spence hoped he would not be asked to name them.

"Good. I would like you to consider me among them."

Spence did not know what to say; he was embarrassed, but could not think why he should be. "I'd be glad to have you as a friend, Adjani. I mean it." The words were genuine.

No one spoke for a few moments. Adjani sat gazing at Spence as if he were reading his future in his face. Spence felt a strange excitement stir within him and the room grew fuzzy and indistinct. At the same time he was aware of a heightened sensitivity to his situation. An unseen presence had entered the room. He could feel it—a force which charged the atmosphere of the tiny room with electricity.

When Adjani spoke, his words cut through to Spence's heart. "I see a darkness around you like a cloud. Would you like to tell me what is troubling you?"

CHAPTER SIXTEEN

SPENCE HEARD the fading echo of a roar like thunder. He could not decide if he had indeed heard the sound or only imagined it, for it shrank away to become the sound of his own blood pounding in his ears. He dropped like a stone through an infinite darkness, falling and falling, turning over and over, spinning slowly through the void.

How long he had fallen he could not determine. Time had no meaning in this formless space. But presently he glimpsed—far ahead as in a tunnel a long way off—a single beam of white light. The light grew stronger and larger as he spun closer, growing until it filled his eyes with a gentle radiance. He could see it quite clearly—a large luminous disk, moonlike against the forever-darkness all around.

As he watched, the disk changed slightly. He noticed that it had features which resembled human features. The disk swept closer to him, or he to it, and he realized that it was not a moon at all, but a human skull.

The skull's black, vacant eye sockets rotated slowly toward him to fix him with their hideous blank gaze. He could see it clearly now, looming ever closer, filling the void with its wan, ghostly light. He saw that the skull was rushing upon him and at the same time that he was shrinking.

Great wrenching spasms of fear shook his body—he imagined he could hear his teeth rattle in his head. His heart hammered against his ribs and his tongue stuck to the roof of his mouth as he fought to cry out.

Spence diminished as the skull swept toward him, growing larger as it came. Now it filled his field of vision—its eyes were huge black pits opening before him. He put his hands out as if to stop the terrible collision, but when he parted them he saw that he was spinning into one of the empty eye sockets.

The gleaming white teeth in the skull's bony jaw flashed as the mouth opened and began to wag. He heard a thin, cold laughter emanating from between the skull's bare teeth—the horrible fleshless sound of ghostly laughter. He clamped his hands over his ears, but it was too late; the sound had gotten inside his head where it reverberated endlessly.

Now he could see the scaly, pitted ridge of bone which formed the brow, and the triangular hole of the nose with its jutting sliver of bone slashing out from it. The eye hole seemed instantly to expand as he toppled through its yawning, craterlike aperture.

At the moment he fell into the monstrous eye socket, Spence's world flashed red—as if he had plunged beneath the surface of a sea of blood. His falling, shrinking, plunging motion abruptly stopped and he felt suspended in the weird crimson glow.

Slowly he became aware of the fact that he lay on a solid shelf of rock, his cheek flat against smooth, cool stone. The deep red color emanated from the stone itself. His terrible fear subsided.

Spence raised his head slowly. He looked at his hands, bringing them before his face in the blood-red glare as if they might belong to someone else. But they were his hands, and seeing them unaltered calmed his fluttering pulse. He stood uncertainly and gazed around him.

He took one step and his legs gave way beneath him; he was still too shaken and dizzy to walk. He pushed himself up on his hands and knees and waited until his head cleared. In this position, staring down at the stone beneath him, he saw something which caused his jaw to drop in amazement. He rubbed his eyes.

When he worked up his nerve to look again it still remained. He bent to examine it once more to make sure his eyes had not tricked him in the strange light. His breath came in long, shaky gasps of excitement as he brought his face closer to it.

Yes, there was no mistake. Before him in the red dust of the rock floor was a single naked human footprint.

Spence heard a shout echoing from the high, vaulted roof of the cavern, and realized with a shock that it was his own voice, crying out over and over: "It can't be! It can't be!"

The day dragged away like a wounded snake pulling its injured length painfully along. Spence felt every slow tick ebbing away as if it were wrung from his own flesh.

He had been in a sour mood upon waking and knew that he had dreamed again. This depressed him thoroughly. Somehow he imagined that, in light of his resolve to deal squarely with the problems besetting him, the dreams would not affect him any longer.

He was wrong. If anything, they troubled him more deeply than ever.

He worked the shift away in a silent, smouldering rage. Tickler felt the heat of his anger and kept well out of range. The meticulous little man watched his every move from a distance as if Spence were a lab specimen that might at any moment show signs of blossoming another head; his bright, beady eyes followed his master around with keen, if secretive, interest.

Spence waded through a magcart of neglected administrative work and hoped that Tickler had no intention of lingering after the shift ended. He had to bite his tongue on several occasions when he felt inclined to suggest that Tickler leave for the day. *No, an inner voice cautioned, act as if nothing is amiss, nothing out of the ordinary. Business as usual.*

There was a reason for Spence's reluctance to open himself to Tickler's fussy scrutiny: he wanted the next two days to go especially smoothly. He wanted to maintain the appearance of stability and order right up to the moment of his departure. He wanted his leaving on the Mars trip to come as a complete surprise to anyone who might have reason to be interested in such an event—especially Tickler.

If he had been asked, Spence could not have given an explanation for adopting this course of action. Very likely he did not know why himself. He told himself it was because he distrusted Tickler, but he never stopped to consider why that was, or what Tickler had done to earn such ill will. In Spence's mind he represented a vague uneasiness which sent out vibrations of veiled suspicion like certain nettlesome vines sent out creeping tendrils.

At last the shift ended and Tickler approached his chair quietly, with his hands held limply in front of him as if they were wet gloves he had just hung out to dry. "Is there anything else today, Dr Reston?"

Spence did not bother to consult the digiton above the console; he knew Tickler would not have approached one nanosecond before the specified time. He pushed back his chair and rubbed his eyes in a show of fatigue. "Oh, is it time to quit already?"

"I don't mind putting in an extra shift—"

"Thanks, but it isn't necessary. We've done a good day's work. Call it quits and we'll hit it again tomorrow. We can ready the equipment for the session tomorrow evening then. Good day, Tickler."

Tickler peered back as if he were trying to read a message that was written on Spence's face in a foreign language. "Are you sure there's nothing else?"

Spence shook his head and smiled as broadly as he could. "You sure are a workhorse. No, I can't think of a thing that can't be done tomorrow. You're free. I'll see you tomorrow."

Tickler did not reply; he only dipped his head in a smarmy little bow and then hurried away like a rat heading back to his burrow after a night in the pantry. Spence watched him go and then went to the portal himself. He cleared the access code on the doorplate and reset it with a new code so that he would not be disturbed.

"Now to business!" he muttered to himself as he sank back into his cav chair behind the console. Throughout the day as he worked, the thought kept nagging him that he should check out the riddle of the identical scan more thoroughly. Actually, the urge was not a new one—it had nagged him before, but he simply had not had time to do anything about it until now.

He fell to with a will. He retraced in his mind the steps he had followed to discover the similarity of the two scans in the first place. As to what the significance of the supposed similarity could mean, he was still at a loss for an answer. But deep inside he believed it to be important in some way. What he proposed to accomplish next was to establish that it had been no glitch, no momentary foul-up in the electronic circuitry or in the program which had fed him spurious information.

Spence picked up at the point where he had made his strange discovery three days before.

"MIRA, Spence Reston here. Ready for command."

"Ready, Dr. Reston," said MIRA's feminine voice.

"Compare all PSG Seven Series LTST entries. Display entries with similarities with less than one percent variability."

He sat back to wait, tapping his fingers on the table before him while MIRA worked. MIRA—the initials stood for Multiple Integrated Rational something or other which he could not at the moment remember—was the largest of a breed of biotic computers whose circuitry was in part derived from organic molecules—protein grids which had been integrated with electronics. She was faster, smarter, and more creative in a dozen ways than any computer before her.

Within seconds the wafer screen spelled out the message, which to Spence's grim satisfaction matched the previous one: PSG Seven Series scans 3/20 and 5/15.

There it was again. The chance that it was a computer error ceased to be a possibility. Glitches did not repeat themselves. The chance that it was a kink in his program was also remote. The command was well within the program's range of flexibility.

Retracing his steps completely, he opened the yellow log book and matched the two disputed scans. They were, as he had previously discovered, quite different.

Next he pushed the inquiry a step further and went to the cabinet, getting out the tray of spools for the week of 5/15 and the tray for the week of 3/20. He set the trays down on his nearby desk and fished out the spools in question. He snapped the seal on each of them and rolled out a portion of the scan. The four red wavy lines undulated evenly across his desk. He matched up two intervals and placed one tape over the other and held them to the light.

The two scans, viewed one through the other as they overlapped one another, were clearly different. He could see peaks in one where there were valleys in the other. Laid one on top of the other all similarities between them ceased to exist. He checked the interval again and even tried to force the comparison by matching peaks and valleys, but could not. The scans were simply quite different one from the other. MIRA had apparently goofed after all.

But there was still one more wrinkle to check: the bubble memory. As an added backup to the overall design of the project, Spence had recorded each scan on a bubble plate. This was the source of the numbers entered in the log book. The rising and falling motion of the scanner's red ink lines was recorded within the thin sealed cartridge whose magnetic bubbles were interpreted by the computer as a continuous series of numbers. For every place the needle rested on the paper tape, there was a corresponding number. By reading the numerical values the computer could reconstruct the wavy lines on the paper tape.

He opened the bubble file and pulled the cartridge for the two sessions. He popped one cartridge into each of the slots in the memory reader of the console and gave the display command.

Instantly the numbers on the plates began filling the screen. He quickly scanned the columns and his breath caught in his throat; the two scans were exactly alike!

He dropped into his swivel chair and propped his feet up on the edge of the table. He stared at the rows of identical numbers on the screen and then closed his eyes, retreating into thought.

Here at last was the corroborating evidence he had been seeking—only instead of helping to solve the mystery, it deepened it. He began to think through the steps of his experiment and how it was recorded in all its various stages to determine how a situation such as the one glimmering at him from the wafer screen could ever have happened.

Given the fact that it was impossible for any two scans to be perfectly alike—even the same man on the same night could not produce two identical scans—he was forced to reckon the evidence an error, either human or electronic.

Now, with the evidence of the bubble memory, the likelihood of an electronic error diminished to the point of infinite improbability. The cloud of doubt in which he had so far carried his investigation began to condense into suspicion: *someone* had been tampering with his records.

The longer he thought about it, the more suspicious he became until the unproven hypothesis hardened into certainty. Someone *had* been tampering with his materials. Assuming that much, the next question was *why?* Why would anyone want to sabotage his experiment?

No, that was the wrong approach. Not sabotage—alter. That seemed closer to the mark. Why would anyone want to alter the evidence? And why these particular scans, in this particular way?

To puzzle this latest wrinkle in this confusing development he got up from his chair and shoved it across the room. He began pacing with his arms folded across his chest and his head bent down as if he expected the answer to form itself upon the floor.

The answer, when it came, hit him like a closed fist between the eyes; it nearly knocked him down.

The simplicity of it staggered him—it was so obvious. The scans had not been altered; they had been duplicated. The scan of 5/15 was a copy of scan 3/20. That was why they were identical. What about the other pieces of the puzzle? The tape, the log book, the main computer memory? Those simply had been manufactured to fill in the gap.

Spence's mind raced ahead like lightning along a once-traveled path.

The morning of 5/15 had been the morning after his first blackout when he awakened in the sleep chamber. That much he remembered clearly. He remembered Tickler remarking that the scan had gone well that night. He also remembered that he had not actually seen the scan at that time; it was not until after breakfast that he examined it. Plenty of time for someone to manufacture the missing pieces and place them in position.

Was the scan of 3/20 somehow significant? Probably not. It had just been selected at random from among the first of the experiment's records. It was used to fill in the gaps in the bubble memory and the data base memory.

What about the paper tape and the log book? That was the easiest part. Those had simply been created wholesale. The figures in the log book were dummies and the paper ribbon probably bore the signature of someone else's brainwaves.

Spence, swept up in the heady whirl of intrigues real and imagined, staggered to his chair and collapsed as if he had just run a thousand meters. He had it—the answer, or the beginning of the answer—and knew that he had it. Proving it was another matter, but he was not interested at present in proving anything. He was happy just to know.

His elation proved short-lived.

Within moments the other question reasserted itself? Why? Why had these things been done?

Clearly he stood at the beginning of the maze. Where it would lead he did not know. But at last he felt strong enough to face whatever he might find.

On an impulse he turned and punched a code into the ComCen panel. There was someone he had to see before another moment passed.

CHAPTER SEVENTEEN

WHEN TICKLER left the lab he did not go directly to his quarters across the corridor from the lab. Instead he put his head down and scurried as fast as his feet would take him to the main axial and then took a lift tube to the eighth and topmost level of the station. He rode the tram along the inner ring radial until the track dead-ended at a blank white wall. Next to a large pressure port in the wall a large sign painted in orange letters read:

DANGER!

CONSTRUCTION AREA

PRESSURE SUIT REQUIRED

AUTHORIZED PERSONNEL ONLY!

Adjacent to the port hung a row of baggy pressure suits limp in their racks like deflated men. Tickler stepped across the trafficway and wormed his way into one of the bulky suits and disengaged it from the rack. He then punched a code into the access plate of the portal and stepped quickly through as soon as the panel slid open wide enough to admit him.

He waited inside the small air lock for the pressure to equalize and then popped the valve. He emerged from the little room into the breathtaking blackness of space. He stood blinking for a moment, looking up into the expanse above him at the stars shining steadily down with their icy light.

Bare spars, like the ribs of an ancient sailing vessel, stuck up out of the darkness. Some of these were hung with rows of red lights to mark portions of the station now under construction. Over the rim of the station's smooth flank floated a work platform loaded with sheets of metal and other materials, all secured beneath steel net to keep them from floating into space. Several robotrucks hovered nearby, tethered to the platform with steel cable.

Not a workman could be seen at any of the several sites, so Tickler proceeded toward a huge cylindrical projection standing at the midpoint of the construction area. Across the top quarter of the cylinder a diagonal band of light, lengthening as the station rotated toward the sun, slashed into the darkness. Ordinarily the whole area would be ablaze with floodlights, but the shift was over and a new one would not come on for a few hours. Tickler had the site all to himself. Still, he wasted no time, but moved ahead quickly and carefully, his magnetic boots clinking over the honeycombed temporary trafficways set up like scaffolds all around the area. He headed for the cylinder.

When he reached it, he paused only long enough for the portal to slide open to admit him. Once inside and through the air lock he hung up his pressure suit on the rack next to another already waiting there and proceeded. A lift tube carried him into the upper section of the silo, and when the panel slid open he stepped into a bare apartment of immense size. At one end a light shone in a pool on the floor. Within the pool two figures waited. One of the figures resembled an egg.

"You are late!" snapped the egg as Tickler approached.

"I came as quickly as I could," explained the breathless Tickler as the egg slowly revolved to display the wizened features of Hocking. "He kept me working all shift. I couldn't very well ask him to excuse me without arousing suspicion, and—"

Hocking grimaced and cut off the excuse. "I have been in contact with Ortu. He is not pleased with the progress we are making. I have taken the blame for our failure upon myself."

"Failure?" Tickler asked, as if he had never heard the word before. He looked to the other figure standing to one side of Hocking's pneumochair. The young man in a cadet's jumpsuit stared back dully.

"I expect," continued Hocking, speaking slow and crisply, "that you and Kurt will find a way to make this up to me. Well?" The eyes flashed from their sunken depths.

Tickler spread his hands. "We have done all you have required of us. I fail to see how we could have anticipated the setbacks arising from the subject's stubbornness."

"I'm not talking about that," cooed the skeletal Hocking. "I am talking about the breakdown in monitoring the subject's every move. Between the two of you he should never be out of your sight for a moment. Do you know where he is right now?"

"Why, yes. He's in the lab."

"Oh? Do you know this for a fact? Could he not have left the lab as soon as you did? Could he not, in fact, have followed you here?"

Tickler looked worried. He cast a quick glance behind him to see if Spence had indeed followed him to Hocking's secret chambers.

"See!" Hocking shouted. "You do *not* know! Reston has consistently moved about the station at will, and yet I have stressed time and again how necessary it is to keep him under surveillance during the induction period. It is only by the merest chance that he is still with us!"

Tickler did not speak; he gazed sullenly at the floor.

"But I am raking over old ground. Suffice it to say that if you cannot watch him more closely than you are at present I will find someone who *can* . . ." He allowed the threat to trail off menacingly.

"Now, then," he continued, "I have been thinking. By this time tomorrow we must have everything prepared to try another induction. Reston is ripe for it now, I can feel it. I have given him additional image cues while in dream state. We will increase the psychomotor quotient of the *tanti* this time—we have, I believe, underestimated our subject's mental strength and willpower. That should not hinder us again, however."

"If it does not kill him," muttered Tickler darkly.

"I heard you perfectly, Tickler. You might as well speak up. I am willing to risk killing him, yes. I'd prefer it to allowing him to slip away again. We cannot suffer that to happen. That is why I want one of you to be stationed with him when the induction takes place."

"No!" Both men gasped at once and looked apprehensively at one another.

"You idiots! The projection will not harm you—it is not tuned to your brain wave patterns. I want you there to keep an eye on him and to prevent him from escaping again."

"I don't know if it will be that easy. He was acting very strangely today. I think he may suspect something."

"What can he suspect?" Hocking glared at his hirelings. "Answer me! Unless you have been careless again, I cannot see how he can suspect anything."

"Maybe, but I was with him today. I tell you he does."

Hocking dismissed the warning with an impatient jerk of his head. "What if he does suspect something? By tomorrow at this time it won't matter what our brilliant young friend suspects. It will be too late! He will be ours!"

The sun shields were nearly closed when Spence stepped into the garden. The slanting bands of golden light falling through the trees resembled a kind of tropical aurora which flushed everything with heightened color. This was Spence's favorite time to come here—just before the shields closed and the garden received its nocturnal rest.

He hurried along to the center of the garden and the benches on the greensward. As he had hoped, the benches were empty; not another soul was to be seen anywhere. He settled himself on the last bench to wait. *The only thing missing is mosquitoes,* thought Spence as he listened to the racking squawks of one of Central Park's half-dozen macaws.

He closed his eyes and breathed the humid air deep into his lungs, tilting his head back to rest on the bench. He was still in this attitude, eyes closed, head thrown back, when Ari found him.

"I *know* I haven't kept you waiting *that* long!" she said. "How dare you pretend to sleep."

Spence's head snapped upright as his eyes flew open. He jumped to his feet. "I didn't hear you come up." He looked at her and stood uncertainly, gazing intently at her fair face, even lovelier in the soft golden light of the garden. He tried to read her feelings in her eyes, but could not.

"Ari," he said, after an awkward moment, "thanks for coming. After what I did you had every right to refuse, and I wouldn't have blamed you."

She did not make the moment easier for him, but stood there looking at him implacably.

"I *am* sorry. I . . . I treated you terribly." His eyes sought hers and his voice became hushed. "I've never asked another person to forgive me, but I'm asking you now. Please, forgive me."

The smile that transformed her face came like the dawn to his long, dark night of despair. All the way to the garden he had tortured himself with six kinds of fear and doubt as to the outcome of their meeting. Her voice over the ComCen speaker had been icily polite, giving away nothing that he could use to bolster his sinking ego. But her smile banished all his dark thoughts.

"Oh, Spence, I've been so worried about you. Furious, too, mind you. But more worried than mad."

"I acted like an ass. Running out of the cafe that way—I don't know what I was thinking of. I'm sorry . . ."

"You're forgiven. Now, what is so urgent and secret?"

He drew her to the bench and sat her down. He looked around him as if he expected spies to be lurking in the shrubbery. She could see that his face was flushed with excitement. His slightly wild-eyed look was creeping over him again. She bit her lip. "What is it, Spencer?"

"I have proof that I'm not going crazy."

CHAPTER EIGHTEEN

"YOU'RE GOING to have to trust somebody." Ari's voice was firm. "You can't go it alone."

They were sitting in her father's reading room. A plate of sandwiches sat untouched on the low table in front of them. Spence stared at the walled ranks of books as if he might find a title among them that would tell him what to say next.

"I need time to sort this out," he said at length. "There are too many pieces missing."

"I don't like it, Spence—this running away. It isn't safe."

He swung around to peer at her with a puzzled look. "I'll be all right," he said lamely. "I need to get away from here for a while, that's all."

"What makes you think that if someone is tampering with your experiment they would stop there? They could hurt you, Spence. For whatever reason, you could get hurt very badly."

He had no answer for that. The same thing had crossed his mind many times in the last few hours. "Ari, all I know is that if I *stay* I will be hurt. I've got to go someplace out of reach to figure this thing out."

There was a finality in his tone that did not invite further discussion. Ari sat with her hands in her lap, legs drawn up beneath her. She studied her clasped hands and said, "I'll miss you."

He smiled. "I'll miss you, too. Believe me, if I thought there was another way, I'd take it." He drew a deep breath. "I won't be gone long; you'll see. I'll be back in no time at all."

"I don't call three-and-a-half months no time at all." She colored slightly and admitted, "I was just getting used to having you around."

"We'll pick up right where we left off, I promise." He looked at her steadily and said, "If I stayed you wouldn't want me around. It would be more of the same. Worse maybe."

"You're probably right. Perhaps it is better this way." She turned her head away quickly. He moved closer and touched her shoulder tentatively.

"Are you crying?"

"No!" she sniffed. "I'm allergic to good-byes."

Spence put his hand to her chin and turned her face toward him. A moist trail glistened on her cheek where a tear had fallen. He wiped away the spot and bent his head and kissed her very gently.

"That's for missing me," he said shyly.

Ari smiled and sniffed, rubbing the heel of her hand across her eyes. "The secret's out now, isn't it?" She looked at him again and he felt his insides turning to warm jelly. "Be very careful, Spencer. Don't let anything happen to you."

"I won't . . . ," he managed to croak.

"Spence, I will pray for you every day." She folded her hands unconsciously. "I have been praying for you ever since we met."

He felt as if he had just stepped into a warm shower. His skin tingled with a strange excitement and his heart tugged within him. He wished that he could say that the would pray for her, too. But he knew that such a statement would ring false. It would cheapen her sincere belief. And though Spence himself had no such beliefs, he did not see any good reason to trample on hers.

"Thank you, Ari," he said at last. "No one has ever said that to me before."

They sat for a long time in silence. Finally, he rose uneasily to his feet and said, "I guess I'd better go. I've a lot to do if I'm going to leave tomorrow night."

"Am I going to see you before you go?"

"I hope so. I'll come by here before I head down to the docking bay. Now you're sure—"

"Yes, you're cleared. And no one outside of Captain Kalnikov knows you're going."

"Good."

"But Spence, shouldn't you tell *somebody*? Someone should know."

"You know. Everyone else will find out after I'm gone."

Ari sighed. "All right, if that's the way you want it."

They moved to the portal and Spence pressed the access plate. "I'll see you tomorrow," he said, ducking quickly outside.

"Good night, Spencer." Ari waved. He waved back and the closing panel broke the spell between them.

He hurried back to his quarters feeling like a cat burglar returning after a night's work. A thousand details had to be attended to before he climbed aboard the transport headed for Mars; between now and then he had precious little time to spare. He would need to work through the night.

He had just closed the door to the vidphone booth at ComCen when the call came through. He sat down and leaned into the camera slightly, resting his elbows on the shelf before him. The flat square screen flickered to life in quick bursts of blue light. He smiled when the red light above the screen came on.

"Spence, it's Kate. Are you surprised to see me?"

He had not expected to see his sister, and for a few seconds could only stare at the image on the screen. In fact, he had imagined so many emergencies which might have provoked the call that he was a little disappointed to see her.

"Your sister, Kate—remember?" She smiled nervously.

"Kate, are you all right? Is everything all right?"

"I know I should have given you more warning. Yes, everything's fine. No emergencies. You sound angry."

"It's just that it's in the middle of the night here—"

"I'm sorry. I forgot. It's three o'clock in the afternoon down here." Spence forced himself to smile in answer to her anxious look. "Don't worry about it. I don't mind. I wasn't sleeping anyway. When ComCen said I had a call coming through, I assumed something terrible had happened to Dad or one of the boys . . . you know."

"Everyone's fine, Spence. I just wanted to talk to you—I hope I'm not interrupting one of your experiments . . . "

"No, no; I'm not working tonight."

"Well, I feel so awkward. I mean, just think, you're a million miles out in space and here I am talking to you like you were across town or something."

"Wait 'til you get the bill. You won't think I was all that close then." He paused, studying her face on the screen. Though only two years older than he was, Kate had always been the wise, benevolent elder sister. He saw her now, a mother of two growing boys, looking more than ever like a matron. She bore little resemblance to the picture of her he carried around in his head.

"You look tired, Spence. Are you feeling all right?" she was saying.

"I'm fine. I've been working a little too hard, that's all."

"Dad said you'd had an accident."

"It was nothing. I bumped my head."

The conversation seemed to dry up at that point. Kate licked her lips. She was trying to bridge the gap of all those miles by staring very hard into the vidphone screen. Spence realized it was not a separation of miles but of life that she was trying to cross. She was trying to imagine his life in that place. Clearly, it was beyond her.

"Why did you call, Kate?" he asked softly.

"Are you angry? Don't be angry, Spence. You'll think it's silly—"

"I won't think it's silly, and I'm not angry. Believe me. Now go ahead and tell me."

She appeared as if she were about to confess a scarlet sin. "Spence, Tuesday's Dad's birthday."

A pang of guilt arrowed through him. He did not feel guilty for forgetting his father's birthday; he had done that often over the years. He felt guilty because the event meant nothing to him. He did not care, and Kate's reminder made him face the fact that other sons *did* remember; they did care.

"I'm sorry," he said flatly. "I forgot."

"That's not why I called. Not to remind you. Well, yes it is, but not how you think. Dad says that you told him you're going on some research trip."

"I told him that, yes. I remember."

"Anyway, he's got it in his head that he's never going to see you again. You know how he gets sometimes. No amount of talking will convince him. He says he's sure something terrible is going to happen to you on that trip—he doesn't even know where you're going—and that he'll never see you again."

Spence could see his father sitting in his faded red chair mumbling and fretting over his son's imagined demise. It was one of the stock images of Spence's childhood and he hated it.

"What do you want me to do, Kate?" he asked, wishing that his mother was still alive. At least she had been able to soothe his father's irrational fears; she had been the cooling balm poured out upon the fevered brow of her husband.

She answered hesitantly. "It would be nice if you would call him and wish him happy birthday. That way he could see you and hear your voice. It might convince him that you're still okay, and that you're thinking about him."

"I'd love to do that, Kate, but I can't. I'll be on my way to Mars by then. I'm leaving tomorrow night and I won't be back for some time." He did not feel like rehearsing the details of his trip with her.

"Mars! Really, Spencer? That's fantastic. Wait until I tell the boys—they'll be so thrilled." Her enthusiasm died almost at once. "But what about Dad?"

"I'm sorry. He'll just have to understand."

"But isn't there *something* you could do, Spence? Anything?"

"I could record a call and have it sent then. I could also send a souvenir of the station—he might like that."

"Would you? It would make him so happy. I'm sure whatever you could send would be fine. It isn't the gift, it's the thought that counts."

But it was Kate's thought—and that was the whole point. "I'll get something on the next shuttle."

"Just send it to me. We're having a little family party for him on Tuesday night. I'll take care of everything."

"Fine. You'll be notified about the call. I'll make sure they give you plenty of time to get to the base."

There was a strained pause. "Well, Spence, I'd better go. Take care of yourself, now. And call when you get back. I know two boys who will want to hear their Uncle Spence tell 'em all about it."

"I'll do that, Kate. Good-bye."

"Good-bye, Spence."

The screen went dark. He sat for a moment gazing into the flat gray square. Then he stood stiffly and left the booth, feeling very hollow and alone, as if every liquid gram of compassion had been wrung out of him in the pitiful effort of conversation with one of his family members.

He wandered back to his quarters gray-faced and eyes burning from the exhaustion of his long day. He stopped briefly at the Visitor's Center to browse among various souvenirs and memorabilia offered as mementos of a trip to Gotham. He selected a small, cast aluminium replica of the space station which was mounted on a grayish stone—part of an asteroid or a moon rock—and designed undoubtedly to be used as a paperweight.

He paid for his purchase, rattling off his account number to a bored clerk who dutifully punched in the data.

"You want it wrapped?" she asked, stifling a yawn.

"No thanks, I'll eat it here," he said, and stuffed the object into a zippered pocket and shambled off to his night's rest.

CHAPTER NINETEEN

MAINTAINING the ruse of "business as usual" proved harder than Spence imagined. For one thing, Tickler seemed especially interested in his plans for the next run of experiments set to begin that night.

"When shall I tell our assistant, Mr. Millen, to join us?"

"Oh, at the usual time. I see no reason to deviate from our norm. Do you?"

"No, sir. Not at all. I just thought that you might have plans which would necessitate rescheduling. In that case I should know about them, that's all."

It was all Spence could do to keep from smirking. "I realize I have been somewhat unpredictable, Tickler. But I'm turning over a new leaf." He turned toward his officious assistant and a lopsided grin stole over his face. "Starting tonight you'll notice a dramatic departure from my usual habits."

Tickler bent his head to one side and sucked in his breath as if he were about to press the matter further, but then thought better of it. That left him holding his breath with his mouth open.

"Was there something else?" asked Spence cheerily.

"Ahh—no." Tickler exhaled like a leaky balloon. "I am quite satisfied." But he stood there blinking his tiny beady eyes as if he expected to be asked to stay to tea and would be disappointed if he were not.

Spence guessed he was waiting for additional information regarding his plans. He decided to end the conversation. "Well, then, If there's nothing else, I suggest we both get busy. There is a lot to be done before tonight. You may wish to catch some sleep before we begin. It could be a long one."

"Of course." Tickler turned and scuttled away. Spence watched him take up his place at the far end of the lab opposite his own work station.

All he needs, thought Spence, *is whiskers and a tail, and the rodent family would have a new patriarch.*

Spence had no intention of showing up for the evening's session. But as the shift came to an end he made a point of remarking to Tickler, "I'll expect you here promptly at the beginning of the third shift. I want to start at once."

To this Tickler replied, "Punctuality is my middle name, Dr. Reston."

"Of course it is," said Spence. "I had always wondered."

Tickler left and Spence dashed to his quarters and began stuffing his belongings into a travel frame, the soft-sided, collapsible carrier of lightweight design used exclusively for shuttle travelers. They were a status symbol back on Earth, identifying seasoned jumpvets. Naturally, they were copied by numerous manufacturers and sold to anyone who wanted one badly enough to pay the outrageous sums these frames fetched. His own bore the company logo in silver on the side and had been given to him prior to the jump.

Although allowed to take two frames with him on the trip he decided to squeeze by with one. He did not care to be bothered with unnecessary baggage. Only at the last minute did he decide to take along his camera.

When it was ready he called housekeeping and asked them to send someone to take it down to the docking bay for him. He did not wish to be seen lugging his frame through the station; he had played it close this far and did not want to risk giving himself away so near to the payoff.

Within the hour a page came to take his frame down for him.

"Do you know who I am?" Spence asked the young man.

"No, sir." He acted as if it was a question he heard often.

"I'd appreciate it if no one else knew either. If anyone asks, you never saw me and the frame belongs to Dr. Packer. Got that?"

"Got it."

Spence handed him a stack of coins for his trouble. "Here, have one of whatever it is you guys have these days on me."

"I never saw you, sir."

"Right."

The kid disappeared pulling the frame through the portal.

Spence went back to his quarters and carefully arranged everything to appear as if he had only stepped from the room and would be returning any moment. Why he went to the trouble he did not know. And he told himself that he was being ridiculous. But having adopted the undercover posture he found himself enjoying the intrigue.

He left the jumpsuit he had been wearing the night before hanging over the chair. Scattered papers lay on his desk, and a mug of cold coffee sat on the table beside the bed. The bedclothes themselves he left rumpled.

When at last he had satisfied himself that everything looked normal, he tiptoed out and left the lab. He had no sooner crossed the threshhold of the portal than he ran smack into his assistant, Kurt Millen.

"Kurt!" he gasped, nearly knocking the young man over.

"Excuse me, Dr. Reston. I didn't see you coming. We're always bumping into one another."

"Yes—" Spence's mind raced to think of a way to escape without arousing suspicion. "I . . . I was just on my way to the commissary. Would you like to join me?"

For one sickening second he thought the cadet would accept his bogus offer.

"Thank you for inviting me, Dr. Reston. But I've got some things to do—Dr. Tickler left me a list of chores. I'd better not."

"You're sure? Just a cup of coffee? I'll buy." Spence fearlessly played the charade to the ragged edge.

"Maybe some other time?"

"Sure—no problem. I won't be a minute." He turned and started away. "I'd better go grab a place in line so I can get back."

He left the cadet standing in front of the lab entrance watching him. Spence kicked himself for overacting his part. He had quite possibly created suspicion where no suspicion existed before. So, to make it look good he strolled dutifully along to the commissary and went inside to stand in line for a few minutes.

He then left, darting back into the trafficway and losing himself in the between-shift throngs heading to and from the cafeteria. He suspected that Kurt would try to follow him. He told himself the notion was absurd, but dodged into a tube and changed levels a couple times anyway, arriving at Ari's door glancing over his shoulder and peering into every shadow.

"Spence! Oh, I'm so glad you came. I was afraid something had happened."

"Something almost did. But there's no problem now." He stepped quickly inside and came to stand in the middle of the room with Ari. They stood face to face, both pretending to be coolly friendly and neither one succeeding.

"How long can you stay?"

"Just a few minutes. I should get down to the bay before the others start boarding—just in case."

"I understand."

"Ari, I wonder if you could do me a favor while I'm gone?" said Spence suddenly.

"Of course, anything."

"My dad's birthday . . . I got him a souvenir, but I forgot to send it. Could you make sure he gets it? I left it in my jumpsuit in my quarters."

"I'll take care of it right away, Spence. Don't give it another thought."

Delicate silence followed this exchange. Ari looked at her hands, clasping them and unclasping them. Spence watched her as if she were practicing magic.

Finally she raised her head shyly. "I'll miss you, Spence. I miss you already and you're not even gone."

"I'll miss you, too. I've been thinking that—"

Suddenly she was very close and his arms were around her, pressing her to him. She murmured softly and he smelled the fresh, clean scent of perfume in her hair.

"Spence, you'll be gone so long . . . "

"Not so long. It'll pass quickly. You'll see." The words came out in a rush, and it was all he could do to keep his composure. Why this turmoil, this confusion over a mere girl? *What's come over me,* he thought to himself.

"Well, I'd better go," he said at last. He was beginning to fear that if he stayed with her any longer he would not be able to leave.

She released him and composed herself, putting on a cheery face and manner.

"I'll think about you every day."

She took him by the arm and led him to the door. "You run along now. I know you're going to have a beautiful time of it—running around in your little space suits all of you, playing scientist."

"I'll come back and tell you all about it." He laughed and his voice made a hollow sound.

"I planned to go down to the bay with you, but I won't. I don't want you to see me cry."

He turned her face to his and kissed her gently. "Good-bye, Ari," he whispered, and then darted away. She heard his footsteps in the corridor and listened until they merged with other sounds. Then she went back to begin her wait.

The docking bay hummed with activity. The boarding tube had been attached to the transport which bore the name *Gyrfalcon* in glittering gold letters across her bulging bow. Skids of supplies and baggage—most of it scientific instruments in cargo frames—were being shoved aboard. Outside the station a small army of maintenance men swarmed the surface of the transport, their arc lights playing over the sleek, black skin of the ship as they moved through their preflight check. It looked like a great black whale patiently enduring a precise grooming by a platoon of tiny silver fishes.

On the big chronometer above the boarding tube he saw that there was less than an hour to blast time. A few of the younger cadet passengers were standing around the bay looking jittery and laughing loudly. Spence allowed himself only a few seconds more to take in the rush of activity around the great space ship. Then he slipped in behind a roboskid loaded with dehydrated rations and entered the boarding tube feeling like a stowaway, half expecting someone to challenge him with a "Halt! Who goes there?"

No one did. No one seemed to notice his arrival at all, which produced a peculiar sense of disappointment for Spence.

He reached the end of the brightly lit tube and entered the hold where dozens of men labored to position all the stores and baggage and lock them into place within huge cargo frames. He threaded his way through the confusion and started toward the head of the ship and the passenger quarters.

A few yellow-suited maintenance men moved along the ship's central gangways trailing black-and-green striped hoses and wagons with odd-looking metallic boxes with flashing lights which emitted chirps and clicks as they slid along the floorplates. Spence also saw the royal blue jumpsuits of the transport's crew who were standing at their stations or talking quietly to one another as the yellowsuits fiddled efficiently around them.

He found an open gallery of seats with their safety webs hanging loosely draped over the headrests as if giant spiders had been busy during the night. He walked across the compartment and came to stand before an observation port to look out upon the space station he had just left. The activity in the docking bay had intensified in the few minutes since he arrived. He could see through the huge observation bubble into the docking bay where some thirty or so cadets had gathered and were waiting to board. A great many others had come to see them off, and a host of yellowsuits were dashing here and there in last-minute preparations.

"So! You are anxious to go to Mars, yes?"

He turned to greet the hulking form of Kalnikov, the captain of the transport. The burly giant crossed the gallery in two strides and shoved out a great meaty paw which squashed Spence's as the two shook hands. Kalnikov looked like the classic Russian weight lifter — broad shoulders above a sinewy back, thick arms, and fists that could probably crush stones. His voice rumbled out from deep within his barrel chest.

"Yes," Spence began to confess, "I was just—"

Before he could finish the man slapped him on the back with a bone-jarring blow.

"Haw! I was that way my first time, too! It is a delicious feeling! Enjoy!"

"Thank you," Spence replied when he regained his breath. The stout Russian turned and pounded away; Spence could hear his voice shaking the floorplates as he bellowed his delight at being space-bound once more. He heard a snatch of song as it boomed out in the corridor:

"God of shining galaxies
Lead me from this place.
Lord of starfields fly with me,
Beyond the edge of space . . . "

Spence couldn't help smiling. He could feel the hum of electricity starting to flow and tingle on his skin; he was as excited as any green cadet. For the first time in many days he felt alive.

Kalnikov's voice echoed down the gangway. "Welcome, my friends! Come along! We are going to enjoy this journey! Come along!"

For a moment Spence entertained an absurd image of God, the Creator of the universe, as a big Russian pilot, calling his cadets to join him in a fantastic flight of discovery.

"All right," murmured Spence to himself. "I'm ready. Lead on."

CHAPTER TWENTY

"WHAT DO you mean!" Hocking screeched.

"We . . . that is, he . . . never showed up," Tickler stammered.

"How could he *not* show up? He never left the lab. That's what you said. Millen watched him the whole time, you said."

"Not all the time, no," said Kurt slowly, very much aware of the danger he was in at that moment. "He went to the commissary for a few minutes."

"You were not to let him out of your sight!"

"It couldn't be helped . . ."

"Oh? And why not?" Hocking demanded. Color has risen to his cheeks, staining his pale flesh with a crimson tinge in the low light of his quarters. Snaky veins stood out on his forehead, and he appeared as if he might burst with rage and frustration.

"I watched him until he got in line at the commissary and then went back to wait. I couldn't let him see me watching him, could I?"

"Ortu will hear about this! I will not keep this from him. This time you'll have to face him yourselves. Unless—"

"Unless?" Tickler leaped at the first sign of hope that they might somehow avert the wrath of the shadowy and severe Ortu.

"Unless you find him immediately. You have four hours."

"We can't search the whole station in four hours," Millen whined.

"You'll find a way," hissed Hocking. "I want him found. Quickly. Do you hear me? Or else Ortu will deal with you."

"We'll find him," promised Tickler.

Without waiting for Hocking to change his mind both men hurried away to begin their search. They donned pressure suits and made their way back across the construction site. Once back inside the station they hung their suits on the racks and stepped into the tram.

"It's all your fault!" muttered Tickler thickly.

"My fault!" Kurt glared at his companion. "I watched him as you instructed. You told me to search his quarters as soon as I got a chance—with him in the commissary I had a perfect chance. He wasn't going anywhere. He told me he'd be right back. Even invited me to go along with him."

"You should have gone—the search could have waited."

"Where were *you*? You could have followed him yourself."

"Obviously we wouldn't be in this mess now if I had!"

"Something's happened to him, I tell you. I saw him waiting in line at the commissary."

"Shut up! I don't want to hear any more! All that matters now is that we have to find him—and fast!"

"Where should we begin?"

"I don't know. He could be anyplace by now."

"I told you we should have gone to Hocking at once—as soon as he didn't show up for the session," Millen moaned.

"What difference does it make now what you told me? We could not risk making Reston suspicious. He knows something is going on. He's hiding somewhere."

"Well, he can't have gone far."

"He's on the station somewhere, and we have only four hours to find him. Wait a minute! I have an idea! I know where to start looking!"

The tram whizzed away on its magnetic cushion as the two began their frenzied search of Gotham.

Ari felt strange in Spence's rooms. She had never been to his quarters, or even the lab. Now everything she saw seemed heavy with the presence of him. She was afraid to touch anything lest she somehow disturb his memory.

She shook the feeling off. "He's only gone on a trip," she told herself. "He hasn't *died*."

But the eerie morbidity still lingered like a chill in the small room.

He could have at least made his bed, she thought. She bent to the task, but drew her hand back from touching the blankets. *No, leave it as it is. Leave everything as he left it.*

The funereal atmosphere of the room was about to stifle her and she wanted only to get away. She found the model of the space station in the pocket of his jumpsuit where he said it would be. She fished it out, replaced the jumpsuit and left the room, stepping back into the darkened lab.

"What have we here!"

"*Oh!* Oh! You scared me," cried Ari as the lights went on and she found herself in the grasp of Tickler. Kurt stood at the portal with his hand at the access plate.

"I did not mean to startle you, miss. I thought you might be a prowler."

Ari gasped and blushed. "I . . . I was looking for Dr. Reston."

"Are you a friend of his?" Tickler still held her arm tightly.

"Yes, are you his assistant?"

"I am Dr. Tickler. What did you want to see him about?"

"Oh, something personal. But it's all right. I can come back some other time."

"Yes, perhaps you'd better." Tickler regarded her carefully, his eyes stealing over every inch of her. "What is that you have there?"

"This? It's just a paperweight," she said uncertainly. She resented Tickler's attitude. "Now if you will excuse me . . ." She pulled her arm free from his grasp.

"Of course, I'm sorry. It's just that we cannot be too careful, you know. The work is very important."

He stepped aside and Ari passed with an air of offended dignity. Inside she was frightened by the way Tickler had treated her. She began to see why Spence wished his mission to remain a secret, and she did not regret the lie she told to cover her reason for being there.

She reached the portal and went through without looking back. Once out of sight she hurried down to the ComCen section to place Mr. Reston's paperweight in the mailframe of the next shuttle down.

"Follow her," said Tickler as soon as she left. "I want to know what she's doing with that model."

Kurt went out at once and slipped unseen upon her trail.

The middle-aged woman's blue eyes stared out onto a green expanse of lawn bordered by high hedge rows and softly swaying willows. A light breeze lifted the leaves of a lilac bush near the open French doors. She sat primly in a large overstuffed chair, her hands folded in her lap. Wrapped in her shapeless cotton print dress of faded blue she looked like a doll grown old waiting for her young mistress to come back and rescue her from loneliness and love her once again.

"Mrs. Zanderson . . . " a voice at the door intoned gently.

The woman did not move; there was not a flicker of response in the vacant blue eyes.

"Mrs. Zanderson?" A white-uniformed attendant slipped into the room silently and came to stand by the chair. "It's time for your medication, Caroline. Here now."

The nurse held out a green capsule in a white paper cup and placed it in the woman's hand. She took the hand and lifted it toward the woman's mouth and tipped it in.

"There, now. Would you like to go for your walk this morning?"

The woman stared unmoving out the open doors.

"All right, then. Let's get up now. That's right. We'll have a nice walk before lunch. Come along. That's right."

The nurse pulled her gently to her feet and with a hand under her arm guided her out onto the broad green lawn. As they crossed the threshold the woman looked back to her room as if she had left something of inestimable value behind and feared for its safety. "My chair!" she cried.

"Your chair will be safe while we're gone. It will be there when we return."

The woman accepted the attendant's assurance. She turned back to her stroll with a look of grim determination as if she were embarking on a walking tour of the continent. She tilted her head toward her nurse and confided as one with a dark secret, "They are waiting for me back there. They want my chair, you know."

"We won't let them take your chair. Don't you worry about it."

"You don't believe me. No one believes me. They want my chair."

"Who wants your chair, Caroline? Tell me all about it."

"You're playing with me. You don't believe me."

"Then you tell me. Who wants your chair?"

The voice became a dry whisper. "The Dream Thief—he wants me, but he can't get me. So he wants my chair. You won't let him take it, will you?" The deep blue eyes went wide.

"No, no. He won't get your chair. And he won't get you, either. We'll fix him. Don't you worry."

They walked out upon the lawn in the yellow sunlight of a clear, cloudless day. Several other patients strolled the grounds under the watchful eyes of attendants in white. Mrs. Zanderson calmed under the warmth of the day and forgot her agitation of a few moments before. Recognition drifted back to those troubled eyes.

"Why, I know you—you're Belinda."

The nurse smiled and nodded. "That's right; you remembered."

"Is my Ari here? I want to see my little girl."

"Ari is all grown-up now, remember? She isn't here now, but she'll be coming to see you soon."

"I have to see her right now! I must warn her!"

"Warn her, Caroline? What would you warn her about?"

"The Dream Thieves, silly. They are after her, too. I know it. I can feel them. They're after her. You don't believe me, do you?"

"I think you're getting yourself all worked up over nothing, Caroline. We won't let the nasty old dream thieves get your Ari, will we? No. Of course not."

"You're making fun of me!"

"No, I'm not. Maybe we'd better go inside and lie down for a little while before lunch. You'll feel much better after a little rest."

"No—no! I'll be good. Let's walk some more. I won't say anything else. Please, let's walk."

"All right, Caroline. Just as you say. We'll walk—but we won't talk about the dream thieves anymore, shall we? You just let me take care of them for you. Look at the pretty flowers, Caroline. All the red ones and yellow ones—aren't they beautiful?"

"Yes. Beautiful."

Mrs Zanderson had withdrawn into her shell. She stared ahead dully; her features appeared cast in gray stone. After a short tour of the grounds the nurse brought her back to her room where she once again took up her vigil, gripping the arms of the faded red chair with her thin hands like an eagle guarding her clutch.

CHAPTER TWENTY-ONE

ALL THE pictures Spence had ever seen of the red planet failed to do it justice. Mars shone with a rosy glow like a big, pink harvest moon, its mysterious canals traced in dark red across the surface. Against the black of space with its litter of stars the planet seemed serene and inviting.

The transport streaked ever nearer and the red orb grew larger by the hour, but the *Gyrfalcon* was still two weeks away from rendezvous.

"It's something, isn't it?" Spence recognized the voice and turned to meet his friend.

"That it is, Adjani. I know I'm supposed to be nonchalant about this sort of thing, but I can't help staring at it—so strange, so alien."

"I'll tell you a secret: everyone else feels exactly as you do—even Packer. He lets on that he's seen it all before and could not care less. But I've seen the look on his face when he thinks no one is watching. He's as taken with it as anyone else." Adjami spoke in his light, rippling voice, his black eyes glowing with the sight before them.

Spence tore himself away from the window and took Adjani by the arm. "Come on, let's go get something to eat."

They walked out of the gallery and along the cramped corridor aft to the galley. There were several groups huddled over steaming mugs at the long tables. A chronometer over the galley window at one end of the rectangular room read 1:25.

"Good," said Spence. "We've got an hour of burn time left. We can still have some coffee and a bite to eat like regular human beings."

Kalnikov accelerated the transport periodically during the voyage.

During these times the thrust of the engines produced the effect of gravity for the passengers and crew. Then the galley filled with people who were tired of sucking their meals out of vacuum bags and sipping their drinks through tubes in zero gravity.

They filed past the galley window and picked up mugs of coffee, sandwiches, and thick squares of crumbly brownies. They settled themselves at one of the tables and wolfed down the sandwiches.

"You're looking much better, Spence."

"I'm feeling much better. I guess I'm an astronaut at heart—this trip agrees with me."

Spence and Adjani had become close friends in the long days of the trip. They had spent endless hours talking over Adjani's magnetic chessboard until Spence felt he could trust the slim Indian with his life. He had been thinking of revealing his secret to him for several days, and had decided to risk it the moment they sat down to eat. Adjani sensed this and provided the opportunity. He watched his friend quietly, waiting patiently for what Spence would say.

"I guess you already know that I was under some kind of pressure back there." He jerked his head to indicate Gotham.

"I sensed as much, yes."

"You read my mind that first time I came to see you. It scared me a little. I'm glad we've had some time to get to know each other here, because I want to tell you about it."

Adjani said nothing, but leaned forward a fraction and inclined his head in a listening attitude.

"I don't know how to say this without sounding like a raving madman. But trust me, Adjani, and hear me out." Spence took a deep breath and launched into his story from the beginning right up to the moment he boarded the transport in secret. Adjani sat still as a stone—only his eyes showed that spark which indicated that he attended every word.

". . . I couldn't tell you before. I was afraid you wouldn't believe me." Spence sipped his chilled coffee and watched his listener for a reaction.

"What you have told me disturbs me greatly, my friend. I wish that you had told me sooner—perhaps that afternoon in my quarters. This is a very dangerous game that you have become involved in."

Spence viewed Adjani's grave features with alarm. He had not expected the reaction he was receiving. "Surely you don't think . . ."

"If it were just a matter of what I think, you would be right to tell me to mind my own business. But what I have to say to you is not conjecture. I have seen it with my own eyes."

He clasped his hands in front of him and his sight turned inward as he lost himself to his tale.

"When I left school to return to my own country you can imagine how excited I was. I had heard my father talk about the mountains of India and the quaint villages perched on the sides of hills and on the edges of chasms. I was eager to see the land of my fathers, to walk where they had walked.

"But I was naive, my friend, dreaming of idyllic golden lands. I went to the mountains of Nagaland and I walked through villages that have not changed in a thousand years. But instead of quaint and happy peasants I saw people suffering unspeakably, people trapped by something so terrible it twists their minds and hearts. Do you know what it is?—fear. A fear so great that it drives them to take their own lives in despair. They die by the scores every year, throwing themselves screaming off the mountains to crush out their lives on the rocks below and so stop the terror. Many more hundreds collapse under the strain. Their minds snap and they become little more than automatons."

"But what are they afraid of?"

"They have a name for it: Supno Kaa Chor. Translated it means Dream Thief."

"Picturesque."

"It is no joke. These people believe that there is a god—the Dream Thief—who creeps from house to house in the night and steals the dreams of men while they sleep. He replaces their dreams with his own, and thereby sows the seeds of madness. They say he lives in a mountain place in the Himalayas where he keeps his stolen dreams locked in a great ruby which is guarded by six black demons from the underworld.

"It is said that when a person has no more dreams left in him the Dream Thief sends him into the night to take his own life."

"You don't believe that nonsense, surely."

"I believe there is something behind it, yes. It is real; I have seen its effects. I have seen the mindless wander the hills, screaming in terror in broad daylight. I have seen the broken bodies collected from the dry streambeds below the cliffs in the morning after the Dream Thief has passed through.

"Whatever it is, it is real."

"But you can't think that I—that I have anything at all in common with a bunch of frightened hillfolk."

Adjani eyed him strangely. "I am a connection man, remember? I make a living providing connections between seemingly unrelated facts and information; it is my job to suggest what does not readily occur to others. I am telling you what I believe is possible. It is up to you to discover whether there is something to be gained by examining what I have told you."

Spence stared at Adjani's grim expression. He was inclined to doubt the connection his friend had suggested; but for the obvious foreboding Adjani seemed to feel, he would have dismissed it outright.

"What do you think I should do?" he asked.

"We must work out a plan of action and a way to keep you safe until we can get back to Gotham to investigate."

"But I am in no danger here." Spence dismissed the notion with a sweep of his hand.

"You are in great danger, my friend. You yourself have felt it or you would not have come on this trip as you did. You know there is truth to what I say."

A buzzer sounded, signaling the end of burn-time gravity in five minutes, and everyone in the dining room rose and took their utensils and dishes back to the galley window. Spence slurped up the last of his coffee and stood. He hesitated, looking down at Adjani's upturned face and the concern written there.

"All right. I'll do what you say. Where do we start?"

Hocking glared at his henchmen; his eyes, red-rimmed from lack of sleep, burned out from his sockets like hot coals. His voice shook with anger and frustration.

"Three weeks he's been gone! Not a trace of him! Not a sign! And we have learned nothing from that slip of a girl. Mr. Millen, have you received an answer to that tracer you put on the package she sent?"

"It came in only an hour ago."

"Well, what is it? I'm waiting."

"The package was sent to Dr. Reston's home—rather, his father's home. It contained only the model and a birthday card. Nothing else."

"Hmm—that is interesting." The egg-chair spun around slowly in midair as Hocking pondered the meaning of this latest shred of information. Neither of the others spoke; they did not dare break in on their leader's thoughts. They had endured Hocking's fits every waking hour for three long weeks, and they feared for their lives. But suddenly Hocking spun around to face them and his deathly countenance lit with a wicked glee.

"Gentlemen!" he announced. "Our slippery water rat, Dr. Reston, has jumped ship. He has tricked us!"

Tickler shook his head. "How could he? We have watched every shuttle and checked every manifest—he never left the station. There is no other way out."

"There is *one* other way, you fools! The transport!" Hocking grimaced and his eyes blazed. "He's on that transport to Mars!"

"He was not listed on the manifest, I tell you. I checked it a dozen times. Not even under an assumed name."

"How we have underestimated our friend, gentlemen. Of course he is on that ship. He arranged to have himself put aboard outside normal channels—probably that bubble-headed girl acted for him. She is Zanderson's daughter after all. There is one quick way to find out: I'm going to pay a little visit to Zanderson himself."

Tickler frowned doubtfully. "Do you think you should?"

"Do I not? It is time he remembered who his keepers were. Yes, I'll go and remind him myself. And I'll find out whether Reston is on that ship—as I'm sure he is."

Hocking stopped and leered at his associates. "Then we shall plan a little surprise for Spencer . . . to celebrate a successful journey. When he lands on Mars we'll be ready for him."

CHAPTER TWENTY-TWO

SPENCE BOARDED the landing pod with Packer and a half-dozen of his third-year men. He swung weightless into one of the seats lining the bulkhead and strapped himself in, pulling the safety webbing over him and fastening it tightly all around. He stared down at the magnificent red-gold sphere of Mars filling the port below him—so large had it grown in the last few days that no more than a slice of its curve could be seen.

The pod was strangely silent; the cadets, ordinarily brimming with dash and bravado, seemed veiled in their own thoughts. Every face wore a look of rapt wonder. Spence suspected that he himself appeared as goggle-eyed as the rest of them.

Olmstead Packer swam into the center of the pod and called his group to attention. "Hear ye, hear ye!" he said, wheeling slowly through the air. "We will wait until everyone is suited up before popping the hatch. I want to check each suit myself before you step out on the surface. I've got a yellow sticker to put on each helmet that lets me know I've checked you out. Anyone who fails to get his suit checked won't get another chance to play outside. Understood?"

The shaggy red head turned to regard Spence and Adjani as well. "That goes for you, too, gentlemen. Same as for all first-timers."

Just then a rattling shudder passed through the pod followed by a low-pitched vibration which built to a muffled roar and died away almost before it began.

"That'll be one of the other pods going down now," said Packer as he dived for his seat. "Happy landing, gentlemen!"

All braced themselves for the blast that would send them streaking toward the surface of the Red Planet. They heard the thrum of the engine and then a whoosh as if gale force winds had passed over them. In the same instant they felt themselves pressed gently back into the jumpseat cushions as the illusion of weight returned.

To Spence it seemed as if they fell like a rock dropped from a mountain peak. The burnt orange of the Martian landscape spun crazily as the pod descended, looming larger and ever larger in the port until individual landmarks could be discerned. They fell alarmingly close to the surface, considered Spence, before he remembered that Mars' atmosphere was very thin and did not extend far out into space. Still, it seemed as if they would smash down upon the red rocks rushing up at them. At the last minute the pod turned itself around and the engines sent forth a staccato burst to slow their descent.

The next thing he felt was a slight bouncing jolt—as if he were aboard an old-fashioned elevator which had reached its floor. He half expected a chime to sound and the doors to open. Instead, the pod erupted with the cheers of the cadets who threw off their webbing straps and jumped to their feet to clap one another on the back in the jubilation of all travelers who arrive safely at their destination.

From the racks behind each seat they took down the elasticized surface suits and began wriggling into them. The suits designed for Mars were simple, tight-fitting polymerized one-piece elastic suits much like ocean divers wore. All the necessary pressure was supplied by the girdling effect of the elastic. A mushroom-shaped helmet attached to a wide neck seal on the suit completed the ensemble. The helmet had a hemispherical visor which allowed full vision in every direction. At the back of the helmet a built-in canister held oxygen pellets for extended rambling on the surface of the planet.

When all helmets were in place, the hatch was popped and each explorer filed past Packer who stood at the portal and affixed his yellow triangular stickers to each helmet as he checked each suit. Spence stood last in line behind Adjani and, after the once-over by Packer, stepped out into the rust-colored world.

He bobbed down the steps of the hatch and walked a few paces in the red dirt that powdered beneath his feet. His motions were exaggerated and springy—an effect of the reduced gravity of Mars. He grinned from ear to ear with the exhilaration of just being there, a human being treading on alien soil. He felt strong, invincible—also an effect of reduced gravity.

He scanned the horizon of the planet and was surprised to find how close it was and how sharp the curve. He turned to scan the points of the compass. Everywhere he turned the same dull red, brick-colored dirt met his gaze, as if he were lost in a monochromatic desert. Rocks of various sizes poked through the red soil; some of these were a shade or two lighter or darker than the dirt around them, providing the only contrast he could see.

At the horizon the sky burned a brilliant blue, as if infused with fire. The blue gradually darkened to jet black directly overhead. Spence soon found that this changed dramatically depending upon the time of day. At high noon the sky was pink. At sunset it glowed with golden warmth at the horizon while stars shone hard and bright above like gems spilled out upon a cloth of blackest velvet.

Low in the sky one of Mars' tiny twin moons hovered above the faraway mountain range. At least Spence took it to be faraway. Without a heavy atmosphere to distort images and clothe them in misty shrouds, objects and landforms on Mars appeared hard-edged and distinct whether close at hand or faraway.

Across a stretch of the arid soil he viewed a loose assemblage of buildings huddled, dome-shaped like a cluster of toadstools—the terraforming installation, one of five on the planet—but whether it stood two kilometers or ten distant, he could not tell.

He heard a buzzing in the air and turned to find its source. He was surprised to see Packer standing atop the hatchway with his helmet in his hands shouting at them as his face grew bright red.

"Take off your helmets!" he called. Through the helmet's insulation the words sounded as if he were shouting at them from one end of a very long hose.

Tentatively Spence grasped the sides of his helmet and gave it a sideways twist. He heard the pressure hiss away and felt his ears pop as if he had suddenly leaped to a high altitude.

He took a breath and found that he could not stop inhaling.

"It's all right," Packer said a little breathlessly. "Just breathe easy. Don't overdo it. Relax and let your body adjust to it."

There were oohs and ahhs all around as the cadets experienced this wonder of breathing the thin Martian air.

"I wanted you to see that you can breathe without a helmet if necessary. The atmosphere is still mostly carbon dioxide—that's why your lungs feel as if they can't get enough. But we have been able to enrich the atmosphere by a few percentage points. There is enough oxygen to support life for short periods of time if you do not tax it. You could not run or even walk quickly before you passed out. But you will not die of suffocation, either, if you don't exert yourself.

"Your more immediate danger is the temperature. I'm sure you are all aware that during the day the temperature this time of year is a uniform 25 degrees celsius. As the sun goes down the temperature plunges to minus 105. Your suits offer some protection from the violent swing in temperature, but they are not designed to be used during the chill of a Martian night."

Packer raised his helmet over this head. "All right, put your helmets back on and let's track it to the installation." He pointed toward the cluster of buildings.

Spence raised his helmet and paused to breathe once more the incredibly dry, thin air, tasting its metallic tang on his tongue. He closed his eyes and drew it deep into his lungs where it burned with tingling fire. It seemed almost as if he were standing on a mountaintop—the effect was the same.

"Remarkably like the Himalayas," said a voice beside him.

He opened his eyes and grinned at Adjani standing at his elbow. "I was thinking of the Rockies, myself. I've never been to the Himalayas."

They replaced their helmets and Spence tasted the sweet oxygen as he breathed it in. He adjusted the voice amplifier so that he could speak to Adjani—Adjani did the same—and they trudged off behind the bouncing column of cadets with Packer in the lead.

The terraforming project was in its fifth year on Mars. At the present stage it took the form of enormous greenhouses filled with broadleaf plants genetically engineered to be virtual oxygen factories. The greenhouses pumped in the carbon dioxide of Mars and flushed out the oxygen waste of the plants. Beneath the greenhouses nuclear reactors maintained optimum temperatures, heating the plants through long, impossibly cold nights.

The greenhouses were established and working according to plan. This trip inaugurated phase two of the project: melting the enormous polar ice cap of the planet.

There was water on Mars; the first Voyager probes had discovered that. But it was mostly locked up with the carbon-dioxide ice at the poles. Although some minute part existed as water vapor, it was not enough to sustain plant life. By melting the polar ice, it was hoped that enough water vapor might be released to allow the planet to begin rebuilding an earth-type atmosphere. As the amount of oxygen and water vapor in the atmosphere grew, the temperature would stabilize and the mineral-rich soil—though dry as desert sand—would perhaps support some varieties of plant life, and later animals and eventually man.

Terraforming was a bold idea that seemed bound to work, given enough time. Packer planned an expedition to the poles to view various sites where nuclear devices might be planted to melt the dry ice. He was anxious that the terraforming of Mars be complete within his lifetime.

"I want to see my grandchildren romping over the lush, green landscape of Mars," he told his cadets. He was far more taken with this project than with the plasma drive. Still, the first colonies were decades away.

Little red clouds of dust rose from the tramping feet of the cadets as they moved along the trail. By the time they reached the installation, an octopus arrangement of buildings with the central barracks surrounded by the long rows of greenhouses radiating out from the center like arms, everyone was covered with the fine rusty grit. They moved along the translucent shells of the greenhouses and Spence could see flashes of green from within, completely out of keeping with the dullness of their surroundings.

The occupants of two other landing pods had already reached the installation and were pulling tractors with high, wide wheels out of hemispherical sheds. Cadets under the direction of project leaders were heading back to the pods to begin hauling in the provisions. The rest were given chores to do to ready the installation once more for human occupancy. Spence, Adjani, and Packer entered the bomb-shelter entrance of the barracks and made their way through the tube to the air lock and to the installation's nerve center.

Packer took off his helmet and inhaled deeply. "Ahh! Smell that fresh air! It comes from the greenhouses."

Spence took his helmet off as Packer waved his hand over a console set in the wall near the air lock. Lights winked on in a ring around the circular room. Overhead a shield peeled away to allow sunlight to enter and warm the interior of the sunken sphere. "All the conveniences of home," said Packer.

"If your home happens to be Antarctica," quipped Adjani.

"Think of it! In a few years this whole area will be nothing but greenhouses as far as the eye can see. We'll turn this place into a jungle of life—careful, of course, to introduce only the most beneficial of plants and organisms. The place will be a paradise."

"It's too late," said Spence. "*You're* here already."

"Look what you've done to him, Adjani! He's as bad as you are. Why am I treated like this? What have I done to deserve it?" He broke off his wounded-elephant act to direct them around the cavernous interior of the living unit. "Come on, I'll show you where to hang your hats."

Spence glanced at the wall console where a crimson signal had bloomed in one corner. "Does that red light mean anything?"

"What's that? Oh, that one. It's a meteorological signal. Must be a special weather report coming in." He keyed a code on the console's pad. The data screen lit up green and began scrolling sentences.

"There's a Simoom blowing up near the equator. It could reach us by tomorrow morning. We'll have to stay inside a few days at least and keep the shields up."

"A Simoom?"

"A storm—wind and sand. A sandstorm such as you've never seen before. It's like a gigantic sandblaster. Winds up to four hundred and eighty kilometers an hour. If anyone were to wander out there in that—why, you'd be *erased* in seconds! Provided you weren't blown clean away first."

"Incredible," said Adjani. He looked around at the superstructure of the building.

"Don't worry," laughed Packer. "These structures are wind-tunnel tested and the shields can withstand anything short of a direct nuclear attack. We're safe enough inside. We just have to stay undercover until it blows itself out."

By nightfall all the provisions and equipment frames were stored away and the barracks hummed with life; the interior of the dome resembled an ant colony. They ate a common meal and then split off into their work groups to begin mapping out the tasks for the following days. Spence and Adjani, without any direct assignment, stole away to the director's lounge to relax and talk.

Spence noticed that Adjani had stuck close to him since they landed and even now regarded him with a watchful eye.

"Do you think the Dream Thief will try something tonight?" he asked as Adjani came to stand beside him. He gazed down at a holographic map of the Martian landscape encompassing the region thirty kilometers in a circle around the installation.

"I was thinking how great the mountain is—Olympus Mons. Twice the size of Everest. Why? Do you feel something?"

"No, but you've been my shadow ever since we landed; I wondered if there was a reason."

Spence recalled the conversation between them and the plan they had agreed upon. He was to alert Adjani the moment he felt anything at all peculiar beginning to happen to him. Adjani would then take whatever steps were necessary to prevent Spence from doing any bodily injury to himself. It was a simple plan, but it would have to do until they returned to Gotham to begin tracking down the cause of Spence's troubles.

Adjani gazed down at the holomap. "Sinai—the desert of Moses. Here we are, wanderers in an alien wilderness, searching for a home in a foreign land. History repeats itself once more, eh?"

"I wonder if this place has a god, too?"

"Spence—"Adjani turned a solemn face to him. "You asked me if I thought the Dream Thief would come again tonight. The answer is yes, I do think so. He has left you alone during the trip, but I think it likely he will try to reach you. We must presume he will try tonight."

It was true, Spence had not been bothered by the dreams or blackouts since leaving Gotham. He had begun to feel that by leaving he had escaped altogether. Adjani's mention of trouble struck a raw nerve.

"You don't think I'm safe even here?"

"No, my friend. You will not be safe until the Dream Thief is stopped."

"At least you believe he *can* be stopped. I was never so certain."

"Of course he can be stopped. But we must keep you safe until we find the way. And remember, if I am right in my assumptions yours is not the only life in danger. Others may depend on what happens to you. We must keep you safe."

CHAPTER TWENTY-THREE

SPENCE STUMBLED doggedly across a rocky, alien landscape. Over his shoulder Deimos, a beautiful, serene blue-white globe, rose full in the black sky. Spence winced in pain as needlelike shards of tiny cinders sliced the flesh from his knees. Blood bubbled from the minute tear in his surface suit.

He shivered and wrapped his arms across his chest for warmth. Staring down at his feet he saw that he stood on a barren ledge of rock, red in the glow of the rising sun. Around him lay diamonds glittering with an icy glare. With a shock he realized that they were his tears, frozen where they had fallen upon the bare rock. He raised his hands, replaced his helmet once more, and continued walking.

How long he walked or how far he did not know. High overhead white wisps of clouds like tattered veils raced through a black sky, blown on the winds of the coming storm to disappear beyond the rim of the horizon. He heard the howl of the wind as it roared through the emptiness above. He wanted to run, to see where the fragile white clouds went. But as he stirred himself, a heaviness sapped his strength. His legs would not obey. He leaned into it, felt himself pushed back as by a great hand, and realized it was the wind. Each step dragged more

slowly than the last. He looked around him and saw red sand beginning
to run in hissing snakes around him, blown on the gusting wind.

He crawled to the top of a nearby dune and toppled over the other
side into the wind shadow. He felt himself sliding down and down. He
struggled to rise to his feet as the dry red sand sucked at his limbs. The
sand rattled down on him from the crest of the dune as the wind
whipped it into a stinging fury. He sank back, too cold and tired to
move. The sand pelted down on him in a steady rain, burying him beneath a fine red blanket.

He screamed and his voice rang hollow in his ears. He looked and
saw that he was trapped in a great glass bubble—the bubble of his
helmet, now beginning to frost over on the inside from the warmth of
his breath.

The sand seemed to fall out of the black sky, burying him alive. He
felt the gritty sting as it pelted against his surface suit. He heard faintly
the dry, bristling hiss as it struck his helmet.

He screamed again and heard the awesome ring of silence and
knew that his cries could not be heard beyond his helmet. His teeth
chattered with the cold which dragged him down into a lazy stupor. He
was drifting to sleep. Sleep, his last great enemy, had conquered him.

Spence came to slowly, by degrees, his senses sluggish as if he had
been drugged. A bright light filled his eyes so that he squinted to keep it
out. When it did not go away he opened his eyes and looked around.

At first it did not occur to him where he was or in what condition.
He heard his own even breathing filling his ears with a steady rhythm,
and knew he wore his surface suit and helmet. But his body was stiff
and frozen into a fixed position. He tried to raise one arm and found
that it came free with difficulty. He raised the other arm and pushed
himself gradually into a sitting position.

With a jolt he realized were he was: Mars! He had wandered out
onto the surface alone. His dream had been real! His stumbling trek
across the Martian landscape was no nightmare; it had happened.
What is more he remembered it, though he remembered it as a dream.

Before that, however, only blankness and unknowing: another
blackout.

Spence rose to his feet, scooping sand away from him. He crawled
to the top of the dune and looked out over the red desert, fighting down
the panic he felt rising within him. Nothing could be seen of the installation, not a glimmer in any direction.

The winds had calmed, but away toward the south—at least he
considered it a southerly direction—the sky bore a distinct brownish-
red smudge as if a prairie fire burned out of control just beyond the

horizon. Overhead the sky was tinged with a pinkish cast which meant it was approaching noon, or just passing it.

Here was a problem. Clearly he could not sit by and wait for a search party to find him, and he could not walk in every direction at once. He glanced at his suit's chronometer on his right forearm and set it on elapsed time mode, figuring that at best he had only seven hours before the temperature dropped and he began to freeze.

He decided to start walking toward the mountain peak he saw rising into the clear air, so close it looked as if he could touch it with an outstretched hand. He remembered the holomap and the fact that Olympus Mons, the tallest peak on Mars, stood some thirty kilometers distant from the installation. If he could reach it there was a chance he could see the installation from its slopes. It would be a race, for it meant travelling fifty or sixty kilometers in seven hours—eight hours at the most. To even have a chance at making it back to the base in time he would have to travel at a pace of seven or eight kilometers an hour.

Without wasting another second, he turned himself toward the mountain and began marching off in long, ground-eating strides.

He walked for hours, it seemed to him, and the great flattened cone of Olympus Mons did not seem perceptively changed. Periodically he had stopped to look around him lest he miss some sign of a search party, or some indication that he might be moving nearer to his goal.

On one of these reconnoitering stops he became aware of the fact that the brown smudge on the horizon to the south had grown considerably. It nearly filled the southern quadrant, towering several kilometers into the sky by his best estimation. As he stood gauging the size of the disturbance he felt the horror of realization creep over him—the Simoom! The storm was sweeping in on wings of awesome fury, racing toward him.

Spence began to trot in an awkward, bouncing gait, doubling his pace. He had to reach the mountain before the Simoom struck. It was his only chance.

The first gusts of wind pummeled Spence like angry fists. Around his legs the sand sang away like steam escaping from a pipe. The force of the coming storm impelled him on, lifting his steps and blowing him forward. He lurched ahead drunkenly, exhausted, sweating inside his surface suit. His tongue stuck to the roof of his mouth in thirst. He stared at the dull brown overcast which crept over the sky like a discolored shade. The sun burned through with a throbbing white glare as he dragged himself on.

He walked mechanically now, not attending to his steps, not caring whether he reached the mountain or not. He despaired of ever seeing the installation through the thick clouds of red dust whipped up by the

Simoom's winds. Spence walked now to keep from thinking of the grisly end waiting for him just a few hours away.

On and on he walked and the wind howled around him, filling the sky with dust and blotting out the land. Tiny projectiles—grit, sand, and shards of rock—threw themselves into him, slicing at him. He could feel their sting through his surface suit and knew that it was only a matter of time before the steady blast tore the suit away from his body, stripped it off like a second skin to leave him naked in a deadly rain.

Packer's grim forecast echoed in his ears: "You'd be erased in seconds." Spence rehearsed the torturous details of such a death: flesh stripped molecule by molecule from his bones and then the bones themselves battered to pieces and scattered still warm over the surface of the planet to be ground into powder.

The scene held a grisly fascination for him, though he knew that it would likely be his own fate. It was that or death by freezing. Those were his choices.

The sun was lowering in the sky and already the wind whistling around him held a chill. Soon the temperature would plummet and he would stop moving as his body heat evaporated. This at least seemed preferable to the other death.

He stumbled blindly now. The dust obscured everything beyond the plastic perimeter of his visor. The rattle of tiny missiles filled his helmet like the crackle of static and his thoughts turned toward those who would mourn his death: his father would take it hard, of course; and his sister. Adjani would feel badly, but it was difficult for Spence to imagine the brown genius actually grieving over him.

Ari, of all he could name, alone embodied the sole regret of his heart. She alone he cared for. And he would never see her again—never see those bright blue eyes, never see her golden hair shining in the sunlight, or feel the cool touch of her long fingers as she brushed his face—the awful certainty of their separation saddened and frightened him more than death itself.

He hoped that in some small way he would leave a void in her life which would never be filled by another, that she would remember him fondly and weep when she heard the sad news of his death.

He remembered the words she had said the night before he left. He could hear her voice speaking to him once more: *Be very careful, Spencer . . . I will pray for you every day.*

Prayer cannot help me, thought Spence, then reflected that probably very little else would help either. At least prayer would not hurt. The idea seemed somehow appropriate to him now, and proper. He wished that he had the right words to say so that his first, and likely last, prayer would not be the feeble simpering of a dying agnostic.

He felt a rush of emotion and the tears brimmed up in his eyes to roll down his cheeks inside the helmet. He could not brush them away. With the tears came the words, "I'm sorry, I'm sorry . . ." which he repeated over and over again. "Forgive me," he whispered. "Help me."

That was the prayer he prayed, though why he was sorry, and for what he should be forgiven, his heart alone knew.

Scarcely had the words crossed his lips when he felt himself slammed to the ground by a blast of cold wind with the force of a rocket thruster and the scream of a beast in agony.

He lay unmoving as pebbles and small stones tumbled over him. He could not raise his head much inside his helmet, but with the cold sweeping over him he knew he must keep moving to remain warm. Snakelike, on his belly, he inched forward.

He had not gone far when he felt the wind lessen. He pushed himself to his knees and stood. He tottered a few more steps and the wind hit him again, this time tumbling him forward and rolling him in a ball.

He felt himself rolling and rolling, as if all support had been yanked out from under him and he would go on forever. But he did not stop rolling, and it was then that the wind no longer assailed him. He had fallen headlong into an arroyo—one of the small canals which creased the surface of the planet. Here he was out of the wind and safe from the blast of windblown projectiles.

He could see only slightly better than before; thick clouds of dust filled the arroyo, rolling in on the wind. Spence put his head down and scuttled forward over the rocky terrain of the dry river bottom. Darkness increased rapidly and he could feel the cold increasing its hold with the setting of the sun.

Gradually he became aware of the downward slope to his path. The arroyo deepened and, from what he could see when the dust clouds parted, widened as it grew into a rift canal.

He walked woodenly on with no other thought than to keep walking until he dropped from hypothermia. He knew that death would follow quickly and he would not feel it. That at least was preferable to being blasted into particles by the wind.

The grade descended rapidly and then flattened out completely. Spence stopped and at the same instant the billowing clouds of red dust parted. In the last glimmering light of day he saw before him a sight which made his mind reel. His knees buckled as he made to draw away.

He had wandered to the very edge of the rift. He now stood on the brink of a canyon stretching out before him hundreds of kilometers and carved deep into the crust of the planet. Another step would have sent him plunging to his death.

His reaction to this new danger was purely physical. In his mind the prospect of falling to his doom held less significance for him than it might have at another time. He was simply too exhausted, and too benumbed by the cold to care anymore; a fact, he noted, that indicated hypothermia was already beginning to affect him.

It would not be long now.

So this is what it is like to die, he thought. To feel the life force slipping away and to be acutely aware of it. He wondered if he would find the release others talked about, if he would meet his mother among the ranks of souls who had passed into the great beyond—or whether those, like so many other things, were simply the superstitions of a fading age.

He had no particular thought about the moment. He noticed how the shadows deepened to violet on the canyon walls and how the depths of the canyon were already sinking into darkness as black as any pit. Simoom wind above him shrieked like all the demons of hell released to vent their fury on the desolated land.

There came a rumble beneath his feet, a vibration of the rock shelf on which he stood. He turned to look behind him and his eye caught a glimpse of a churning mass moving down the rim of the rift toward him.

A rock outcropping, eroded by the wind, had broken free and started an avalanche that was now sweeping down the side of the canyon toward him. Spence had time only to throw himself to the ground before he was swept away in the sliding jumble of rocks and dirt.

The rock slide carried him tumbling far down into the canyon. Miraculously, the grinding, twirling, thundering mass did not crush him outright. When the slide stopped he lay panting on the topmost layer. Rocks and pebbles continued to pelt his body, but he had neither strength nor will to move.

The cruel Martian night closed its fist around him and he knew no more.

Part II
TSO

CHAPTER ONE

"IT's NO use, Adjani. He's gone. We've got to turn back."

Packer's big hand flipped a switch and he talked into his headset. "Sandcat 2 to Sandcat 1—we are returning to base. Repeat. We are returning to base. Over."

"Just one more pass along the rift valley," pleaded Adjani. His eyes did not leave the thermograph screen. The Sandcat swayed on its springs as the Simoom screeched around them.

Packer, blue in the light of the thermoscreen, turned his face toward his friend. He placed a hand on his shoulder and gripped it firmly as if to establish a physical hold on reality. In a voice deepened with fatigue and sadness, he said, "It is twenty below out there and only an hour after sundown. In another hour it will be fifty below. The storm is bucking to full force by morning—we haven't seen the worst of it yet. We lost visual four hours ago, and the thermograph shows a solid blue field. If we don't head back now, *we* won't make it."

He paused and added, squeezing the shoulder once more, "It's over."

"I let him get away. I am responsible," protested Adjani.

"You're lucky he didn't injure you for life. There was no stopping him. God knows we've done everything humanly possible."

"He's out there somewhere—alive. I know it. I feel it."

"If he is still alive, he's past help." Packer turned the Sandcat and watched the instruments as he punched the return course into the on-board navigator. He took his hands from the wheel and let the computer guide them home.

Adjani buried his face in his hands and began rocking back and forth in his seat. Packer turned away. Neither one spoke for a long time. They sat and listened to the rattle of the sand and rocks upon the shields.

The radio on the overhead panel squawked to life. "Kalnikov at I-base. MAT units 1 and 2 return to I-base immediately. Acknowledge."

The message was repeated and Packer responded, giving their ETA to the base. There was a long pause; static crackled over the speaker. "Your loss is to be regretted . . ."—more static—"I am sorry." The transmission was lost once more to the storm. Packer reached up and switched the radio off.

"I guess I'll send a report as soon as we get back to base. I don't exactly know the proper procedure—this has never happened before."

"Couldn't we wait a few days? I want to look some more."

"Sure, we can wait. But it won't make any difference."

"I would like to find the body at least."

"Adjani, the storm is likely to blow for days. By the time you are able to search again there would be nothing left to find."

"It is the least I can do. Please . . ."

"All right. I won't stop you."

They sat silent until the computer flashed the outline of the installation on the vidscreen. "We're almost there," sighed Packer heavily.

Adjani turned with an urgency, laying a hand on the big man's arm. "Please, let us pray for him now. Before the others . . ."

"Of course."

Both men bowed their heads and Adjani spoke a simple, heartfelt prayer as the Sandcat entered the installation compound, safe from the storm.

Spence lifted his throbbing head. His limbs were numb; he could no longer feel his hands or feet. Heavy vapors of sleep tugged at him, luring him to slip lightly away on their easy-flowing stream to oblivion. For a moment he nearly gave in and let the stream take him where it would, but something about giving in that easily rankled him.

With an effort he pushed himself up, shifting the debris which had settled over him. He placed his unfeeling hands on the ground and steadied himself. Gritting his teeth with jaw muscles stiff with cold, he straightened and swayed unsteadily on his knees. Overhead the bright disk of Deimos shone down on him—the Simoom had abated for the moment, allowing the ghostly light to spill down into the rift canyon.

He looked around him as rattling shudders racked his body. His muscles were contracting violently in their last effort to produce life-saving warmth. These contractions would pass soon, he knew. And then he would lie still.

Spence did not want death to find him sitting down. He stood on wooden, unfeeling legs and tried to walk. The loose debris shifted and he was thrown down the incline of the canyon still further. His helmet struck a rock and he stopped.

He lay there exhausted, staring up at the black sky of Mars, imagining that he was the first man, and possibly the last, to ever lie awake under a Martian night sky.

The convulsions gradually lessened. He felt a tingling warmth spread through his frame—the illusion of warmth, the last remnant of his body's defenses exhausting itself.

A misty darkness closed around him, narrowing his field of vision, blurring the edges with a velvet softness. But the stars above, in the center of his sight, still burned hard and bright. Untwinkling, unmoving, unlike stars at all. It was as if the eyes of the universe watched him to see how a man died.

"No!" he shouted, hearing the empty ring of his voice in his helmet. "No," he said again; his voice was but a murmur.

Watching the stars he saw a pale white mist pass over them like a diaphanous veil. He thought it a trick of his failing eyesight. Then he saw it again—just the faintest trace of color against the night, the frailest of silken threads.

Odd, he thought. *What could produce such a phenomenon?*

His scientist's brain turned over this bit of novelty. He raised his head and saw, a little below him on the slope, a silver tracery on the rocks, glowing in the light of the moon.

On nerves and determination alone he stirred his useless limbs and half-slid, half-swam to the spot. He touched a gloved hand to the faint white outline of the stuff on the rocks. It gleamed in the clear light. "Crystals," he muttered to himself. "Ice crystals. Frost."

All around the immediate area he noticed the white hoarfrost, and below, the wisps of mist rising out of the ground.

Scarcely thinking or attending to what he was doing, he scrambled further down the slope and found himself peering into a pitch-dark hole. A fissure in the canyon wall had opened up, perhaps due to the rock slide earlier. Out of this fissure the slightest trace of pearly mist rose into the deathly cold Martian atmosphere.

The crack was just large enough for a man to squeeze head and shoulder through. Without thinking a second time, Spence thrust himself into the opening.

He found the hole beyond somewhat wider as he wriggled awkwardly into the opening. He inched forward into the blackness bit by bit and discovered the crevice dropped away at a sharp downward angle. He sat down and used his heels to pull himself along, sliding on his seat.

Down and down he went.

I have chosen my own grave, he thought. *My bones will not be blown to dust on the winds.*

The thought strangely cheered him.

Deeper into the brittle crust of the Red Planet he went. Sometimes sliding, sometimes walking nearly upright, calling on his will alone to move his body. Blind as a cave bat he moved, abandoning himself to all else but the moving. Onward; deeper and deeper still.

How long he walked, how far he burrowed, he did not know. The blackness around him penetrated his mind, covering it with itself, removing all thought, all memory, leaving only the present moment and the raw will to move on.

When the first ghostly glimmer reached his eyes out of the darkness around him, he thought it a trick of his failing mind: his faltering brain cells firing off minute electrical charges and somehow producing light in the cortex or optic nerve.

But the faint greenish glow did not fade. Instead it grew stronger. Spence, shuffling forward like a zombie, willing his legs to carry him along, stumbling over the uneven downward pathway, stayed on his feet and moved toward the gleam he saw in the distance.

He reached a spot where the glow seemed brightest and found as he came upon it that the faint light was a reflection on a blank wall of stone. He placed his hand upon the stone and saw the green cast on his glove.

He turned to see what produced the glow, as one reeling in a dream. What he saw rocked him back against the wall in disbelief: a wide tunnel glowing with interlacing veins of living light stretched before him. The thin green color glistened on the walls and roof of the gallery like a luminous dew.

Spence tottered into the tunnel and pressed his face close to the rock surface, as close as his helmet would allow. The glowing stuff oozed from the rock, clinging there like a slime. He thought of the phosphorescent plankton and algae in the oceans of Earth.

Can it be? he wondered. *Have I discovered life on Mars?*

CHAPTER TWO

THE TUNNEL, glowing softly with the light of the tiny green organisms, stretched beyond Spence's sight. It was smooth and round, and large enough for a man to walk erect without touching the top or sides. Its circular symmetry reminded him of a water conduit; the notion occurred to him that the shaft had been formed long ago by the water which had once run in the arroyo above.

He stepped into the shaft and started walking, not knowing or particularly caring where it led. As he moved along he saw that the green light wavered as he passed, as if his passing disturbed the tiny luminescent creatures. The glow dimmed as he drew near and then flashed brighter behind him. The creatures, if creatures they were, apprehended his presence.

He moved on; it seemed like hours that he pursued the unbending downward course of the shaft before he noticed a slight curving of the tunnel walls ahead.

When he reached the place where the curve began he noticed a gap in the floor of the shaft. Not a large crack—one he could jump across if he were careful about it, but dark so that he could not see how far down it went.

Spence reached out over the edge of the hole and after a few moments felt a tingling sensation in his fingers as warmth began to seep through his gloves.

The fissure was a natural vent which carried heat from a deep reservoir beneath the crust of the planet, perhaps from some ancient volcanic source or, reasoned Spence, from the molten core of the planet itself.

With shaking hands he grasped his helmet and gave it a sideways twist and lifted it off his head. He felt the warmth drift out of the hole and wash over his frozen features. This was perhaps the source of the fragile mist he had seen on the slope of the arroyo trough.

He replaced his helmet momentarily and took a lungful of air; then, stepping away from the crack he blew it out and watched the steam roll away in great billows. Clearly, the tunnel was still desperately cold, but by contrast with the surface it was a virtual tropic. It was at least warm enough to keep the tiny glowing algae alive. He doubted whether it was enough to keep himself alive for any length of time. Without real warmth the cold would eventually get to him, if more slowly than it would at the surface.

Spence, balancing himself carefully, leaped with extreme caution over the crack and trudged off, feeling every weary step deep in his bones. He wondered how much longer he would be able to keep going and feared that if he stopped to sleep he would not wake up. The cold would overcome him. Pushing the thought aside he gritted his teeth and moved on.

After a while he noticed that the green glow shining around him grew brighter. Looking at the walls of the tunnel he saw that the strange organisms grew in greater profusion. Perhaps it meant that the shaft was becoming warmer. He continued on.

Soon he walked, not in a faint glow, but in the green half-light of a moon-bright night. The light-making creatures clustered in thick colonies over every available inch of surface, radiating a steady green fluorescence which made him feel as if he walked inside a beam of light.

He welcomed the illumination, but the floor of the tunnel was now so covered with the algaelike organisms that walking became a hazard. His unsteady feet, aching with the rigors of his ordeal, slid as on glare ice while he propelled himself along the shaft. He fell often, each fall wearing him down further; it took him longer to regain his feet each time. He began to think that the next time he would not rise again.

But he did rise again. Something urged him on, kept him climbing back onto legs wobbling with pain and fatigue. Again and again he rose, sliding, stumbling, staggering ever downward into the bowels of the planet.

The tube twisted and turned like a snake. It sank in sharp downward angles and he lay on his back and slid like a man on a sled. He followed it without thinking where it would lead him.

Where the tunnel walls pinched together he wormed his way through. Where crevices opened in the floor, he found the strength to get across. Where the roof lowered he went on hands and knees. He kept moving.

Time lost significance. He lost all comprehension of the passing hours. His suit's chronometer, shattered in the fall into the arroyo, presented only a fixed present—time frozen, as if his life had stopped at that moment. Past, present, and future merged into one mingling amorphous element through which he moved as through water.

Once he came to himself as he felt the floor drop away beneath him, his feet kicking out from under him. He landed heavily on his back and glimpsed the shaft falling away in a near-vertical drop.

He had stepped over the brink without knowing it.

The tube was smooth beneath him, and the light-emitting algae cushioned his slide somewhat as he picked up momentum, sliding faster and faster, riding the curving conduit deeper into the Red Planet's heart.

The exhilaration of this wild ride burned the clouds from his mind. He felt adrenalin pumping into his bloodstream, rousing him from his torpor as the shaft raced by him, blurring his vision.

It seemed to him that he was falling into a gleaming green infinity, hurtling faster and faster, whizzing into a radiant unknown.

The luminous algae tore away in flashing streamers from his hands and feet to splatter over him like foaming light, covering his faceplate, blinding him. He wiped at the visor and cleared a small area just in time to see the shaft bottom out.

He braced himself for the impact and felt the tube curve and level out as he hit the bottom with a bone-cracking thump. He skidded out, arms and legs flailing, rolling over himself as if he'd been tossed from a speeding vehicle.

When at last he raised his head to look around he saw that he was in an enormous cavern. He pushed himself up on elbows and knees and winced from shooting pains in his head and back.

The cave was a vast bubble-shaped dome flattened on the bottom. Its roof arched at least a hundred meters above the floor; the walls, curved and smooth, lifted upward gracefully.

He rose stiffly and, feeling as if every bone in his body had been rearranged, began walking the length of the domed vault. The dim bluish-green light bathed him in the illusion of walking on the bottom of the sea; he fully expected schools of fish to swim by at any moment.

He reached the further wall and discovered that the cave had several smaller conduits leading out of it, and large drainlike holes in the floor. These smaller tubes were squat, roughly half his height; if he were to continue his journey it would have to be on hands and knees.

He quaked at the thought. His muscles already drooped with exhaustion and strain. He sank to the floor and lay down in front of one of the drain tubes. In moments he was sound asleep.

CHAPTER THREE

TWO DOORS stood at the end of a long, dark passage, shimmering with a cool blue light. Spence approached the doors and as he came nearer his heart began to race, pounding in his chest. Sweat rolled off his forehead and burned in his eyes. He wiped his face with his sleeve and walked on.

Now he stood before the two doors and it came to him that behind one of the doors Ari waited to embrace him, to soothe his troubled spirit and heal his wasted body.

Behind the other door a monster with large yellow eyes hulked ready to pounce and devour him.

He wept with anguish over the decision he must make, and cried out for someone to help him, but his voice rang hollow in his ears.

He stepped forward, placed his hand on the old-fashioned doorknob and turned. The door creaked open on ancient hinges and he peered apprehensively into the room. It was empty.

Spence crept into the room and as he crossed the threshold the door closed behind him. A mist came boiling out of the walls and floor, rising in a cloud before him.

Within the cloud lightning flashed in red streaks and he could see a shape dimly emerging as if it were being knit together out of the stuff of the vapors. He watched as the shape took on human form.

Then the clouds receded, falling away in curling tendrils to reveal a creature remarkably manlike, but born of a separate creation, the child of an alien god.

He trembled in its presence as the thing, motionless, towered over him head and shoulders, its smooth, golden skin gleaming with beads of moisture. He felt a tremor pass through him as the man-being drew its first breath deep into its lungs. Spence sank to his knees before it, transfixed with awe and fear.

Then as he gazed through trembling fingers up at the stern, spare features, the eyelids flickered and raised slowly. Two great yellow eyes glared down at him and he shrank away from their terrible gaze. He threw his arms over his head and tried to hide himself from their sight.

But the being saw him, saw through him, weighed his soul with its piercing sight and found it sadly wanting. It raised one long, multi-jointed arm toward him and opened its wide mouth to pronounce judgment.

Spence screamed, clamping his hands over his ears . .

The tremor seeped through the rock floor of the cavern, accompanied by a strange sighing roar. Spence, still groggy from his exhausted sleep, lay for some moments trying to remember where he was.

The rumble increased and the roar grew louder, banishing the last traces of sleep from his brain. The floor beneath him vibrated steadily. He had never stood on the slope of an active volcano, but that was the image that came to mind as he rolled up to kneel quivering with fear and uncertainty.

The thin air inside the cave convulsed as tremendous jets of water, rushing out of the sinkholes in the floor, erupted in gushers fifty meters high. The explosion knocked Spence sprawling as the floor rocked with the aftershock and tons of water rained down.

Instantly he was swept into the narrow opening of the conduit, kicking feebly against the swirling flood and slamming full force into every curve of the pipeline until he learned to relax and let the water take him.

On and on it carried him. Eventually it no longer filled the conduit; he could see a bubble forming on the roof of the tunnel. The bubble expanded until it covered a quarter of the pipe, and then half, and then it left him stranded on his stomach as it dwindled away.

He slipped off his helmet and cupped his hands to get a decent drink, but succeeded only in wetting his gloves. That, he reasoned, was better than nothing, so he held up his hands and let the water drip off his fingers into his mouth. He repeated the process several times, managing only to arouse his thirst the more for whetting it.

On hands and knees he continued his trek and arrived at the junction of a larger tunnel just as his muscles, every fiber screaming for relief, threatened to give out. This larger passageway stretched away on either hand into dark shadowy distance, slanting upward on the right and downward on the left.

He tried the upward course, but it proved too slippery, and each attempt brought him sliding unceremoniously down again before he got a dozen paces. He decided to stop before he lost his footing altogether and went skittering into the dark corridor behind him.

He was just about to resign himself to having to take that course in any event when he spied higher up in the tunnel wall a small aperture he had not noticed before. This opening suggested itself to him as an acceptable alternative and he decided to give it a try.

The decision nearly killed him.

Twice he reached the edge of the opening and failed to get a proper handhold, sliding back onto the floor both times. The third time he managed to tear away some of the algae around the rim of the opening for a better grip. He dug in and held on while he brought his feet beneath him, hoping to use them to drive himself up and into the opening. It nearly worked.

He gathered himself for the push and then let fly. His head rose to the level of the bottom of the opening and he thrust an arm forward while his feet kicked against the smooth, slick stone wall. Then he brought his other hand around and grasped the lip of stone. It was then he felt himself falling backwards to the tunnel floor below.

The fall progressed in slow motion. His hands raked the stone and then empty air as he twisted catlike in mid-fall, sank backward, and dropped in a heap to the floor.

The impact knocked the wind out of him. For one horrible moment he could not breathe, and then air rushed in in great windy gasps. His ribs felt as if they had been staved in, and his shoulder throbbed where he landed on it.

What he failed to accomplish with strength and dexterity he achieved with patience and cunning.

Using every inch of body surface to increase the amount of available traction, he imagined himself a slug and oozed up the curving side of the tunnel toward the opening. He felt his handhold and pulled himself up centimeter by painful centimeter until he could lean into the opening and squirm in on his belly.

This new tubule also rose at a slight upward grade which forced him to concentrate on every step—one misstep would send him sliding out into the main tunnel like something expelled from a cannon. He doggedly placed one foot in front of the other and, arms outspread like a man walking a tightrope, labored up the passageway.

This tedious method of locomotion wore on him, taxing already tired muscles to the limit. He longed to sit and rest, but the incline offered no advantage there. He lowered his head and pressed on, ignoring the pains shooting through his thighs like fire.

A kind of benumbed melancholy overtook him, which he recognized as the sum of a number of factors—stress, fatigue, hunger, and pain not the least of them. Each step was a struggle against creeping despair; he longed to just sit down and let his fate roll over him like breakers upon a desolate shore. But he did not give in.

He slept again and awoke still exhausted but clearheaded and with a gnawing emptiness in his stomach. He was fiercely hungry, but the prospects of doing anything significant about it appeared depressingly slim. He resolved to push all thoughts of food and eating out of his mind.

The attempt proved largely unsuccessful. Like the tongue that has just discovered the still tender gap where a tooth used to be, his mind returned again and again to probe the subject despite the pain it caused him.

Under such extreme conditions hallucinations were perhaps to be expected. Still, despite this knowledge and his training in the ways of the human brain, the hallucination stopped him dead in his tracks.

Unremarkable as hallucinations go, it nevertheless hit him with a wounding impact, as if the thing had exploded in his face. He tottered on his heels for a moment and then stepped backwards into the wall behind him where he slid slowly to the floor, eyes starting from his skull in shock and disbelief.

There before him, glimmering faintly across the corridor, stood a door.

No snarling, hydra-headed monster could have alarmed him more than this simple architectural object. At first he thought it must be an optical illusion, a trick played by overtired eyes. Then he knew he was experiencing a hallucination—seeing doors where he desperately wanted them to be.

Following this observation, it dawned on him that persons undergoing hallucinations did not percieve them as such while in the very grip of them.

A door! His mind reeled. What could it mean? Indeed, what else *could* it mean?

Feverishly Spence began tearing away the algae by handfuls, digging it out with his gloved fingers from around the imagined threshold. What emerged was an object of stone cut from the same stuff as the surrounding walls with no external markings of any kind. He would have considered it a novelty of nature except its smoothness, roundness, and perfect symmetry argued against a natural artifact. But he could not be sure.

He lifted off his helmet and smacked it into the slab. He listened to the echo pinging away to the dim recess of the tunnel. He also heard a hollow sound beyond the barrier; it was not a dead end.

Overcome by a burning curiosity to see what lay beyond the supposed door, he leapt at the slab and began pushing with all his might, succeeding only in shoving his feet out from under him. Then he knelt before the door and tried to worm his fingers into the cracks at the sides. He arched his back and strained until he thought his heart would burst—and the slab began to move.

It slid a few centimeters, and he felt a gush of warm air from behind the door. The algae on the floor around him flushed brightly. He smelled the stale dry air flowing out; it had an odd taste which he could not place—sweet, yet rancid. The air of a tomb.

Once more he attacked the door with a fury. He was rewarded for his labors when at last the stone rolled back another few centimeters and he was able to squeeze his shoulders through.

He forced himself through the narrow opening, dizzy from the lack of oxygen and gasping for breath. He collapsed on the floor and lay down, panting while waves of nausea from his over-exertion slammed into him.

A faint, reddish-gold radiance fell over him as he lay gazing upward, though where this might come from he could not readily tell. The walls around him were smooth stone and dull red in the ruddy twilight of the mysterious light.

After a while the wracking nausea subsided and he was able to raise his head and look around. There was not much to see. The passage, bone dry and dusty, continued upward at a steep angle directly ahead of him. In order to find out more about his new surroundings, he would have to haul himself back onto his weary legs and climb that incline.

Shaking with fatigue he squirmed onto his side and made to push himself up. His hand brushed something in the dust—a small ridge of stone. He looked down and saw between his hands the faintly outlined depression of a footprint.

CHAPTER FOUR

THE FOOTPRINT lay squarely in his path, outlined in the red dust thick upon the floor. A trick of the light, he thought; some odd stone formation. But he stared at it as if he expected it to disappear.

Spence leaned down over the print and carefully, as any archeologist would, blew away the dust. Then, with the tips of his fingers, ever so lightly, he brushed away the thicker silt that had accumulated.

The print remained, inexplicably pressed firmly into the stone—a print of an upright creature: quasi-human. Narrower and longer—it looked like someone had taken a man's foot and stretched it out of proportion. And it had only four small toes. On close inspection he decided that it was not missing any of its toes, as from an accident; it had been designed that way.

He looked around to see if there were any other prints nearby, but there were none. He did discover that the print lay in the bottom of a slight depression boundaried by two smooth banks, as if at one time long ago an underground stream had trickled along this course.

Spence sat in the dust, his mind reeling.

This was the discovery of a lifetime—of several lifetimes. Probably the most important find in the last two hundred years. In the last thousand!

Life on Mars! He, Dr. Spencer Reston, had discovered life on Mars. Beyond a shadow of a doubt, Mars had once been home to something more significant than glowing algae. The thing that made that print walked upright like a man, perhaps thought as a man, was conscious of itself.

The implications of his discovery sorted themselves out only gradually. Once the dimensions of his find emerged in their immensity, the finer details could be seen. The print very clearly had been made ages past counting in order for it to have solidified into stone. If other articles of Martian civilization existed they would most likely be dust and ashes, unless fossilized.

Of course, he argued, the print need not necessarily belong to an inhabitant of Mars at all. It could just as well belong to an intruder like himself. This did not diminish his enthusiasm in the least, nor belittle his discovery. The thing was extraordinary no matter how one viewed it, but it did cause Spence to slow somewhat and consider how little he knew about the print or how it had come to be there. Clearly, he had pushed speculation beyond reasonable limits for a scientist. He would have to have many more facts to substantiate his theories, to even begin to develop any theories.

One print alone was not enough. He needed more to go on. One print alone was almost worthless. What he needed were bones, artifacts—any of the normal archeological building blocks.

Deathly tired, his mind beginning to wander, he crossed his arms on his chest and fell asleep beside the footprint with thoughts of red Martians crawling blithely over the landscape, besmeared with chalky red dust like pygmies, and himself towering over them saying something ridiculous like, "Take me to your leader."

The ache in his gut was back when he awoke, and his throat burned. A thick, gummy film had formed in his mouth, foul-tasting and nasty. His tongue felt large and uncooperative. He had heard stories of men dying of thirst in the desert whose tongues had swelled, turning black in their mouths and choking them in the end. He wondered if this was how it started.

Grimly he got to his feet, swaying dizzily. Black spots swam before his eyes. Hunger had become a demanding force, and thirst an ever-present fire. He knew that he had little time left before he collapsed in a faint. After several such collapses he would rise no more.

He considered returning to the tunnel behind the door where the algae grew in such lush profusion. It occurred to him that he might be able to eat them and sustain himself.

The only drawback to this plan was that the algae could well be poisonous. One mouthful could cause him to end his life retching out his entrails in a cold sweat, or send him screaming in agony to crush his head against the stones to stop the pain. These were the milder scenarios he imagined—less pleasant possibilities occurred to him which he did not care to entertain.

Spence decided that if he had found no water by the time he slept once more he would return to the passage beyond the stone door—he now considered it a door in every sense of the word—and eat the algae, come what may. He would by that time be on his last strength and it would not matter which way his life finally ceased. At that point he would be willing to gamble, but not before.

So he lurched off once more, climbing up the passageway. Not more than a few meters up, the tunnel ended and he stepped into a vast underground cavity of enormous proportions. He began walking, head down, shoulders forward, arms swinging loosely at his sides.

Soon he was pleased to discover that his gnawing hunger had eased. He felt clean, lean, purged of a heaviness that weighed on his body and spirit, electrically alive.

Spence knew this to be the sensation associated with a fast. Medically, the effect was well recognized. Still, he could not help feeling the intense emotional impact of the phenomenon. He felt, for lack of a better word, spiritual.

At intervals along the route—he decided to move directly ahead, keeping the tunnel at his back—thick columns of stone rose from the floor like the trunks of trees. He wondered at these but they, like the slab door, seemed to be natural formations such as one might find in any cave. There was no reason to believe they were not exotic forms of stalagmites peculiar to the Martian lithosphere.

And yet the sprout of suspicion had already woven its snaking fibrils deep into his consciousness. What if they, like the footprint, were *not* natural?

The implications were too extraordinary to entertain for any length of time. But increasingly the suggestion of trespassing occurred to him. How he had struck upon that particular word he could not say, but it seemed appropriate.

He felt like one trespassing on private ground. A grave-robber desecrating a pharaoh's tomb. He imagined that at any moment a whole phalanx of spear-toting soldiers would come swinging into view from behind one of those strange columns. He had visions of plumed horses and chariots dragging him through the village square while the screaming alien populace jeered, "Thief! Grave-robber! Desecrater!"

These daydreams he knew to be associated with his deprivation. He had begun to feel his thirst once more—the tiny amount of water he had scooped from the conduit floor was not enough to sustain him. He needed a real drink badly.

He hoped that the flood which had washed him through the tunnel could be located again. There was water on Mars; maybe not much, but it existed. He had navigated it; finding it again was a project becoming uppermost in his mind.

Gradually, as he walked along the dull red cavern floor, listening to his own footsteps pattering away into the darkness, the roof of the cave sloped away and with it the rust-colored lichen clinging to its surface. The lichen, he discovered, gave off a pale aura like the algae in the tunnels.

He made his way along through a dim and hazy light of ruddy gold which reached him as sunlight through the flaming canopy of autumn trees. But here the trees were stone and no leaves scattered before his feet.

He fell into an easy rhythm of walking, trying to maintain a steady course forward. The tempo of his steps carried him along.

After a few hours of walking he slept again, and then once more after that—still unwilling to give in and return to the tunnel and the algae. Each time he slept less and woke less rested than before. He supposed this to be the effect of his fast. His body was beginning to turn on itself for nourishment. He felt lightheaded, airy, spiritlike, pure.

In his journey through the Martian underground Spence's eyes turned inward and he gazed upon his life with the kind of aloof objectivity he usually reserved for his work, with the same meticulous scrutiny and the same relentless curiosity. Only this time the subject was himself.

Though considered a fast-rising star by most, he nevertheless knew himself to have fallen far short of the mark. There were others he knew who had accomplished more, received higher praise, garnered more of the glittering prizes he sought, whose names were better known and respected more than his own. The resentment he felt for those fortunate others had hardened into a burning, almost ruthless ambition to surmount their achievements—an ambition Spence had always prided himself on, thinking it a virtue and a means to his personal fulfillment.

Now, considering his circumstances and the shallowness of his inner being, he viewed that ambition for what it was—a flame which had consumed nearly all his better qualities to fuel itself. Compassion, generosity, joy, even love—these had been given to the fire and it had all but consumed them. And now what had he to show for his pains?

Nothing of lasting value. Nothing that would live after him. All had been directed inward, feeding the flame. That he had any redeeming qualities left at all seemed to him something of a miracle, so much had been given to the all-consuming fire.

In this delicate, suggestible state he felt the loss of all those years of determined self-denial—the endless studying, working, striving. The waste appalled him.

He had been convinced that the only success in life came through achievement. As a scientist he trusted only what he could see and examine. "If it cannot be measured," a professor had once told him, "it is not worth thinking about."

He had laughed at the time, but now he saw clearly that the joke was on him. He blindly bought that empty philosophy, as did so many of his young colleagues, though they called it by different names and dressed it in altruistic rhetoric. Of course, he had told himself that his goals as a scientist were helpful to mankind and therefore worthy. But a real concern for his fellowman never entered into it. The goals were merely milestones on his private road to success.

The question he kept coming back to, the one uppermost in his mind at the moment, was a question of ultimates. What, ultimately, had he done with his life? Had it been wisely spent?

Sorrowfully, no. Spence, confronted with the naked facts, was forced to conclude that his life had been pretty much one long self-aggrandizing binge. And it had contributed nothing to anyone but to make him a dour, selfish gloryhound.

In short, it had been, except for momentary lapses, a life not worth living. Spence, his logic cool and keen as a computer's, stared unblinking at the conclusion and marveled that he should have tried so hard to save such a sorry life as his own.

There came over him a feeling of shame, of guilt so thick it clothed him like a garment. Never in his life had he felt guilty for anything. That he should feel so now, when there was absolutely nothing to be done about it, was the final irony.

He dimly remembered a sort of prayer, uttered out of the frustration of the moment, as he had wandered in the wilderness desert of Mars not so long ago. That prayer came back to him now and mocked him, as his own lack of faith in anything beyond human ingenuity mocked him.

See how the worm turns! his ghostly accuser seemed to say. Faced squarely with its own mortality, the creature grasps at any straw. Where, O foolish one, is your dignity? Where is your self-respect? Do you not have courage enough even to end your life as you lived it? What right do you have to call upon one you never worshiped, never believed, never acknowledged? You lived by your beliefs—die by them!

Spence felt a chill in his chest as if an icy hand had closed around his heart. As much as he wanted it to be otherwise, he had to admit the accuser was right. For the first time in his life he saw himself for what he was. The sight sickened him. He desperately wished that somehow all that had happened could be reversed, that he could be given a second chance.

The hope died stillborn in his breast.

He reflected sadly that there were no second chances. And his plight was beyond reverse, beyond help, beyond hope.

In this way, absorbed in his pitiless introspection, Spence came into the city.

CHAPTER FIVE

THAT IT was a city he had no doubt. He had not noticed that for the last four kilometers or so the roof of the cavern had been arching away gradually. By the time he reached the outskirts of this alien habitation he could not see the ceiling. He had been lumbering along oblivious to his surroundings when he saw something glimmering in front of him. Spence had raised his eyes and found himself standing before a weird assemblage of structures.

If pressed for a description, Spence would have said that the city appeared to him like a termite nest. He recalled pictures of the inside of such a nest from an entomology textbook, and looking upon the strange, elongated and flowing structures brought back the same image to him. On further inspection, though, the graceful interwoven cells looked like nothing at all that he had ever seen. And they gave not a hint of what kind of resident might have inhabited them.

This discovery brought none of the heady rapture of the explorer who believes he has found Eldorado at last, nor of the paleontologist who chances upon an unnamed saurian. He did not even feel the same elation experienced upon finding the footprint.

He just stood unmoving in his tracks, shaking his head in disbelief and wonder. It was simply too much to take in all at once. He did not know how to react.

When he came to himself again he began threading through the winding pathways among the hivelike habitations, under curving arches and over half-buried burrow hills. He soon lost himself in the refined tangle of bending, interlacing shapes, as a small child in an enchanted forest.

His way was lit by the radiant lichen clinging to the sides of the dwellings. It was as if he moved through an elven world sparkling with magic and whispering voices. The voices were the swish of his steps as he passed hollow or curving shapely walls.

The more he saw of the city—formed of some kind of adobelike material such as ancient Indian settlements but harder, more durable—the further he walked, the more beautiful it seemed to him. And colorful. The dwellings were of various subtle hues: oranges, reds, violets, and browns in various subdued tones; delicate earthen, or rather Martian, hues of ocher and sepia, madder and rust and buff, softly shimmering in their own faint light.

There were apertures and openings which he took to be windows and doors. These were of various shapes, all in keeping with the surrounding curve of the wall or archway of which they were a part. For this reason Spence could get no precise impressions of what the residents themselves might have looked like.

He poked his head into the darkened interiors of several dwellings and saw nothing at all to further the identification process. The rooms were the inner version of the outer structure, molded and graceful and, for all he could see, clean-swept and empty.

In his reverent ramble through the interlacing forms he struck upon a wide, meandering pathway between two ranks of towering structures. This he took to be a central trafficway.

The domiciles on either side of this street rose to a considerable height above the smooth, even surface he walked upon. Some of them branched over it in sinuous arches or tubes which wound snakelike to join a building on the other side.

The notion came to him that if he followed this trafficway he would end up in the center of the Martian city.

He was not wrong.

Within an hour of discovering the place he stood blinking in the center of a wide expanse surrounded on all sides by the queer architecture. The sheer alien beauty of the place still overwhelmed him. He had begun to think that the Martians, whatever their outward appearance, had been an elegant, peace-loving civilization. Such was the effect of the architecture on him. He did not for a moment consider that there might be any Martians still around. Everything he saw indicated a civilization which had long ago ceased to exist.

He sat down to rest on a smooth, mushroom-shaped projection, one of many which randomly dotted the central clearing. His vision blurred and wavered; he knew he was seriously dehydrated now. Dizziness played over him and he felt suddenly weaker, as if he were beginning to disintegrate. He imagined an exploring party of the future wandering into the square and finding his bones, and mistaking him for the last remaining Martian.

As Spence sat holding the last unraveling threads of his strength his gaze happened to fall on one of the hives across the square, set apart from the others. For some reason the structure took on an importance for him—he felt himself drawn to it, though outwardly it did not differ from any around it. It was roughly mound-shaped with bulging sides rising upward to become bulbous compartments and chambers.

Spence nodded in his remote inspection of the building. His eyes closed and he slid from the mushroom pod and rolled onto his side and fell asleep.

He woke at once. He would have sworn his head had barely touched the ground before his eyes snapped open again. But the burning in his throat and the throbbing in his head told him differently. He had perhaps been asleep for some time, but the pain was not what awakened him.

Someone called his name. And it sounded as if it had come from the hive across the square.

The word had been so quickly spoken he could not say that he did not imagine it. But unlike imagined voices, this one hung in the air as a present thing. Spence slowly lifted off his helmet and put it down.

The air in this part of the cavern, though dry and stale, seemed more conducive to oxygen breathing, for he found he did not gasp as before. The deathly silence of the place alarmed him. He heard nothing at all, not even the suggestion of an echo. At least inside his helmet he had heard the constant, rhythmic pattern of his own breathing.

All at once it came to him that he had drifted off to sleep because his oxygen had run low in his helmet—the pellets had given out. If not for the voice which had stirred him once more he would never have awakened again. He would have suffocated in his sleep.

He stood looking down at his helmet with a mixture of relief and longing. He did feel relieved to have escaped this subtle death after braving so many other, greater dangers. On the other hand, it would have been a peaceful, painless death—to sleep and not wake up again to the ache in his stomach and head and the stinging fire of his thirst.

As he stood contemplating whether or not to put on his helmet again and so end the game, he heard his name again. He heard it ring in his ears and register in his brain, but it came from another place, though where or how that could be he could not say. The dying often hear voices, he reminded himself. Such occurrences were well documented.

But Spence felt an inner tug at him toward the hive-shaped dwelling across the quad. He stepped forward hesitantly, uncertain whether to give in to his hallucination so easily. He shrugged, remembering that he had nothing at all to lose, though he knew he would find nothing of interest or of any possible value to him within. All the other hives he had peered into had been uniformly barren.

Still, the inexplicable pull directed his steps and he gave himself over, lacking the strength to fight it. In a few moments he stood gaping at the exterior of the hive and at the darkened hole of the entrance.

Spence swayed unsteadily on his feet as he shuffled in and knocked against something standing just inside the door. It was hard and unyielding and he went down in a heap, without the strength to fall gracefully.

Darkness dwelt in the cool interior, had dwelt there undisturbed for perhaps a thousand centuries. He sank back on the floor and let the darkness cover him, surrendering to it, become a part of it. He longed to just lay there panting and never stir again. But his curiosity overcame him.

What had he bumped up against when he entered? It was flat and hard and he still felt the chill of it against his side where he hit it. What could it be?

If it was to be his last act, so be it. But at least he would know what he had found. He dragged himself to his knees and lurched forward across the floor toward the unseen object. His cheek struck a hard, flat edge and he pressed his palms against a smooth surface and raised himself up.

Now what? he wondered. *I have found something here in this dark place . . . now what?*

He thought to try moving it with the idea that he might be able to take it out into the relative light of the cave. But try as he might, in his weakened state he could not budge the thing, nor even find a place to grasp it.

He let his hands run over the surface of the object to give him some idea of its size and shape. He felt like a blind man trying to guess the nature of an object he had never seen. He discovered it to be uniformly smooth and rather boxlike, its surface composed of flat planes joined at shallow angles like plates of armor or the facets of a gemstone.

Spence brought his hands once more toward the top of the rectangular object and felt a long cylindrical portion rise from the plane of its surface. Following the cylinder up he discovered it was surmounted by a large sphere. He found two more cylinders and spheres at either end of the rectangle.

Now he was thoroughly intrigued. He stood abruptly—too quickly for his condition—and the dizziness flowed over him in a dark wave. He staggered backward and fell against a smaller object directly behind him. The thing caught him at the back of the legs just below the knees and he toppled over it. The sound of a brittle crash filled his ears.

He was there in the darkness, listening. For there had been something else in that crash that he heard. Something he had been listening unconsciously for since he first entered the tunnel. He recognized it now, but it seemed out of place and almost eerie in the silence.

In the darkness, somewhere close at hand, he heard the wonderful liquid splash of water dripping on the floor.

CHAPTER SIX

"JUST GIVE me one more day. Just one more. What does it matter? You can send your report in the morning. That's all I ask."

Packer, hunched in a form-molding chair at the radio console, tilted back and looked at his friend. Their eyes met and held their gaze. "All right," sighed Packer. "I quess it doesn't matter that much. You've managed to put it off a week already. But you have to tell me why—I don't understand it, this obsession of yours. You must know there's nothing left. It doesn't make sense, Adjani."

The slim brown man nodded thoughtfully and then spoke, lowering his voice cautiously as if he feared he would be overheard. "I had a dream last night," he whispered. "I saw him—Spence. He was alive in some kind of cave or something. He was hurt, but he was alive."

"And you believe this dream of yours?"

Adjani nodded slowly.

"Why? Tell me."

"God sometimes speaks to his people in dreams and visions. I believe this is a sign that I should keep on looking."

Packer frowned. He fingered the switches on the panel before him idly. "A sign? Aren't you being a little melodramatic?"

"I don't know what you mean—"

"Nothing, really. Don't mind me." Packer swiveled away. "Look, you go on and do whatever it is you think you have to. But I've got to tell them he's missing at least. And I want you to be on call for some of the sessions, okay? The rest of the time it's up to you. You can even stay here while we're planting the probes. Deal?"

"It's a deal." Adjani remained slouched against the console, smiling down at the burly physicist.

"Now what? You want the keys to my car?"

"I was just thinking that you'd like to believe, too. You'd like to think that he's still alive, wouldn't you?"

"Sure—who wouldn't? To die like that—"

"That's not what I mean and you know it. You would like to believe about the dream. Admit it."

"All right. I admit it. Yeah, I'd like to believe that there was something out there watching over us. I wish I could believe it."

"Well, *wanting* to believe is just a step away from believing. Isn't it?"

He turned and disappeared along the banks of telemetry equipment which formed the communications nook.

"Spooky Injun," muttered Packer as he rose and pushed the chair back and shambled off to check on the progress of his boys who were assembling the probes for the next phase of the terraforming project.

Hocking's thin fingers fluttered over the tray of his chair, brushing the tiny knurled impressions. A whine like that of a dog in pain seemed to waver in the air, rising rapidly out of audible range. A circle of light appeared on the floor before him and the egg-shaped chair glided into it and hung there.

In a moment the air around the chair crinkled with a tinkling sound like needles dancing, or slivers of glass breaking. Then, in a spot midway between ceiling and floor, a dull glow appeared and spread into a gleaming blue halo. The interior of the halo sparkled as shapes collided and shifted within it, forming themselves out of pure light.

Hocking waited as the shapes resolved themselves into the familiar features of his dreaded mentor.

Ortu sat with his old head bowed, the folds of his yellow skin hanging slack, eyes closed, unmoving. He appeared wholly without life, but Hocking knew better.

Slowly the hairless head rose and the eyelids opened. Two yellow eyes stared out with cold, reptilian malice. The thin, lipless mouth, drawn into a straight line, frowned, the edges bending down at slight angles. Nothing Ortu did expended the merest fraction more than the absolute minimum of effort whether in thought or motion. He would do only that which was necessary to accomplish his ends, nothing more.

"The broken man summons his master. Why?" The words were cut from ice.

"You asked me to report to you following the latest attempt."

"Yes?"

"We located Reston . . . on Mars." At the last word Hocking sensed a prickling of interest on the static features of his master—the merest spark in the dull yellow eyes. "I attempted the mindlink as instructed. It failed—or at least I have not been able to reestablish contact. He, of course, may be dead."

"You bungled the procedure again!" Ortu snapped. "I warned you!"

Hocking glared back. "I did as you instructed. It was no fault of mine. Reston is resourceful, but there is some sort of interference where he is concerned. *No one* has survived three projections."

Ortu hesitated, something Hocking had never before witnessed. But when he spoke again his voice was flat and controlled once more. "There may be something in what you say—an interference. But we must make certain whether he is dead or alive. Find out and report to me."

"I will do as you say."

The sparkling halo dimmed and faded from view. Hocking saw the ancient features dissolve once more into pools of diffuse light to vanish as the wreath melted away. The pneumochair spun and whisked itself away. Hocking smiled darkly and muttered, "I think it is time to find out just how much Miss Zanderson knows."

Spence lay sprawled on the floor of the hive with the brittle pieces of whatever he had fallen over scattered around him. A hard mass of something pressed against his left leg—the remains of the object that had tripped him. From this source he heard the dripping sound.

He reached a trembling hand into the darkness and felt the jagged edge of an object near his elbow. Gingerly he traced the ragged rim with his hand, careful not to cut his glove, lest the liquid prove corrosive. Next he bent his head over the opening his glove had traced and sniffed the contents of what he imagined to be a jug-shaped article of some size. He smelled nothing at all, so lowered a hand inside.

Yes, the receptacle did contain liquid of some sort. He withdrew his hand and brought it close to his face and sniffed again, and then cautiously, knowing the peril, touched a finger to his tongue.

It was water.

Spence nearly jumped out of his surface suit. Shivering with excitement he removed his gloves and threw them aside, hunkering over the top of the vessel. He placed one hand inside and lifted a tiny sip to his lips.

The water tingled on his tongue like electricity. He let it seep into his parched tissues and then cupped his hand for another drink. In this way he eventually quenched his thirst; it took some time, for he was careful not to spill even the tiniest drop. He did not know how long the water would have to last him and he wanted it to go as far as possible.

When he had finished he sat back and, holding the vessel with one hand so that it would not tip over and spill out the remaining ration of water, he fumbled on the floor for his gloves with the other hand. His hand brushed over a raised platform set in the floor. Three oval objects decorated the surface of the platform; they were smooth to the touch like glass, and Spence did what any child born on Earth would have done: he placed his fingers on the center oval and pushed it.

Suddenly the interior of the hive blazed with white light and the air sang with a superhigh-pitched hum. He threw his hand over his eyes and fell on his face.

He waited. Nothing happened.

He cautiously raised his head and saw before him on a low pedestal an oblong object shaped like a coffin and bearing three narrow cylinders topped with spheres. The spheres were transparent and filled with liquid. On the floor beside him sat his own broken sphere next to the low base on which sat the ovals, one of which he had pushed and which apparently had illumined the place. It was this low base or console of sorts he had stumbled over, breaking off the sphere which may have been attached to it.

The light which had blazed so brightly emanated from beneath the pedestal of what looked more than anything like a translucent sarcophagus. It gleamed darkly, its facets like shining scales of a reptile showing gray as the light came through and around them.

He rose and went to it, rubbing at one of the plates as he would have rubbed at a fogged window pane, trying to peer inside a forbidden room. The contents, if any, could not be clearly made out.

Spence turned once more to the small console. He had pushed the center oval with some effect. Now he chose the oval stone on the right and carefully pressed it.

Again the high-pitched hum and as he watched, eyes riveted on the sarcophagus, one of the three spheres of liquid slowly began trickling through the cylinder and into the murky depths of the mysterious box. When the first sphere was empty the process was continued with the second sphere, and likewise by the third in its turn.

Spence tiptoed to the oblong box and pressed his face to the dim plates. He saw an indistinct mass of intricately interwoven material. It was fibrous and reedy, shrunken and withered, vaguely man-shaped like a mummy. But it was not a mummy. The thing lay in about six centimeters of liquid on which floated, as far as he could make out, a thick film of dust.

He supposed the device to be some kind of machine for growing food. It was the first thing that came into his mind, for with the light and water and the floating nutrients the apparatus reminded him of a greenhouse in miniature, though a greenhouse of a design he was sure no man on Earth had ever seen.

He waited for the last of the liquid in the third globe to trickle into the greenhouse chamber and then he went back and pressed the third oval.

The hum which filled the room now made a deeper sound, and he imagined the interior of the hive growing warmer almost immediately.

He went to the growing tank and placed his hands on the sides. It did feel warmer to the touch, but he could not be certain. He waited for a little while and nothing else happened, or seemed about to.

He decided to conduct a hive-to-hive search to see if he might turn up any more of the strange greenhouses. This he did and was disappointed. Finding no more of the devices nor anything else of interest, he returned somewhat dejected to the first dwelling.

During his search Spence had puzzled over the voice that had beckoned him and thus brought him back from the brink. Twice he had heard it—the first time it had awakened him from the sleep of death just in time. The second utterance had directed him to the hive which, alone of all the others, contained the growing-machine and the water. This had also saved him.

Spence had once seen a map of the world drawn by a sailor in the eighth century. The map conceived of a flat world where known perils were clearly marked. Toward the edges of the world, where the boundary between the known and the unknown had been drawn, the mapmaker had written the words, *here be dragons.*

Anyone who spoke of the supernatural within Spence's hearing he summarily lumped into the same cast as the ignorant and superstitious Byzantine sailor. Regarding religion, Spence had slightly more respect, but only a shade more. He considered it in its milder expressions a form of harmless do-goodism, the refuge of weaker minds perplexed and frightened by the world they saw and their own inability to change it. It was a psychological holdover from a time long past when men, yearning for order but not knowing how to create it, conjured up a Supreme Being who was not affected by the daily ebb and flow of change, who was not part of the confusion because he stood outside it. And if he did not help resolve the chaos of the world, he at least did not add to it and so was conceived to be benevolent in his dealings with his creatures.

He allowed that faith in this God-Being was a minor virtue of sorts, in the same way kindness to dumb animals or small children was a virtue. He did not mock it as a rule—such virtues had a place in the world—but he did not find anything in it to recommend it for himself.

And yet, he had prayed—if one could call it a prayer—to this same Supreme Being in his own moment of doubt and pain. This, he concluded, had been the act of a drowning man, one who might not have believed in life jackets, but who was nevertheless willing to try one as a last resort before the waters closed over his head forever.

He had done it out of weakness, and understandably so.

But the *voice*—that was something different. He had *heard* it. He could not argue it away; its presence still lingered in his mind.

Spence settled down in the room with the growing-machine to brood and wait for any new developments. He would sleep and wait; if nothing more seemed forthcoming he would take his water and retrace his route back through the tunnels, or try to find another way back to the surface. The latter plan seemed to offer more promise since he doubted he would be able to climb back up along those tunnels with any success: the walls were too smooth and slippery and steep.

CHAPTER SEVEN

THE TUNNEL, glowing gently with a subtle blue-green shimmer, wound up and out of the planet's interior. Spence, clinging with fingers and toes to the slippery surface had, by sheer strength of nerve and will, dragged himself up to the very entrance of the underground shaft. Before him, glimmering coolly, stood two doors.

As he approached the doors he understood that one door led out onto the surface of the Red Planet and the other contained the answer to his dreams. With this realization came a moment of dizzying indecision. His heart began to race. Sweat beaded on his face and neck.

Which one should he open? Which freedom did he desire more?

He raised himself and placed his hand on the knob of the door nearest him and stepped into an empty room. At once his heart sank—he had been tricked. There was nothing here to help him.

But as he stood blinking into the room's dim interior, a mist gathered, boiling out of the floor in front of him, rising in a dense cloud.

The vapors churned and he saw red sparks like lightning darting in thin streaks, and he could see a shape dimly emerging as if it were being knit together out of the vapors. He watched as the shape took on a vaguely human form.

The cloud receded, falling away in curling tendrils to reveal a creature remarkably manlike but fashioned out of different stuff entirely.

The thing, motionless, towered over him, its smooth, hairless skin gleaming golden and wet with beads of moisture. He felt a tremor pass through him as the man-being drew its first breath.

He felt the urge to turn away, to run and hide himself from its presence, but he could not move; he was held by an inescapable force. He buried his face in his hands and peered through trembling fingers at the stern, spare features. The eyelids flickered and raised slowly, and two great yellow eyes, like those of a cat, glared down on him. He shrank away from their sight.

But the monster saw him and saw through him, piercing him to the innermost recesses of his heart. It raised one lanky arm and opened its mouth to speak.

He fell to his knees as if to beg for mercy from the creature, but it stepped forward with surprising quickness for something so tall. It scooped him up in strong arms and carried him into the darkened corner of the room, which suddenly changed into a wide, brightly lit corridor with an arched ceiling, joined by other corridors which led away from it at regular intersections along the way.

The golden being carried Spence effortlessly with long, sure strides and at last came to a great domed room which was filled with exotic-looking machines and strange instruments. He placed Spence in a kind of bowl-shaped chair and put a thin transparent shell of a helmet on his head. The creature bent over a low bank of spheres mounted atop one another and Spence felt a warm sensation sweep over him.

The creature looked at him and asked, "Who are you? Why have you come?"

The pain was a laserknife that sliced through his brain, carving it neatly in half in one effortless stroke. One moment Spence had been standing atop one of the taller domed hives searching the underground cavescape for anything resembling an entrance or exit. The next thing he knew he was laying on his side with the pain bursting in fireballs inside his head.

He had plunged through the thin shell of the structure when the portion he was standing on collapsed with a brittle crack under his weight. He landed on his side and when he made an attempt to move, the pain had exploded in dazzling colors.

He lay back panting for a long time until the pain subsided enough for him to roll over and put his hands on the floor to push himself up. The effort left him head down, retching with dry heaves. He fell into a fit of coughing and tasted blood in his mouth when he was finished. He looked down and saw flecks of blood in the thick dust. With a stab of horror he realized that he had broken one or more ribs and that at least one of the broken ribs had punctured his lung. He fell back and a long sobbing wail burst from his throat; tears rolled down his cheeks as he rocked back and forth in the debris around him, howling in despair and agony.

Sometime later, whimpering with pain at every step, he dragged himself back to the first hive and lay down near the water sphere. The hours blurred and ran. The fire in his side increased unbelievably. Spence teetered on the brink of consciousness, often tipping over the edge. Fever raged as he coughed and the lung filled with fluid, threatening to suffocate him. Any but the smallest movement brought crescendos of pain booming through his body. His chest felt as if it were clamped between white-hot pincers.

Spence lay in a dream world, half awake, half swooning in his own sweat. He roused himself periodically to sip water from the sphere and then fell back weakly following each exertion.

Time passed; he had no idea how much time. The already confused hours merged together and he could not easily tell his waking moments from dreaming ones—they all fused and mingled like beads of wax on a heated plate.

It was during one of his rarer waking moments that he heard the pulsing hum of the machine next to him; actually, it occurred to him that he had been hearing it for some time. He turned his head and shifted his body slightly to get a better view.

The gray translucent sides of the coffinlike box had grown murky, as if clouds of vapor swirled within. As he watched he saw tiny flashes, like red lightning arcing from point to point within the plated box, illuminating the interior.

Stirred by this sight he inched himself closer and slowly, painfully edged high enough to press his face against one of the lower plates to peer inside.

He saw a bubbling mass of gelatinous material, glistening in the light of the tiny flashes. The oozing stuff had covered the dry reedy material with a quivering layer that gave off a heavy vapor like a steam. He noticed the dim outlines of a form beginning to take shape—a form that was vaguely familiar.

Spence drifted in and out of consciousness, waking, sleeping, fainting. Weakened by hunger and the agony tearing at him like a ravenous beast, he could not be certain of what he was seeing or when. The room, his thoughts, the pain, the machine—all took on the airy illusory quality of one of his dreams.

Reality dissolved around him.

He moaned, howled, and sang crude songs; he laughed like one demented and wept like a lost innocent. He heard strange sounds: sighs and gurglings, groans and rasps, and long quaking wheezes. He could not be certain that all these did not emanate from himself, but they seemed to come from within the growing-box.

At some point the light from the sarcophagus's pedestal changed from white to a rosy pink, bathing the room and Spence in the ruddy illusion of vitality. Soon afterward the upper portion of the machine separated from the lower portion. There was a rushing gasp of escaping vapors and the room was filled with an acrid smell like burnt rubber.

He lay with his head lolling on the floor, choking and gagging. But as the interior of the plated box cleared, he raised himself feebly over the edge to look inside.

He saw a body stretched out in deathlike repose—humanoid, with limbs and torso like a man's, but remarkably elongated. Its features, and the details of its body, remained unformed as if it were made of clay and only partly finished. There was no sign at all of life—the thing could have been a statue whose sculptor had been called away before finishing his work.

Twice more in lucid moments Spence looked into the machine. Each time it seemed that the thing had become more developed, though the exact changes were hard to pinpoint.

By the hour he became weaker and more unstable. The pain in his chest was a constant piercing throb. He lay curled around his water sphere, without the power to raise his head. He slept long and fitfully, his sleep tortured by the torments of a broken body and troubled spirit. He dreamed strange and fantastic dreams and saw things which terrified him.

In one of these frightening visions he ran down a stinking, garbage-filled street pursued by shrieking black demons with flashing teeth and shining eyes. Nowhere could he hide or escape them. They followed him in a pack like wolves, snarling in evil rage.

In what might have been another dream he saw the form of a golden being rise from the gray-plated coffin. He saw the moisture glistening on the smooth, hairless skin, and he heard the swift and sudden inhalation of air drawn into its lungs. He saw the eyelids slowly raise to reveal two large, almost luminous yellow eyes which regarded him with a coldly reptilian stare.

Then he was aware of smooth walls in the lighted corridor sliding past him and he thought he was back at Gotham, riding in one of the trams. He turned his head and saw a long, three-fingered hand gripping his shoulder and he looked up into the huge yellow eyes.

When next he regained consciousness he was in a room filled with odd-looking devices and he was surrounded with a filmy substance which hung over him like a limp tent made of cobwebs. The tent glittered and pulsed with energy. He glanced down and saw a red, ragged gash in his side surrounded by putrid green-black flesh, swollen and disfigured. His flesh was skewered by two long white needlelike objects which caused a tingling sensation in his bones.

Then he dreamed that he stood under a wide blue canopy atop a high mountain and felt the cool air whipping at his clothes. He saw an ancient castle set on a peak just above him and black birds circling slowly in the air, keening their sharp disapproval. A voice formed words inside his head that danced and made sparkling images, but the words had no meaning and the images were utterly foreign to any realm of his experience.

And then there was only darkness—blessed darkness and release.

CHAPTER EIGHT

THE MESSAGE had been puzzling enough, but the young man standing before her was no less cryptic. Ari regarded his smiling face suspiciously and answered slowly, "I'm not sure I know what you're talking about. I haven't seen Dr. Reston for several weeks."

Kurt nodded reassuringly. "I understand. Dr. Reston wished his whereabouts to be kept secret, but he has communicated with us and wanted me to contact you."

"You said you had a message from him?" Ari stated firmly, not giving away her sudden flourish of hope.

"Yes, I was just getting to that. He said that he was fine and to tell you that he missed you very much. He was looking forward to getting back and seeing you."

"Is that all? Did he say anything about his work?"

"Oh, yes. He said that his work was going very smoothly, and that he was very glad he'd gone—apart from missing you, that is. I take it he likes you very much."

Ari ignored the comment, but the young man smiled so sincerely she felt like an ogre for suspecting him. He obviously was telling the truth.

"I think so," Ari admitted.

"And you like him—I can tell. Did you know he was going to Mars?"

"Certainly, I—" Ari paused, glancing quickly at the cadet's face. He seemed genuinely interested. "That is, I suppose I did. He doesn't confide in anyone very much, you know."

"You can say *that* again. I just figured he might have told you—that birthday gift and all. We didn't even know he'd gone. Don't you think that was odd of him to sneak off like that?"

"Was it that big a secret then?" asked Ari. "I assumed he told those who needed to know."

"It must have slipped his mind," Kurt laughed. "Well, I better be going." The panel slid open and the young man made to leave. "By the way, is there anything you want me to tell him for you—in case he contacts us again?"

Ari smiled and shook her head. "No, nothing that can't wait. Just tell him to be careful and that I'm anxious to see him again."

"Will do. Good-bye, Miss Zanderson. See you around."

"Good-bye, Mr. Millen." The portal slid shut.

The whole visit seemed innocent enough, but she could not help feeling that something more, something unspoken, lay behind it. After all this time, why had he come? Why now? Furthermore, something he said sounded suspicious to her. What was it?

She hoped she had not given Spence's secret away. Perhaps she was just being overly protective. Perhaps Spence had resolved his problem as he hoped he would and wanted to let her know. He would have sent his cadet with a message. It was plausible enough.

Then why couldn't she accept it? Surely, there was something more here than simple female vanity. Ari had had the impression that when Spence decided to break silence *she* would be the first one he contacted. She felt betrayed, but told herself she was just being silly. Beside, she should be happy that he was all right.

But *was* he all right? Why did she question it? The thought nagged at her the rest of the day, whereupon she decided that since she had no reason to doubt the sincerity of the young man or his message she should forget it.

Spence viewed his surroundings with a kind of groggy half-awareness, as if he had been drugged and then beaten senseless and left in a congealing heap. What or who had done the beating he did not recall. Assuredly it had been something large and mechanical; perhaps he had mixed it up with a shuttle scrubber.

Oddly, he felt no pain; in fact, he felt nothing at all. It seemed as if he had been disconnected from his body and hovered somewhere very close to it, but far enough away not to have to share its misery. A thin, gauzy veil separated him from his senses, as if he were visiting a sick friend for whom he had only slightly more than the usual amount of empathy. The sensations he felt seemed more properly to belong to someone else. He was more than happy to let them go; they had not held particularly pleasant associations.

A sound like a crystal chime reached his ears and he felt himself enveloped in a snowy white cloud which shut out all sight, all sound, all thought. He knew himself to be conscious, but beyond that he had no thought at all—a state like sleep, only brilliantly light rather than dark.

He floated in this feathery state of unknowing for an eternity.

Then, tinning in the distance far away he heard the chime again, and the blazing white cloud which had held him for so long began to dissipate. He was back in the strange room again, covered with the filmy energy tent. Spence glanced down at his side and saw that the needles were gone and all that remained of his vaguely remembered injury was a rosy pink scar along his ribs.

He looked around the oval-shaped room for his surface suit, but could not see it anywhere. Only then did the full impact of what had happened break in on him. He had been carried to this place, ministered over, and nursed back to health. The dreams of his delirium had not been dreams at all. The creature from the growing-machine had cared for him.

He lifted the clinging web and was about to stir from the nest where he lay when he glanced up and saw a humanoid well over two meters tall watching him from a doorway. The thing gazed at him steadily with keen interest, its long, triple-jointed arms crossed over its narrow chest.

Spence recognized the golden, finely pebble-grained skin, the huge yellow eyes and the elongated body as the being from his dreams. He felt no fear of the creature, only amazement that this meeting should actually be taking place.

The creature, clothed in a loose-fitting garment of a sandy color that glinted in the light, came to him in graceful strides. It stood towering over him, its eyes burning as if it would devour him with its hungry look. Spence realized he was looking into the face of a Martian.

Feeling a little like a character out of a corny old science-fiction movie, he raised his hand in greeting.

The Martian opened his wide, thin-lipped mouth and a sound like a sustained and fluid chirp issued forth. Ringing, reverberating, the liquid tones reminded him of a treeful of nightingales breaking into song at once.

The Martian stared at him, expecting some kind of response. But before he could think of a suitable reply the Martian, still staring intensely, made some physical adjustment in its speech organs and then said, in a voice that trilled like bubbling water, "Who are you? Why have you come?"

Spence passed a hand before his eyes in disbelief. When he looked again the being still loomed over him, its spare features almost sparkling with fierce intensity. He decided that the harsh, reptilian quality of the Martian's aspect was due to the fact that it had no hair, that the face, with its thin, almost nonexistent nose, was dominated by the huge brilliant eyes. Also, he saw a narrow double row of gill slits along either side of the Martian's exposed chest.

They stared at one another for several minutes before Spence, realizing he had not answered, managed to croak out, "I am Spencer Reston. I am from Earth." He had almost forgotten how to speak.

The Martian then turned with a dry rustle of his clothing and scooped something off a nearby pedestal table. He turned back and held out the flat, ovoid object. Spence took it and looked at it and saw that it was a three-dimensional photograph of astonishing depth and clarity. It showed a grouping of stars as viewed from ground level; low brown hills showed on the horizon. It could have been any grouping of stars in the galaxy, but Spence guessed it was a constellation viewed from Mars. Still, it meant nothing to him. He shrugged and handed the object back.

The alien did not take it but pushed it at him once more and when Spence looked the picture had changed to another scene; this one he recognized easily. In remarkably vivid holographics—so lifelike it was as if he held a window which opened onto the universe—he saw the Sol system.

He nodded enthusiastically and pointed to the third planet from the sun. "Earth," he explained as he might to a dull-witted child. Immediately the scene shifted once more and he was peering at Earth's great blue globe with its swirls of frilly white cloud encircling it.

The alien loosed a low whistling word which rose at the end; then with but a moment's pause said, "Earth."

Spence realized he had just received his first lesson in Martian. He was mystified.

"Who are you? How do you know my language?" he asked slowly.

"I am Kyr. I have . . . assimilated," the word rolled out oddly, "your language skills while you were healing. I hope this causes you no anxiety. It is easier."

The creature, as alien as anything Spence could have imagined—not so much in appearance as in character and bearing—stood conversing with him like a native. It passed all comprehension.

"You saved me. Why?"

"Life is precious and must be conserved. You had nearly ceased to be."

"Thank you. I am grateful." He hoped the alien understood him well enough, for he meant it sincerely. "Are there more like you?"

The Martian reflected for a moment and something like a smile flitted across the thin lips. "Yes. Many seedings by now."

The creature—for some reason Spence considered it a *male* creature—allowed that this was not what Spence wanted to know. "But that is not what you asked. You wished to know if there are more of my kind here now. No, not for many Earth years. I am the only one. I am the last."

"Why? Where are they? Where did they go?" There were so many questions he wanted to ask, they gushed like a fountain into his mind; he could not ask them all at once.

The alien handed him the picture generator and Spence saw a bright array of stars slanting across the center of the field. It could have been the further rim of the spiraling Milky Way galaxy.

"To other stars?"

"Yes." The Martian nodded.

"Why?"

"Ovs could no longer support her people. Our atmosphere shrank, the waters dried up. To survive we built the underground cities and then, when we became skilled enough to venture to nearby stars, we left in search of other worlds."

"Migrated to the stars . . . but why? What caused your atmosphere to change?"

Kyr indicated the picture device and Spence saw once more the solar system he had seen before, but on a closer inspection he saw that it contained ten planets orbiting the sun in orderly fashion, rather than the nine he knew.

"Our neighbor, Res, was struck by a large mass that passed close by Earth and Ovs, causing disturbances in the atmosphere and rotation of the planets. Debris rained down, and clouds of dust from the explosion covered both planets for many Earth years. Ovs suffered more serious damage."

"Where was this Res?"

"Here." A long multijointed finger pointed to the fifth planet from the sun.

"The asteroid belt!" said Spence with some excitement. "We've long theorized a planet there."

"We were struck by many of the pieces; so was Earth. Your planet has been struck many times in the past, but luckily was not much popluated during these events. Each time it has been recreated.

"Here it was . . ."—no human word seemed adequate—"catastrophe. Very much life was destroyed—plants, animals. Whole cities died. Ovs could not recover."

Spence's mind reeled. This little bit of information could answer so many questions about the great upheavals and cataclysms in Earth's past. He wondered what else the Martian could tell him. And what of Martian life—philosophy, art and literature? Did they have these things? Did they know of their origin? What kind of spaceships did they travel in? What secrets had they possessed while men still roamed the Earth in nomadic tribes?

There was so much to learn Spence fell silent, speechless. The possibilities were awesome, and he was hopelessly inadequate to the task.

"You must sleep now," Kyr said. "We will talk again. I would hear how you came here and how you knew to rebirth me."

Without protest, though his brain was reeling with excitement, Spence lay back in the oval nest and the alien lowered the energy net over him once more. He slept at once, blissfully and soundly.

CHAPTER NINE

"WHAT PLACE is this?" Spence stood on a sort of skyway overlooking a spreading underground metropolis undulating in graceful asymmetry—hives, hollows, arches, pinnacles, and spikes—stretching out as far as the eye could see under a great glimmering golden dome.

"Tso. It is the largest of the underground cities built in the Third Epoch. On Ovs there have been four epochs: *Vjarta, Kryn, Ovsen,* and *Soa.* In your words the Water Epoch, Dust Epoch, Stone Epoch, and Star Epoch."

The underground city held an eerie beauty for Spence, though seeing it now reminded him of nothing so much as bones, as if he were gazing into the fabled Elephant Graveyard.

In the last few days—Spence called them days—Kyr had guided him through the ancient city and had instructed him in the culture of the vanished race. Each new bit of information struck him with the force of a mind explosion. Each new fact was a revelation. Spence had learned a great deal; enough to know that to learn the rest would take a lifetime—ah, but what a lifetime!

He turned to his tall friend. That had been one of the first things he had learned; the docile, peace-loving, kindly beings were friends, not enemies of man. Brothers under the sun.

He gazed at the form of the being beside him and felt a sadness for him. "Why did you stay behind? Why didn't you go with your people?"

Kyr fixed him with an indecipherable look. "I am a Guardian. It is my life to preserve the memory of our kind in the solar system, so that any who come—as you have come—will know and remember.

"I was chosen among others to guard the secrets of our past, lest anyone come after us and use our discoveries unwisely. You see, there was much we could not take with us and to destroy it would have been unthinkable. The Guardians were chosen to keep watch over all that was. Now I only am left." Sadness accompanied this last admission; Spence felt it and turned the conversation.

"When did your people leave? How long ago?"

Kyr pondered this for a moment. "Several lifetimes," he replied at last. "Three or four thousand of your years, maybe more. I cannot be sure until I have visited the—" He paused and chirped a word that sounded to Spence like *krassil* and then continued. "That I must do soon. I must make certain no one has entered there."

"Then let's go. I'd like to see it." Spence, feeling remarkably fit thanks to Kyr's healing care, was eager to see all he could of Martian wonders.

The *krassil* turned out to be part museum and part time capsule. It was a huge, cone-shaped hive in the center of a cluster of smaller hives, and it had been sealed long ages past against this very day.

Kyr walked several times around the enormous structure while Spence sat on one of the mushroom-shaped objects which abounded throughout Tso. After his tour Kyr stepped aside and tilted back his head, loosing a long, whining note that split the air like a knife.

Spence clamped his hands over his ears and watched.

Kyr waited for a few moments and then repeated the procedure, this time in a slightly lower register.

The vibration of the Martian's voice shook the very ground beneath their feet. Spence realized then how powerful the beings were. He watched as a sizeable crack opened in the smooth, shell-like surface of the hive. Kyr went to the crack and began pulling away chunks of material which concealed a door.

He stood before the door and in his whistling tongue chirped a few words to it. The door magically slid aside.

A voice-imprinted lock, thought Spence. Such things were in experimental use on Gotham now. The Martians then were not as far advanced technologically as he had first thought.

Spence entertained this notion for a few seconds before remembering that he was seeing the state of their science four thousand years ago. Technology on Mars had frozen the day they left.

He chided himself for the vanity that lay behind his mistaken observation and for presuming to compare two such different civilizations. Then Kyr reemerged from the *krassil* and beckoned to him to follow.

Spence entered through the oblong doorway and stepped into the interior of the *krassil*, crammed to the ceiling with singular objects, all looking as if they had been placed there only moments before and their owners would return to take them up again at any time.

There were things impossible to describe—many of them looked like they had been grown according to some freakish horticultural method rather than manufactured. Most of the Martian artifacts he saw possessed this natural, rather organic quality.

This had caused Spence to do some wild theorizing on the origins of the Martian civilization. Man had belonged to the mammalian order on Earth, but it did not necessarily follow that that should be the regular course of things at all. The Martians might very well be part of the botanical branch of the Martian life tree, or the reptilian—he was not sure which they resembled the more. Maybe they came from some otherworldly synthesis of both.

While Kyr busied himself with what appeared to be an inventory of sorts, Spence wandered among the strange assemblage of objects—objects at once bizarre and eerily fascinating, whose uses could only be supposed by the most astounding leaps of imaginative fancy. His curious eyes devoured all he looked upon greedily, like a man whose sight has just been restored after a long period of blindness.

He came after some time to a further part of the *krassil* where an arched opening led into a small alcove. Inside, set on a rough base of stone, stood a large graceful object which immediately captured his attention. It looked like delicate, interwoven, semitransparent wings. He stepped into the alcove and the sculpture—if that is what it was—instantly lit with a rosy light and began to slowly move.

Spence watched as other colors gradually came into play along the sculpture's transparent surface: yellow, blue, and green. These tones began to melt into each other in complex patterns as they swirled over the sculpture's elegant form until the form itself and the color became one. The hues mingled and blended, forming more subtle shades, now flashing boldly, now subdued.

He was riveted to his place, drinking in the astonishing beauty of the art piece. He could not take his eyes from it. The thing held him with a hypnotic power as it spun and resolved itself into endlessly intricate patterns of light and color, each more graceful and lovely than the last. He felt a welling up inside him of emotion, a yearning so strong that it resembled a hungering pain—a pain that bordered on bliss.

It was a feeling he recognized as belonging to the apprehension of beauty, but one he had rarely, if ever, felt. Presumably others were so moved when they looked upon a classic work of art or listened to a beloved symphony. He had seldom had such experiences; the feeling was foreign to him and perhaps therefore more powerful and bewildering.

He could not look away. The light scupture reached out to him, binding him fast with threads of wonder. He felt nearly faint with rapture.

This, thought Spence, was what the poets felt, the love that burns its victims in flames of ecstacy. Oh, to be so consumed—it was past enduring, yet he longed to endure still more.

That he could be so affected by the sight of any created object he would have denied. But that obstinacy melted away in the certainty that he was experiencing a work of consummate beauty.

Tears formed in his eyes and his heart swelled nearly to bursting as the dry rivers of his soul began to flow with streams of joy. The passions he felt unlocked within him could not be contained. He wanted to leap, to dance, to weep and shout and exhaust himself in singing. Shudders of pleasure coursed through him; he heard a strange music ringing in his ears and realized that it was his own voice giving free vent to his pleasure in spontaneous song.

The sculpture, as if sensing his joyous outpouring, moved more swiftly in response. The brilliant shades spun and changed, weaving themselves together and parting in intracacies beyond reckoning.

It seemed to live, growing larger and more luminous, throwing off flashes of light and filling his tear-filled eyes with shapes too wonderful to behold.

At last he could take no more. He closed his eyes, but still felt the shifting colors of light playing over him. A voice nearby said, "This is *Soa Lokiri.*"

Spence turned to see Kyr standing beside him. He had not been aware of the Martian's presence.

"It is beautiful." He returned his gaze to the shimmering display. At length he said, "What is *Soa Lokiri?*"

"It means Starmaker. It is an artwork in homage to Dal Elna, made by the hand of one of our most revered artists, Bharat."

"Starmaker." Spence repeated the name, nodding to himself. "It is aptly titled. But who is Dal Elna?"

Kyr tilted his head sideways, looking at Spence closely. "Dal Elna, the All-Being."

"All-Being? You mean God?"

Kyr's head began weaving from side to side. "That word does not communicate to me."

A pang of guilt squirmed inside Spence. Possibly the word held no meaning for Kyr because it held no particular meaning for him. Whatever means Kyr had used to, as he said, *assimilate* Spence's language, he had only received Spence's vocabulary and only the meanings Spence himself attached to the various words at his command. *God,* for Spence, was an empty word. It did not communicate.

"The word *God,* I think, is what men call the All-Being."

Kyr merely looked at him.

"I have never been so moved by anything in my life. Bharat is a most extraordinary artist. Are there more of his works here?"

"No. This was, as many considered, his greatest. It alone survived the Burning."

"That's tragic. I would like to have seen more." He looked back at the sculpture. He now imagined he could see the hot points of stars forming in starfields, worlds bursting into creation, and more. There was a pattern to it—a greater pattern than could be taken in all at once. "I feel as if I were always on the verge of apprehending it, and yet . . . not at all," Spence said.

"That is the greatness of the work. Bharat has mirrored Dal Elna's mystery and given visual expression to the greatest single truth of our philosophers: *Rhi sill dal kedu kree*. It means: In the many there is One."

Spence repeated the words with a slow shaking of his head. "You'll have to explain that to me. I don't get it at all."

"Many hundreds of lifetimes ago our philosophers reduced their theories to this one axiom. It cannot be expressed more simply. But I will think about it and find a way to explain it to you."

They left the alcove and the kinetic sculpture silently. Spence went on tiptoes like a priest leaving the holy of holies. He was conscious of a sharp longing, almost a loneliness, as if he had left the presence of the Deity himself. He felt cut off.

He turned to view the sculpture a last time, but the alcove was dark and the slender object still. He wondered if he had imagined the patterns and color. The ache in his heart told him that he had encountered a masterpiece, and that, as an onlooker at a miracle, he, too, had been inwardly changed.

CHAPTER TEN

CAROLINE Zanderson called for a pen and paper, something she had not done in the eleven years she had been at Holyoke Haven. The request caused a sudden rush of the asylum's staff as they tripped over one another to fulfill it. Mrs. Zanderson, wife of the director of GM Advancement Center, was a most perplexing case.

Of all the patients she seemed the most normal, and the most severely disturbed, depending on the time one happened to see her. She was often remarkably lucid and calm, calling everyone by name and glowing with a genuine vibrant charm. But her good days were separated by periods of extreme anguish and depression. Her highs were balanced by the lowest lows.

When her madness came upon her, the charming sophisticate became a hunkering crone. Her personality disintegrated; she neither knew who she was nor where she was. She became fixated on the strange force she believed to be torturing her, possessing her, stealing her sanity.

That is why, when she called for a pen and paper, the staff fell over themselves in their haste to provide it. The act signaled a beginning perhaps to one of her good periods, and there had been few of those in the last year.

"Is that you, Belinda?" Mrs. Zanderson heard a slight commotion at her door and turned toward it, peering around her faded red chair.

At the door a white-uniformed nurse was speaking to another patient, a woman in a light blue flowered dress who strained ahead eagerly, clutching a worn cloth suitcase.

"The ship has not come today, Mrs. Mawser," the nurse intoned gently.

The woman turned a suddenly stricken face to the nurse, her eyes wild and fearful. "I haven't missed it? Oh! Ohhh . . ."

"No, no," the nurse soothed, placing her hand on the woman's back. "You haven't missed it. We won't let you miss the ship when it comes. Now you go back to your room and unpack. It's almost time for lunch."

The woman shuffled away with the suitcase, muttering as she went. The nurse watched her go and then stepped lightly into the room.

"Caroline, I've brought your paper and pen—and an envelope, too."

"An envelope?" The blue eyes were pools of lead in her face.

"You'll need an envelope if you are going to write a letter. Remember?"

"Oh, yes. I'll need an envelope. May I have the paper and pen now, please?" She took them and moved to the tiny antique writing desk that stood by the French doors. Without another word to the nurse she began. After several strained attempts she wrote:

My Dearest Ari,
    Don't be alarmed at receiving a letter from your Mother. I have long wanted to write to you and thank you for all the wonderful letters and gifts you send, but I have not been up to it for a very long time. I do think of you often, of course—when I am myself, that is.
    I am writing now to tell you something very important. Please listen to me and do as I ask. You are in great danger, my dear one. The greatest possible danger! The Dream Thief has

turned his eyes on you and he wants you. Even now his hands are stretching after you. Be careful. Please, be careful!

You must take steps to protect yourself. Come to me and I will tell you what to do. I dare not put it in a letter—his eyes are everywhere. But come soon, my darling. Please, before it is too late.

Always my love,
Mother

When she had finished the letter she read it through several times and then folded it neatly and placed it in the envelope and addressed it. She then called for the nurse again.

"Good, Belinda, you're here. Take this letter and make sure it is mailed properly. Mail it yourself, please. It's important."

"Of course I will, Caroline. I would be happy to. Oh, I see it's to your daughter. I'm sure Ari will enjoy hearing from you. It's been a long time since she has been here, hasn't it? I'll mail the letter today, right after lunch. Would you like to come down and eat now? We're having a nice chicken salad. They say it's very good."

"I think I will have some tea in my room," Caroline said, slumping back into her overstuffed chair facing the doors. "I'm a little tired right now. Maybe I'll come down later."

The letter drained her, as if the amount of concentration necessary to complete it had depleted an already scant reserve. She closed her eyes and rested her head on the white crocheted doily of the chair. Her muscles went slack and she fell asleep at once.

"That's right," said the nurse. She crossed the room and closed the doors. "You take a little nap and I'll look in on you later." She crept out of the room, placing the letter on the top of a large bureau near the door.

Spence sipped the broth, a warm, brown liquid that tasted of cinnamon. He did not mind the thin soup—undoubtedly it was very nourishing—but it did not fill him up as he would have liked. He was hungry all the time. Kry had explained that it would be some time before food could be grown and produced, but that in time they would have something more substantial to eat.

That had brought up the subject of his leaving.

"I should return to the surface soon," remarked Spence in a tone he hoped was casual.

Kyr only peered at him intently, and so Spence launched into a full account of how he came to be there, including the fact that he had friends waiting for him, worrying about him, back at the installation. He did not know how long he had been underground, but he reckoned it to be nearing the time when the work party would begin preparing to return to the transport for the journey back to Gotham.

"I understand. But there is much I would show you still."

"I will come back as soon as I can. I'll stay years if you like. Believe me, I want to learn everything you can teach me. And there are others—hundreds of others—just like me who will come."

Kyr had not received this in the way Spence intended. He seemed to become restive and, after a session of head waving, sat back stoically with slender hands in his lap.

After he had finished sipping his ration of broth, Spence asked, "Have I said something wrong? Tell me if I have not understood you."

At that the Martian picked up his bowl of broth and drained it and stood, hoisting Spence to his feet with a strength that astounded him.

"I must be patient. You do not know what you are saying, because you do not yet understand. Come; I will show you."

Kyr strode off on his long legs at a ground-eating stride. Spence had to jog along behind just to keep up. When they reached the *krassil* Spence was wheezing and puffing, and dizzy from the exertion in the oxygen-weak atmosphere.

Kyr entered the *krassil* and Spence followed with a hand pressed to his side, doubled over as if with a stomach ache. "Sit down here," instructed Kyr, and Spence saw a semicircle of indented hollows shaped into a low bank before a flat portion of the curved wall of the hive. He sat down in one of the hollows and waited.

Almost at once the interior of the hive darkened and a sound, eerily sweet, like violins with the voices of birds, or the songs of whales, filled the chamber, rising and falling in regular rhythm like breathing. It was, as Spence had come to understand, Martian music, and like their architecture and everything else of Martian design, it was free-flowing and organic.

In a moment the portion of the wall directly before him dissolved, becoming transparent, and he was gazing out a huge window into a lush, tropical landscape beyond. A soft breeze stirred the leaves of extremely tall, spindly shrubs while a flock of storklike crimson birds flew overhead in a sky of shining blue. Low mountains glimmered in the distance and raised rounded peaks skyward.

Everything he saw was tinged with a golden aura; the light itself shimmered with a golden hue, enriching all it touched. Then he saw a herd of long-legged grazing animals with giraffelike necks and small round heads moving as one across a vast open plain. Behind them, carrying slender poles, he saw Martians, tall and lithe and bronze in the sun, running with the herd.

The amazingly lifelike images on the screen pulled Spence immediately into the drama of this scene. He realized that he had embarked upon a journey back through the ages of an alien planet and its vanished life. The holoscreen spun out its stream of magic images in a sweeping pageant of color and beauty he could never have imagined.

He saw the formation of the first cities and the panorama of a civilization blossoming unhindered in a world of peace and harmony. The cities grew and water vessels traversed the globe, plying the great waterways, the Martian canals, and linking the gleaming white cities in commerce. Later, airships filled the sky and great colorful objects that looked like giant kites or winged dirigibles elegantly plowed the air.

Next came a parade of the most fantastic creatures he had ever seen, all strangely familiar, bearing at least the rudimentary resemblance to the animal life on Earth, but unique and wholly different at the same time. Birds and fishes and mammals of an endless variety appeared in their natural habitats as the music swelled and sang and the procession continued.

Spence saw the Martians themselves in their cities and in their homes—engaged in various inexplicable occupations which he guessed to be working, playing and learning. These were not separated or isolated tasks, but apparently went on simultaneously, children and adults together all the time.

He felt a tug of longing and a sharp regret that he had not known *this* Mars, though he knew he must be seeing it exactly as it had been millions of years ago.

Then the sky darkened and the ground shook with violent explosions. Fire swept the planet as huge flaming meteorites rained down. Gradually the vegetation browned, withered and blew away. The broken cities crumbled to dust and the once-lush landscape was transformed to desert. The great circling bands of water shrank away and dried, leaving huge canyons and flat lake pans of cracked, baked mud. The birds and animals disappeared.

The scene shifted and he saw the excavations of the tunnels and the vast underground chambers which would house the cities. He saw a job of construction on a scale he could not conceive. He witnessed the rebirth of life beneath the surface of the planet and saw these cities flourish after their own fashion.

Still, he could not forget the stirring beauty of the planet that had been. It haunted the soul with a felt presence.

At last, he saw the gleaming starships rise like silver orbs from the dead flatlands of the Red Planet. By the thousands they floated up like bubbles hung in momentary farewell and then streaked off into the black sky above.

And so they were gone. The music, a soft sigh of mourning, drifted away and Spence sat staring at a blank wall once more.

He did not move or speak for a long time. He let the memory of all he had seen wash over him and carry him in its flood. How long had he been sitting there, he wondered. A few hours? It seemed a lifetime.

Spence heard a soft snuffling sound nearby and turned to see Kyr kneeling on the floor behind him with his face raised upwards, his eyes closed and damp trails of tears streaking his angular cheeks.

Spence wanted to weep, too; he felt a sense of grief at the loss of what had been, yet he had never known it.

"I weep for the dead," said Kyr at last. "And for those who never saw our world as it was in its beauty."

"Did you see it? I mean, in the good time? Did you?"

The Martian shook his head. "No. My father's father may have lived through the time of the fire, but most likely it was his father before him. Many great dynasties were wiped out. The fire rain lasted for many Earth years."

"Kyr, how *old* are you?"

The Martian thought and said, "Your question does not have a ready answer since we measure our lives differently than you. But I think you would say two thousand Earth years."

"Counting the sleep?"

"No. Only counting the time I have been alive. You see, a Martian may live ten thousand of your years or longer perhaps."

"You don't grow old and die?"

"I don't know what you mean. We grow, yes. We develop all our lives, not physically—that takes only a little time. Several of your Earth years. But mentally and spiritually we grow always. Our *vi* grows with us."

"*Vi?* I have not heard you speak of that before."

"*Vi* is our . . ." He paused, searching Spence's vocabulary for the proper word. "Our true selves. Our souls."

"No one on Ovs *ever* dies?" Spence's voice rose incredulously. Even granting the fact that the lower gravity on Mars might have the effect of radically increasing the life span of its inhabitants in the same way it increased their stature, Spence could not believe they did not know death.

"Death? No. We can be killed—disease, accident—the burning killed entire cities. Or we may simply cease to be. Those who have grown great in wisdom may decide it is time to take up their *vi* and join Dal Elna. It is a choice everyone must eventually make."

"Then what happens?"

"I do not know. I have not undergone the change. But a wise one may call his friends around him to celebrate his decision and he then imparts all he has learned in his life to those he loves. In a little while no one will see him anymore. He becomes one with the dust and goes to be with Dal Elna, the All-Being."

Spence glared at the alien in disbelief. "Then why didn't you join Dal Elna when you ceased to be?"

"When did I ever cease to be?"

"When you were in the growing-machine."

"The *emra*?"

"Yes, that box of yours where I found you."

The Martian made his laughing sound. "I had not ceased to be. I was . . . " No word came.

"Sleeping?"

"No, it is not the same thing."

"Dormant?"

The creature waved his head and contemplated the meaning of the word. "Yes, dormant."

"But I looked in there and saw nothing but dust and dry fibers."

"The material of my body can be reborn many times."

Spence could not fathom such a possibility, but then reflected that there were plants on Earth, desert plants, that possessed the same abilities. Several lower life forms also carried the seed of life with them even though they remained paper-dry and dormant for years between cycles.

"What happens to you while you are dormant?"

"I do not understand your question. I exist, but I do not exist in the same way as before. I am not conscious."

"But what keeps you from dying? And why do you wake up knowing who you are? If you are recreated, why do you remember your past life?"

Kyr spread his hands wide in a gesture of great humility. He said, "The questions you ask are questions for Dal Elna himself. Are all Earthmen as inquisitive as you?"

Spence admitted that there were many things he had trouble accepting and that the All-Being's role in creation was one of them.

"So I have come to believe. But I will find a way to help you see."

"You have already shown me much." He gestured toward the blank screen where only moments before the splendor of a glorious past had unfolded before his eyes. "I understand now why Tso must remain a secret. The sudden explosion of interest would destroy it."

"One day, when your world has regained the peace that it lost long ago, Tso will be revealed. Until then it is better that such secrets remain hidden."

"And you trust me with this secret?" Spence experienced a fleeting doubt that perhaps the Martian had no intention of allowing him to return to tell the tale.

"Yes." Kyr reached out a long hand to him. Spence took it. "I must trust you, for how can it be otherwise? I cannot prevent you. Dal Elna himself will hold or give as he sees fit."

"Kyr, how much do you know of Earth and its people? Have you ever been there?"

"No, but others have. In the days before the starships your planet was visited. Many times. But when we discovered it inhabited by sentient beings, not unlike ourselves, we knew that we could not look for a home there. No one ever went back after that; it was forbidden."

"Forbidden? Why? I would have thought friendly contact with a higher intelligence could have been very beneficial to primitive Earth societies."

"There were those among us who took that view. But in the end the leader of the Earth expeditions argued very persuasively against going back. His name was Ortu, and he was one of the great leaders of his day. It was his view that the primitive Earthmen should be allowed to develop in their own time. Dal Elna, he said, had not meant for us to interfere with others of his creations."

"So no one ever went back?"

'Never. Even the watcher ships were withdrawn. Ortu said that was necessary if we were ever to keep peace here on Ovs. Otherwise the temptation to step in and save Earthmen in times of distress would be too great. They had to survive on their own, if they were to become strong."

"And then the migration began?"

"Exactly. With Res destroyed, we knew there to be no other inhabitable planets in this solar system. The stars offered our only hope. Again, Ortu led the development of the starships and even led the first wave to leave Ovs."

Spence nodded slowly. "And now I, too, must think about leaving Ovs."

Kyr turned and led them out of the *krassil*. "I have something to show you before we talk of leaving. Come, there is much more to see."

Spence followed his lanky host through the silent, vacant pathways of Tso and tried to imagine what it had been like when the tall, graceful Martians had lived there and the narrow trafficways rang with the chirrup of their voices and the floating sounds of their eerily beautiful music. He was immediately overcome with a heavy sense of loss and loneliness, as if someone he loved very much had died.

CHAPTER ELEVEN

THE LAST three days had been a blur of activity to Spence. He felt as if he were a sponge that had absorbed ten times its weight, he had seen and experienced so much of ancient Martian culture. Now he and Kyr stood looking at a large model of the Red Planet which had the area of the underground cities marked on its surface.

He frowned as he looked at the terrain. "I don't see anything I recognize." The model, of course, had been made before the Martians left; it was several thousand years old. "The surface features have changed a lot."

They walked around the perimeter of the sculptured replica.

"Wait a minute," said Spence. "Where is that great volcano?"

Kyr thought for a moment about what the word meant and then pointed a long finger to an area between two dry canal beds.

"At the time of the Burning, several small volcanoes erupted in this area. It is not far from Tso."

"Could it have been active since then? I mean, really active?"

"It is possible, yes."

"Then I think that is what we call Olympus Mons. That is the mountain I was walking toward when I got lost." He studied the model carefully, noting the huge canyon directly to the west of the giant Mariner Valley, a hole so big it could have swallowed the entire Rocky Mountain range and still have room for the Grand Canyon. According to the model the outskirts of Tso lay near one of the tributary troughs which fed into this canyon system.

"I think this is where I came upon the tunnels. Right here. Since I didn't tumble into the canyon, the installation must lie somewhere in this area." He pointed to the smooth plain eastward.

"Kali," said Kyr.

"What is that?"

"It is a smaller underground settlement which housed the workers building the starships. It is not shown here. The plain is where the starships were built, and from there they left Ovs forever."

Spence had the picture in his mind of hundreds of ships rising like silver balloons into the pink sky of Mars to disappear like fragile bubbles into the void. "Then this is where the last of the Martians left and the first of the Earthmen came. Because, unless I miss my guess, this is where the installation is."

"Kali is connected by tunnels with Tso, as are the other cities. I will take you there."

Spence had been feeling a greater and greater reluctance to leave Tso and its lone inhabitant. He wanted nothing more than to stay and learn all the secrets of the vanished race.

"I wish I didn't have to go," he said. "I would give everything I own just to stay here with you."

"Then you must return one day when you can stay."

"I will come back. I promise you that. There are treasures here worth more than anyone on Earth can imagine." He meant the remark as a compliment, but it seemed to have the opposite effect on Kyr. The alien began waving his head from side to side.

"Did I say something wrong?"

"Your words remind me that I will be alone . . ." He turned away before finishing the thought.

"What will you do when I leave? Go back to sleep?"

"No, I will not sleep again. Contact has been made between our planets. I must now begin the vigilance."

Spence realized the sacrifice Kyr had made to remain behind. "I will come back, Kyr," he vowed. "Somehow I will."

Kyr looked at him closely and said, "No creature knows his destiny. Even rivers change their courses in time. I will not hold you to your promise. It is not yours to make."

The Martian turned and placed his hand on a smooth, globe-shaped object and it opened, revealing two small disks. Kyr handed one of them to Spence, who took it and turned it over in his hand.

It was a rather flat, roundish thing which looked like nothing more than a seashell which had lost its grooves and fluted edges. It had a warm feeling in his hand.

"Do you feel the power in it?"

"I feel a warmth from it. What is it?"

"This is a . . ."—he searched for the word—"a *bneri*—a signal device. I am a Guardian. Now that you have awakened me I must guard you, too. If ever you have need of me you have only to hold this in the palm of your hand, think about me, and I will know of your need. I will come to help you."

This mystified Spence more than anything he had seen on Mars since he arrived.

"How is it possible?"

"I could explain the . . . the science of the device to you, but it would take time. As for the other—traveling to Earth is no problem. The vehicles of the old explorers are preserved here; I can travel anywhere I wish to go."

"But why would you want to protect me?" He still could not believe it.

"Because you know the secret of Ovs, and of its cities. And because you are my friend, and the first to have joined our civilizations. In time that will be an important thing to both of our worlds."

Spence did not know what to say. "Thank you, Kyr. I will take this and use it if ever I have such need."

"Now we will eat together once more before you go. I will prepare for you a real meal. Yes," he replied to Spence's surprised look, "the first of the *rhi* has been grown. We will eat our first real Ovsin meal together."

"But not our last," said Spence. "Not our last."

The gleaming domes of the installation shimmered in the hard, bright light of the sun. Overhead a rosy pink tinge crept into the sky. The dull red dust lay powdery and still. Not a whisper of a breeze stirred so much as a particle anywhere. Nothing moved around the installation and for a moment he feared the work-and-research party had gone back to Gotham.

The air on the surface had less oxygen than Tso, and Spence felt himself growing lightheaded and decided to sit down and rest before continuing on toward the base only a kilometer further.

Kyr had left him slightly less than three kilometers away. Spence had not wanted Kyr to come too close lest they be seen and the secret exposed. So after a sad parting he had begun walking alone.

He wished he had his helmet at once. He had set off at too quick a pace and almost fainted. After a brief rest he adjusted his stride accordingly and drew near the cluster of buildings in agonizing slow motion. Now he was almost there. And he wondered why he saw no signs of activity—recent or otherwise—anywhere around the installation.

He climbed back to his feet and struck off again feeling tired for his short walk, and very apprehensive.

As he came nearer he noticed a red plume of dust rising high into the air on the far side of the base. It looked like a dust geyser or red smoke drifting on the wind, but there was no breeze.

In a moment the plume had come near the cluster of domes and stopped there. Spence guessed a vehicle of some sort had driven up. Soon he saw a tiny figure moving among the buildings. It disappeared inside.

Someone is home, thought Spence. He was not alone after all. He turned and peered back behind him as if he would see Kyr watching him, urging him to go ahead and rejoin his own. He saw nothing but the dull red rock-strewn pan of the desert.

In another hour he was stepping into the shadow of the first long greenhouse. He had returned.

Adjani had finished the day's search and returned to the installation dejected and disappointed. The high hopes with which he began the day evaporated like dew in the heat of the sun. He had showered—one of the few genuine luxuries on Mars—and settled down to eat after a quick scan of the daily log. The wafer screen showed no messages from Packer and company since he had been gone. He munched a handful of the tiny, pelletlike nutribiscuits that they all ate and washed it down with cold fresh water.

He was thinking about tomorrow's search, the last he would be able to make before leaving Mars. In ten or twelve hours Packer and the rest of the crew would be back, and then they would secure the installation and make ready to leave. There was one more pass he wanted to make along the rift valley to the west. If he found nothing, as he now feared, he would allow that Packer was right and that nothing would ever be found.

This was his thought when he heard the whoosh of the outer air lock. He turned, expecting to see Packer and a dozen of his cadets standing in the lock. Instead he saw a lone figure without a helmet standing in the shadow at the far end of the glassed-in chamber.

Adjani moved quickly, his senses pricked like a cat's on the hunt. A rush of excitement stirred him as he recognized the figure even before his mind could attach a name.

"Spence!" he gasped as the lock opened and his friend stepped unsteadily into the room.

"Adjani. It was you . . ." Spence was assailed by a strong outpouring of emotion. He fell on his friend's neck and hot tears of relief spattered the green of his jumpsuit in dark splotches.

Adjani, too, cried and laughed and shouted for joy.

"Spence, you're alive! Alive! I knew it—in my heart I knew it! Thank God! You've come back!" The lithe Indian fairly danced in circles around him.

Spence threw off his gloves and wiped at his eyes with the heels of his hands, looking boyish and embarrassed. "You missed me, huh?"

Adjani threw his head back and laughed as if that were the funniest thing he had ever heard. "Missed you? No, not at all. I can't believe it. You're *alive*." He laughed again.

"Where is everybody? I expected a bit more of a welcome than this."

"They have all gone to the North Pole—rather they should be on their way back from there now. We are leaving tomorrow. I thought we would have to leave you forever." Adjani fixed him with a firm look.

"I know I have some explaining to do. Actually, it's better that it's just you and me. You can help me think through what to say to the others. That has been on my mind since I found out I was coming back."

"Found out?" asked Adjani with some surprise. "Did you doubt it?"

"Plenty!" said Spence. "I never thought I'd see this place—or any other—ever again. I was a dead man more times than I care to think about."

"Well, come, tell me everything. Are you hungry? I'll fix you something. Sit down. Rest—you look like you've lost weight. You look exhausted. But you look better than I've ever seen you." He paused, standing over Spence and grinning from ear to ear.

"Welcome back, my friend. Welcome back to the land of the living."

CHAPTER TWELVE

"I DON'T believe it. I don't believe it." Packer recited his litany once again. He sat in the chair where he had collapsed upon entering the base, and stared at Spence as if he were seeing a ghost. His mouth hung open and his eyes bulged slightly, making him appear first cousin to a cod. "I just don't believe it."

"You didn't think you had seen the end of me, Packer? I paid for a round-trip ticket."

"I can't believe it."

Spence gave Adjani a conspiratorial smile. "That's Packer, always the keen conversationalist."

Packer then leaped up and proceeded to give Spence's back such a pounding that Spence wished he had stayed quite out of range of the burly giant. "Reston, you old fox. How did you do it? Tell me that. How did you ever do it? Look! Not a nip of frostbite on him! How did you do it?"

Spence then proceeded to give Packer a version of the story he and Adjani had carefully constructed between them. He said that he had stumbled into a warm-air shaft which kept him from freezing to death and also allowed him to distill a small amount of water vapor—enough to keep him from dehydration—by using his helmet.

He told how he had walked every day to try and find his way back, the trail having been obliterated by the storm. He could only walk as far as he could return in the same day. That way he could be back in his warm air vent by nightfall. Each day he had gone out a different way and on the last day had been fortunate enough to have been spotted by Adjani and picked up.

"Adjani, why didn't you radio us when you found him?"

"I started to, but you were already on your way back. We decided to let it be a surprise."

"Surprise! Well, I'll say it is! Spence, I sure am glad to see you. I thought you'd bought your ticket that first night. I was sure of it. And then the storm and everything. I *don't* believe it."

"I never thought I'd see this place again, either. I had almost given up hope of finding it."

Packer grew serious; his eyes, still twinkling, regarded Spence sharply. "What made you do it, Spence? What made you run out into that sandblaster out there? I can't figure it."

Spence lowered his voice; there were others gathered around that he did not wish to involve in his private affairs. "I think you're entitled to a full reading on that score, Packer. I think I'd like to wait until we can sit down and talk it over."

"I understand. No pressure—just curious."

"Adjani tells me I'm back in time to help close up."

"Yes, indeed. You made it back just in time. We're leaving as soon as we can seal up this compound. Shouldn't take but a few hours. You *are* fit to travel, aren't you? You look like you've lost twenty pounds—"

"I'm fit enough. I'll have nothing to do but rest once we're aboard."

"That's another thing! I have to radio back to Gotham and let them know we found you. I'm afraid I gave up on you, Spencer. I told Com-Cen you were missing, presumed dead. That's one mistake I'll gladly correct pronto."

"No! I mean, couldn't we let it wait for a few days?"

Packer's eyes narrowed. "There's some trouble, isn't there? I'm dense, but not *that* dense. You want to tell me about it?"

Adjani spoke up. "Again that would be better discussed in private between friends. All right?"

Packer shrugged. "I'll hold off sending the report, but you two are going to have some explaining to do as soon as we're under way." He smiled, his features relaxing into their normal benign smirk. "I don't care if you've nipped the Crown Jewels, I'm just glad you're back."

Olmstead Packer turned to those gathered around and yelled,

"Let's get this show on the road! I want everything stashed, stowed and shipshape in three hours. Kalnikov is bringing the transport into alignment now. Personally, I don't want to spend another night in this chicken coop. Let's go!"

The cadets let out a whoop and the place swung into a ferment of activity. Adjani settled himself at a nearby computer terminal and reactivated the drone program which ran the installation in the absence of human caretakers. Spence went back to his bunk in the team leader's quarters and picked up his still-packed frame from the bed he had never slept in.

It seemed like ages ago that he had wandered half-crazed out into the cruel Simoom. And everything that had happened after that seemed like a dream. But now, as he stood looking at his belongings, he was once more acutely aware that he was still vulnerable to the mysterious blackouts, and still no closer to solving the enigma of their cause—his flight had been futile from that respect. His sanity dangled by an all-too-slender thread. He did not know how much more he could take before that tenuous thread snapped!

Ari sat up in bed with a start. The dull ache that had driven her, after weeks of dogged endurance, at last to bed had finally disappeared. The churning emptiness had gone and she felt almost herself once more.

The awful news about Spence had been a shattering blow. For days she had done nothing but sit in her room while the cruel words "presumed dead" tore at her heart. She cried until tears refused to come, and then entered a state of benumbed indifference to life. Her father, at wits' end, summoned doctors who advised sedatives which she would not take.

But this morning she told herself that her vigil of grief was over, that she would face the day with resolve and put her life back together. The effect was like a cool wind rising in the night to blow away a long, sultry hot spell. This weather change in her brought with it renewed hope that somehow, some way her life would resume, even flourish.

It was this change, so fresh, so startling in its suddenness, that brought her awake out of a leaden sleep. And she had a feeling of waking to unfinished business—knowledge which seemed to dance just out of memory. Like a butterfly it flitted close, but when she tried to capture it, to hold it and remember, it darted away again.

Ari hummed with the feeling that she knew something very important, though she could not remember what it was. The feeling hounded her all day.

She rose and went about her morning routine with a lightness and cheer that would have delighted any who had seen her. She filled her small room with a sunny radiance that splashed against the walls and chased the shadows—as if a window had been opened on a new spring morning full of golden sunlight and glowing promise.

She wondered what the change could mean. An answer to prayer? Thankfully, she accepted it as such and launched into her day relieved, refreshed and revived.

"Daughter, you look absolutely reborn!" her father shouted when she met him for breakfast. The director always took breakfast in his own dining room while he skimmed the news of the world which Com-Cen gathered from various satellite news services and patched together for him in a special vid-disc edition of the *Gotham Times*.

"I feel *much* better today, Daddy."

"You look marvelous, my dear. Simply wonderful. Oh, I can't tell you how good it is to see you like this. I was beginning to think that . . . Well, never mind. Breakfast?"

"I'm starved!"

"I daresay. You haven't eaten a mouthful in two weeks!"

"Not that it has hurt me any." She laughed and her father watched the light sparkle in her deep blue eyes once more.

"Nonsense, my dear. You're but a whisper of a girl already." He reached for her hand and kissed it gallantly. "I am glad you have come back, Ari. I was deeply afraid I'd lose you."

She smiled and clasped his hand in both of hers. "I won't ever leave you, Daddy. Not like that."

Both of them knew what lay behind the veiled reference: Mrs. Zanderson; his wife, her mother. It was simply too painful a subject to be spoken about in open terms; they had invented a code language to help them speak about it without stirring up old, unwanted memories.

"So! Sit down. I'll ring you up some breakfast. What will it be?"

"I'll have some of whatever you're having, please. And the sooner the better."

"Orange juice?"

"Gallons." She settled into her chair next to her father's. "And some of those scrumptious croissants—if there are any left."

Director Zanderson rang the silver bell at his elbow and a pink jumpsuited kitchen attendant swished into the room with the crisp, formal movements of a military conscript. The director was the only person on GM to have his own serving staff and kitchen; everyone else ate at the commissary. He gave the man their breakfast order and sent him away.

"Oh, and Henry, no croissants for me. I'm meeting with the AgDiv heads this morning." He turned back to his daughter. "They say they have invented a new protein potato or some such thing and they want me to pass judgment on it. I'll probably have to eat my weight in potato steaks. Would you care to accompany me, dearest?"

"I thought I'd go for a swim. I haven't been near the pool for ages. I could use a little sun, too."

"Quite right. Just the thing to put the roses back in your lovely cheeks."

"But enjoy your new potato. Sounds promising."

"Oh, I'm sure it's fantastic. It's just that every other week or so they seem to come up with something bigger and better than the week before. A bigger carrot, better rabbits—I don't know what. I'm afraid it's getting harder and harder for me to work up enthusiasm like I used to. And the *smell* down there would knock you over."

She smiled cheerily. "It's the price of progress, Daddy. Just keep thinking maybe they'll come up with a way to make your nutristeak taste like real beef."

"Now that's something I'll crow about. By the way"—he paused, his manner growing serious. "I meant to tell you before, but—"

"What is it, Daddy?" The smile faded.

"The *Gyrfalcon* is due in sometime today or tomorrow. I think that's what Wermeyer told me yesterday. I thought you should know so that if you heard it somewhere else it wouldn't come as a shock." He patted her shoulder and gave her a kind, fatherly look. "I hope I haven't ruined your day."

"I'm not going to let anything ruin my day. Yes, the wound is still tender, but I thank you for telling me. Don't worry. I'll be all right."

The servant brought in two large trays and set them before the diners. Ari, true to her word, tackled a cream cheese omelette with vigor; her father drifted back to his perusal of the morning's news.

After seeing her father off to his office, she went to her room and slipped on her bathing suit and made her way down to the garden level to walk in green solitude before going to the noisy, kid-ridden pool.

The quiet pathways wending among the growing things, and the clear unobstructed view of the garden sweeping before her in the distance to vanish around the curve of the station lifted her spirits once more to their previous level; soon she was soaring again.

Something is about to happen, she told herself. *Something good, I know it.*

CHAPTER THIRTEEN

"I HATED lying to him like that. I don't enjoy this at all," moaned Spence. He and Adjani sat face-to-face in the empty galley over half-full cups of cold coffee. Kalnikov was making his final burn for home.

"There was no other way. You know that. We've been over and over it. Why do you keep bringing it up?"

"I'm sorry, Adjani." Spence looked at his friend's usually fresh, untroubled face. Now he saw dark circles of fatigue under the black eyes and lines of concern pulling the edges of his mouth into a perpetual frown. "And I'm sorry for mixing you up in this. I had no right—"

"I gave you the right when I asked you to be my friend. Don't ever question it, Spence. Never. Understand?" Adjani lowered his voice—it seemed that they had talked in lowered voices the whole of the trip back. "I know what you think, but you could not have held such a secret inside you for long. It is too great for one man to bear."

"You think Packer is satisfied with the explanation I gave him? He seemed skeptical."

"Leave Packer to me. I've known him for a long time. I'll talk to him again, but don't you say any more. Stick by your story—at least until we figure out what to do next. Will you promise me that much?"

Spence sighed and nodded slowly. "I promise. I won't do anything rash or stupid—at least not without asking you first. But I didn't expect it to be this hard. Really, I—"

"Did you think you had returned from a Sunday picnic? Your life has been changed. You will never be the same, Spence. You have seen things no man has ever seen and you know things now that can . . . well, change the world. And you can't tell anyone."

Spence stared dully ahead, eyes unfocused, remembering the long sessions he and Adjani had put in during the five-week journey back to Gotham. Now, only a few hours more before docking, they were rehearsing it all again.

He had told Packer a story about his having a fight with Adjani and how he had wanted only to get out of the installation for a few minutes to cool off. He hadn't known Adjani was hurt, and hadn't meant to hurt him. The storm blew up and he became disoriented and couldn't find his way back. Spence admitted to having violent spells of anger and frustration lately—probably due to overwork—and that something had touched him off. Adjani had had the misfortune of being in the wrong place at the wrong time.

Packer accepted this version of the events in much the same way he accepted Spence's version of his miraculous survival on the surface of an extremely hostile planet—he nodded a good deal and puffed out his cheeks and rubbed his hand through his wiry thatch of copper-colored hair and at last said, "I see. Very interesting." And that had been that.

Packer had not questioned him further about either incident, and that is why Spence felt he had not been believed—Packer had seen through the shabby lie and been too hurt to press the matter further. He wanted to come clean and explain everything just the way it happened. Adjani counseled against this and was still of the same opinion: wait and see.

"You're right, of course," said Spence at length. "It's just that I, ah . . ."

"I know, I know. You feel very alone right now. Don't worry. I'm with you. Together we'll work this out."

Spence wondered if Adjani knew or guessed there was more to his story than tunnels and a lost city. He had not told him about Kyr— partly out of obligation to the Martian, and partly out of fear that he would not have been believed. This, too, was eating at him. He wondered if he should tell Adjani about Kyr now, or wait for a better time. He decided reluctantly to wait.

He looked glumly into the dark brown stain at the bottom of his cup as if peering into his future and not liking the color of what he saw.

"You think I'm still in danger, don't you?" he said at last.

"Yes, I do. I see no reason to think otherwise." Adjani leaned across the small table. "As soon as we get back I'm going to request data on the Naga superstitions of Northern India and run it through MIRA for a profile. We may see something there that can help us."

"All right. What do I do in the meantime? Go on as if nothing had happened?"

"Precisely. Nothing did."

"You know, all the while I was in Tso I didn't dream—I mean other than normal dreams. And no blackouts, either. What do you make of that?"

"I don't know. But it is another fact to be considered in our theory."

Spence raised his eyes slowly. "I'm afraid, Adjani. Really afraid. I don't want to go back there. I feel as if he's waiting for me—this Dream Thief of yours—and as soon as I set foot back in Gotham, I'm lost. Powerless."

"Far from it. We will fight him, Spence. And we will win."

"How do you fight a dream?"

"God knows," said Adjani firmly, "and he will aid us."

The signal for return to weightlessness sounded, and Spence and Adjani got up and replaced their cups in the covered bin. For the remaining hours of the flight Spence kept to himself for the most part—the only time he laughed was when a few of the cadets pooled their leftover water ration and created a floating swimming pool in one of the empty cargo holds. Then they all took turns diving through the hanging globule of water.

One of the favorite tricks was to immerse the body completely in the floating sphere, withdrawing arms and legs carefully into the mass of water, and then to swim inside it like fish in a bowl. The effect was hilarious and brought gales of laughter whenever someone accomplished it. Spence, along with nearly everyone else aboard, stripped down to his undershorts and joined in the fun, forgetting for a while his dark secrets.

The rest of the time he sat alone or lay in his safety webbing brooding on his problem; it seemed to increase as they drew nearer the station. He had succeeded in forgetting about it while on Mars—other things, like bare survival, helped him forget. But now it all came back to him and the sense of hopelessness and dread ballooned as the transport streaked toward rendezvous.

Surely, even God—if he existed, which Spence was not yet willing to admit despite what Kyr and Adjani believed—even their God could not help him now. And if he did exist he would not have allowed him to get into such a mess in the first place. That was how he thought about it. Case closed.

Spence half expected the docking bay to be filled with wives and sweethearts and screaming children all waiting eagerly for their husbands and lovers to return from their voyage. It surprised him to discover that aside from a few girlfriends of cadets and the docking crew the area was empty. No cheering crowds, no joyous welcomes.

The absolute routineness of their deboarding disappointed him, but he knew that it was best if he was seen by as few people as possible on his return. It was for that very reason he had donned a cadet's uniform. He also reminded himself that since he was supposed to be missing, no one would be meeting him. Still, as he disembarked and walked quickly through the milling cadets he found himself searching the faces for one in particular he hoped to see.

He hoped Ari would be there, though he felt foolish for even thinking it. He also remembered with a shock that she most likely considered him dead.

What have I done to her? What have I put her through?

He resolved to go to her at once and started off to find her, but checked himself before running ten steps. It would be dangerous to be seen too soon. He would have to wait and arrange a meeting at a safe place.

Feeling like a spy, and not a particularly glamourous one, he slunk away unobtrusively, lugging his travel frame with him. He regretted not thinking of a way to bind his flightmates to secrecy about his reappearance. That, if it could have been accomplished, might have been a valuable card in his hand. On further thought, however, it would have increased the interest in his case which would have spotlighted him. The best course, the one he was on, was just to lay low and keep out of sight.

He at last reached his quarters; after trying various means to determine whether anyone waited for him inside the lab, he had pressed his ear against the panel and listened for a long time before punching the access plate. The panel slid open at once—there had been no entry code entered in his absence.

He went in.

The rooms, dark and quiet, seemed unusually so to Spence. No one waited for him; the control booth was empty. He guessed no one had been around for several weeks.

He had ignored Adjani's protests to stay far away from the lab; he wanted to see it, to see if it was as he had left it. He would not feel he had made it back until he saw his own room. He would join Adjani later.

He moved across the lab silently and went into his personal quarters to look around. Everything appeared exactly as he had left it—that is, as far as he could remember that he left it. Yet the room looked strange and new. Everything was the same, yet altered and different. Spence felt a telescoping of time upon entering, like he had just left it but a few minutes before and now had returned to find it subtly changed. All that happened since he last stood in the room now belonged to a weird, fantastic dream. He awakened from the dream to find himself in his own room, but a room he no longer knew.

It had not been a dream. If he doubted its reality he had only to dip his hand into the inner breast pocket of his jumpsuit to pat the smooth shell-like object Kyr gave him. No, it was no dream.

He slipped his travel frame under the bed without bothering to unpack and sat down in his chair to decide how best to reach Ari. He decided to leave a message for her to meet him in the garden near the fountain.

Spence tapped the message into the ComCen panel and signed it Mary D.—one of Ari's friends. He hoped it would bring her without question.

Then he lay on the bed and fell asleep.

He awoke in a better mood and shrugged off his clothes and stopped himself from putting them in the laundry chute. Instead he threw them under his bed and stepped into the sanibooth and just as quickly out to don a fresh blue and gold jumpsuit. Then he crept from his rooms into the main trafficway and hurried down to meet Ari in the garden.

By the time he reached the garden level his heart was tripping along at an alarming rate. He glanced guiltily around and then stepped off the pathway and into a shaded nook out of sight to wait for her.

He heard steps along the pathway and voices and peered from his seclusion to see two members of the secretarial section gaily flouncing along in full gossip. He swallowed hard and noticed a lump in his throat; he had not been so affected by meeting someone since fifth form when he asked Beatrice Mercer to the Young Astronaut's Annual Dinner Dance. The absurd feeling that at any minute his onetime dancing partner would appear grew unbearable. He shrank back further into the shadows.

He waited; beads of perspiration formed on his forehead from the humidity and his hands grew clammy. *I'm falling to pieces. I'm acting like a fourteen-year-old on his first date.* He forced himself to take deep calming breaths, and then felt woozy and mildly hyperventilated.

When he felt he could no longer stand the waiting he heard the crisp, unmistakable footsteps of Ari pattering along the pathway. She had come. He smelled the fresh scent of lemons a split second before he saw her and stepped from the bower.

It was to Ari's credit that she did not collapse in a dead faint on the spot. Her hands fluttered like frightened birds to her mouth; her eyes grew round, showing white all around; her lovely jaw dropped open and a little pinched scream passed her lips.

"Eeee!"

"Hello, Ari." He had tried to think of something in some way appropriate for this meeting, but that was the best he could come up with.

"*You . . .* how? Oh!"

The next instant she was in his arms, her trembling hands touching his face, squeezing his flesh as if to make certain that it was solid, alive. He clung to her and filled his soul with her living, breathing essence.

"Spence, oh Spence . . ." she said over and over.

He felt a wet spot on his neck and when he pulled her from him to look at her at arm's length he saw the tears rolling down her cheeks.

"Forgive me," he murmured, drawing her to him once more. "There was no other way. I had to—"

"Shh, don't talk. Don't say anything. Oh, darling. They said you were—oh, you're not! You're *here!*"

"I'm here."

"I never thought I'd see you again." She broke from him and expressions of pain, anger, and mingled joy crossed her face in complex patterns. "I never hoped, never dreamed . . . I cried for you. How I cried for you. For so long no word. Nothing."

She looked about to stomp off in anger at his thoughtlessness. He groped for the words to tell her of his own sorrow at hurting her, but there were no words. He hung his head.

The next moment he felt her cool hand on his cheek and he raised his eyes to meet hers. "I never thought I'd see you again, either," he said. "I—I'm sorry. I love you."

Ari pressed herself to him in a tight embrace. "I love you, too, Spencer. Never leave me again."

"We have to get away somewhere private where we can talk. No one else on Gotham knows I've returned—yet. I'd like to keep it that way for a little while longer if I can."

"Come on, I know a secret place here in the garden where we can be alone. I discovered it when I first came here. No one else seems to know about it."

She led him along, his hand clamped tightly in her own, to a place where one of the little artificial creeks bubbled out from a fern-covered bank. She parted the ferns and jumped lightly across the water. Spence followed her and found himself in a cool green shade sweet with the smell of gardenias. He looked around and saw bushes of the fragrant flowers luminous against their waxy dark green leaves.

Ari pulled him down onto a soft bed of long grass. For a moment all he heard was the burbling of the brook nearby and the rush of his own pulse in his ears. Then he was kissing her and nothing else in the world existed but the moment and the kiss.

When they parted Ari looked at him, drinking in his presence with dark blue eyes now sparkling with happy excitement.

"Now, then," she said, drawing her knees to her chin and circling them in her arms. "Tell me everything. I want to hear it all."

"It scarcely seems to matter anymore."

"I don't care. I want to hear it. I need to hear it, Spence."

"All right. I won't leave out a single thing," he said and then remembered that the most important part of his tale, his sojourn in Tso with the Martian Kyr, the whole incredible miracle that was, he could not tell her. His heart sank at once.

Ari must have seen what transpired mirrored in his features. "What's the matter, love?"

"There is something I can't tell you right now,"

She did not make it easier for him. "Oh?" she said, and looked hurt and disappointed.

"At least not yet."

"I understand." She did not understand at all.

"I promise you'll know soon. I don't want there to be any secrets between us ever. For now, though, this is how it must be."

"Of course." Ari brightened at once. "You know best, Spence. Tell me all you can, then. I won't press you for details. It's just that you've been away so long, I want to know what you were doing every minute since I saw you last."

Spence took a deep breath and began relating to her all that had happened since he left, starting with the journey and eventual landing on Mars, then on to that first night and the blackout that had sent him wandering lost on the surface with the storm rising around him. He told of the exhaustion, of nearly freezing to death, of his plunge into the rift valley, and his discovery of the crevice and tunnel. Then he stopped, uncertain what to say next.

"There's something in that tunnel you don't want me to know about."

He nodded. "That's right. I shouldn't say any more right now."

Ari stared upward into the leafy canopy overhead; a ray of sunlight slanting through the branches caught her hair and set it ablaze with golden fire. "All right," she said softly. "Even though I'm dying with curiosity, I won't make you. It doesn't matter. All that matters is that you're here with me and safe."

In the shelter of the hidden nook the two lovers held each other and talked in low, intimate tones, pledging themselves to one another again and again until the closing sunshields cast the garden into a semblance of twilight.

"We'd better go," said Spence, drawing Ari to her feet. He held her close and kissed her once more. "That's until I see you again."

"When *will* I see you again?"

"Tomorrow, I hope. Here. We'll meet here at the same time as to-day. If I need to get in touch with you before then Mary D. will leave a message."

"You're not going back to the lab?"

"No, I'll be staying with Adjani. You two are the only ones I can trust right now."

"You make it sound very dangerous."

"Well, I think it's best to assume so until we can figure out this whole thing. My keeping out of sight for a while longer might be just the break we need."

"I'll do whatever you want me to. You know that."

"I know." He drew her to him and kissed her lightly. "That's good-bye. Until tomorrow."

"Tomorrow." She slowly turned away and parted the ferns closing the entrance to the shady alcove. "Sleep well, my love. Don't let the Dream Thief get you."

For a moment the words did not register. Then they began to burn themselves into his brain like a laserknife through soft butter. An icy tingle crept up his scalp. "What did you say?" His voice had become a rasping whisper.

CHAPTER FOURTEEN

ARI FROZE in place. "What is it, Spencer? What's wrong?"

"What did you say just then? Say it again."

"I said, 'Don't let the Dream Thief get you.'"

"Where did you hear that?" He stepped close to her and pulled her back into the deepening shadows.

"I don't know . . . we've always said it. It's—" Her eyes shifted away.

"It's what? Tell me!" He gripped her arm tightly.

"Spence, what's wrong? You're scaring me!"

"It's what?" Spence persisted. He lowered his voice and forced a calmer tone, letting go of her arm. "Tell me. It's important."

"It's just something my mother used to say. That's all. I must have heard it from her. Why? What does it mean?" She gazed at him with troubled eyes, her brow wrinkled in concern.

"I—I'm not sure," he said at length, avoiding her eyes. "It just seemed important somehow . . . I don't know." His tone softened and he smiled to reassure her. "I'm sorry if I frightened you. It surprised me that's all."

Ari nodded uncertainly; the cloud still hung over her features. "All right. If you're sure, Spence, I—"

"Don't think about it anymore. I'm all right. Just let me think it over. I'll tell you if I come up with anything tomorrow."

"Good night, Spence." She waved and was gone. Spence heard her footsteps recede along the pathway outside and then stepped out of their hiding place and left the garden by another route.

Adjani sat cross-legged on his rumpled bed. He was barefoot and appeared more than ever the wise, all-knowing guru dressed in his flowing white kaftan, his hands placed palms together, fingertips touching lightly. He had been silent, listening to Spence's recitation of the facts. Now Spence waited for his verdict.

"So here it is," he said at last. "Another fact to be connected. How will we make the connection? That is the primary question."

"I can't see it myself," offered Spence. "Maybe it's just a coincidence."

"Please, there is no such thing as coincidence. Not in science. Not in the plans of God. The connection must be made and perhaps it will be useful to us."

"Ari's mother—the woman isn't even alive anymore. How can she help us?"

"Ari herself might know more than she thinks she knows. We should find out."

"I still don't see how I could possibly be connected with some weird superstition in the mountains of India somewhere, and to a woman I've never even met—who has been dead I don't know how long."

"Stranger things are possible. You yourself thought there was a connection or you wouldn't have reacted the way you did. Subconsciously you fastened on it."

"How could I help it? I mean first you mention it, and then Ari—it gave me a jolt at first. I thought it might be a clue, but I'm not so sure now."

"And I think you're just afraid to face what you might find."

"Afraid?" Spence could not prevent the sneer that came. "What makes you say that? If I was afraid I wouldn't have told you about it."

"I think you might fear prying into your lover's past," said Adjani carefully.

Was it that obvious that he and Ari were in love? "I don't recall ever mentioning anything to you about that."

Adjani laughed and the tension which had built up in the room floated away on his laughter. "You didn't need to say a word. It is written all over you, my friend. Anyone with eyes can see it—I just happen to know her name, that's all."

"You're shrewd, Adjani. I'll give you that. You'd make a great spy."

"What is a scientist but a spy? We're detectives, all of us, scratching for clues to the riddles of the universe."

"What are we going to do about *my* riddle?"

"Simple. We'll ask Ari. She may be able to tell us more about it."

"You know, now that you mention it, it is a little strange. Ari never talks about her mother. I gather it's still a painful subject—her death, I mean. I wouldn't want to hurt her for anything."

"Then we must be very discreet and gentle in our inquiry. That should not prove too difficult, should it?"

"I guess not. There's still something I don't like about this, though. It makes me nervous."

"A warning, perhaps?"

"Warning?"

"We may be probing close to the heart of the matter."

The egg-shaped chair spun in the air as Hocking gazed upward at the clean blank ceiling, as if he were searching for cracks or specks of dirt. Tickler and his assistant sat slumped in their own, less-mobile seats gazing upward, too, in imitation of their leader. But they had less on their minds.

"The transport is back and Reston has not turned up." Hocking repeated the facts of the case so far. He shot a quick, disapproving glance at Tickler. "It would probably have been a good idea to have watched the docking and disembarkation of the passengers. But that, I suppose, would never have occurred to you."

Tickler grew sullen. "There was no reason to. He has not been seen or heard from since the message. And if he was here he'd have to turn up sooner or later somewhere. He's gone."

Hocking's eyes narrowed. "He disappeared—broke contact—on the first night they landed. Yet the report of his disappearance did not come until a week later. Doesn't that strike you as odd?"

"I don't know. I hadn't thought about it."

"You don't think period!" exploded Hocking. "*I* have to do all the thinking for all of us."

Tickler looked away. "I'm getting sick of this—this constant badgering. Just tell us what you want us to do, will you? I can't be responsible for Dr. Reston's whereabouts anymore. He's gone. Most likely he fell over a rock and broke his neck."

"Possible—but I don't think so. I believe Reston is very much alive, and something tells me he has returned to Gotham. I think we had better check with that young bubblehead, Miss Zanderson. If he is alive he will have tried to contact her; she may know his whereabouts."

"Kurt can go talk to her," growled Tickler, "but it's a waste of time. I say we should begin looking for a new subject right now."

Hocking whirled to face him. "Since when are you in charge here? You'll do as *I* say! Or do I have to remind you who holds the reins of power, hmm? I thought not.

"We will begin looking for a new subject when I have satisfied myself that he is indeed gone. But need I remind you that Reston possesses certain highly refined qualities—he is unique—probably not one in a million like him. We have searched long and hard to find him, gentlemen. And his contribution thus far has advanced our work enormously. I do not intend to give up now until I know for a definite, absolute, undeniable fact that he is dead."

Tickler muttered under his breath and avoided Hocking's eyes. He did not wish to feel the terrible sting of the power Hocking had referred to. Once had been enough for him; it was enough for most people.

"Any further observations, gentlemen? No? Then report back to me as soon as you have questioned Ariadne. I want you to talk to some of the cadets on that trip, too. They can confirm our suspicions. You may go." The chair spun away from them and the two beleaguered underlings crept away.

Hocking heard the sigh of the partition closing and then silently cruised to the panel himself. "Perhaps another visit to Miss Zanderson's father is in order," he said to himself. "Yes. It is time we had a little chat."

CHAPTER FIFTEEN

"ADJANI! Wake up!" Spence jostled the arm of his sleeping friend. A low murmur passed the Indian's lips as he rolled over. "Adjani!" he persisted. He went to the access panel and brought up the lights.

"What is it?" Adjani sat up rubbing his eyes, and then snapped fully awake. "Are you all right?"

"Some watchdog. Yes, I'm all right. I remembered something.'

"In your sleep?"

"I don't sleep much anymore. What difference does it make? I remembered something—it may be important. When I first came here I met someone, a very unusual person—he had a pneumochair—"

"Those things aren't cheap."

"A quadraplegic, I think. His name—I can't remember his name. But he asked me about my dreams."

"He did?"

"Well, he didn't come right out and ask me. But he seemed to suggest that he knew about them. He implied as much; at least that was the feeling I got at the time."

"What made you think of this now?"

"I don't know. I was laying there thinking about what you said about there not being any coincidences and this just popped into my head. Here was a coincidence where there shouldn't be one. I don't know. *You're* the connection man. You tell me."

"A quadraplegic in a pneumochair will be easy enough to track down in any case. We'll try to find him tomorrow." He yawned and lay down again.

"What's wrong with right now?"

"I'm sleeping right now. Besides, if you haven't noticed, it's third shift and everything is shut down. We wouldn't get very far on his trail just now. Go back to bed and try to get some rest. Tomorrow may be a long day."

"Sorry if I interrupted your beauty sleep, mahatma."

"It is but the buzzing of a gnat, my son. It is nothing. Go to sleep."

Director Zanderson passed through the outer office and smiled warmly at the receptionist. He entered his office and hurried by Mr. Wermeyer's empty desk, glancing at the near corner as he went by to see if there were any messages for him. He saw a small red light blinking on the ComCen panel set in the desk. He stopped and punched his code. The wafer screen lit at once with the message.

It was a note from Wermeyer; it read: Brodine called to thank you for your support of their AgEn project. I quote: "Means so much to me and my boys to know the boss is behind us." End quote. They're sending the first crate of spuds to you. Reply?

The director tapped a key and entered the words "potato pancakes." He then cleared the display and proceeded to his office.

It was only when he reached his high, handsome desk with its satiny walnut top that he noticed he was not alone. He turned and jumped back a step.

"I *am* sorry if I startled you, Director Zanderson."

"What are you doing here?"

"Is that any way to greet a friend?" Hocking smiled his grisly smile. "I hope you don't mind. I had to see you, and since no one was about I let myself in."

It occured to the director that he would have to have the entry code changed at once. "What do you want? I thought you said you'd never come here again. You said you had what you wanted and you wouldn't bother me any more."

"Something's come up, Director. I need some information. That's all. Just a little information."

"What makes you think you can just come sneaking in here any time you want and bully me around? I can have you thrown out of here."

"Now, now." Hocking clicked his tongue and chided, "You agreed to our little arrangement long ago, didn't you? It would be showing poor form to begin getting all indignant and officious at this late date. We've kept our part of the bargain. We expect you to keep yours."

"What do you want?" Zanderson scowled at his unwelcome guest.

"I want a modicum of consideration," sniffed Hocking.

"Ha! You won't get that from me."

"I thought I made myself clear last time we talked," Hocking intoned menacingly. "You are a powerful man, director. With powerful enemies. What they might do with the information I could give them . . . Well, who knows what they might do? There is, of course, one quick way to find out, isn't there? But you don't want me to use it, do you?"

Zanderson closed his eyes and turned away.

"I thought not," Hocking soothed.

"I made a big mistake in letting you come here. A big mistake."

"I wouldn't worry about that. It wasn't really your choice." Hocking smirked haughtily. The chair rose higher in the air.

"What do you want?"

"I want to know the whereabouts of a certain Dr. Spencer Reston."

Zanderson gulped and stared blankly at his guest. "Him? Why him?"

"Let's just say he has become something of a topic of conversation lately. I would like to know where he is."

"He's missing," said the director delicately. "I'm afraid that's all I can say right now."

"Do you expect to say more later?"

"No. I mean, I don't know. We haven't even notified his family yet."

"And why is that? Do you think he's likely to turn up soon?"

"No, I don't." The director shook his head sadly. "Dr. Reston is dead."

"Then why haven't you notified his family? And why has there been no announcement to this effect?"

Director Zanderson touched fingertips to his temples and sank into his chair. "You don't understand," he said wearily. "In the case of suicide we don't exactly like to rush to press with the news. It isn't good for the Center."

"Is that what you suspect? Suicide?"

"I am afraid so."

Hocking watched his man intently and decided that he was telling the truth. He assumed a bright, reassuring tone. "See how easy that was? Not unpleasant at all. I shall be going now." The chair floated across the room toward the door.

"I don't want to see you again," Zanderson said to the retreating figure. "Do you hear me? Stay away from here."

Hocking did not answer and the chair kept right on going. As the door panel slid closed the director thought he heard a grim, ghostly laughter coming from the other side. He sat motionless in his chair for a long time after the sound of that laughter had died away.

The two men slipped along the trafficways of Gotham trying to be as invisible as possible. They moved with the crowd of technicians and construction workers, the dark one keeping a wary watch ahead on all sides, the light man keeping his face averted, eyes on his feet.

When they were certain they were not being followed they slipped unnoticed into an empty axial and hurried on. As they approached their destination they stopped and waited. Upon hearing a slight noise and voices speaking low as a portal slid open they dived into a nearby maintenance alcove and waited until the footsteps trailed away down the corridor before emerging to press the buzzer on the access plate.

Ari, having just gotten rid of one visitor, hesitated before answering the door. She expected to hurry off to meet Spence soon and considered that probably it was best to ignore the buzzer and hope that whoever it was would go away. But it buzzed again, more insistent this time, she thought, so she went to the panel and lightly tapped the entry key.

The panel slid open and she saw a slight dark man and another behind him hidden in the shadow.

"Yes?"

"Excuse me, Miss Zanderson, I—"

"Oh, it's you, Dr. Rajwandhi." She paused. "I, uh—was just about to leave . . ."

"Please, I understand. Is your father here?"

"Why, no. He is at his office, I imagine. Or at a meeting somewhere. If you need to see him, I would suggest—"

He cut her off. "Thank you. Is anyone else here?" He answered her suspicious look, saying, "Please, the purpose of my questions will immediately become clear."

She peered past Adjani to the man lurking behind him. A hint of worry glinted in her eyes. "No one else is here. I'm alone."

At this the man behind Adjani moved into the light and both men hurried through the door.

"Spence!" squeaked Ari in surprise.

"Sorry for the charade. I had to see you at once."

She saw a strange fire smouldering behind his dark eyes and stopped; she had been about to greet him with a kiss. Instead, she froze, her hands halfway to him. "What is it? Something wrong?"

Spence took one of the outstretched hands and led her to the reading room where they all sat down together. "No," he told her, "nothing's wrong. I remembered some details that might help us. I couldn't wait. I'm sorry if we frightened you."

They sat on the couch beneath the green abstract and Adjani pulled up the low table and sat facing them.

Now that he was here, Spence did not know where to begin. Adjani helped him. "Our friend here has been awake all night pestering me with impossible questions. For the sake of a restful sleep tonight I suggested we come to see you."

Ari smiled. "For a sleep researcher he doesn't seem to do much of it, does he?"

"And he makes sure no one else does, either, I assure you."

"He's right. I couldn't sleep last night. I kept thinking about what you said yesterday—about the Dream Thief. I told Adjani about it. We think it might be important."

Ari suddenly paled. Spence could see her withdraw a little into herself. Her tone became guarded. "Certainly. I'll tell you anything you want to know."

"Who was with you just now?" asked Adjani. The change in subject came so abruptly, both Spence and Ari looked at him sharply.

"What?" they asked in unison.

"When we came up a moment ago someone was just leaving. Your father, perhaps?"

Spence frowned. "That doesn't concern us, Adjani. Anyway it's none of our business."

"But you are wrong, my friend. It might concern us entirely."

Ari held up her hands. "It's all right. I was going to bring it up myself anyway because I thought it was a little odd.

"Spence, it was that lab assistant of yours."

"Kurt Millen?" He said the name as if it were a foreign word he did not know how to pronounce. "What did he want?"

"Now that you ask, I don't know. He didn't say exactly. That's what was odd about it." She paused; a look of deep concentration crossed her face. When she looked up again her eyes glittered; her tone was hushed excitement.

"Oh, Spence! I remember something—it's been haunting me for weeks and I couldn't for the life of me think of what it was. I think it's important."

"What is it? What do you know?"

"I think I know who's out to get you!"

CHAPTER SIXTEEN

CLOUDS OF incense colored the murky air a dull, dirty brownish gray. The pungent scents of sandalwood and patchouli mingled, creating a single heavy dusky stench. But the inhabitant of the closed chamber seemed not to mind the oppressive atmosphere.

He sat cross-legged, his hands folded in his lap, head erect, eyes closed, sight turned inward. He appeared the very essence of the meditating guru with his paridhana, yellowed with age, wrapped in swaddling fashion around his wasted body. His sunken chest and bony shoulders heaved only occasionally as if breathing were not so important to him that it needed regular attention.

The hairless head on its long slender neck floated on the clouds of incense filling the room. A tiny brass bell sat on the grass mat before the ancient figure. With a slow, snakelike movement the guru slid a hand out to grasp the bell and ring it. The hand had but three long fingers.

In a moment a white-haired servant came running, his thin sandals slapping his naked feet in mock applause. The man, dressed in muslin shirt and trousers, entered the room bowing.

"Yes, my master. I am here."

Ortu opened his eyes languidly and cast his dreadful yellow gaze upon the creature scraping before him.

"I will eat now. When I have finished I will see my disciples."

"Yes, Ortu." The servant hurried away and shortly there sounded a bell clanging from some further recess of the guru's castle.

In a few moments the white-haired servant returned with a tray of food in bowls: rice and green tender shoots, and a thick pungent broth. These he laid at the feet of his master and retreated silently. Years of humble service had taught him that one did not linger in Ortu's presence unbidden.

Pundi, the servant, hurried away to fetch Ortu's disciples. Every master had disciples, Pundi knew. Wise men always attracted sincere students who wished to learn the paths of wisdom from one whose feet treaded the higher paths. He himself, though now a servant, had in his youth been a disciple of a great seer who had become a Brahman.

But the disciples of Ortu were unlike any Pundi had ever heard of. They were not human; they were not even alive. Ortu's disciples were six hollow gems, great black stones which contained only dust within their cleverly carved interiors. These stones sat in six teak boxes which had been made to hold them. The teak was very old and had words carved in the design which Pundi did not recognize.

It had been years since Ortu called for his disciples. The last time, Pundi remembered, there had been reports of demons loosed in the hills. Sacred cattle had been found dead and calves stillborn, nursing mothers' milk turned sour, snakes mated in the village squares and the shrines of the gramadevata were overturned.

He shuddered to think what might happen this night after Ortu met with his disciples. But he did not hesitate a moment to fulfill his master's wish. One did not hesitate before such a stern and powerful master.

He crept to the special room where the stones were kept and drew the key from the leather thong around his neck. The treasure room contained many ususual objects which seemed both exceedingly old and yet new somehow—as if their time of use had not yet come. But he never dallied to wonder at these things; it was enough to be allowed just to see them when he occasionally entered to fetch one or the other of them for Ortu.

His eyes fell on the large gopher wood chest which contained the six smaller boxes of teak. He picked it up by its brass handles and carried it away to his master.

Ortu's eyes flicked open when the last of the boxes had been placed before him. With a twitch of his hand he sent Pundi scurrying away.

He gazed at each of the black glittering gems as he opened each box in turn. A sound like the hiss of a serpent drifted into the air. He held his hands over the six black stones and, with his head weaving back and forth, began to speak in a strange chirping tongue.

His lids closed slowly over his enormous yellow eyes and his ancient head, with its skin dry as old parchment, sank to his chest. The odd, three-fingered hands remained outstretched over the gemstones in their boxes.

The drifting brown haze of incense scattered as by a cool breeze entering the chamber. A low moan or hum rose into the air; the sustained note came from deep in Ortu's throat. The thin band on his head—the *kastak*—began to throb with a bright pulsing light.

One by one, so softly it could hardly be noticed at first—little more than a stray beam of light striking a facet here and there—the six black gems began to glow.

"You what?"

"I think I know who's out to get you—that is, I think I have a pretty good idea."

Spence's stupid expression gave way to one of incredulity. "How?"

"It came to me just now. Your question sort of triggered it."

"Let's have it!" said Spence excitedly. Adjani leaned forward from his perch on the coffee table.

"You asked who was here—"

"Kurt, right."

"But that wasn't the first time he's been here. He came to see me one other time just after you had left aboard the transport—no, I remember clearly now, it was several weeks after you'd left."

"What did he want?"

"I'm getting to that," she said a little impatiently. "Let me remember it exactly." She closed her eyes and her lovely features scrunched themselves into a frown. "All right, yes."

"Proceed," said Spence more calmly.

"Your Mr. Millen came to me and said they'd just received a communication from you, and you'd given him a message to pass on to me."

"What was the message?" asked Adjani.

"Nothing, really. He said that you'd told him to tell me that you missed me and you'd be seeing me soon—something like that."

"Seems pretty harmless to me," said Spence, "only I never sent any messages."

"I thought it was a little odd, but he seemed like such a nice guy, and there was really nothing ususual about what he said. It made me feel a little uncomfortable, though."

"Uncomfortable how?"

"Well, I was under the impression when you left that if any messages were going to be sent they'd be sent to me."

"You're absolutely right."

"Why was this?" asked Adjani.

Spence replied, "We had agreed before I sneaked aboard the transport that if anything happened I'd contact her and no one else."

"Actually, there were to be no messages at all unless something important came up," continued Ari. "But Kurt seemed so nonchalant about it—he knew all about the trip and everything and he knew that . . . that you and I were seeing each other."

"He knew that?"

"He seemed to know so much I figured you'd told him. I thought maybe you really *had* sent a message and explained everything to them. Why not? It made sense after all. He said you'd told him your work was going smoothly and everything was fine. I figured maybe you were . . . you know, feeling better. So I just accepted what he said."

"Did you tell him anything?"

Ari gave Spence a perturbed look. "I hope I've got more wits than that! Besides, it wasn't like he was looking for information anyway. He asked me if I knew you were going on the Mars trip. I told him I supposed I did, but that you didn't confide in anyone very much. It's true, Spence, you don't."

"Is that all? Apart from the fact that I never sent any such message, you'd think it was all on the up and up. You're right."

"No—that's not all. Here's the thing that I just remembered." Ari grew very intense. The other two waited to hear what she would say. "Spence, they knew about the birthday gift."

"That little paperweight I sent to my dad?"

"That's right. I haven't mentioned it, but they caught me when I went to get it from your room. Remember? You asked me to send it for you."

"I remember. What happened?"

"Nothing, really. They came in as I was leaving. I told them I was just looking for you."

"Good. And then?"

"And then I left. But they saw the paperweight."

"So?"

"So, that's just it. They saw a paperweight. But when Kurt came to see me he said *birthday gift*. Spence, I never told them that. I called it what it was, a paperweight. I swear it."

Spence's eyes grew round with recognition. "You're right! Good Lord, you're right! But how could they know?"

"They must have had it traced somehow," put in Adjani. "Are you quite positive there was not another way they could have innocently received this information?"

"I'm positive *I* didn't tell them," she said a little crossly.

"Well, this *is* interesting," said Spence darkly.

"Very interesting," murmured Adjani.

For a moment they all sat ticking over the facts in their minds. No one spoke. Finally the silence grew unbearable. Ari said, "What happens now?"

Spence shook his head slowly. "I wish I knew."

CHAPTER SEVENTEEN

"I JUST don't get it," muttered Spence. "Oh, I'm not doubting your story. It just doesn't make any sense. Why would Tickler and Millen be out to get me?" The initial shock had worn off and the three were once again lost in conversation, trying to untangle the deepening mystery.

"You have to admit their behavior certainly seems suspicious," said Ari.

"For a fact." Spence scratched his jaw absently. "But it seems beyond them somehow—I mean, Tickler's not the kind of man to plot sabotage. He's nothing but a fussy old grudger—a drone."

"What about the quadraplegic?" asked Adjani.

"I could believe anything of *him*," said Spence. "He gave me goosebumps."

"What quadraplegic?"

"I'll tell you," said Spence, turning to Ari. "But first I'd like to know why Kurt came to see you again just now."

Ari lifted her shoulders. "Like before, there didn't seem to be any particular reason. At least, he made it seem as if it was not at all important. He just said he'd heard you were missing from the Mars expedition; he stopped by to pay his respects. That's all. And to see if I knew any more about it."

"It seems innocent enough."

"Of course they would want to give that illusion," offered Adjani. "What did you tell him?"

"I told him that I was very sorry and that I didn't really know any more about it either. The whole thing being so sudden and all, and the formal reports not being filed yet." She glanced at the two men worriedly. "Did I do right?"

"You did fine. It's hard to see what they could have learned from that." Spence reached and took her hand.

"Don't be too sure." Adjani raised a warning finger. "They may not have been after information at all, but were looking for an emotional reaction to confirm what they already knew or suspected."

"Blazes, Adjani! You seem to have quite a talent for this espionage stuff."

The Indian smiled broadly. "It is part of the oriental mind, sahib. But from now on we are all going to have to adopt this way of thinking. We must suspect everyone and trust no one. Do not accept anything at face value until you have probed below the surface. We must become very sly dogs if we want to catch these foxes."

They fell to discussing various theories as to why anyone would want to meddle with Spence's work, or with Spence himself for that matter. But the talk proved pointless since no one really had anything more than bare speculation to go on. Spence explained to Ari about his chance encounter one day with a quadraplegic in a pneumochair at a lecture. He finished by saying, "What I'd like you to do is check the records of personnel and visitors for anyone answering that description."

"That's easy, Spence. I can tell you right now there isn't anyone like that on GM. I've been updating the personnel files for the furlough assignments for next year. Anyone with a special disability like that would have been in the primary group—that's the high-stress group who must be considered every quarter regardless. They can put in for furlough at any time and not wait for the rotation. There are a few partially disabled—but no one that severely handicapped."

"From what I saw of him he wasn't at all handicapped."

"What about visitors?" asked Adjani.

"Possibly, but I don't think so. Any visitors like that would have to be cleared. Sometimes, you know, their devices interfere with certain radio frequencies and such. You two would know more about that than I do, but I know they have to get advance clearance from the director's office. No one like that has come through since I've been here. I usually handle Daddy's correspondence myself—things of that nature, anyway."

"Well, could you check it out again just to be sure? We need to be positive."

"All right. No problem." Ari smiled cryptically.

"What?"

"I'm sorry. I just couldn't help thinking that this really is a mystery, isn't it? An adventure."

"Not to me it isn't." Her glib tone offended Spence.

"Oh, I didn't mean anything by it, Spence. You know that. It's just that I've never been involved in anything so exciting."

"I hope the excitement doesn't prove fatal," said Adjani.

Ari's eyes grew round. "Do you think there's a chance of that? Is it *that* serious?"

Spence nodded solemnly. "Until we figure out what's going on we'll all be in danger. We still don't have the slightest idea what this is all about. Not really."

"You're right. I'm sorry.

Adjani, sitting back casually, swiveled toward Ari and abruptly asked, "Ari, was your mother ever in Sikkim?"

"M-my mother?" she managed to stammer out.

Spence was about to protest this ill-advised and rough handling of an obviously delicate subject, but Adjani held up a hand and kept him silent. "Sikkim is in India. A small province in the north, high in the foothills of the Himalayas."

Ari bent her head as if examining her fine long nails. "I know where it is."

"Oh? Not many people do."

"Yes, my mother has been there. You might say she grew up there."

"Tell us about it, please."

"Is this—" Spence started. Adjani cut him off with a sharp look.

"How did you know?"

"You mentioned the Dream Thief to Spence. He told me you said it came from your mother. And since it is a fairly obscure local legend, I assumed she must have been there at some time or known someone who had."

"My grandfather was a professor of hermeneutics at Rangpo Seminary. They lived there for twelve years and left when he became dean of West Coast Seminary. She was sixteen when they came back to the States."

"Do you know anything more about it?"

"Not really. She never really talked much about it—it's just something she said." Ari's voice had become almost a whisper, her tone strained.

Spence wondered at the transformation in her; it had happened so swiftly. Only a moment ago she had been her lighthearted, enchanting self. Now she appeared pale and shaken under Adjani's questioning.

Adjani, eyes intent, watching her every move, asked gently, "When did your mother pass away, Ari?"

The girl was silent for a long time. Finally she raised her head slowly and looked at the two men cautiously as if trying to decide how to answer the simple question. Spence saw something in her blue eyes that told him she was fighting a bitter battle somewhere inside her.

"She—" Ari started and then stopped. Her head fell once more. Whichever side had won the battle, it appeared to Spence that Ari had lost. "My mother isn't dead."

"What?" Spence could not help it; the admission took him by surprise. "You told me she *was*."

"I said she was no longer with us—and she isn't. I wanted you to think she was dead, I admit it. That's what I always say."

"But why? I don't understand."

She buried her face in her hands. "I'm so embarrassed."

Spence was mystified. He could never have believed this bright, angelic creature capable of such duplicity.

"About eight years ago my mother became ill—her mind started going. She began having these attacks of insanity. She'd be perfectly calm and normal one moment and the next she'd be screaming and crying and carrying on something terrible. It was frightening."

Ari, avoiding Spence's eyes, drew a long shaky breath and continued.

"There was nothing to be done for her. Daddy took her to all the top doctors in the country. No one could help her. Oh, it was awful. We never knew when another attack would come, and they got worse and worse as time went on. She would run away sometimes and it would be days before we found her again. She wouldn't know where she'd been or what she'd been doing or anything.

"Gradually her good periods shrank away and we couldn't watch her anymore. Daddy was up for the promotion to director and wanted to accept the job—it was his life's goal. There was nothing to be done for Mother but put her in an institution. She's been there ever since."

"But why let everyone think she was dead?"

"I don't know. It just seemed easier at first, telling people that . . . Then they don't ask questions. It was Daddy's idea, really. I think he couldn't stand the idea that Mother would never be right again. He preferred having the uncertainty settled one way or the other.

"Then, after it got started we couldn't very well tell everyone that she was really alive. So we kept it up. I think Daddy was a little afraid that if anyone on the Board ever found out different there'd be an investigation and the whole thing would come out."

"Would he lose his directorship?"

"I don't know. Maybe—if someone wanted his blood badly enough and there was a scandal or something."

Adjani, eyes narrowed, had listened to every word Ari said without moving a muscle. "When did she tell you about the Dream Thief?"

"Oh, I don't know. That was what she always told me when she wanted me to be good. She said if I didn't behave the Dream Thief would get me. Like the bogeyman or something. Later, when I was a little older, she'd put me to bed and say, 'Don't let the Dream Thief get you,' like that. It was just something she said. I didn't know where it came from.

"One time I asked her about it. She said she'd heard it when she was a little girl in India. There was some kind of superstition connected with it, but she didn't know or remember what it was."

"That was all she told you?" asked Adjani. He peered at her over his laced fingers.

"That's all. She ordinarily didn't talk much about India and growing up. I gather she didn't like it there very much. She was sick a lot as a little girl—once, when she was twelve she almost died. She was in a coma for a month."

"How did this happen?"

"Fever, maybe. She never said." Ari, more at ease now that the secret was out, glanced at her inquisitors and asked, "Is this important, do you think?"

"It may be," said Spence. Adjani nodded. "See, when you mentioned those words to me in the garden yesterday something snapped —like a rubber band stretched too tight. I had never heard of this Dream Thief and then here, both my best friends were talking about him. It seemed like too much of a coincidence."

Ari cast a questioning look at Adjani. He answered it, admitting, "Yes, I know about the Dream Thief. But what I know goes beyond children's tales of bogeymen and superstition." He told Ari the story he had heard on his visit to his homeland, and related the things he had seen.

When he finished Ari shook her head. "No wonder you nearly jumped out of your skin. I don't blame you. I would have, too."

"You couldn't have known what you were saying," Spence soothed. "But it still doesn't add up at all. Instead of arriving at an answer we seem to be creating more questions, more loose ends."

Adjani shrugged. "That is to be expected. Difficult problems are not solved by easy answers. Very likely we will have to work very hard to penetrate this mystery."

"Where do we start? It seems like we're kind of out on a branch right now."

"True, you cannot go back to your lab just yet—not with those two skulking around," said Ari.

"Perhaps it would be best to follow the thread Ari has given us," said Adjani, "to see where it will lead."

"Where *does* it lead? The only other person I can see that would know anything about any of this is Ari's mother. You don't mean that we should—"

Adjani nodded. "Precisely. I believe we must pay Mrs. Zanderson a visit.

CHAPTER EIGHTEEN

OLMSTEAD Packer sat heavily in his chair reading the latest findings of a battery of tests which had been carried out in his absence. He grumbled and muttered into the bushy red beard, regarding the material with sour disapproval. It seemed that, from the evidence, nothing had gone right while he was away; it would all have to be done over again.

He got up and poured himself another cup of coffee from a jug on a bookshelf overflowing with magcarts, printouts and stacks of coded discs. A chiming tone sounded from a wedge-shaped instrument in his desk and a clear, crisp voice announced, "Dr. Packer, there is a gentleman waiting to see you. He's from an investigation firm."

"Oh?" That sounded interesting. "Send him in. I've got nothing to hide."

Almost before he could set the jug down and turn around the panel of the outer office slid open and a large egg-shaped object glided into the room. It was a pneumochair and in it sat a skeleton of a man grinning a deathly grin at him which chilled Packer like a sudden icy blast.

"Professor Packer?" said the skeleton as the chair came to hover a few inches from the edge of his desk.

"Yes. I'd ask you to have a seat, but I see you already have."

The skeleton laughed. "Very good. I'll have to remember that one."

"What can I do for you?" Packer dropped back into his seat and folded his hands on the desk.

"I am from the United Federal Insurance Group, investigation division."

Packer raised his eyebrows. "Oh? Something needs investigating?"

"That is what I'd like to find out." The man in the chair tilted his head to one side, studying the physicist behind the desk. "I believe you know Dr. Spencer Reston, do you not?"

"Why, yes. Yes, I do. That is, before the accident."

"Accident?" The skeleton man's eyes narrowed. "Could you tell me about it, please?"

Packer hesitated, his large hands fumbling over one another on his desk. The insurance investigator noticed the man's reluctance and said,

"Oh, I assure you this is not a formal investigation. I was merely making our quarterly audit—you can understand that with an account this big, well—" He rolled his eyes to include the whole of the space station. "And someone mentioned the loss of one of our insureds—that is, one of your staff members. I merely thought that while I was here I might as well do a prelim and save some time later. No doubt a claim will be filed in due course and our company will schedule a formal inquiry. But . . . I'm sure you understand."

Packer nodded uncertainly. He was not sure he should tell this investigator anything at all, but figured a refusal would arouse undue suspicion where there was none to begin with. Besides, something about the investigator made him nervous and a little suspicious. He decided, out of loyalty to Adjani, to stick to the story he and Adjani had agreed upon.

Packer cleared his throat. "Well, he wasn't one of my staff members."

"Oh? He was on the research trip, correct?"

"Correct. But he belonged to a different division—BioPsych, I believe."

"But you were party leader, were you not?"

"Yes, of course. But that is not at all ususual. Often members of other divisions are invited along. As many as transport space will allow."

"I see. Do you know what happened to Dr. Reston?"

The question came so quick that Packer did not have an answer ready. He bluffed. "I suppose so."

"Don't you know for a certainty?"

"Not really, no." Packer lied and felt his stomach knot in tension.

"Then what do you *suppose* happened to him?"

"I suppose he froze to death."

"Would that not be extremely unlikely, professor?"

Packer was beginning to feel as if he were a criminal under cross-examination. Perhaps talking to the investigator had not been such a good idea in the first place. He took a deep breath. "Not at all. It would, in fact, be quite the opposite—very likely. A fair certainty. For one caught outside of shelter in the Martian night, inevitable."

"I see. Is that what happened to Dr. Reston? He was caught outside of shelter?"

"Yes."

"That's what I find so unlikely, Professor Packer. I keep asking myself why would an intelligent man like Dr. Reston allow that to happen to him? It simply doesn't add up."

Packer glanced at the desk as if he held a hand of cards and was trying to decide how to play them. He sighed. "I will tell you something, Mr.—ah . . ."

"Hocking."

"Mr. Hocking. This is off the record, you understand. I am not qualified to offer any kind of analysis of Dr. Reston's condition."

"I understand. Continue."

"Dr. Reston was a very disturbed man. It is my opinion that he did not know what he was doing when he went out that night."

"Could he not have found his way back? He surely could not have wandered very far."

"No, you wouldn't think so, but then with the storm and all . . . who really knows what happened?"

"You never saw him again?"

"No. Not a trace. We searched for eighteen hours before the storm brought a halt to the rescue operation. It was three days before the wind let up enough to venture outside again. And by that time . . ." He shrugged heavily. "There was no point."

"I see."

"All this is in my official report," Packer said gruffly. "If you want to know any more about the incident, I suggest you look it up." He felt he had said enough and that it was time his visitor left.

"Well, I think that's all for now. Thank you for your help, Professor Packer. I appreciate it. May I call on you again if any questions come up later?"

"Of course." His tone was even, noninviting.

"I will do that. But I don't anticipate the need for a lengthy investigation. Most likely you'll never see me again." Hocking's chair backed away from the desk and whirred toward the door. "Oh, there is one other thing." He fixed Packer with a crafty gaze.

"What's that?"

"Do you think it was suicide?"

"Who told you that?"

"Director Zanderson mentioned the word, I believe."

"Well, I wouldn't know. I wouldn't like to comment on that."

"Just wondering." The pneumochair half turned in the air. "I don't suppose there is a chance that Dr. Reston could still be alive?"

"Not the slightest." Packer rose and came around the desk. "Good day, Mr. Hocking." The interview was concluded; Packer wished he had terminated it a whole lot sooner. He had a dark suspicion that Hocking saw right through his flimsy answers.

Ari felt unseen eyes upon her all day. She imagined spies around every corner. Though she saw no one and nothing out of the ordinary as she walked along the winding garden pathway, she nevertheless made doubly sure that no one followed her.

She paused, looking both ways along the path and then skipped over the little brook and entered the green seclusion of the fern nook.

"Oh, you're here already," she said upon entering. Spence greeted her; she saw by the look on his face that he was eager to learn what had been discovered from her detective work.

"Where's Adjani?"

"He couldn't make it. He had to work. But never mind that. What did you find out?"

"Good news and bad news. The good news is that we can all make the jump down with the next shuttle. They're bringing up a dozen extra construction workers this next trip. They've added an extra row of seats in the cabin. There are only twenty-five scheduled to go down this trip, so those seats will be empty. I've already obtained three travel vouchers. We're all set."

"When does it get here?"

"The shuttle will get here on Thursday—two days from now. It leaves next morning."

"All right. It'll have to do," said Spence. Ari could see he was deep in thought, making rapid mental calculations.

"Have to do! It's blooming terrific! Do you have any idea how hard it would be to get aboard a shuttle any other time? You'd have to wait months for an extra seat. The schedules are tight, my dear. Impossibly tight."

"I'm sorry." Spence smiled and looked at her as if he had not seen her before this moment. "I guess I'm a little preoccupied."

"Is that what you call it? Preoccupied? I call it bossy." Her lip protruded in a pretty pout.

"I said I was sorry."

"Oh, you're no fun. I was only teasing."

Spence gave her a sharp look. She hurried on. "The rest of my news isn't so terrific. I've looked and looked, but there is no record of anyone like you described on GM in the last six months."

"He was here all right. I saw him." Spence was fighting the belief that he dreamed up the mystery figure.

"No one doubts that you did, dearest. But there is simply no record that anyone answering your description was here. Obviously he was here without authorization."

"Authorization? Who would have to authorize him?"

"GM ground base. You see, he'd need clearance for that pneumochair of his because of its magnetic field or whatever."

"He couldn't get aboard without it?"

"I don't see how. The only other way would be for Daddy to offer clearance."

"He could do that?"

"Certainly; if he wanted to. But he never has."

"He got on board somehow."

"Well, if he did someone else must have seen him. He was in a whole room full of cadets, wasn't he? What class was it?"

"I don't know," Spence moaned. "I can't remember. I wasn't there for the lecture. Anyway, confirming his existence isn't the point. *I* saw him—so what if the whole colony saw him, too? I want to find out who he is."

"Are you sure it's important? I mean, it won't change anything one way or the other, will it?"

"I don't know what's important or what's not important any more. Everything's getting so confused. But yes, I feel it's important in here—" he thumped his chest. "Don't ask me why, I just do."

Ari stepped close and laid a cool hand against his cheek. "It's all right, Spencer," she soothed. "No need to get heated up over this. We're with you. We'll work this out, you'll see."

Spence calmed under the girl's touch. He peered deep into the cool blue eyes and brought his hands up behind her neck.

"You are an angel."

"Spence, can't we tell Daddy about all this?" Her look implored him and he understood how hard it was for her to keep secrets from her father.

"Soon. Very soon now we'll tell him everything. I promise. But right now I'd rather as few people know about any of this as possible. There will be less chance of a slipup that way."

"All right. I do so hate to deceive him like this. I feel so guilty."

"You're not deceiving him. Anyway, we'll tell him soon enough."

They kissed then and held each other for a moment. Ari broke away first. "I've got to get back to the office. I'm watching Mr. Wermeyer's desk today. He's conducting a tour for some plastics manufacturers. They've got a congressman or lobbyist or some sort of high muckymuck with them. If you see any of them, stay out of the way; they'll talk your leg off."

"I thought that was your dad's job—to entertain muckymucks."

"Usually it is, but he's in seclusion today for some reason. I haven't even seen him." She smiled brightly. "Will I see you tonight?"

"Yes. Tonight."

She blew him a kiss and vanished through the ferns. Spence watched her slim form blur as it merged with the green and gold of vegetation and sunlight beyond the shady hollow. He sat down and began going over the new information once again. He wanted to make sure he did not forget anything in order to give Adjani a complete report.

Hocking, eyes lit with triumph, twitched with excitement. "Gentlemen," he said, his voice booming through the speakers at either side of his head. His two henchmen looked at each other, uncertain how to interpret their unpredictable master's mood. "I have great news. Our inquiries have borne fruit."

The tidings, whatever they were, had put their chief in a munificent frame of mind. They grinned slyly at one another and waited for Hocking to tell them what he had discovered.

"Dr. Reston"—Hocking drew the name out in a long, sibilant hiss—"our wayward young genius, has been found. He is here on GM this instant, and very much alive!"

CHAPTER NINETEEN

"STAY IN here and don't move," whispered Adjani. "I'll see who it is and get rid of them."

Adjani had changed the access code to the door of his quarters and someone trying to punch in the old code had set off its signal. Spence, going through the drill, stepped inside the sanibooth and closed the panel to a crack so he could hear who it was.

In a moment he heard Adjani sing out, "It's all clear. You can come out."

Feeling like a burglar who had been discovered, he opened the door and crept out. The first thing he saw was Packer's fiery head bobbing excitedly.

"I don't like it," the big scientist was saying. "It's getting out of hand."

"What's up?"

"All we need is a little more time," Adjani explained.

Packer addressed Spence. "I had a visitor today. An inquisitive fellow from the insurance company. You were high on his agenda."

"Oh?"

"He was nosing around and found out about your disappearance; thought he'd check it out while he was in the neighborhood."

"What did you tell him?"

"I told him you'd joined a monastery—what do you think I told him?" Packer's jaw thrust forward angrily; his face was flushed and red.

"Hold on. I know you've stretched your neck out as far as it'll go on this. But don't go turtle on us now. A few days more is all we need."

"We're making great progress," Adjani offered.

The scowl on the big man's face dwindled away, soon to be replaced by a slight, impish smirk. "You know, I do believe I twisted the old boy's tail just a bit. It wasn't really necessary, but the guy acted like *I'd* made off with his precious Dr. Reston. He tried to give me a real professional cross-examination, but I cut him off pretty quick."

Adjani and Spence looked at each other.

"Besides," Packer continued, "this guy gave me the willies. Him in that pneumochair and all shrunken up like that. He looked like a skeleton!"

Packer stared at his listeners. "Hey, what's the matter?—I say something wrong?"

Two great curving hemispheres, blue in the light of a silvery moon, rose up like incandescent mountains—smooth, pale, and surrounded by a zigzagging wall which fell around them in a seamless black barrier. Spence looked and saw a tower, a thin heaven-poised finger, between the two domes shimmering darkly in the moonlight.

He sat on a stone ledge separated from the palace by a deep gorge. Between him and the palace, swinging in the wind rushing out of the chasm, hung an ancient bridge made of twisted rope and wood. He could hear the wind singing through the ropes and saw the frayed ends blowing on the breezes like an old woman's hair. The frail structure creaked as it danced, and the sound was a ghostly falling laughter which echoed away into the inky depths below. In Spence's ears the sound became the voice of his enemy jeering at him, daring him to cross the crevice on that bridge and come to the palace to face him.

He huddled with his hands around his knees, shivering in the chill night air, but then rose and went to the swaying bridge, gripping the frayed ropes with his hands and placing one foot cautiously on the footboards. At his first step the bridge bounced wildly. Spence drew back.

In a moment he worked up his courage again and stepped gingerly out onto the bridge. The laughter seemed to well up from the chasm below as he heard the roar of a crashing cataract, like the sound of an angry beast thrashing in its dark den. He closed his ears to the sounds and kept his eyes on the far side and walked on step by cautious step.

He reached the middle of the bridge and felt the sharp winds buffeting him, rustling his clothing. Then everything was still; the night sounds faded and a gentle warmth seeped into the air.

A new sound reached his ears—the sobbing of a young woman. He looked up and saw Ari standing on the far side of the brink. Her tears fell in liquid gems and sparkled on her cheeks. She was crying and lifting up her arms to him. Her long yellow hair was white in the moonlight and it drifted like moondust.

"Ari!" Spence cried and heard the name repeated again and again far below him.

He raised his foot and put it down and felt himself step into the air. His foot failed to touch wood and he fell, plunging headlong down into the gorge, spinning helplessly down and down. He screamed in terror and anger and saw the form of his love turn into that of a wizened old man who peered over the edge and laughed at him. The rocks rang with laughter, and he shut his eyes and screamed to keep out the hideous sound.

Then he was on his knees in a dirty, stinking street, narrow between the crumbling facades of buildings. The moon shone between the buildings from above and he could see far down the canyon-street to where it ended at a broad gray river.

He began walking toward the river and felt a pang of terror clutch at his heart. He looked behind him and saw nothing, though he heard the rush of muffled feet.

He started to run.

The feet ran with him and he saw on either side of him dark shapes flitting by to become lost in shadow. He peered over his shoulder and saw a churning black mass sweeping ever nearer to him.

He came to a courtyard bounded on all sides by a high wall. He stood in the center of the yard on crumbling stone, one hand pressed to his side, breathing hard and feeling the burning stab of pain in his side. All at once he heard them, his pursuers, coming down the narrow street behind him. He turned and saw hundreds of narrow yellow eyes and the curved white slivers of bared teeth. He heard an enormous slavering growl tearing up out of a hundred throats as the dogs sprang on him, their jaws snapping, hackles raised, ears flattened to their angular heads.

The dogs leapt as one and he felt himself sinking. The stone was cool against his cheek and he heard the ripping of his clothing and flesh as the beasts lunged for him. He felt their teeth in him and the white-hot searing pain . . .

"Spencer, hear me now. This is Adjani. If you can hear me, say 'yes.'"

"Yes."

"You are dreaming, Spence. It is only a dream. Do you understand?"

"A dream."

"Don't fight the dream, let it come. In a moment you will awaken and remember your dream. I want you to remember it."

"Remember." The word was soft and mushy. Spence was deep in his dream.

Adjani knelt close beside him, his lips to his ear. He spoke slowly and with authority, as a hypnotist would speak to his subject.

"Spence, I want you to wake up now. I'm going to count to three, and when I reach that number I want you to wake up. Do you understand?"

"Yes."

Adjani counted off the numbers and Spence awakened to see his friend standing over him.

"Adjani!" Fear and relief mingled in his voice. "I was dreaming!"

"Yes, I know. I heard you cry out in your sleep."

"You woke me up—"

Adjani nodded.

"It was terrrible. Horrible. Oh!" Spence made to rise up, but Adjani placed a hand on his chest and held him down.

"Tell me about it. Quickly, before you forget."

"I won't forget this one." He proceeded to tell his dream in vivid detail.

"Yes, very frightening," murmured Adjani when he had finished.

"Very. I remembered, Adjani. I remembered everything. I've never been able to do that before."

"I gave you a hypnotic suggestion. I thought it might help us."

All at once the significance of what Adjani was saying broke in on Spence's sleep-dulled brain. "The Dream Thief!"

Adjani nodded slowly.

"They know I'm alive. They're trying to get to me again."

"Was there anything in your dream that might give a clue to who they are or what they might want from you?"

'I don't know—it all seems rather bizarre. Dogs and castles and bridges . . . it doesn't mean a thing to me." He shuddered involuntarily as he remembered the flashing, slashing teeth tearing into him and heard again the sickening crunch of his own bones. "But it was so real! I've had lucid dreams before, but they were nothing like this. It was really happening."

"Maybe I shouldn't have awakened you so soon."

"I'm glad you did! They would have killed me!"

Adjani glanced at him sharply.

"Hold it!" Spence protested. "You don't think they actually could—no, it's impossible! You can't kill someone with a dream. Can you?"

CHAPTER TWENTY

THE SNUBNOSED taser gun seemed very natural in Tickler's hand. He held it steadily and surely; there was no hint of nervousness or jitters. It occurred to Spence that he had handled the weapon before under similar circumstances.

Spence had been waiting in Adjani's room for Adjani to return. "I'll fetch Ari and be back in a few minutes and we'll go over our plans for the trip down tomorrow," he had said and slipped out.

When he heard the signal Spence answered the door and found, not Ari and Adjani, but Kurt and Tickler, wearing the red and black jumpsuits and caps of the GM security force.

"You!"

"You have led us a merry chase, Reston." Tickler smiled a thin, snaky smile. "But now you're coming with us."

"I'm doing no such thing," said Spence. Then Tickler had drawn the taser—a mean little gadget which expelled a tiny electrified dart, instantly rendering its victim paralyzed and unconscious for two or three minutes.

Generally speaking there was no escaping a man armed with a taser.

"You will do as *I* say from now on, Reston." Tickler mouthed the words with special relish. It was clear he enjoyed his role as tough guy.

"Put that thing away, Tickler. Are you crazy?"

"Not crazy, doctor. Concerned. We've been very worried about you. When you didn't return from Mars we thought we'd lost you. It turns out that we were wrong. Happily so. Now that you're back we mean to hold onto you for a while."

"What is this all about? What do you want with me?" Spence hoped to keep them occupied until Adjani returned. It was his only hope.

"You *are* inquisitive, aren't you. But we have no time for questions now. There's someone waiting to meet you."

"Where are you taking me? I demand to know!" Spence shouted shrilly.

"Your demands mean nothing. Keep your voice down or we'll carry you out of here. Come on—" The taser waved him ahead. "Get moving."

"Just a minute. I need my shoes." Spence indicated his stockinged feet.

"Get his shoes for him," Tickler said. Kurt went into the other room where Spence had been resting. The assistant came back with his shoes. "Put them on," ordered Tickler. "Only you won't really be needing them once we get where we're going."

Spence took the shoes and sat down at Adjani's desk. He placed both shoes deliberately on top of the computer keyboard. He took the first shoe and put it on. When he picked up the second shoe he deftly tapped the ComCen key; the monitor flashed on across the room. Neither of the intruders noticed; their backs were to the screen.

Spence stood and said, "So you're taking me down to the docking bay, huh? Then where? Not back to Mars, I hope." As he spoke he pushed the DICTATE key and hoped that Adjani had the machine programmed the same way he did.

"No place as far as all that," answered Tickler. "You'll find the trip anything but boring, I assure you." He jerked the nose of the gun toward the door. "Now, get going. And I warn you, Reston—don't try anything or I will make you very uncomfortable. We have a vehicle waiting outside."

"Nothing but the best for the condemned man," said Spence. He hoped the machine had picked up their conversation.

"You're taking this very well," said Tickler. "I hope you have abandoned any notions of escape. I will not hesitate to use this on you. I've used it before."

"I bet you have."

Millen led the way into the corridor and took the driver's seat of a small electric car. Tickler and Spence sat facing one another in the back as the open vehicle moved noiselessly away with its red light flashing to warn oncoming pedestrians to stand aside.

"He's gone," said Adjani as soon as he entered the room. "Something's happened."

Ari looked stricken. "You mean they've taken him?"

"Right. But maybe we can still catch them."

"Look!" Ari pointed to the ComCen screen on the wall.

"Bravo! He left us a message." Adjani leapt to the computer console and tapped in instructions for an audio replay.

This is what they heard:

" . . . far as all that. You'll find the trip anything but boring, I assure you. Now get going. And I warn you, Reston—don't try anything or I will make you very uncomfortable. We have a vehicle waiting outside."

Then they heard, "Nothing but the best for the condemned man." There was a rustle and the faraway sound of people moving in the room. The first voice, faded and indistinct as the party left the room, said, "You're taking this very well. I hope you have abandoned . . ." The rest was lost as the portal slid shut.

Ari turned wide, horror-filled eyes upon Adjani. But her voice was calm and steady. "Do they mean to kill him?"

"I don't think so. Not yet, anyway. His reference to the condemned man was to let us know that he was under armed guard, I think."

"Where will they take him?"

"They mean to leave the station, I would guess—back to Earth somewhere."

Adjani bent over the computer keyboard and closed his eyes, his fingers poised above the keys. Then he smiled and his hands began moving over the keys in swift, precise movements.

"Come on!" he shouted, jumping away from the desk. "Let's hope that will hold them until we get there."

"What are we going to do?"

"I don't know yet. Come on!"

Kurt nosed the security car into a recharging berth just outside the entrance to the docking bay. Tickler took the opportunity to warn his prisoner once more. "We are leaving Gotham, Dr. Reston. Do not attempt to attract attention. Security has already been advised that we are transporting a seriously disturbed prisoner."

"You think of everything."

"Shut up!" snapped Tickler. "Move! And remember, I'm right behind you."

Kurt picked up a long bundle from the driver's seat of the car and led the way into the air lock. Red lights warned them that the outer doors were open. Spence was shoved forward to the long line of pressure suits hanging in their racks. He squirmed into one under Tickler's watchful eye and wondered whether the suit might stop a taser dart. He decided that it probably would not but that if the right opportunity presented itself he might chance it.

While Tickler donned his suit, the cadet held the taser on him.

"This will go down on your achievement report, you know," he quipped. The young man spit on the floor. "Not much for achievement, I guess. Oh, well, there's always computer maintenance."

"Shut up!" Kurt growled. "You've caused us enough trouble as it is. I don't have to listen to your smart mouth."

"It's all part of being a kidnapper. Occupational hazard."

"Shut up, I said! So help me I'll let you have it!"

Spence said no more, figuring he had pushed his luck about as far as it would stretch for the moment. Tickler rejoined them, looking like a deflated snowman in his suit.

"What's the matter, Tickler? Didn't they have one your size?"

"Put your helmet on," he ordered, and pushed the bleed switch.

He was still fumbling with the helmet when he heard the whoosh of escaping air. His ears popped and his nose trickled a thin pink thread of foaming blood before he got the helmet secured. Tickler had popped the valve at once rather than wait for the air to bleed off slowly. It was a dirty trick.

"Ready?" Tickler leveled the taser on him again and shoved him forward.

They walked out of the air lock and into the cavernous docking bay. Ahead of them, across a wide, empty expanse of gleaming duralum, two ships waited. One, the transport *Gyrfalcon,* dwarfed the smaller six-passenger shuttle—the one used by the director for his trips back and forth to board meetings and other special occasions. Between them and the ships waiting at the end of the tether ramps only a few roboskids moved about on their programmed errands; there was nothing to offer an escape.

They've thought of everything. They even picked a time when the maintenance crew is away and the outer doors open. That meant, of course, that anyone entering the docking bay would have to don a pressure suit and thus be slowed down considerably. Most likely any attempt to save Spence would come too late—he was not even sure if there *was* an attempt being made to save him.

Tickler pushed him across the floor toward the small shuttle. Halfway to the vehicle Spence saw a large figure emerge from the *Gyrfalcon* and come toward them. He thought the huge, hulking form vaguely familiar.

Closer, the figure raised an arm to them and stepped into their path. Through the helmet's wide face plate Spence recognized the smiling, good-natured face.

"Ah! Dr. Reston! It is good to see you again!"

"Hello, Captain Kalnikov. It's good seeing you again, too."

Kalnikov, his manner easy and unconcerned, looked at the two men with Spence. He smiled, showing even rows of large white teeth. "Are you and your friends going somewhere?" the Russian asked, his booming voice sounding tinny and distorted as it overpowered the helmet's radio.

"Yes, we are," replied Spence vaguely. "A little trip. Allow me to introduce you." Spence fastened on the stalling tactic which Kalnikov offered him.

"That won't be necessary," said Tickler sharply.

"Oh, nonsense," objected Spence. His mind raced for a way to let Kalnikov know he was in trouble. "I'm sure we have time for a little chat. Captain, I'd like you to meet my two former assistants—Dr. Tickler and Cadet Millen. Very thorough, both of them."

"Charmed," said Tickler. His eyes strayed to the shuttle.

"Have you ever been aboard the *Gyrfalcon*, gentlemen?" Kalnikov asked.

"Thank you, no," said Tickler. "Perhaps some other time." He moved as if to continue on his way. Kalnikov stopped him, laying a big hand on his shoulder.

"Do not think that it would be an imposition, please," said Kalnikov. His smile remained, but his eyes had grown cold. "I would be happy to show you around."

Tickler hesitated. Spence saw the hesitation and pounced on it. "We'd be delighted! Why don't you take us aboard?"

As they moved toward the great transport, he felt an electric charge of excitement run through him. The game had been moved to neutral ground and now he had a chance to score a few points of his own.

He had just put his foot on the boarding ramp when he heard another familiar voice inside his helmet. "Spence! Wait for us!" It was Adjani. He turned to see two bulky figures emerge from the air lock and dash across the floor. A quick glance to Tickler's face showed that his kidnappers were getting worried.

They waited while Adjani and Ari drew up. "We've been looking all over for you, Spence," said Adjani.

Ari, with a strange, defiant scowl on her face, pushed her way through the others and came to stand beside him. "You promised to take me to lunch today. Remember?"

"Gosh, I clean forgot," said Spence.

"All right!" barked Tickler. His voice buzzed in their helmets. "Enough of this charade! Get back all of you!" He drew the taser again and waved it at them.

Kalnikov stepped forward, thrusting Spence and Ari behind him. "That is such a little gun. And it has only one sting. How will you stop all of us, I wonder?"

Tickler nodded to Kurt who brought up the cloth-wrapped bundle he was carrying. The cloth slid off to reveal a stun rifle.

"Does that answer your question? Now back off, all of you. Reston, step over here."

"I'm sorry," said Spence. "Nice try, everybody." He made to step around Kalnikov and as he passed the Russian pilot a strange thing happened.

Kalnikov raised his arm and his glove suddenly shot off his hand

and flew into Tickler's face. There was a muffled whoosh and Tickler gasped as instantly a jet of white foam splashed over him.

Before anyone could speak or move, the foam jet was turned on the cadet and his face plate obliterated beneath the white mess. Spence saw his two antagonists reeling and heard their voices swearing into their microphones; then Kalnikov was herding everybody up the ramp into the transport.

Spence reached the top of the ramp first and turned to pull Ari through the portal. Adjani jumped through and then he ducked inside. Kalnikov was right behind him shouting, "Close the hatch!"

Just as the Russian reached the hatch he staggered, his eyes rolling to the tops of his sockets and eyelids fluttering. A strangling noise came from his throat, his head snapped back and his arms flung themselves wide as a convulsion passed through his mighty frame. He collapsed onto the ramp and Spence saw the taser dart sticking out of his still-twitching body.

He did not wait to see more but jumped through the hatch and ran into the interior of the ship. He saw Adjani motioning to him and he ducked after him into the next section.

"I couldn't get the hatch closed," said Spence as they huddled together in the next compartment. "They'll be in here in a second."

"I've got an idea," said Adjani. "Follow me."

Aware that their pursuers could hear every word in their own helmets, Adjani motioned for them to proceed aft. Inside the next compartment he pushed Spence and Ari into deck tubes and sent them and himself to the level below.

The three hurried further aft through the transport. They could hear Tickler and Millen, their rapid breathing and grunting loud inside their helmets; it made it seem as if they were inside their suits with them.

"Stop where you are!" shouted Tickler. Spence turned just in time to see the scientist level the stun rifle at him. He threw himself to the deck and rolled into the next compartment. Adjani punched the access plate and the door slid shut. Spence looked around—they were in the hold of the transport. Along the sides of the hold were the hatches of the empty landing pods. Adjani gestured excitedly toward the first hatch.

Ari dived into the pod with Spence behind her. Adjani jumped through and Spence threw the switch to seal the hatch. They were now safe within their own spacecraft. Adjani pressurized the cabin with a flick of a switch and waited a few moments until the light on the switch changed from red to green. Then he grabbed his helmet and gave it a sideways tug.

"Now what?" asked Spence. They could hear Tickler and Kurt pounding on the hatch outside.

"Get strapped in," said Adjani. "Hurry!"

"You can't be serious! We won't get anywhere in this."

"Where do you want to go?" asked Adjani, heading for the small pilot console.

"Earth, I guess. Wasn't that the plan?" He stared at his slim, brown friend buckling himself into his seat.

"This is a landing pod, isn't it? Well, we're going to land it. Now get yourself strapped in."

It had not occurred to Spence that the landing pods could make such a trip, but they could at least get out of Tickler's range and then figure something out. "Okay," he shouted when he had thrown the straps over him. "Just one more thing: you sure you know how to drive this bucket?"

"The question does not deserve an answer. Everybody ready? Hold on!"

There was an immediate rumble as the pod jettisoned from the transport. A pressure forced them back in their seats as if a giant hand had pressed on them. "I'd give a month's pay to see Tickler's face right now. I'd hate to be in his shoes when he reports to his boss."

Ari had been quiet since they entered the pod. Spence looked at her and she looked back, forcing a small, tentative smile.

"I'm sorry I've mixed you up in all this. You could have been hurt back there."

"I was mixed up in this a long time ago—from the day I met you. I'm all right."

'You sure?"

"I'm fine. I just haven't had much in the way of combat training."

"Don't worry. That's behind us now." Spence tried to sound assured, but his tone fell short of persuasive. The truth was he felt their troubles were only beginning.

CHAPTER TWENTY-ONE

HOCKING'S gaunt face had taken on the coloring of a ripe tomato. He appeared ready to burst. But when he spoke, his voice was ice. "You let him get away! Fools! Idiots! You let him escape. Ortu will hear about this! Oh, yes he will. And I hope he deals with you as you deserve. I won't stop him this time!"

"Please!" cried Tickler. His moleish face was contorted in fear and anguish. "It wasn't our fault. That Russian pilot, Kalnikov—he *knew* about it."

"How could he know? Unless you were careless. You gave Reston an opportunity to warn them."

"There was no way he could. I swear it! Please, believe me!"

"You've ruined everything. Reston will be that much harder to catch now that he knows we're after him. He won't be taken by force, that's certain." Hocking swiveled away from his two quaking underlings. He seemed to relax somewhat as he pondered the situation. When he spoke again, it was mostly to himself. "No, it must be something subtle. It would be better if he came of his own accord. Yes, he must come of his own will—that way he can be guided more easily, and he will be receptive to the stimulus."

Tickler sensed a ray of hope in Hocking's change of demeanor. "That girl—we could get her."

"Would he follow her?"

"To the ends of the earth," said Tickler.

"He's in love with her," put in Millen.

Hocking's eyes sparked with interest. A thin, skeletal smile drew his lips taut. "There may be something in what you say," he mused. "Perhaps this is precisely the opportunity we've been looking for."

Then he snapped, "All right! This won't be easy—we don't even know where they're headed yet, so we'll have to improvise. Here's what we'll do . . ."

The discussion that followed was brief; it ended with Tickler and Millen bolting for the door and dashing away to carry out their new orders, glad for the moment to have saved their skins.

As soon as they had gone, Hocking propelled himself to ComCen console across the room. He tapped in a code and waited. Seconds later a voice said, "Wermeyer, here."

"The takeover is begun. You will put Phase One into operation at once."

"So soon? But—" The voice was a whisper.

"Immediately! This is the chance we've been waiting for."

"They are to be held upon landing. They have stolen a spacecraft. They are fugitives. You are the director of this station; you can order their arrest. You will do so."

Director Zanderson, his round face pale with fear and worry, fumbled for words. "I—I don't know if that's ah, possible."

"Oh, it is possible. In fact it is precisely what will happen."

"I don't want Ari involved in this. She's not part of it. She doesn't know anything. Leave her out of it."

"We're not interested in Ari. She'll be turned loose immediately." Hocking could see he was finally getting through to the frightened man and so softened his tone to a persuasive coo. "Of course, she shall be spared any unpleasantness."

"What about the others? Reston and Rajwandhi? What have they done to you?"

"They have stolen some very expensive secrets—a kind of tech theft, if you will. We want them stopped before they sell what they know."

"I still can't believe it of them. Are you sure?"

"Positive. Why else would they run away like they did? I did not mention it before because I did not want to alarm you, but I think it possible that they intend to use Ari for ransom in case there is trouble."

This last remark drew a quick, worried look from the director. "They wouldn't dare!"

"They are desperate men."

"To think I trusted Reston; I grieved for him—and to think he was alive all this time, hiding here."

"Yes," said Hocking. "Now send that order."

Director Zanderson pressed a button and leaned over his desk and spoke into the wedge. "Mr. Wermeyer, have ComCen clear a signal for me to ground base."

In a few moments his assistant's voice replied. "Done. The signal's open. Channel two."

The director pushed another button and a tone code sounded over the speaker in the wedge, and then a lady's voice said, "ComCen GM ground base, can I help you?"

"This is Director Zanderson. Get me head of security. This is urgent."

"Thank you," said the lilting voice. He might have been ordering flowers.

A second later he was talking to head of security for the GM ground base. He diplomatically described the situation and ordered the man to apprehend the two suspects and hold them. His daughter, he said, was not to be touched. He was to be notified as soon as they had been taken into custody. The security chief offered his assurances of a clean and professional grab, promising his utmost cooperation and that of his men, and asked for details of the craft and its ETA.

"It should arrive at five o'clock this afternoon your time. That's fourteen hundred GMT."

"I'll notify you personally as soon as they are safely in hand, Director. Don't worry about a thing."

"Thanks, Chief Tatum. I'll be waiting for your call."

Hocking's henchmen were waiting when he returned from his talk with Zanderson.

"I am an absolute genius," crowed Hocking as he swept into the chamber. "I was magnificent!"

"He bought it?" inquired Tickler, wringing his hands.

"He took the bait like the big fish he is," smirked Hocking. "Ah ha!" he laughed suddenly. "You should have been there. It was priceless. I have him convinced that they have kidnapped his precious daughter. He's putty in our hands, gentlemen. When the time comes he'll follow like a lamb."

Tickler allowed himself a smile at their good fortune. He turned to Millen who beamed back at him.

Hocking continued. "Of course, I'm not for a moment forgetting your failure in this matter. But I will excuse it this time. It seems to have brought about a turn of events even better than we could have hoped for. Now *they* are the ones with the GM ground force on their tails, not us. And Zanderson is so confused he doesn't know what to believe. Their stealing that landing pod clinched it."

"What's next?" asked Tickler. He was becoming caught up in his master's contagious good cheer.

"We get ready to move out. There won't be much time—we'll have to strike and strike fast. Ground security has been notified, but if we can find out where they intend to land we may be able to save ourselves a lot of trouble. I will return to Zanderson's office to wait—I don't want to let him out of my sight. I'll be there if any calls come through."

"What about Kalnikov?" asked Kurt. "Won't he talk?"

"He can say anything he chooses; it won't matter. I was able to convince Zanderson that the taser belonged to Reston and that Kalnikov was in on the conspiracy. He accidentally got shot by his own side and left behind. Whatever he says will be assumed to be a lie. Besides, Williams has him wet-sheeted in one of his wards. No one will be seeing him for some time."

"Then this is it. The takeover has begun."

"That's what I've been telling you, gentlemen. Very soon now the station will be ours."

Adjani nursed the landing pod along a precision course which allowed for no margin of error. The fuel cells of the small craft had not been designed for extended flight, but since they had no intention of returning to the station Adjani figured, with the help of the on-board navigation computer, that there would be enough to get them down safely and with some speed. Spence and Ari were trusting that he was right.

"They will undoubtedly be waiting for us," said Spence. "There's no telling what Hocking has been up to. It's four hours since we left. They've had time for almost anything."

"I think we ought to call my father," said Ari. "We could let him know we're okay and warn him about Hocking and the others. He could also get us landing clearance at the base."

"I don't think it will be safe to land at the base. We'll have to choose an alternate landing spot." Adjani bent over the computer monitor and tapped the keyboard quickly. "We can land anywhere within a radius of twenty-five kilometers from the base if we want to be on the safe side. Otherwise, just pick your spot and I'll do my best to put her down anywhere you say."

"In other words, you don't know *where* we're going to land, do you? It's a shot in the dark."

"I wouldn't say that at all. We're safer in here than in the shuttle. It's just that the computer memory isn't charged with coordinates for landing in the continental USA."

"Oh," said Spence. "So what do we do?"

"I could put us into orbit—we'd have time to pick out a place on our first couple of passes before our orbit started to decay."

"I take it big cities are out."

"Not at all. This machine was designed to land almost anywhere. We just won't have enough fuel to be picky. Anyway, we wouldn't want to come down in Pittsburgh rush-hour traffic. Why? What are you thinking?"

It's just that since we'd planned to go to Boston anyway, why not try Boston Metro? Land on one of the old abandoned airstrips. They're running mostly rocketjets out of there now anyway."

"Daddy could get us clearance, I'm positive," put in Ari. "He could get us our coordinates, too, while he's at it."

"Why didn't I think of that?" mused Adjani.

"You two aren't the only ones with brains, you know," Ari said with a flip of her head.

"Precisely."

Adjani fiddled with the ComCen pac and in a few moments raised the signal channel for the space station. He matched the landing pod's signal and then sent the ID code. A second later the clear calm tones of a ComCen operator rang out.

"Hello, Daddy?" Ari chirped as soon as the call had been put through to his office.

"Ari! Darling! Are you all right?" There was the concern of a distraught parent in the director's voice.

"I'm fine, Daddy. Really, I am. You probably know all the details by now—"

"I know what's been going on, my dear. Believe me, I've taken steps to remedy the situation."

Spence and Adjani exchanged questioning glances. Perhaps Tickler and Millen had been caught.

The director continued. "It must have been awful for you, my dear."

"I'm fine. Don't worry about me."

"Where are they taking you? Do you know?"

"We're going to try to set down at Boston Metro. Can you get us clearance? We also need the coordinates, Daddy. I think if you can get those two things for us, nothing will go wrong."

"I'll do anything you ask, dearest. Anything." There was a long pause. "Are they treating you all right?"

"Of course! Don't be silly. We're going to see Mother. Daddy? Are you still there?"

Another long pause ensued, and then the director said in a voice shaken or surprised, "I'm here. Why, Ari?"

"It's really too complicated to explain right now. But I'll call you when we're through. Don't worry, it'll be all right. Just promise me you won't get your blood pressure up."

"I promise, dear. And I'll have the clearance and coordinates transmitted as soon as possible."

"Thanks." She glanced at Spence and Adjani and then said, "I guess that's all for now. I'll call you after we've seen Mother and I'll tell you all about it."

"I'll wait for your call, dear."

Ari said good-bye to her father and turned to the others. "He didn't sound too good. He's terribly worried, I can tell. He didn't even ask about either of you."

"I suppose I'd worry, too, if my daughter was galloping all over the

galaxy shooting it out with ill-tempered ruffians. Of course, he's worried."

"You know," said Adjani slowly, "I think he thought we had kidnapped you."

"What makes you say that?" Ari laughed. "He would never believe
such a thing. How could he?"

"How was that?" asked Director Zanderson.

"Perfect," replied Hocking. "You were perfect. Very convincing."

"I guess I'll call Ground Security and have them picked up at
Boston Metro."

"Not so fast! I have a better plan, Director. I believe I'll go down
and apprehend them myself."

"You? But why not—"

"Tut, Director. I assume you would rather keep this thing as quiet
as possible? With your daughter involved, you must consider the effect
of such publicity."

"I don't trust you, Hocking."

"Then come with me, Director. Yes, that's splendid! We'll go
together."

CHAPTER TWENTY-TWO

To ONE who had endured the artificial interiors of Gotham
and had left his footprints in the rock-strewn red dust of Mars, the
sparkling white mansion with its three-story white columns and its red
brick wall joining the white gravel drive across a lawn of smooth-
shaved green grass looked to Spence inexpressibly old, almost
medieval. Holyoke Haven, only shouting distance from the sea, had not
changed at all in three hundred years. Once the home of a wealthy
owner of sailing ships, it now sheltered, as a safe harborage, the troubled souls who roamed its corridors and muttered along its hedgerows.

Spence was surprised there was no fence. "They don't need one,"
explained Ari. "The patients here are very well looked after. Each one
has an attendant with them virtually every minute of the day. They are
very exclusive; they don't take violent or dangerous patients."

He would have been further surprised to learn that those stately
walls housed the relatives of fine old families, kings of commerce, and

politicians—weird sisters whose presence in public would have proven embarrassing and perhaps unsafe.

They walked quietly down cool hallways after registering at a small antique desk with a kindly elderly lady who wore a large purple orchid pinned neatly to her pink uniform. "Your mother will be so glad to see you, Ari. And your gentlemen friends, too." The old woman sent them off with a light flutter of her hands, as if to cookies and milk in the parlor.

Spence found the juxtaposition of the grand manner of the place against the grim insanity of its patients a little hard to bear. He was haunted by the feeling that he had been and, for all he knew still was, very close to taking up permanent residence in such a place. Still, it was far from the snake pits of fifty or a hundred years ago. With a morbid interest he found himself reconnoitering the asylum with the air of a value-conscious consumer and feeling a little like a potential lodger on a rental tour.

Then they were standing before a wooden door and Ari was knocking gently. The door opened and a round smiling face peeked out. "Ari! How good to see you!" The nurse glanced beyond her to the two young men. "You've come to see your mother, of course."

"Of course. Belinda, I'd like you to meet my friends." She introduced Spence and Adjani and said, "Is Mother up to a visit?"

"She's been asking about you today." The nurse opened the door wider and ushered them in. Her eyes round with animated disbelief, she said, "And here you are! I never would have believed it. She said you'd come—and here you are!"

"Thank you, Belinda. You may leave us. I'll call you when we're finished."

"I was just about to take her for a walk on the lawn. Perhaps you would like to do that with her."

"Yes. We'll chat first and then a walk would be just the thing. Thank you."

The attendant clearly wanted to linger nearby, but Ari adroitly pushed her out of the room and closed the door so they would have privacy.

"Mother?" Ari crept close to the old red chair. The woman sitting in it had not so much as glanced at them all the time they had stood at the door. Now she turned toward them for the first time.

Spence recognized the mother of his sweetheart; they were as alike as mother and daughter could be, as close as look-alike sisters. The woman was trim and youthful, though her hair had faded to a darker blonde and tiny lines creased the corners of her eyes and mouth. Her eyes were just as blue as Ari's but they were different: wary, furtive, somehow sly. This is what shocked him: they were the eyes of a wild and hunted creature.

"Ari! You've come! Oh, at last you've come. Did you get my letter?"

The woman reached out her hands and Ari stepped in and hugged her mother. It could have been a normal homecoming. Spence turned away and looked out the wide open French doors onto the placid lawn outside.

"I didn't get your letter, Mother. Did you write me a letter?"

"I did." She shook her head fiercely, and then looked puzzled. "At least, I think I did. Didn't I?"

"It doesn't matter; I'm here now. What did you want to tell me?"

"Tell you?"

"What did you want to tell me in your letter?" Ari spoke to the woman in calm, patient tones as if she were a child, a shy, apprehensive child. Spence began to feel that their trip had been for nothing. He could not imagine they would get any useful information.

"How nice you look, darling. How pretty you are. I'm going to make you a beautiful new dress. You'd like that?"

"Of course, I'd love it. What did you want to tell me in the letter?"

"About the Dream Thief, Ari."

At this Spence faced around at once; maybe they would discover something after all.

"What about the Dream Thief, Mother?"

Adjani, who had been hanging back, came to stand beside Spence between the woman and the French doors.

"Who are these men? Do they work for *him*?" She shuddered as she said the word. Clearly, she referred to the Dream Thief.

"No, they're friends of mine. But they want to know about the Dream Thief. They want to know about him so they can stop him. You would like that wouldn't you, Mother?"

"No one can stop him!" cried the woman. "It's too late! Too late! He is too powerful! He was here, you know. He came to see me." She suddenly adopted a sly, conspiratorial tone.

"He was here? Dream Thief?"

"Yes. He came to see me and he said he would come back."

"What did he wish to see you about?"

"To give me a present. A beautiful little present."

"Where is the present? I don't see it." Ari looked around the room.

"He will bring it when he comes back. He said he would. I must wait and do as he says."

"When was the Dream Thief here, Mrs. Zanderson?" asked Spence.

"I don't know you, young man," the woman replied as if Spence were a stranger who had accosted her on the street.

"This is Spencer Reston, Mother. My friend, remember? And this is Adjani. He's my friend, too. They've come to see you to ask you some questions."

The woman looked at them closely as if she wanted to remember them in order to describe them later. "I'm glad to know you, gentlemen." She offered her hand. Both men took it in turn.

"How nice to meet you, Mrs. Zanderson," said Adjani. There was not the slightest trace of condescension in his manner. "Could you tell us about the Dream Thief? I'd very much like to know."

Slowly she came to herself, as out of a daydream. "Oh," she sighed softly, "have I been carrying on again?"

"No, Mother," replied Ari. Her mother reached up and patted her hand absently.

"I hope I haven't embarrassed you in front of your friends." She smiled ruefully.

"Nonsense," said Spence. "We'd like to help you if we can."

"I wish I could believe that; I'd very much like to be helped."

"Suppose you just tell us what you know about the Dream Thief." Adjani spoke normally, but he seemed to radiate a warmth and, Spence thought, a love which drew the woman out and settled her mind. He had never witnessed anything like it; Adjani's influence was magical.

"It was many years ago now." The bright blue eyes held a faraway look as memory came flooding back across the years. "I was a little girl. My father was a professor; very stern, very upright he was. There was just me and my mother. I used to play outside every day with the children. We lived way up in the mountains, maybe seventy-five miles from the city, in a tiny village called Rangpo.

"It was beautiful there. The seminary was an old monastery, I think. It had the most beautiful courtyards and gardens. My father taught there and we had a little house nearby. I can still see the little purple wildflowers that grew along the road. Passion flowers we called them; I don't know what they were. And safflowers—red and yellow, all over the hillside. It was lovely.

"There was an ancient palace nearby. We used to go sometimes to look at it. But only from a distance. You couldn't go there; it was too dangerous. The bridge was very old and decrepit. I used to wonder what kind of treasures lay inside it. There was certain to be gold and rubies—all the children said so. But they said the palace was guarded by the demons of the Dream Thief, and they watched over the treasure and whoever dared to touch it would be stricken down dead.

"One time I asked my father about the demons. He said it was just backward superstition, the kind we had come to wipe out. But none of us ever went to the castle or even near it. We were too afraid."

Spence noticed that the woman's voice had become softer, higher. She was experiencing her childhood again. Ari, in rapt attention, sat at her side with her hand clasped in her mother's. Very possibly she had never heard the story of her mother's childhood before.

"But you did go there, didn't you, Mrs. Zanderson?" Adjani said. The woman nodded.

"Yes, but I never told anyone about it. I was afraid." Her eyes showed the depths of that old fear.

"What happened?"

"It was a few days after my twelfth birthday. My mother told me that I was a young lady now and that I could start making up my own mind about things. I decided that I wanted to go look inside the castle and see the treasure. Father had said there were no demons, so I went. I was grown-up, so I didn't tell anyone.

"The castle was a long way; by the time I got there it was late afternoon. The shadows of the mountains were creeping into the valleys. I went across the bridge and it held me up. I went up to the castle and looked through the holes in the gates. There was nothing there. The courtyards were empty and full of dried leaves; the stones were all moss-covered and rotting away. It looked as if no one had ever lived there. I began to believe that there *were* demons—I never really stopped believing in them, despite what my father said.

"I heard something strange, like singing, only not like any singing I had ever heard before, coming from one of the buildings inside the walls. It grew louder and I waited to see if someone would come. I hid behind a bush outside the gates, but no one came.

"I could not get in the castle—the gates were locked and the walls were too high. Anyway, I don't think I really wanted to go in at all. I just wanted to look inside and see what I might see. But I waited until the music stopped and when nothing else happened I started to leave. I did not want to be out alone in the hills after dark. That was when the Dream Thief came, they said. He was an evil god and a powerful one. My father said there was only one God and he was love. But my friends said that he was only for the Christians.

"So I started back. I started to run and I ran toward the bridge. The shadows had grown long across the path and I stepped into a hole and fell down, twisting my leg. It was not a bad injury; it just hurt. I sat down in the path and rubbed my leg, knowing I would have to hurry back and hoping my leg would not hurt too much.

"As I was sitting there I heard something—not music this time, but something else, a strange sound. It came from the castle and it sounded like a great bird rustling to flight, yet it crackled like fire.

"I looked back over my shoulder to the castle and then I saw him, the Dream Thief. He was standing outside the gates and he was looking at me. He was very thin and tall and he had long arms. He turned his head and he saw me, and I looked at his two great yellow eyes. He didn't move or come near me, but I could feel him calling to me. I could feel it inside my head. I don't know how this was, but I heard him even though he did not say a word."

Mrs. Zanderson's voice had become a whisper. "Then behind him I saw three great black things—all hunched up like giant insects, but they had wings folded over their bodies and they came out from the castle to stand beside the Dream Thief. I felt him speak to them, but I could not understand what he said; it was just a feeling I got that he was talking to them. Two of them turned away and flew off and the other one came toward me. I knew then that he meant to come and get me. I jumped up and started to run.

"I reached the bridge and, without even stopping to think, dashed across it. I found the path on the other side and ran as fast as I could. I looked back over my shoulder and the demon stood on the far side. I kept running and when I looked back again he wasn't there. I thought he'd gone away. But—" Her voice pinched off suddenly.

"What happened then, Mrs. Zanderson? It's all right, we won't punish you," said Adjani. He spoke as one would to a child who feared the wrath of a parent for some imagined transgression. "You can tell us what happened."

The woman's eyes had gone empty. She was no longer in the room with them; she was reliving the past. Her face suddenly twisted into a contorted mask of terror. Her hands became claws which clutched the arms of her chair, her body rigid. When she spoke again it was a trembling whisper. The others had to lean close to hear the words; they held their breath.

"A shadow came over me and I looked up and saw the most hideous face—right above me. The demon stretched out his wings over me and reached for me. I felt his hands tear at me as he scooped me up from the ground. He clutched me in his arms—they were hard and brittle like insect arms. His wings buzzed as he flew; this was the sound I had heard coming from the castle. He carried me back to the Dream Thief and put me down on the ground. I was too scared to scream; I scarcely knew what was happening.

"The Dream Thief reached out a hand and touched me on the head and then all went black. I don't remember anything at all, just his hand reaching for me, his fingers touching me.

"The next thing I knew I was laying in the road just outside the town, not far from where we lived. I don't know how I got there, but the sun was almost down. It was a red, glowing sunset and the whole sky burned red and orange as if it was on fire.

"I got up and ran home and never said a word about what had happened to anyone. I really could not remember it very well anyway, not to tell about it. Just sometimes in my dreams it would come back to me. And sometimes I would feel the Dream Thief trying to call to me—I would feel his voice inside me. No words at all, just a feeling, and thoughts I knew were not my own. But I never went back.

"About a week later I got sick and the fever came on me. I could feel myself changing through the sickness. I was a different girl, but I kept it to myself and never told anyone about the changes I felt inside. I stopped playing with the other children. I stayed in my room and locked the door so the Dream Thief couldn't get me. I had bad dreams and couldn't sleep sometimes for several nights.

"And then, during one of my fevers, I slipped into a coma and slept for a long time, although it didn't seem very long to me. When I opened my eyes again I had forgotten all about the Dream Thief and his demons. It was like it never happened—only I knew it did. Inside I knew it, although I could not remember it or think about it. I just knew that something was there—deep in my mind, deeper than any other memory.

"I didn't get sick any more. After a while we went home to America and I tried to forget all about living in India. I tried to block it out of my mind . . ."

When she finished the room was silent as a tomb. No one moved or breathed; no one wanted to break the spell that had grown. But Spence had a question that needed asking—something the woman had said triggered an image in his mind.

"Mrs. Zanderson? What was the castle like? Can you describe it?"

"Yes," she replied, speaking in the same faraway voice, as one in a trance. "It was a strange castle, but it had a pretty name: Kalitiri. It had a high stone wall which kind of weaved back and forth, not straight. Inside the walls I couldn't see the main building very well but there were two large domes, round like globes, and a tower, thin and tapering. It was very tall. The gates were wooden but old. The wood was black and scarred, as if by fire or battle. I don't remember any more."

Spence only nodded. "Thank you. That has helped me very much."

Mrs. Zanderson seemed to come to herself then; she slumped back in her chair and her head fell forward. A long sigh came from her lips and she raised a shaking hand and rubbed her face. She looked around at the three visitors and smiled wanly.

"Oh, are you still here? Ari?"

"We're still here, Mother. You've been telling us about your girlhood in India."

"Oh? I don't remember. I hope I didn't ramble on. You didn't let me ramble on, did you?"

"No, no. I only hope we haven't tired you out." Ari's mother looked as if she could fall asleep at any moment. Her face was drained of color and her lids drooped heavily over her eyes.

Adjani stood and motioned to Spence. "Ari, we'll take a little walk out on the lawn. You can be alone with your mother and join us when you're ready."

The two men left through the French doors and walked out onto the green expanse. When they had moved away from the building a short distance, Spence touched Adjani on the arm. "Did you hear? Did you hear what she said?" He gripped Adjani's arm hard in his excitement. "I've seen it—the castle—in my dream! It exists! She's been there; she knows. It's real!"

Adjani nodded.

"And the Dream Thief, Adjani. She's seen him, too!"

"Have *you* seen him?" Adjani regarded him closely.

Spence hesitated. "Well, there's something strange about that—" A woman's scream cut him off.

"Ari!" cried Spence. "Come on!"

The two raced back across the lawn and into the room. It appeared nothing had happened. Mrs. Zanderson still sat in her chair, but her head fell to one side and she breathed deeply and evenly. She was sound asleep.

Ari was nowhere in sight.

Spence did not stop to look around. He dashed through the room and into the corridor beyond. He looked both ways up and down the long hallway, but saw only a woman with a suitcase creeping along the far side of the wall. He went to her.

"Did you see anyone run from this room?" He pointed to the room he had just come from.

The woman looked at him with wide, unseeing eyes. He knew then that his question was hopeless. "Is the ship coming? I must hurry to meet it. I must not be late."

He ran to the entrance and asked the receptionist if she had seen anything. "No," she told him. "No one has come in since your party."

"What about before?"

"No one all day."

He raced back along the corridor to Mrs. Zanderson's room. He looked in the open doors of the rooms he passed and saw the rooms were empty. One door was closed. He grabbed the doorknob and burst into the room.

An elderly lady turned to regard him with a motherly smile. She held a potted plant in her hands and caressed the plant's shiny leaves. She was not wearing a stitch of clothing.

Embarrassed, he quickly closed the door and returned to where Adjani was waiting for him.

"I can't find her," Spence puffed. "No one has seen her."

"You won't find her. She's gone." Adjani held out his hand and Spence saw a small black object—a little stone carving. "They meant for us to find this. It is a clue to where they are taking her."

"What is it?"

"I'm not sure. But I know who can tell us—my father."

Spence, mystified, looked at the carving and back at Adjani.

The day seemed very dark and cold, as if the sun had been blanketed in the sky. He felt a sharp sting of fear pierce him like an icy chill.

"We've got to find her, Adjani. Before anything happens to her. We've got to find her!"

CHAPTER TWENTY-THREE

THE TRIP to London from Boston left Spence nervous, irritable, and upset. Heat, fatigue, and worry joined forces to make him even more uncomfortable than he already was. On top of everything else he had a headache that wouldn't quit. His head throbbed every time he moved and drummed with a steady pulsing rhythm of dull pain. In short, he was miserable.

The last twenty-four hours were a blurred scramble. He and Adjani had chased over half of Metropolitan Boston to catch a plane to London to meet Adjani's parents and dine with them. Adjani's mother had insisted on fixing her son and his friend a meal they would both remember, although neither one professed to being at all hungry.

They ate a chicken pilau which contained okra and some other vegetable Spence could not identify over saffron rice. A cool yogurt and cucumber sauce helped soothe the fire of the curry. Fish baked in tents of paper and served with dill, peanuts, and chutney highlighted the meal. There were stacks of chapatis, the traditional flat bread of India, and endless cups of sweet milk tea.

Spence enjoyed the meal enormously and ate his share with no additional urging after his first polite nibblings. Following dinner Adjani's father took the two aside into his study. The Rajwandhis lived in spare, almost ascetic style in a small four-room apartment in an old building near the university. The room which housed the professor's library and served as a den when need occasioned it bore the stamp of a meticulous scholar.

Books lined shelves floor to ceiling. A small desk covered with a dyed yellow and green cotton cloth sat in one corner with papers stacked squarely in the center next to a great open dictionary. A single large window looked out upon a dusky cityscape where street lights began to twinkle as stars in a firmament of gray cement.

Professor Chetti, as his students affectionately called him, settled into an armchair and waved Spence and Adjani to seats on either side facing him. Looking somewhat out of character he took up a pipe and filled it with tobacco and lit it, savoring the first few puffs in silence.

"It is my English vice," he said at last with a happy chuckle.

He fished in his pocket and brought out the curiously carved stone charm Adjani had found in Mrs. Zanderson's room.

"You wish to know what this is, eh? I will tell you. It is very interesting. I have not seen one of these in many years and never outside a museum."

He got up and walked to one of his bookshelves and scanned the rows of books for a moment. He drew out a book and returned to his seat. He thumbed the pages of the book and smoked his pipe and then said, "Ah!" He turned the book around and offered it to them. "You see? Here." He pointed to a picture on one of the pages.

Spence looked at the picture and saw a carving of the exact figure Adjani had found. It was of smooth black stone and looked like a man with the body of an insect. The one in the book had a tail like a snake and wings partly outstretched. Its arms were drawn up over its head and it held a circular object in its hands.

"What is it?" asked Spence.

"It is an arca, an icon, a charm, you might say," answered the professor. "In many places in India it is believed that one keeps a demon away by wearing a charm such as this, representing an even greater demon."

"Fighting fire with fire," said Adjani.

"Yes, in a way. This is a Naga, a snake spirit. One of the older of the demons. And this one is itself very old. Look at the fine detail. You can see the eyes and eyelids, the mouth and nostrils, even though it is very small. Even the scales of the tail are individually carved. Yes, this one is very old. Later carvings are simpler, more stylized." He turned it over in his hands, regarding it with keen scrutiny. "Where did you get it?"

"It was found in the room of a friend," said Adjani vaguely.

"I see—you do not wish me to know." Chetti shrugged. "All right. But whatever you do, don't lose this. It is a very valuable piece."

"Tell us about the Nagas," suggested Spence. The scholar's words had struck a responsive chord in him.

Chetti settled back in his chair and laced his fingers together. "I would happily tell you all I know; the problem is where to start. It is a very long, confusing story. But I will try to make it understandable." He launched in at once.

"India is an ancient country of years beyond counting. The peculiar cultures of many peoples have mingled together over time, like the waters of streams flowing to a central river, and have created what is India today.

"But it is still possible to take short trips back along some of these tributaries, although many of them are lost to us forever. Such are the Nagas. Little is known now about where the belief came from. It may have originated almost spontaneously among many of the hill tribes of northern India.

"The mountains of the Himalaya were looked upon by these ancient people as the homes of gods and demons and other strange beings. They believed that in the high hills and among the snowcapped mountain peaks magic cities lay hidden from mortal eyes. The gods lived in these cities and went about their own business, for the most part staying away from men.

"There were three main groups. The Nagas, or snake spirits, dwelt in an underground city called Bhogavati and there guarded great treasures. They were usually represented as at least half human. They seemed to have special protective powers, possibly owing to their function as guardians.

"Then there were the Vidyadharas, or heavenly magicians. These created the magic cities of the high Himalayas and could fly through the air and transform themselves at will. Little is known about them; they had little to do with men.

"But some were more approachable by human beings; they were called the Rsis, or Seers. These were legendary wise men. Some say they were at one time mortals who became so wise that they were translated into heaven to become gods. Other accounts state that they were leaders of the Vidyadharas who could be petitioned by men in times of trouble, or who appeared during special times set aside for the purpose of teaching or instructing men in better ways of living.

"There have been many Rsis—the word now applies to anyone who is thought to possess great powers of magic or psychic ability. But the original Seven Rsis are thought to be the very ancestors of all the gods, and men too. They are mentioned by name: Marici, Atri,

Angiras, Pulastya, Pulaha, Kratu, and Vasistha. They came from heaven and built the magic cities to live in because they liked the Earth, having watched it from afar.

"The leader of the Wise Ones was a Rsi called Brasputi. He is a strange figure in the old legends—almost never represented in carvings or painting, and then in an odd, misshapen way—long arms and three-fingered hands. It was he who led the gods to the high mountains—they came in the fantastic *vimana;* that is, their aerial car—and who founded the philosophy of their civilization. That is to say he handed down the laws of government among the gods. He is the only one to be identified by a sign in the sky—one of the planets. Probably Jupiter or Mars. And Brasputi it is who rules the demons of the hills, although this was added perhaps much later."

Spence sat spellbound as Adjani's father talked. The names fell to his ear with an exotic, otherworldly ring. He visualized a time back in the dim and misty past of a newborn world where these beings walked and held commerce with men who worshiped them as gods. But there was also a strong suggestion of something else in his mind, which Chetti's words called up from his own, more recent past.

"What's the matter?" asked Adjani, studying his friend closely. "You look like you've seen a ghost."

"Not a ghost—a god." Spence shook himself out of his thought. The next instant he was standing before them, eyes burning with excitement. "It fits! It all fits! How could I have missed it?"

"Missed what?"

"Adjani, I have something to tell you. If I had told you sooner, maybe we wouldn't be in this mess right now. I haven't told you all that happened to me on Mars."

"Oh? There's more?"

"Adjani, you haven't heard the half of it."

Part III
KALITIRI

CHAPTER ONE

SPENCE FELT as if he had entered The Land That Time Forgot. India, apart from the glassy modern cities of the western coast and southern interior, was largely a country where poverty and population had united to halt the wheels of progress and even rock them backward a few paces.

It was a land retreating back into the past—almost as fast as the rest of the world advanced.

Spence found the contrast between the crumbling cities and ragged people and his own ultra-advanced space station too hard to reconcile. The foreignness astounded him, numbed him. He resented it, resented the screaming populace that reeked of stale sweat, urine, and other basic human smells. He resented their poverty and blamed them for their lack, although intellectually he admitted that one could not blame the patient for the effects of his disease. Still, his first reaction was a smouldering malice against a people who could allow themselves to sink so far.

In this reaction he was no different from the millions who had gone before him, and millions more who still held the blight of India against India herself.

The rocketplane ride into Calcutta had not prepared him for the scene that would greet him upon landing. He had felt the thrust of the rocket engines and endured the g-forces of takeoff. The plane rose to its peak altitude within ten minutes and began its gliding descent. Out of the small round window he saw the blue-black sky devoid of clouds above him and the crisp crescent curve of the Earth's turquoise horizon. He had placed his palm against the window and felt the heat from the friction of the air moving over the skin of the plane. Then they dropped out of the sky in the steep landing glide to roll to a stop outside a skyport like any other skyport the world over.

Upon emerging from the boarding tube the shock of India hit him hard. One moment Spence had been comfortable amid familiar surroundings, the next plunged into a churning mass of backward humanity. The effect could not have been more startling if he stepped out of the a time machine into the Stone Age.

"What now?" he asked Adjani in a bewildered tone.

"Are you all right, my friend?"

"No, but I'll get used to it." Spence stared dully at the chaos around him—diminutive travelers scurried like cockroaches all over the dilapidated terminal. The din was a muffled roar.

"Follow me," instructed Adjani. He began plowing through the crush as a man wading through floodwaters. "I'll get us out of here."

"In one piece, I hope," said Spence. His remark was lost in the havoc.

Adjani hailed a rickshaw outside the terminal and bundled Spence into it. He yelled something unintelligible to the driver and, with a creak and a sway and a clang of a bell, they were off, worming through the snarled traffic around the skyport.

If Spence's first glimpse of India shocked him, the view from the rickshaw crawling along the rutted streets sickened him.

Everywhere he looked he saw people, an ocean of people: dirty, poor, ragged, fly-bitten, naked, staring, grasping. He turned his eyes from one dismal scene only to witness another, still more miserable. And there were animals: white and brown cattle, little more than ambulating bags of bones covered with hide, roamed among the streets; horses, their large heads bobbing on bony necks, pulled rude carts; dogs, yapping endlessly, dashed between the wheels of careening vehicles; crows and other birds—even vultures—watched the stinking pavements for any morsel to fall, swooping down in an instant to seize the scrap in their beaks and make off with it before some dog or begger could grab it.

At the corners of large intersections were piled great heaps of refuse and garbage containing every kind of filth imaginable, and at least forty kinds of pestilence, thought Spence. On these dung heaps it was commonplace to see a dozen or so of the populace defecating or relieving their bladders while keeping the rats at bay with flailing sticks. Once they saw a huge wagon piled high with carcasses of cattle and horses—the dead scooped off the streets and destined for the rendering plant.

They passed by a railroad depot where nuns had set up a relief station for mothers with babies. Spence could see the sisters' white scarves moving among a sea of black heads that threatened to overwhelm their feeble effort. The cries of starving babies filled the air.

Everywhere, along the road, on traffic islands—every square centimeter of space—trash huts were erected; bamboo sticks for a framework, covered with rags. Bricks pulled up from the street or from a nearby wall established a fireplace. Other dwellings consisted of nothing more than a grimy scrap of cloth or blanket with stones to hold down the corners. On such a scrap a whole family might be encamped beside gutters running with raw sewage.

Billboards depicting smart, well-dressed Indians enjoying soft drinks or cigarettes, or wearing the lastest fashion creations, sheltered masses of naked homeless who lay wrapped in rags beneath their cheerful slogans. Roving throngs of orphaned children ran after the buses and wagons and rickshaws, chanting for coins or food or castoff objects.

The stench of all this—the cooking, rotting, festering, putrefying—hung over the city like a malodorous cloud, reeking in the hot sun. To Spence it smelled like death.

"The City of Dreadful Night," said Adjani. "Look around you, my friend. You will never forget it. No one who comes here ever does."

Spence did look around him. He could not help but look. It seemed to him that he had left the world behind and descended into hell. "It's a nightmare," said Spence.

They passed on through the murky air of Calcutta's human quagmire; past slums and open-air mortuaries with corpses stacked like cordwood, awaiting cremation; past children bathing in the gutters; past beggars collapsed on their haunches in the middle of busy streets; past crumbling facades of once-stately buildings blackened by the cooking fires of the refugees of the streets; past rusting hulks of old automobiles turned into brothels; past squalid, unwashed, infested, decaying habitations of meanest description.

Spence felt that he had contracted some cancerous disease in his soul and would never be clean again. He shut his eyes and lay back in his seat, but he could not cut out the cries of misery around him.

They finally rocked to a stop outside a tumbledown, tarnished building in the center of a commercial district. Spence surveyed the rotting structure, its yellow paint flaking off in great patches like skin off a leper.

"What's this?" asked Spence. The long, tiring ride had made him surly.

"Dr. Gita's home, remember?" Adjani jumped out of the taxi and spoke to the driver, offering him coins and asking him questions in a rapid babble of Hindi. "Come on," he called, motioning for Spence to follow as he strode into the disintegrating building.

Spence followed without attending to his steps and walked into a pile of cow manure lying on the sidewalk. He heard a snicker and scowled in the direction of the sound. A swift movement caught his eye, but he heard only the echo of small feet patter away.

Fuming, he cleaned his boot off as well as he could and made to enter the building. Just as he was about to disappear into the darkened interior, a loud voice boomed out above him. He looked up to see a dark brown face leaning out an upper window and beaming merrily down on him like an oriental sun; a pudgy little hand waved a cheery greeting.

"*Namastey,* Spencer Reston. Welcome to India."

Despite the unpromising exterior and the decrepit stairs swarming with cockroaches and mice, where a family of squatters had taken up residence, Dr. Sundar Gita's rooms were clean and fresh and fairly gleamed with the shining presence of the little man who inhabited them —along with his wife and five daughters. Spence had expected a dingy grime-caked hovel of the kind he had seen on his trip through the decaying city. In his foul mood he was a little disappointed to find the good doctor's rooms light and airy; he almost grumbled at the sight of fresh-cut flowers in a delicate hand-painted vase which brightened the living room.

"Sit down, my guests. Please, sit. We will drink tea," the round man said as Spence entered a square room which was dominated by a wide bed. "Now you can come out!" called Sundar and, turning to his guests, explained, "They have been waiting all day to meet you. They have never seen visitors from America before."

There was a titter of female voices and a bead curtain parted and a parade of dark-eyed beauties came into the room, each one bearing a small tray with something to eat upon it. They lined up in stair-step fashion before their guests, and Gita introduced his family.

"This is Indira, my wife," he said, "and my daughters: Sudhana, Premila, Moti, Chanti, and Baki." As he called their names each bowed demurely and stepped forward with their trays. Spence soon had a plate full of sesame cakes, date cookies, and rice balls balanced precariously on the arm of his low bamboo chair while he held a hot cup of jasmine tea first in one hand and then the other.

Their service completed, the women disappeared into the next room where Spence could hear their chippering whispers.

Dr. Sundar Gita was quite dark skinned, much darker than Adjani. He was short, coming only to Spence's shoulder, and almost as broad as he was tall. His full, round face shone with constant good cheer as if he were lit from within by a warm inner glow. His plump form was wrapped in an ivory-colored muslin suit, and, as if to emphasize his overall rotund shape, a bulbous blue turban topped him off.

As Spence was studying him, there came a loud shout from outside in the street below. Dr.Gita put down his cup and saucer and trotted to the window and leaned out. A quick conversation took place which ended with the doctor shouting, "No patients today. Come back tomorrow!"

He returned to his guests with an apologetic smile. "A linguist must make a living," he explained. "I am also the local dentist."

Spence sipped the rest of the tea and placed his cup on the floor. He felt a light tickle at his wrist and something cool and polished pressed against the inside of his hand. He looked down and saw an enormous snake curled beside his chair. The great gray and brown speckled creature was pushing its wide angular head into his hand.

"Ahk!" Spence yelped, jerking his hand away.

"Rikki! You naughty girl! Come away from there and stop pestering our guests." Gita gave the snake an exasperated look and the reptile slowly uncoiled itself and slithered silently away behind Spence's chair, leaving him with a prickly, queasy sort of feeling. He would almost have preferred having it beside his chair. There, at least, he could have kept an eye on it. Now he did not know when it might jump out at him again.

"Rats," Dr. Gita was saying. "They are such a problem in the city. But Rikki is a remarkable hunter. They do not bother me at all."

"Dr. Gita," Adjani began, "we are grateful that—"

"Please, I am only Gita among you learned men. And the pleasure is mine. When your message came last night I was very much excited to hear of your visit and of course I will help you in any way I can. Your father has been my dear friend all these many years, Adjani. I remember our school days fondly."

"Now." He spread his short hands on his round thighs. "What brings you to Calcutta and to my humble home?"

"I think I will let Spence tell you his story first, and then I will explain."

Gita turned inquisitive black eyes upon his guest and nodded, settling himself with a sigh onto the wide bed. This piece of furniture took up fully a third of the room. Spence realized that the whole family probably slept in that bed.

"What I am about to tell you may sound a bit—well, incredible, but I assure you it is true. Every word. And I ask that what I say will never be repeated outside this room," Spence began nervously. "May I have your promise on that?"

Gita touched his forehead and nodded with an oriental bow of submission. Spence could see the excitement mirrored in the black eyes, though his listener's face had lost all expression.

Taking a deep breath Spence began his tale. He told once again of his dreams, of his wandering lost in the deadly sandstorm on Mars and his discovery of the tunnels leading ultimately to the city of Tso. He told of his thirst and hunger—this made his listener squirm—and of the nightmarish illness. He described the oblong box and his manipulation of the controls, the strange sounds and sights that came from it, and lastly his meeting with Kyr, the Martian, and all the wonderful things he had seen and heard.

When Spence finished, an hour had elapsed like the blink of an eye. Gita sat as one in a trance, spellbound by the magic of his story.

"Truly fantastic," Gita said at last, breaking the fragile silence which had enveloped the room. "I have never heard anything like it. Incredible." He turned to Adjani. "You said I would be amazed, but that is not the half of it. I am astonished beyond words."

After another long silence in which Gita sat staring at Spence and nodding, muttering under his breath, he leaned forward and said, "Now, then. That is but half a tale, remarkable though it is. You did not travel halfway around the world to tell me that. What is it you require of me?"

CHAPTER TWO

NO SOONER had Spence and Adjani stepped out onto the lawn than a knock sounded at the door. Thinking it was the nurse, Ari had gone to tell her that her mother was a little tired and would not be coming down to lunch just yet.

As she opened the door she turned back into the room saying, "You take a little rest, Mother. I'll be back in a moment."

The next thing she knew she was jerked through the doorway. An arm shot around her neck and a hand covered her mouth—so quickly she did not even have time to scream.

"Don't struggle! Don't make a sound!" a voice whispered harshly in her ear. "We are going to walk down the hall. If you try to escape you will be hurt." With that she was dragged away.

Another figure pushed past them and she recognized the man's pinched features and rounded shoulders as belonging to Spence's assistant, Tickler.

When they reached the end of the corridor they paused and turned to Tickler, who was still standing in the doorway to her mother's room. Some signal must have passed between the two men because Tickler reached into his pocket and took out something which he tossed into the room. He then closed the door and came running up the hall toward them.

Ari was shoved out a side entrance marked with a red Emergency Exit Only sign. As the door swung open she heard a woman scream—it might have been her mother; it seemed to come from that end of the hall.

Then she was hustled into the back seat of a late-model tri-wheel which sped off with the man she now recognized as Kurt Millen behind the wheel. She yelled and scratched at the windows, and then at Tickler sitting beside her in the cramped backseat.

"You can scream all you want to, it really won't do you any good," said Tickler. "No one can hear you now. You might as well save your strength; we have a long trip ahead of us."

Ari's eyes were blue fire. She threw herself forward over the seat and tried to jerk the steering wheel from the driver. The car lurched to one side and skidded in the white gravel of the drive. Kurt swore and cuffed her with the back of his hand. "Keep her back there! She'll kill us all!"

Tickler pulled her back into her seat and brought out a taser. Ari looked at the gun and slumped back. "That's better," said Tickler. "I assure you I will use this if there is another outburst."

"I demand to know where you are taking me!"

"We're taking you somewhere where you can talk to your father, Miss Zanderson. He's very worried about you."

"Worried about me! Why? What have you been telling him?"

"Nothing all that serious, but you know how parents can get. I wouldn't trouble myself over it."

"They'll find me. Spence and Adjani will know what happened. They'll find me."

"Oh, we hope so, Miss Zanderson. We hope they do indeed."

The sky glowered with a gray, angry look, threatening rain before nightfall. A chill, shadowy dusk crept across the landscape as the car silently slid off the old highway and up a long, narrow gravel drive lined with towering elm trees, black in the failing light.

The angry sky and dark branches mirrored Ari's mood. She seethed in a silent black rage. *Someone* was going to know how she felt, and soon!

The car had passed up the regional headquarters of GM, as well as every other opportunity of stopping within the city. Instead, the driver had headed out on the expressway toward the country and, hours later, they were creeping up the road to an aging country house.

The house, pale in the yellow beams of the car's headlights, swung into view as the vehicle rounded a bend and pulled into a wide driveway. A falling-down barn loomed nearby, the darkening sky showing through the spaces between its loose boards as through the ribs of a skeleton. A light shone in a single window of the two-story frame house, glowing behind a stained and tattered shade.

On the whole the scene which met Ari's eyes was best described as dismal. But after riding in the car for the several long hours of their trip she ws glad to get out, no matter how bleak the surroundings. She was careful not to let the relief she felt at stepping out onto the crunchy gravel of the drive show in her face or actions. She wanted to maintain a hard, angry appearance. This plan, however, was abandoned as soon as she set foot in the house.

"Daddy!" The next instant she was in his arms and he was hugging her as if she had been rescued from the sea after forty days in a lifeboat.

"Oh, Ari! You're all right! I was so worried about you."

She stepped back out of his embrace. "Just what did you think had happened to me? And what are we doing here?"

Her questions went unanswered, for at that moment a large white ovoid object came gliding into the room. It was a pneumochair, and in it sat a sharp-eyed skeleton of a man, grimacing at them with a malicious twist of his thin lips.

"So, the wandering maiden has arrived. I trust you had a pleasant trip, Ariadne. Yes?"

"You!" she shouted, hands on hips in a show of defiance. She turned quickly to her father, who was wearing a sickly expression. "Daddy, who is this man?"

"Ari, please calm yourself." Her father placed a hand on her shoulder.

"I demand to know what is going on here!"

"You're safe now, that's all that matters, dear."

"Safe! I was safe before those two kidnapped me!" She threw an accusing finger at Tickler and Millen.

"There must be some mistake, daughter."

"There's been a mistake, all right. Daddy, answer me—what's going on?"

"Well, go ahead," said Hocking. "Tell her. She has a right to know."

Her father glanced dubiously at her and said, "Mr. Hocking has been helping me rescue you. I asked him to—"

"Rescue me? I didn't need rescuing. For heaven's sake, Daddy, Spence and Adjani were not holding me. We were escaping *him!*" She glared at Tickler again. "They were trying to kidnap Spence!"

Director Zanderson seemed to shrink into himself somewhat. He looked at Hocking. "Is that true? Answer me!"

Hocking's lips twitched; his eyes narrowed slyly. It was clear he was savoring the moment fully.

"Well, go on."

"Your daughter's absolutely right. It's Reston we're after. You just have the misfortune of being in a position of influence, you might say."

Director Zanderson's mouth dropped open. "I'm aghast!"

"You're more than that, you old buffoon. You are a hostage!"

"You can't do this! Mr. Wermeyer knows my whereabouts. If I'm not back soon, he'll—"

"He'll do nothing. Perhaps he'll tell people you're vacationing, or that you've embezzled the payroll—it really doesn't matter. You might say that from now on Mr. Wermeyer takes his orders from me."

Director Zanderson's face went gray. Ari scowled furiously and her eyes became blue lasers burning out at her captors.

Hocking continued, "I'm afraid that's all the explanation we have time for. I have made some traveling arrangements for us all. Come along, please."

Just then the old house was shaken by the vibration of a jet engine firing up, and a low whine climbed to a scream.

Hocking disappeared through the doorway. Tickler and Millen followed, pushing the Zandersons before them out the back of the house where a small hoverjet was rolling across the grass in a clearing ringed with tall trees.

The plane turned and stopped. A hatch popped open and steps were lowered. The party boarded and the hatch resealed itself. The whine of the engines increased and the plane rose vertically until it cleared the treetops, then streaked off into the night.

CHAPTER THREE

"SUPNO KAA CHOR," said Adjani. The afternoon light slanting in through the woven screen over the window cast a diamond-studded shadow on the walls. Gita sat nodding on the bed like a Buddha. He leaned forward and Spence saw his dark face glistening with perspiration.

"Ah, the Dream Thief," whispered the little man. "It has been a long time since I heard of him."

"We believe," said Adjani, carefully choosing his words, "that he exists. The Dream Thief is real."

Gita did not burst out laughing, nor did he show any outward signs of disbelief—like throwing up his hands or rolling on the floor, which was what Spence expected. Instead, the linguist-dentist flicked his quick eyes from Adjani to Spence and back again in an expression that said he was prepared to suspend all judgment until the facts were heard.

Spence decided then and there that they had come to the right man; he liked Gita from that moment on.

"I see." The Indian smoothed the folds of his trousers. "I suspect you are prepared to support that assertion."

"We are," said Spence. "Kyr told me that their race fled Mars as soon as their technology made starships possible. The Martians went in search of new worlds to colonize, finding none within our own solar system which could sustain life."

"What about the Earth?"

"I asked that, too. Kyr said that they have known of Earth's life-sustaining capabilities for thousands of years. Some of them even visited our planet in times back, but found it already inhabited by sentient creatures well on their way toward domination of the planet. They elected not to interfere with human development. Their mere presence would have drastically changed the course of our history."

"Remarkable."

"Yes, quite. Considering that they could have come and taken control of the entire planet at any time and no one could have stopped them, I think they showed uncommon restraint. It took them several thousand years to perfect interstellar travel; meanwhile they lived in their underground cities and watched the wind and sand erode their planet to a dry red powder.

"But what if all the Martians did *not* leave the solar system as planned?" Spence underscored his point with the thrust of his finger. "What if some of them came back to Earth and established a colony here? What form would it take? How would their presence impact on the local civilization?"

"All very good questions, Spencer Reston." Gita watched him through narrowed eyes, his head thrown back. "Do you have answers?"

"No answers—suppositions. Theories." Spence stood and began pacing as he talked.

"The air of the Himalayas is very thin—much like the atmosphere of Mars must have been before the Martians left. Also those mountains are perhaps the most remote part of the whole planet, except for the poles and ocean bottoms. A colony settling there would never be bothered by curious Homo sapiens.

"But as the Earth became more populated they perhaps would be noticed. Suppose also that as they came and went they encountered various tribes of human beings with which they developed some sort of commerce. Over time these interactions, although rare, would become the subject of speculation and wonderment among the primitive human beings they encountered. And since the Martians lived apart in places inaccessible to normal men, and their ways were far above the ways of men, they would be looked upon as godlike, and their advanced technology would be regarded as magic."

"We have seen this in the last century," added Adjani. "The aborigines of Borneo considered airplanes magic and the white men who flew them were called gods. Any technology very far advanced beyond the accepted explanations of science is viewed as sorcery by the unenlightened."

"True, true," replied Gita. "Most of my patients still believe my drill is a magic serpent whose bite is only too real."

Spence stopped his pacing and came to stand in the center of the room in front of Gita. "Exactly. You would expect all sorts of stories and legends to grow up regarding these gods and their civilization—and all with at least a grain of truth to them."

"Yes, but after all these years . . . surely you don't think there can be any left? Do you? Either they would have died out, or become intermingled with human races. Or they would still be present and in such numbers that we would have known of them from long ago."

"I can't answer that," said Spence. "I don't know. But Martians have incredibly long life spans—thousands of our years. Suppose one is still alive and living here on Earth?

"I reawakened one of them. What if another never slept?"

Gita sat very still for a long time. Only the rise and fall of his full round belly showed he was still with them physically. Then as one starting from a spell he said, "Supno Kaa Chor, eh? The great thief of dreams still among us. Well, why not? It makes sense." He fixed twinkling black eyes on Spence. "I believe you. What do you think of that?"

Spence wanted to hug the man.

"What is more, I'll help you all I can—though I can see that will be far from easy."

"Good!" shouted Spence. "That's terrific."

"Maybe not so terrific," muttered Gita. "Before we are through you may well have reason to curse the day you ever set eyes on me."

Olmstead Packer sat with folded hands in the director's outer office. He was well into his rehearsed speech when a tall, stringbean of a fellow came out of the director's den.

"I'm terribly sorry, Dr. Packer, but the director has asked me to convey his regrets. He has canceled your meeting for this afternoon."

"I don't understand. I talked with him only yesterday."

"Yes, I know. He was suddenly called away on an important matter. He may be gone several days. Is there anything I can do until he returns?" Wermeyer gazed officiously at the big physicist.

"No, I can wait." Olmstead turned to leave. "I only wish he'd have let me know. That's all."

"Accept my apologies. He sometimes forgets these things." The way he said it gave the impression that Wermeyer was used to covering up for the director. With a shrug Packer walked out of the office.

This is strange, he thought as he walked along Gotham's trafficways. First Adjani and Spence disappearing and now the director. A strong hunch told him the two incidents were connected, but how? As he walked along he became more and more determined to get to the bottom of things as he saw them.

"And I know just where to start," Packer said to himself, making an abrupt aboutface in the center of the trafficway. "Kalnikov."

He arrived at the infirmary and stood tapping his fingers on the spotless white counter until the young woman looked up.

"Yes, may I help you?"

"I'd like to see Captain Kalnikov, please. I understand he's still here."

"Yes, of course." The white-clad nurse disappeared into another room behind the nurse's station. She was back in a moment looking at a chart of some sort. "I'm sorry"—she smiled up at Packer—"but your friend cannot receive visitors at this time."

"When, then? Can I come back later?"

"I'm sorry, I can't tell you that. You'll have to ask Dr. Williams. It's his order."

"What's wrong with him? Can you tell me that?"

"I'm sorry. We don't discuss our patients' cases with outsiders," she said. Packer felt a touch of frost in the air. "You'll have to ask the doctor."

"Bring the doctor," said Packer flatly. He was starting to resent the woman's tone.

"I'm sorry, he's not in at the moment." She gave him an icy smile. "Was there anything else?"

Packer increased his drumming on the counter. "No, you've been a world of help," he said and stepped away from the station. He walked to the door and then paused. His hand reached out for the access plate, but he suddenly grabbed his side and moaned.

"Oh, no!" Packer groaned. "Help!" He toppled to the floor in a heap.

"What's wrong?" cried the nurse, rushing out from behind the counter. "Are you having an attack?"

"It's my stomach," wheezed Packer. He squeezed his eyes up and contorted his face. "Oww! Help me!"

"We'll have to get you off the floor," said the nurse. "Can you get up?"

"I think so," panted Packer. "Oww!" He grabbed his middle and rolled on the floor.

"There, there. Easy now. We'll get you into bed and get some tests started. You'll be all right." She laid a hand on his forehead. "You're not feverish; that's a good sign. Shall we try it again?" She put her hands under his shoulders and rolled him up into a sitting position.

With some effort they got him back up on his feet where he swayed precariously and moaned at intervals like a wounded bull moose. She led him into the next room containing three beds, and Packer dropped into the first one.

"Don't move. I'll be right back," the nurse told him and ran out of the room.

Packer waited until the door slid shut again and jumped up out of bed. He approached the figure laying in the last bed.

"Kalnikov?" His voice was a harsh whisper. "Can you hear me?"

The man rolled over and opened his eyes slowly. His stare was dull and glassy. "You're not Kalnikov," he told the man.

Fearing he would be discovered Packer jumped back into his own bed and waited for the nurse to return. She came back in an instant and brought with her another nurse who carried a flat, triangular object which she placed on his chest. "Here, put this under your tongue," the second nurse instructed, pulling a small probe from the instrument.

Packer did as he was told and sighed now and again to add to the effect—as if he did not expect to tarry much longer in this world and did not greatly mind leaving.

"Normal, just as I thought."

Next he felt a prick on the inside of his arm just above the wrist. The nurse studied the machine on his chest and fiddled with a few knobs. "No trace of salmonella. How do you feel now?"

"A little weak," he said weakly. "But the pain is gone."

"Probably it was gas," replied the first nurse. "I'll bring the doctor in when he returns."

"Thank you, you're both kind. If I could just rest here for a moment I'm sure I'll be feeling better in a little while."

"Of course." The nurse packed up her instrument. "I'll check back shortly." She nodded to the first nurse. "She will stay with you for a few minutes."

"You're too kind," said Packer benignly.

"Nonsense." The nurse smiled prettily. "That's what we're here for."

Packer lay back and closed his eyes. The nurse sat on the edge of the bed and looked at him. *This will never do,* thought Packer. *I've got to get rid of her.*

He belched loudly and allowed his eyelids to flutter open. "Could I have an antacid?" he asked. "I think it *was* gas."

"Just as I thought. Sometimes it can be very painful."

"Yes, I have a little heartburn now."

"I'll go get you something. I'll be right back."

As soon as the nurse left, he was out of bed and heading for the door to the next ward. The wards were clustered around the central nurse's station and could be entered by interconnecting doors without going through the station. The next ward was empty, and the next contained three young women who stopped talking and giggled when he tiptoed through. The third ward he looked into appeared empty at first, too. Then he saw a lone figure in the far bed, wrapped head to toe in a white sheet.

Packer, fearing the worst, crept up to the bed and pulled back the sheet. Kalnikov lay flat on his back, his face the color of putty.

"Kalnikov." He shook the man by the shoulder. There was no response. He reached out a hand and placed it against the side of the pilot's neck. The body was warm and a pulse beat regularly in the throat. He jostled the man again.

"Kalnikov, can you hear me?"

There was a slight murmur.

"Wake up! Kalnikov, I have to talk to you. Wake up. Please!" Packer glanced around quickly and went on trying to rouse the Russian. When he looked back Kalnikov's eyes were half open and bore the glazed expression of one heavily sedated.

"Listen," whispered Packer, "I know you can hear me. Don't try to talk. Just blink your eyes if you understand me. Okay?"

The pilot raised and lowered his eyelids slowly and heavily, like the curtain at a Russian opera.

"All right, here we go. One blink for yes, no blinks for no. Got it?"

There came a slow blink; Packer thought he had never seen a slower one. He wasted no time in getting right to the heart of his interrogation.

"Kalnikov, now listen carefully. Rumor has it that you were jumped by Reston and Rajwandhi—is that true?"

No blink.

"Were you trying to help them?"

One blink.

"Hmmm. Were you injured in the fight?"

No blink.

"What? Did you understand my question?"

One blink.

"Then why are you here? To keep you quiet?"

One blink.

Suddenly a voice called out behind Packer. A man's voice, and he was angry. "Just what do you think you're doing? Stop!"

Packer turned to see Dr. Williams striding toward him. Behind him were two security guards with tasers in their hands. The guards were frowning and their tasers were aimed at him.

CHAPTER FOUR

THEY STARTED out at first light. Spence had not slept at all well. If not because of the hungry dogs that roamed in packs barking through the night, it was the sudden chilling expectation that Rikki the rat-catching python would mistake him for a rodent and strangle him. He was up and ready to be off as soon as dawn broke over the iron-blue, smoky skyline of Calcutta.

Gita had been up long before dawn making arrangements and seeing to last-minute details. He returned huffing excitedly and talking in gibberish, his round, dark moon face glowing with pride and good cheer.

"I have secured our passage," he announced. It sounded as if they were attempting a hazardous ocean crossing.

"How long will it take to reach Darjeeling?" Spence asked.

"A week. Maybe two if it rains." To Spence's look of amazement he hurriedly added, "You do not understand our roads. In the rain they dissolve and run away. They become rivers. It would take you a long time to swim to Darjeeling, and all uphill."

Gita scampered around his apartment throwing provisions and personal belongings into sacks and bundling them together. "One bundle for each," he explained. "That way if we must walk part of the way it will not cause too much strain."

Gita looked like a man who had lived most of his life investing in strain-avoidance schemes, and had become wealthy collecting the dividends.

"Is it really as bad as all that?" Spence asked, hardly keeping the naive bumpkin out of his voice.

"Traveling to Darjeeling will be like traveling back in time," Gita warned.

He had arranged for them to join a group of merchants camped about half a mile from his house. These men banded together to travel under the protection of armed soldiers, hired to defend them against the *goondas* and *dakoos*—bandits and outlaws living in the hill country. They would be moving at a snail's pace in rusty old gas-burning cars over once-smooth roads that had crumbled into little more than cattle tracks.

Spence and the others set out walking the few blocks to the caravan in the early morning light, tinged an oily brown from the smoke of ten million cooking fires throughout the city. They stepped carefully over the sleeping bodies of Calcutta's homeless who lined the streets like human pavement. Mange-ridden dogs ran yapping, poking here and there among mounds of putrefying garbage for morsels to eat. A hump-backed cow stood gazing at them with deep melancholy over a dead body where two crows perched on a stiffened arm, clucking their beaks in anticipation. Small children, already awake and crying, clung to their still-sleeping mothers, becoming quiet as the men passed.

The buildings lining the streets wore iron bars at windows and doors, though it seemed on the whole a useless gesture since, by Spence's estimation, anyone with little more than a strong resolve could have toppled them, they looked so tentative.

The three rounded a corner a few blocks away from Gita's house and saw the caravan. Their convoy consisted of five clanking sedans, a small bus loaded with objects of trade, and a jeep carrying three soldiers with old-fashioned M-16s leading the procession. It was already lined up, and the various merchants involved in the enterprise darted here and there to store their goods and pack just one more item on the bus. The soldiers came strolling down the street at a leisurely pace eating their breakfasts wrapped in paper with their fingers. Their rifles were slung on their backs and they laughed heartily among themselves.

This is our protection? Spence wondered.

The whole troop would have been comical if not for the fear Spence saw in the faces of the merchants. To them it was a life-or-death proposition with death an all-too-possible outcome. He found it hard to believe such conditions still existed in a world that was quickly hurtling itself toward the stars. He himself had walked on Mars, and these frightened merchants could not even conceive of such a thing. His world was as far from theirs as—well, as far as Kyr's was from his.

When they had walked the length of the caravan a tall, gaunt Indian with the pursed expression of a man perpetually sucking lemons hailed Gita and met them.

"This is Gurjara Marjumdar, leader of the merchants making this trip." The man bowed low, placing his hands together in the classic greeting.

"Your presence among us strengthens our purpose." He smiled a puckery smile. Later, Gita told Spence that with the money they had paid Gurjara to join the convoy the merchant had already made a profit.

"I have arranged for you to travel in my car," Gurjara said with some pride. "I hope you will be very comfortable."

It was all Spence could do to keep from remarking that perhaps they would be more comfortable if the car had springs. He could already see that the junker rode low to the ground, and as yet no passengers were aboard.

After a few more minutes of frenzied packing and tearful, heart-rending good-byes among the merchants and their families, the caravan, asthmatic engines gasping and sputtering, rumbled off. Gawking street sleepers staggered out of the way as the odd train of vehicles rattled past. Children and dogs ran beside as they wound through the streets, hoping for trinkets and shouting at the drivers to honk their horns—a request the drivers obliged with childlike persistence.

Spence marked their passage through the decaying city with numbed wonder. It was repulsive, and yet somehow fascinating in its lazy, sprawling decadence. He had never experienced anything like it.

Behind the train a small army of ragged wayfarers walked or rode bicycles. They too were making the trip to Darjeeling; though lacking the money to hire a car or other transportation, they were nevertheless anxious to benefit from the presence of the soldiers.

At the outskirts of Calcutta they came to a greasy, noisome river where they stopped, though Spence could not determine why. He and Adjani got out to give their legs a last stretch before the train headed into open country. Walking to the head of the convoy they saw the reason for the delay. A family had set up housekeeping on the bridge during the night—not only one family, but several—and were having to be removed in order to let the cars pass by. The people repacked their baggage and belongings—which seemed to Spence to consist mostly of broken bamboo chairs, rags, and hacked-up oil drums—with a sullen slowness under the urgings of the soldiers.

"Why would anybody homestead a bridge?" he asked as he watched the unusual scene.

"Look around you—where else is there for them to go? Besides, it's close to the water for bathing and drinking—that's why most of them try it. They may even get to stay there a day or two if no one moves them."

Spence looked down at the buff-colored water and grimaced. "They surely don't try to drink that stuff." Adjani didn't say anything, but pointed down along the banks below them.

Every square meter of available space was taken up by crude brush lean-tos and cardboard huts right down to the water's edge. The Hooghly river was both sewer and reservoir to the clamoring masses that crowded its bare earth shores. In the murky light of a new day, as far along the shore as he could see, thousands of river dwellers were going about their daily business; men, women, and children stood naked in the shallows and splashed the foul water over themselves to wash away the previous day's filth.

Near a group of bathers, a starving dog worried a floppy, white rubbery object which Spence at first could not identify. Then with a sick, churning feeling he recognized the thing as a human corpse, bleached white by the river and deposited on the shore.

Spence turned away from the scene with a hollowness in his chest. In a short while the journey resumed. He avoided the accusing stares of the displaced bridge settlers as the car passed them along the side of the road.

For a long time after that he did not say anything.

At midday, though only a few kilometers out of the city, they stopped to eat. Fruit sellers materialized with baskets full of produce to sell to the travelers. Spence was not particularly hungry, but bought two bananas from an old man with a stump leg—mostly out of pity.

Adanji and Gita had gone to confer with Gurjara about the route they would take. Spence sat on the ground in the shade of the car and peeled one of the bananas and munched it thoughtfully.

The air was clearer away from the city, and the land green with tropical foliage. Except for the crumbled pavement underfoot they might have been a safari from long ago exploring an uncharted territory —the sense of the new unknown was strong in Spence.

To the north the foothills rose in even steps leading to the high mountains which showed as little more than a faint purplish smudge in the sky behind the hills. Somewhere up ahead in those hills was Darjeeling, jewel of the mountains. Six days, seven, maybe more away. Rangpo was further still.

Spence sighed; perhaps they were on a wild goose chase. Perhaps Ari was nowhere within a million kilometers of those superstition-breeding hills. Thinking of her, wondering about her, worrying over her had made him sick at heart. He kept telling himself, and anyone else who would listen, that he should have done something to help her. Adjani had pointed out time and again that her kidnapping had been carefully arranged and that she was probably out of the building before they had entered the room.

"What about the scream? That was her scream, I know it."

"How do you know? We both heard what we were meant to hear. We were summoned when our presence was required and not until then. Do you really think that if there had been a struggle we would not have heard it? We were but a few steps from the door and could have rescued her easily if she had been there to rescue. No, they knew where to find her. They were watching her, waiting for a chance to act."

"But why? What is *she* in all of this? Why didn't they take me?"

Adjani shook his head. "I don't know. But we're doing the right thing. We'll just have to trust God to show us what to do when the time comes."

"How can you be so sure?"

"I don't see that we have any other choice—do you? We were meant to follow. So be it. We follow."

Spence felt he had betrayed his beloved. It frustrated him to have to sit in the road eating bananas while she waited for him to rescue her.

He finished the banana and tossed the peel away.

At once there was a flurry of motion at the roadside where he had tossed the peel. Two children—a girl about eight years old and wrapped in a ragged, faded sari, and her brother of about five who wore only a man's sleeveless shirt—dived after the banana skin. They had been watching Spence from a distance and when he threw the peeling, they pounced.

The girl brushed the dirt away from the peeling and pulled a small square of frayed cloth from the folds of her sari. She spread out the cloth neatly and she and her brother sat down.

With patience and care she began pulling the long stringy soft portion of the inner peel away from the skin. When she was done she discarded the outer skin and divided the remains with the boy.

They ate them slowly and with deliberation as if they were munching a great delicacy best enjoyed at leisure. Spence was so moved by the sight that he went to the children and held out the other banana.

The girl's eyes grew big and round and the little boy cowered at his sister's shoulder. Spence smiled and offered the banana more insistently; he could tell by the way they looked at it that both wanted it very much. They were simply too shy to accept it.

So Spence put the banana down on the dirty square of cloth and walked back to the car and sat down. As soon as his back was turned the girl snatched up the banana, peeled it and broke it in half. Both were slowly chewing the fruit when Spence returned to the car.

Adjani and Gita returned and they began discussing their plans for the immediate future. They heard the soldiers call out and the pop of the jeep firing. As they were climbing back into the car Spence felt a tug at his elbow.

He turned to see the little girl and her brother. He started to gesture to them that he had no more bananas when the girl smiled prettily and with some ceremony presented him with his banana peel.

Spence grinned and gave the peel back. Both looked at each other as if unable to believe their good fortune and then scampered off to devour the rest of their prize.

The happy look in the children's eyes warmed Spence the rest of the day.

"It's just a little thing," he replied to Adjani's knowing glance. "It's nothing."

"It's more than you think, my friend."

Thereafter he always made it a point to buy three bananas.

CHAPTER FIVE

"YOU'RE IN a lot of trouble, Packer. Care to tell me what this is all about?" Elliot Ramm, Gotham security chief, crossed his long legs and leaned on the edge of his desk. A penitent Olmstead Packer sat facing him with his hands between his knees and his face long and unhappy. There was a note of smouldering indignation in his voice when he spoke.

"To tell you the truth, Chief Ramm, I don't know myself." He jerked a thumb toward the two guards who stood watching him with cool disinterest. "Maybe you should ask your men. I was just talking to a friend when they came in and grabbed me."

The security chief nodded to his men, dismissing them. "I have your report. You can return to duty." He turned to Packer. "I also have a statement from Dr. Williams. He says that you obtained entrance to his infirmary under false pretenses after you were told you could not see the patient Kalnikov. He claims you were endangering the life of his patient."

Packer grinned sheepishly. "I guess I may have overdramatized a bit."

"Hmph." Chief Ramm picked up a white folder from his desk. "He's pressing charges against you."

"He's *what?*" Packer suddenly became very red. "He's nuts! This is all crazy. Let me talk to him. I didn't mean any harm. It was that nurse of his—she acted too snippy and fresh; I just decided to take matters into my own hands."

A faint smile crossed Ramm's lips; he nodded and shoved a lock of his black hair away from his forehead. "All right, I believe you. You scientists hate to be told 'no' to anything."

"Then I can go?" Packer asked hopefully. He had been in detention for over three hours, and was getting tired.

"I'm afraid it's not that simple. Whether I believe you or not doesn't really make a lot of difference. You see, Williams has filed a formal complaint. It's up to the director to review it and decide what to do."

"Director Zanderson's gone. No telling when he'll be back."

"I'm sorry. You'll have to stay here until he gets back, or—"

"Or what? If there's another way to settle this I'm all for it."

"Or Dr. Williams could agree to drop the charges."

"Then let's talk to him by all means. I'm sure he'll listen to reason."

Ramm held up a hand. "Not so fast! He was pretty steamed up over this. I'd let him cool off a little first."

"But I've got to get out of here. I'm a busy man; I've got an experiment running."

"It'll just have to run without you for a while. You should have thought of that before your performance of Swan Lake in the sick bay."

"All right, I guess I had that coming."

"I'll talk to Williams after a bit and see what I can do."

"I'd appreciate it, Chief Ramm." Packer rose and shuffled to the portal. "You know, there's something funny about this whole thing. I never knew anyone to have to be sedated after getting buzzed by a taser. I thought those things were fairly safe, if you know what I mean."

"I'm sure there's an explanation. I'll check into it. In the meantime you can wait in the outer office until I get this cleared up. I won't put you in the tank."

Packer nodded and left. Security Chief Ramm returned to the chair behind his desk and picked up his officers' report and glanced over it. He tossed it down on the desk, laced his hands behind his head, and leaned back in his chair. He frowned as if deep in thought and then shoved his chair back, rose, put on his red and black cap with its gold emblem, and went in search of the physician.

Ari had never seen her father so shaken. He sat slumped in the seat beside her, face white as the pale sliver of moon that shone in the jet's small oval window. His eyes were closed, though she knew he was not asleep. He was shutting out the reality of what was happening around him.

The plane was not large; their captors sat all around them and watched them incessantly. Although they had not forbidden them to talk to one another, their close proximity tended to limit the exchanges between father and daughter to mere whispers and nods.

She knew there was more to what was happening than she had as yet been told, more than their kidnapping and the trouble with Spence, though he was certainly central to the whole escapade. Her father seemed to know more than he let on, and the way it had affected him was not explainable in terms of his normal behavior. Ari was seeing a new side of her father and it scared her.

She went to sleep wondering what it was that he knew and would not, or could not, tell her.

The plane flew on through the night, stopping only once for refueling at a hoverport in Germany. Ari roused herself and peered sleepily out the window. She saw a golden-gray dawn sky and a ground crew of men in blue overalls wheeling orange machines around the wings of the jet. Across the field she saw a building with signs on the roof in German and guessed they were somewhere in the middle of Europe at least.

When she woke again the blue sky held a fierce white sun above a lumpy landscape of gray and white clouds. She could not see the earth below and had no idea where they were or which direction they were heading. Not that it mattered at all.

Shortly after that she and her father were given a simple breakfast: orange juice and a dry roll. No one else seemed to be eating, so Ari thought they were at least being shown some small courtesy. She hadn't eaten in almost a day, and wolfed down the food in several large bites, then turned to her father.

"Daddy, you're not eating."

"I'm not very hungry, dear. You may have my roll if you like."

"No; you eat something and drink your juice. You have to keep your strength up. No telling when we might eat again, and anyway we want to be alert for any chance of escape."

Her father did not say anything, but his expression gave her to know that he considered any thought of escape pure foolishness.

The jet dropped down through the clouds and landed on a square of concrete near a small town on the edge of a desert. Ari could see brown desolate hills in the distance and the white stucco buildings of the town like bleached bones in the sun. Squat, bushy-topped palm trees and low dusty shrubs stood off away from the landing field like forlorn travelers awaiting transportation that never arrives. There were no human passengers or greeting committee that Ari could see on her side of the plane.

Someone popped the hatch and the cool interior of the craft was assaulted by warm dry air from the desert. Then, one by one, all of the occupants disembarked. Ari and her father stayed in their seats until Tickler came back and told them to get out. They emerged from the plane and walked a few paces along the concrete landing pad.

"Stay in sight!" Tickler called. But other than that admonition no one seemed to pay the least attention to them.

Hocking and his assistants withdrew to the far side of the pad to confer with a group of five or six men in black and white kaftans, fuel smugglers, no doubt. Ari thought she saw a camel's head moving among the shrubbery a little way off.

"I wonder where we are?" Ari whispered to her father. "And what's going on?"

"Does it matter?" The resignation was so strong in her father's voice that Ari spun around and faced him, gripping him by the arms.

"Daddy, tell me. You're hiding something and I have a right to know. It's *my* neck, too. Don't think you're protecting me by not talking. It's too late for that, and besides—I'm a big girl now."

Her words brought him back. He looked at her and blinked, as if recognizing her for the first time since the ordeal started. "Of course, my dear," he said gently. He looked around and saw that they were unobserved. "I'll tell you all I know and what I guess . . ." He paused and looked at her once again.

"Is it about Spence? Tell me. I won't be spared the details no matter how it hurts."

"Spence? Oh, no. I mean, yes—it started there. At first it was him, but not anymore. He doesn't matter anymore, not really."

"Doesn't matter?"

"They told me he'd kidnapped you, that he and Adjani were stealing advanced technology secrets to sell, and I don't know what all. I thought I was helping you, Ari. I never dreamed . . ."

"I don't understand. Why did you believe them? Didn't you know—"

"No," her father said curtly. "I . . . I had to believe them. I had no choice."

"Daddy, who are these people? What do they want from us?"

He turned sad and bitter eyes on her. "It started almost a year ago. *He* came to me"—a jerk of the head indicated Hocking—"and said that there were people who would pay handsomely to know the truth about your mother. I was afraid—I couldn't let that information out. It might have ruined my career. The board elections were only a few weeks away. There had been some mumblings of dissatisfaction among the more conservative board members; my reappointment was by no means assured."

"What did he want?"

"That was the odd thing. Only to come aboard Gotham and observe, he said. We made a deal: I would let him come on board—no questions asked—in exchange for his silence about Caroline. I didn't see him after that. He stayed out of sight."

"Didn't you wonder what he was up to?"

"I didn't want to know! After the elections I forgot about him, put him out of my mind."

"He was there all the time. Spence was right."

"Spence knew about him?"

"Spence saw him once and had me try to find out who he was. Of course I couldn't; there was no record of him anywhere."

Director Zanderson passed a hand in front of his eyes. "I've been such a fool! Now everything's gone."

"What do you mean? We're not finished yet, not by a long shot."

"What difference does it make?" He returned to his whining tone. He looked at her again with eyes showing white all around. "Don't you understand? They are taking over control of the Center! The space station will be theirs."

"Impossible!"

"Far from it. Gotham is totally self-sufficient now. It's quite possible. No one would even know."

"But GM would find out eventually and they'd put a stop to it."

"By then it would be too late. With only a slight modification of the thrusters the station could be moved anywhere in the solar system—the galaxy!"

"They'd go after it. They wouldn't just let it go."

The elder Zanderson shook his head wearily. "Remember, the only craft capable of traveling that far is the transport *Gyrfalcon,* and it's based at the station. It could be years before another craft of that kind could be readied. By that time the station could be hidden somewhere in the asteroid belt or beyond. Why, Gotham would be a true space colony; it could conceivably go anywhere."

The thought of a thing so huge hiding out in plain sight in the empty openness of space seemed ludicrous to Ari. But then, the universe was a very big place.

"What will they do with us?"

"I don't know. I suppose we'll be useful to them until they have secured control of the Center. Then . . . who knows?"

"We've got to do something. We can't just give up hope."

"There is no hope."

"Daddy, we can't just let all those people up there become slaves to this madman. We've got to do *something*. We've got to try."

"It's too late. It's already happening."

"It is *not* too late," Ari said harshly. She took her father's arm and shook it hard. "Spence is still out there and free. He knows about them. He'll try to find us and free us."

"It's too late. He won't know where to start looking—*we* don't even know where they're taking us."

"He'll find us." She gave her father a knowing look. "Spence has as much at stake in this as anyone else, maybe more. And I have a pretty good hunch where we're headed and where he'll start looking."

CHAPTER SIX

THE GUNSHOTS did not wake Spence; it was the bullets themselves—rattling through the rusted hulk of the sedan like lethal hail—that snapped him to attention.

The moon was nearly down—the darkest part of the night several hours before dawn—and perfect for an ambush. The *goondas* had been waiting for the sentries to slip off to sleep before creeping out from hiding in the jungled hills. The attack, swift and professional, caught everyone off guard.

Merchants ran screaming into the night. The horde of barefoot followers scattered in every direction, not knowing where the shooting was coming from. The soldiers fired off quick bursts with their M-16s and someone—perhaps one of the merchants, more likely one of the outlaws—blazed away with a submachine gun.

The scene erupted in such confusion Spence could not be sure who was shooting at whom when he dived out of the back seat of the car onto the road. He collided with the crouching figure of Adjani.

"Ooof!" he said as he went down.

"Stay down!" Adjani pressed his shoulder to the ground.

"Where's Gita?"

"I don't know. When I woke up he was gone. The shooting seems to be coming from those trees across the road."

Spence looked and saw that Adjani was probably right. A thin white trace of smoke drifted from the tops of a stand of tall trees about thirty meters away; a running line of bullets kicked up little clouds of dust as they ripped along the length of the caravan. A few bodies lay motionless between the trees and the line of vehicles, but whether these were dead, wounded, or just keeping down and out of sight he could not tell. He feared the worst.

All at once the shooting stopped. They heard shouts from the trees and then saw the three soldiers walking across the road with their empty hands in the air.

"So much for our protection," said Adjani.

"What happens now?"

"They will take what they want and—we would do well to pray—

they will go their own way." The voice was Gita's. Spence and Adjani turned around and saw the turbaned head sticking out from beneath the car. How he had squeezed his bulk under there was a mystery.

All around them the groans of the wounded rose from the earth, and the foliage on the far side of the road began to waver and shake as the bandits stepped into the open.

There were a dozen or more of them, and probably others still hidden in the trees. They were dressed in dark clothing, making them almost impossible to see as they fanned off along the caravan's length— they were dark shadows against a darker night. The feeble moonlight struck the bare metal of their old guns and glinted with a cold lustre, letting any remaining doubters know that they did indeed mean business.

"We have nothing of value," said Spence. "What can they do?"

"Kill us," replied Gita. "It would be better if we had something to give them."

"Our provisions," suggested Adjani.

"They'll take those anyway. They want more."

"Well, let's not stick around to haggle about it; let's get out of here now." Spence, still on his stomach beside Adjani, began squirming backward behind the car. Adjani flattened himself and followed Spence's lead. Gita, wedged between the car chassis and the dirt road, hissed like a snake. "Stop! Stop! Wait for me!" In a moment he had disengaged himself from his hiding place and was rolling into the ditch after his friends.

They had not run three steps toward the cover of the jungle when a shout and the glint of the moonlight on the long barrel of a rifle halted them. Directly into their path stepped a large, dark figure. His teeth and the whites of his eyes shone in the darkness and he turned the gun toward them and shouted again, more insistently.

Without waiting for a translation Spence turned slowly and, putting his hands in the air, walked back to the car. There they saw that all the merchants were standing in front of their vehicles while teams of bandits unloaded the cargo. From the whining chatter which filled the air Spence guessed they were pleading with the robbers not to wipe them out completely. The *goondas* seemed oblivious to this racket and went about their business wholly unconcerned with the pitiful wheedling of the tradesmen.

Then two bandits were standing before them with rifles leveled. One of them spoke a rapid question to Gita. The little man, quaking with fear, stepped forward.

"He wants to know what we have to give him," whispered Adjani out of the side of his mouth.

Gita was speaking quickly with fear-inspired eloquence. The palms

of his hands could be seen waving ecstatically before him in wild gestic-
ulations.

"What's he saying now?"

"Gita is telling him that we are doctors on our way to Darjeeling to
help a friend. That we have no money or possessions with us. He is
praying that we be allowed to continue for the sake of our friend."

The bandit looked long at Gita and then at Adjani and Spence in
turn. He came to stand directly before them and peered into their faces.
Spence could smell the reek of puyati, the strong home-brewed liquor
made from fermented palm sap, on the thief's breath. His face was
greasy in the fading moonlight.

All at once the bandit whirled on his heel and barked out a short
sentence. In a moment a very large outlaw with a huge white turban
and a flowing, striped coat came striding up with a *goonda* on either
side. Spence guessed this was the leader.

The two bandits conferred with one another briefly and then the
leader turned with a flourish of his coattails and left. Spence thought for
an instant that they would be left alone. But the first bandit roared a
command at Gita which almost sent the little man rolling on his back-
side. Gita scrambled for the car and came out with the sacks bearing
their provisions. He turned to Spence and Adjani with eyes wide and
fearful.

"We are to follow him," said Adjani, nodding in the direction of
the retreating bandit.

"What if we don't?"

"Then he hopes we have lived good lives and thought pure
thoughts, for tonight we will have the opportunity of joining the World
Soul in Nirvana."

"I'd rather not," said Spence. "Let's go."

Olmstead Packer crossed and recrossed his legs, folded and re-
folded his hands alternately and regularly. He was bored with waiting
and apprehensive that security chief Ramm should be taking so long to
iron out the difficulty between him and Dr. Williams. A sense of doom
had settled over the big physicist as he waited; he saw his future growing dim before his eyes, and the hobbling shackles of a prison record
snaking out to claim him.

And yet, the offense was so small, so trivial, so insignificant he
wanted to laugh. This extreme ambivalence of feeling created in the
red-bearded man a curious tension, as if a tug-of-war was being waged
inside him with first one side gaining the advantage and then the other.
And to make matters worse, Packer did not know which side to cheer
for. At any moment, depending upon the swing of mood, either side
seemed capable of carrying the day.

So he sat and tried to keep himself calm while inwardly the battle for the control of his emotional outlook and disposition raged unabated.

He shook his red shaggy head. How had he ever gotten himself mixed up in anything like this? It had all started out so innocently. Or had it? Wasn't it true that there had been something peculiar right from the beginning? Right from the very first moment he had laid eyes on Spence Reston? Didn't all this have to do with him?

Packer was certain that beyond anything else Spence was the cause of his particular problems, and very likely the rest as well. Certainly Kalnikov had gotten where he was because of Reston—*there* was a mystery that begged investigation. Where it all would end, and what it was all about, he could only guess. Physicists did not like to guess.

Presently the outer door slid open and he heard someone speak in the next room. In a moment Chief Ramm was standing over him. Packer jumped up like an eager lap dog and all but barked to be let out.

"Well? Did you talk to him? Can I go now?"

Ramm frowned an official frown. "I'm afraid it won't be that simple. I'm going to have to lock you up for a couple days—until the director gets back, anyway."

Packer's face fell. "You're not serious."

"I'm afraid I am. Come with me, please." The command was cold and left no room for argument.

The security head led the malefactor into an octagonal room with transparent doors set in each of the seven facing walls. These were the doors to the cells. All were empty; crime was not a problem on Gotham.

Ramm took his prisoner to the cell directly opposite the entrance to the room. "In here," he said, punching in the access code. The door slid open and Ramm stepped aside so Packer could enter. "I think you'll be comfortable here. Try not to worry. I'll notify your wife."

"Don't bother," Packer responded dully. "My wife's visiting her sister Earthside. Just tell my assistant what's happened." He looked around at his cell: a small square room with padded walls and a low cav couch built on a ledge. That was it. He turned back and was surprised to see Ramm had joined him in the cell.

Ramm indicated the couch and said, "Sit down. I want to talk to you."

Packer did as he was told.

"This is the only quiet room in the detention center—all the rest are bugged," Ramm explained. Packer kept quiet and waited for what would follow.

"Something squirrelly is going on here. I mean to find out what it is. You'd better give me the whole story, Packer. From the beginning."

Packer stared back blankly. The chief's frown had deepened to a formidable scowl. He guessed the tall policeman could eat his weight in wildcats, and decided not to play any games.

"You talked to Williams?"

"I talked to him. It was like talking to a clam. He's scared of something and he won't open up and let it out. I thought I might see if you could enlighten me."

"I'll try," said Packer and began telling him about what he knew of Spence and Adjani's disappearance—which was not much because he had only heard the same rumors as everyone else.

"Yes," said Ramm. "I've got a couple of men working on that one. Nothing much has turned up so far."

"That's why I went to Kalnikov. Reston and Rajwandhi are friends of mine; Adjani's on my staff. I couldn't believe the rumors about them, and I wanted to find out what happened. I figured Kalnikov was the one person who might know."

"Would it surprise you if I told you that it was *my* order that Kalnikov receive no visitors?"

"It was?"

"It was. He was an eyewitness and I didn't want anyone talking to him before I could. When you turned up in bed next to him, I figured you were mixed up in it. Either you knew a lot more than you were telling, or you had stumbled into something innocently. I didn't know which, but it gave me a chance to go back and talk to Williams again."

"Well?"

"You tell me. I can't make heads or tails of this. All I know is that it doesn't take fifteen hours for a man to recover from a taser jolt. Usually only a few minutes. Williams claims the taser dart struck Kalnikov in the spine and pierced the spinal column, grazing the spinal cord. He says Kalnikov may be paralyzed."

"He's not paralyzed—he's sedated."

"Are you sure?"

"Positive. Kalnikov told me himself. Rather, I got him to tell me—he can't talk, so we used an answer code. I found out that Kalnikov was trying to help Reston and Rajwandhi escape—from what, I don't know."

"He wasn't injured by the taser. You're right there. He thinks he was pumped full of sedative and muscle relaxant to keep him quiet. That's all I could get from him before I was interrupted."

"Hmm. Curiouser and curiouser."

"That's all I know, honestly."

"What about this Reston and the other guy. What's with them? Who were they escaping from?"

"I don't know. Kalnikov might. He saw them."

Chief Ramm stood. "I'm inclined to believe you, Packer. I'm going to check this out. I could release you on your own recognizance, but I think you'd better stay here for a while."

Packer moaned. "Oh, no. I was hoping you wouldn't say that."

"Look, it's more for your own protection than anything else. Until we find out what's going on here I don't want to lose any witnesses. You know as much as Kalnikov now. I don't want you to turn up missing."

"They wouldn't do anything to me—" bluffed Packer.

"Don't be too sure. I've got one man sedated and two others flying around in a stolen landing pod and I don't know why. I'm not so sure whoever's behind this would balk at killing off their witnesses if this gets any messier." To Packer's disbelieving look he said, "It happens. So just sit tight and I'll get you out of here as soon as possible. In the meantime, relax. I'll have some statmags brought in for you to read, and we'll be having dinner in an hour or so. It's on me."

Chief Ramm smiled good-naturedly and went out, leaving Packer to fume in frustration.

"Just one thing, chief," the prisoner called through the faceplate in the door.

"Yeah?"

"Don't *you* go getting into trouble."

The chief laughed. "Don't worry. It's all in a day's work."

"Maybe so, but I have a feeling these guys work mostly at night."

CHAPTER SEVEN

THE HOVERJET dropped once more below the scattered cloud cover and Ari saw the ground for the first time in several hours. She viewed a lush green terrain that looked like emerald velvet rolled out in puckered wrinkles. She could see the shining silver threads of rivers winding along the deep gorges. White birds soared over the verdant landscape in vee-formed squadrons. Seeing them from above with the noonday sun gleaming on their wings they looked like strands of diamonds suspended between the blue sky and the green earth, flashing white fire as their wings sliced the misty air.

Ahead and a little to the left of the plane she could see the sharp hills rise to a promontory surrounded on three sides by jungled slopes and by a lake on the fourth. Further ahead, and blue in the hazy distance, the white peaks of mountains rose, creating a jagged line on the horizon as far as she could see.

The hoverjet made a long descent, passing over the promontory with its cluster of villages crowded at the summit and descending in tiers like stairsteps.

Ari felt she recognized the place, though she had never seen it before.

"Daddy, where are we?" she whispered. Her father was not asleep, though he had his eyes closed and his head rested on his chest.

"Hmm?" He had sunk into black depression and would make only grunting answers to her attempts at conversation.

"Could that be India down there? I think it must be."

This brought her father upright in his seat as his eyes snapped open.

"India, did you say?" He leaned across her and peered out the window. "It's hard to tell. It might be anywhere."

"No, that's Darjeeling down there, I know it."

"Could be," he admitted, regarding his daughter carefully. "What makes you so sure?"

"I just know, that's all. Mother told me about it, described growing up there." Just then, as her mind leaped ahead, it came to her exactly who it was that awaited them at their destination. "Oh, Daddy," she said, gripping his hand. "If we *are* in India it can only mean one thing. We're going to see the Dream Thief."

A short while later the jet's forward progress slowed and then halted as it dropped to a landing below. The vegetation was so dense and the trees so close—she might have reached out and pulled leaves from their branches—she could not see the ground directly below the plane. They seemed to be landing in the forest some distance east of Darjeeling. How far east she could not tell, but the terrain glimpsed through the tall trees as the jet came down gave the impression of rising into mountains all around.

Then the plane bumped gently down and the engines ceased their droning whine. At the same instant warm, humid air flooded the cabin as the hatch popped open. Ari heard voices from outside speaking in the rapid birdsong of Hindi; this confirmed her suspicion that they were indeed in the land of the Dream Thief.

She blinked as she emerged from the cabin. The sunlight fell hot and bright from directly overhead. The moist air seemed to shimmer in waves before her eyes and the green walls of the broad-leafed forest screeched with the calls of alarmed birds and angry monkeys.

She lifted her eyes to take in her surroundings and saw a scene out of the pages of an archeological text. Before her rose walls of massive, crumbling stone, black with age and mildew. Further along the wall a large gate stood open and beyond it a narrow tower struck out into the azure, clouded sky. They seemed to have landed in a courtyard of sorts, inside the walls of a castle.

Ari remembered her mother's description of the Dream Thief's palace and knew that she was there. She looked around with eyes filled with wonder. What had been only a dream was real; the buried memory of an unhappy little girl was fact. It had been true all along—not the imaginings of a disturbed and frightened child.

Three men approached wearing military tunics and trousers of linen. Their dark, almost black skins glistened in the sun and their black almond eyes watched the newcomers warily. One of the men wore a holster on his hip. Hocking and the others stood in consultation with the men for a moment and then Tickler came and said, "These men will take you to your quarters."

He made it sound as if they were checking into a hotel. The men, without a word, led the captives off toward the gate and into a further courtyard beyond. This inner yard was smaller; its walls were draped in heavy vines growing out from and between the stones of the yard, cracking them and prying them apart, heaving them up at angles to each other. The vines had covered everything—stunted trees, standing statues, stone benches, an ancient dry fountain—smothering all beneath a thick green blanket of glossy leaves, like the sheets thrown over the furniture of a house closed for the summer. Ari got the impression that if she stood very long in the courtyard she, too, would soon be covered over to become one of the standing objects she saw around her.

The men marched them across the decaying stones of the yard to a low-roofed portico, then under this to a tier of steps leading up into a darkened entrance. Ari reached her hand out to her father as she tripped going up the stairs. One of the guards caught her in a steely grasp and righted her. His hand lingered on her cool flesh. She jerked her arm away quickly.

They entered a room, dim and cool and quiet as a tomb. Light entered from small clover-shaped windows around a shallow domed ceiling. Dust lay thick and undisturbed on the tile floor of the hall—except for the meandering trails of insects; their footprints in the dust gave testimony to the fact that no one had visited the place in a very long time. They might have been the first visitors in a thousand years.

They were whisked across the hall and into a dark corridor which ended in a long, spiraling flight of stairs. Other, lighter passageways joined the main one at the foot of the stairs, but they went up the spiral which wound round and round and narrowed as it ascended.

At the top of these dark steps they entered a small landing with a circular hole in the vaulted roof overhead. At one end of the landing stood a large wooden door which appeared much newer than its surrounding posts and lintel, with black iron bands forming a large X across its surface.

Her first look at the interior of their cell did not dismay Ari. It was a spacious room, round with lofty, pointed windows and a wide balcony closed only by a curtain of woven wooden beads. There were oriental couches and rattan chairs and several beds piled high with cushions of red, blue and yellow silk. A toilet stall was concealed behind a silk curtain for the privacy of its occupants. There was a marble table with carved ivory chessmen arranged neatly on its polished surface. Nearby, a great glass bowl with a crystal dipper held fresh water; next to it a smaller bowl offered fruit: small wild grapes, bananas, oranges, and several large, greenish-yellow pulpy things she could not identify.

It appeared as if the room had been newly scoured and furnished for their arrival with all the amenities one might find in a charming old hotel. But when the great wooden door slammed shut behind them she knew that they were prisoners and not guests.

"Well, here we are," she said, trying to sound optimistic.

Director Zanderson stirred himself out of his staring reverie to gaze about the room with tired eyes. "Yes, here we are. A gilded cage for the captive birds."

"Look, there's a balcony," said Ari, running to it at once. "Daddy, come out here; you can see the mountains."

"The Himalayas," he said, joining her. "Yes, we are northeast of Darjeeling in the foothills of the Himalayas, somewhere near the old Bhutan border in Sikkim."

"I didn't know you knew so much geography." Ari turned a fresh, enthusiastic face to her father. The sun lit her hair with golden fire. She was trying very hard to draw her father out and cheer him up in the hope that he would abandon his moody despondency. To see him sunk so deep in his depression hurt her more than anything their abductors could have done to her. "Tell me more."

"I don't know much more. I was only here briefly—with your mother before you were born."

"I never knew that. You said—"

"I know what I said." He smiled devilishly. "There is a lot parents don't talk about in front of their children. They lead double lives, my dear."

"Really. I always suspected as much. But now the truth comes out. You've got to tell me all about it."

Her father sighed, as if sifting through the various recollections of a long and burdensome life for one remnant of a memory saved from some long-ago time. "There's not much to tell," he said at last. "It was not much of a trip."

"I don't believe that. Two people—young and in love, frolicking in these secret hills."

A faint smile touched his lips as he warmed to the memory. "Yes, there was something of that. But there was a sadness, too. Your mother wanted so very much to show me the town where they had lived and the seminary where her father had taught all those years. She wanted me to see where she had come from, she said.

"But when we reached Darjeeling something happened to her; she became moody and unhappy. We stayed only a few days and looked around, but she couldn't bring herself to show me all she had planned. It was like she couldn't bear to be here. She became very depressed—that was the first hint of her trouble.

"After we left we never spoke of the trip again, though I could tell that it was often on her mind. She seemed to regard the trip as a fiasco, but I didn't feel that way at all. It was years later, of course, before I began to suspect there was more to it than a holiday ruined by unpleasant memories."

Ari remembered the story her mother had told—it seemed years ago now, but only one day by the clock—and how she sat at her elbow as one in a trance, drinking in every word. "Did she never tell you about the Dream Thief?"

Her father gave her an odd look. "What do you know about it?"

Ari described her visit to the asylum with Spence and Adjani and how her mother had rallied during the visit and had, in one flash of lucidity, described what happened to her in the wild hills. Ari told the story word for word the way her mother had told it, while her father sat with a look of rapt attention on his face.

"Yes," he said when she had finished. "I've never heard it quite that way, but that's pretty much the way I've pieced it together over the years—from little things she'd say. Not that she ever really tried to hide it; I don't think she was aware of it. She had blocked it out completely. But sometimes she'd slip; her subconscious would send out a plea for understanding."

He turned to look at the faraway line of mountains heaving their mighty shoulders skyward. An expression of deepest grief came over his features. Tears gathered at the corners of his eyes and trickled down his broad cheeks. Ari took his hand and pressed it hard. She lifted her other hand to his face. He took the hand and kissed the palm and held it against his lips for a moment. When he spoke again his voice was thick with sorrow. "All these years I thought it was the fantasy of a troubled mind. I never dreamed it could be real.

"The best doctors in the world agreed with me—the treatments, the drugs, the horrible nights of pain when she'd cry out in her terror . . . but it was real, Ari. And it drove her insane."

The air suddenly seemed colder and Ari wrapped her arms around herself and stepped away from the balcony.

Yes, it was real. And it had turned its attention to her, and had brought her within these walls a prisoner. Would she be able to withstand? She wondered, thinking of the one had who escaped, yet the memory of it had eaten away at her sanity until nothing remained but the shell of a formerly beautiful woman.

"Daddy, I'm scared," Ari said, trembling.

He took his daughter in his arms and held her tightly. "I know, dearest. I know."

"What are we going to do?"

"There is not much we can do, Ari. Only pray."

"I've never stopped praying, Daddy. But pray for us now—and for Spence, too. I think he may need it more than we do."

CHAPTER EIGHT

SPENCE HELD the flame in his hands. It burned lightly, fluttering yellow in the soft night breeze. He brought the candle, made of woven cloth and plant fibers dipped in wax, close to his face and felt its warmth lick him.

Beyond the small circle of his light he could see nothing. The night sat like an impenetrable wall all around him. Above, no star gleamed, no moon shed its light—all was dark and Spence was alone in the darkness.

The only thing holding the awful smothering blackness at bay was the little, crudely formed torch in his hand. That a light so small could keep out the dark seemed a miracle.

He had never thought about it before, had never seen this miracle performed. But he witnessed it now, and he marveled at it. Even the tiniest spark was stronger than all the mighty forces of the night.

Strange, he thought, that it should be that way.

Suddenly a quick gust of wind whipped at the flame, and though Spence cupped his hand around it at almost the same instant, it was too late. He saw the flame wink out as the darkness it had been holding back leaped in to devour him.

Like some immense, amorphous creature, the darkness absorbed him into itself. He could sense its exulation at conquering him—a thrill of excitement seemed to course through it as it tightened its grasp on him. He knew, with a horror that exceeded any he had ever felt, that it meant to crush him into nothingness. Already he could feel the suffocating blackness, clamped like an iron fist over him, beginning to squeeze him.

The mind that controlled the darkness, that was itself the heart and soul of darkness, reached out toward him. He recoiled from the contact as if from the slithering touch of a reptile's polished skin. His blood ran cold.

He had touched a mind of utter chaos and depravity, and it made him feel weak and insignificant in its presence. It meant to kill him, but for no better reason than that it meant to kill all things that possessed even the faintest glimmer of light in them.

A long, aching cry tore from his throat, full of helplessness and bleak despair. In that cry he heard all the bitter disappointment and hate and injustice he had ever experienced—the sum total of all his deepest fears and failures.

And he heard the cry lose itself in the darkness, becoming part of it, strengthening it. Spence knew then that the despair and the hate and all the other black nameless fears belonged not to himself—although he had held them and nourished them in his innermost being; they belonged instead to the darkness that covered him now, were part of it, were one with it. Long had they fought within him to extinguish his spark, that portion of light that was his.

Now they had gone back to strengthen the darkness from which they were sprung. Now it would at last crush him.

Spence felt his strength to resist slacken, running away like water. That the darkness should prevail over him was the most monstrous insanity he could conceive. To be snuffed out like his poor candle flame seemed to him the final, unanswerable injustice. And for what? For possessing a tiny gleam of light that he had never asked for, nor sought.

"No!" The shout was defiance. "No, no, no!" He heard his cries die in the darkness.

Then he heard a sound that pierced him like an ice dagger. It seemed to hollow him out, disemboweling him, slashing at his heart. The sound was laughter, originating from within the cruel mocking heart of darkness.

He would be annihilated with the insolent laughter still booming in his brain; his last thoughts would be of the utter senseless waste of his life, echoed in each note.

"God!" Spence cried. "Save me!"

He felt a shudder run through the darkness as if he had wounded it with a blow. And then a single beam of light, finer than a single hair, struck down through the darkness to stand shimmering before him. Spence reached out and touched his finger to the light and felt it sing within him. It was alive, this tiny laser point of light, in a way that the darkness was never alive. It had power beyond all the power of the darkness, and it awakened in him a corresponding power as it infused his own inner spark with new brilliance.

In the light he heard a voice speak to him. "Why do you search in darkness for your life?" it asked.

Spence could not answer it. He could not speak.

"Come into the light," said the voice, "and you will find what you are searching for."

Spence looked up at the shining thread of light and far above him he heard a tremendous tearing sound as if the sky itself were being torn in two. He clamped his hands over his ears to save them from the deafening sound.

Far above him he saw a crack in the darkness and light began to spill in. It seemed to him for a moment that he was inside an enormous egg and light from a greater world outside was pouring in through a crack in the shell.

He heard above the tearing sound the agonizing shriek of the darkness as it was riven apart and burned away by the light. Then he was standing in a pool of light that fell down upon him from above. He raised his face to it and filled his eyes with it.

With a terrific roar the darkness dissolved and ran away and a brilliant white light, brighter than ten thousand suns, blazed. He felt its power and its vibrant, living energy as it danced over him, tingling every pore, every square centimeter of his skin.

Now it was inside him, penetrating his flesh and bones and burning into the fibers of his soul. He could feel it like fire—consuming all impurities, devouring any remaining shreds of darkness which clung to his inner self, cleansing the very atoms of his being.

Spence then knew that he and the light were one; it had done its work in him and he was transformed into a living beam of light. He felt himself expanding and growing without limits, a creature of infinity, without beginning or end, and yet he knew the true living light to be as far above him and brighter as he was himself above and brighter than the darkness it had saved him from.

He had touched the source of life and it flowed within him and through him and always would. It was eternal and so, now, was he. He knew that he was born to be part of it and to live forever in it.

The thought was a song inside him; but there were no words, only a melody which soared endlessly up and up, ever higher, ever more pure.

Spence bent over the sleeping form of Adjani. The forest sounds were hushed; it was an hour yet to daylight, though through the trees above he could see a dull blue showing. Crickets in the tall grass and among the branches of nearby bushes trilled musically, filling the night with their peaceful sound.

"Adjani, wake up!" He heard the slow, rhythmic breathing of his friend and hated to wake him, but his news would not wait. It had to be told. "Adjani!"

"What is it?" Adjani sat up at once—wary, like a cat. "Has something happened?" He looked around quickly but saw no signs of alarm. A bandit sentry watched them from a distance; his rifle rested on his knees. Clearly, they were in the same predicament as before; nothing had changed.

"Adjani, I've seen him!" Spence's hands were shaking and his voice trembled.

"Seen who?" Adjani came fully upright and peered into Spence's face. He saw a peculiar light in his friend's eyes.

"The Creator of all this," he waved a hand vaguely at the jungle around them, "of you and me, of the universe!"

"What?"

"The All-Being—God! He spoke to me!" Spence put an unsteady hand on Adjani's shoulder. Until he had said the words aloud he had not consciously named his vision. The full meaning of what he said broke in on him, jarring him. He lapsed into a stunned silence.

"Spence! Are you all right?" Adjani shook his elbow.

"I'm fine." Recognition came back into Spence's eyes. He lowered his head and grinned sheepishly. "It was only a dream."

"Tell me about it," said Adjani. "I have learned to respect your dreams."

CHAPTER NINE

"I AM HERE, Ortu." Hocking looked at the motionless figure before him. It had been some time since he had been in the palace, and Hocking thought his master appeared even more shrunken and wasted than ever.

"*Why* are you here?" Ortu did not raise his head; he spoke to Hocking as one asleep. Hocking knew Ortu never slept.

"You said you wanted Reston . . . " Hocking began.

"Then why is *he* not here?" The voice was cold, the tone menacing.

"He is coming, Ortu. He is on his way here now."

"How do you know this?" Ortu raised his head slowly. His almost luminous eyes glared out at Hocking with loathing.

"It was not easy, Ortu. I've had to . . . to make other arrangements."

"Silence! Remember who I am! You have failed again to carry out my commands. What do you have to say for yourself?"

"It was my fault. Reston escaped—he tricked us. But—"

"Who are the people you have brought with you? Why have you brought them?"

"They are hostages, Ortu. I thought it best to—"

"*You* thought! I am your master! You act according to *my* will! Or have you forgotten?"

"No, Ortu. I have not forgotten. But the girl—the girl is Reston's girlfriend. That's how I know he will come. With the *tanti* we can bring him. That's what you want, isn't it?"

Ortu seemed to consider this and then said, "Fazlul's men are here. Instruct them that the Governor is to intercept Reston on the road and bring him here at once. I will not risk losing him again." Ortu's head sank once more; his eyes closed.

"As you wish, Ortu."

"And the others—your hostages. You will eliminate them at once. It was foolish to bring them here. We have no use for them."

"Yes, Ortu. I will do as you say."

The incense rose in gray billows filling the chamber where Ortu sat like a statue. Hocking, almost choking on the fumes, gazed around the room he knew so well. As always it held a fearful fascination for him. This was the room where his master lived—Ortu had not stirred in forty or fifty years—and from this room he directed his will.

Hocking again regarded the wizened body before him and felt the heat of anger leap up in him. Ortu was patient beyond all human patience; he had waited a thousand years for his plans to begin to grow. He would wait a thousand more for them to bear fruit. *I cannot wait that long,* thought Hocking to himself. *We have a chance now; we must not wait!*

Hocking had his own plans for the new world order which Ortu had designed and which would soon commence. It seemed ludicrous that one man, the stubborn Spencer Reston, should single-handedly halt their progress, and so close to the realization of their dreams. What was so important about Reston anyway? He was nothing—a worm to be crushed underfoot.

Someone had to be eliminated; Hocking saw that clearly. But it would not be Ari and her father; they would be needed until the station was secured. It was Reston who should be eliminated.

Hocking withdrew silently; his chair floated out on the clouds of incense and away. It was so simple he did not know why he had not thought of it before. Perhaps he had been afraid, but not now.

Very well, he would give Fazlul's men their instructions: Reston must never reach Kalitiri.

Yes, it was nearly ready. Things were falling together nicely. He went away almost humming to himself. His features had assumed that gruesome death's-head leer.

Packer was not asleep when the intruder entered the darkened cell block. He had been lying on his couch staring up into the inky blankness when he heard the outer door slip open. When the lights remained off he knew something was amiss.

As quietly as he could he slid out of the couch and onto the floor of the cell; he rolled to the far wall and lay there waiting to see what would happen.

He waited so long that he began to think that he had only imagined the door opening. He was about to get back in bed when there came a distinct click followed by the slight rustling sound of clothing.

He froze.

Every sense was awake and tingling with anticipation. The hairs on the back of his neck stood up as he peered into the darkness and tried to see any movement at all.

He held his breath.

There came another click and a pencil-thin shaft of blue light jabbed out and seared into the couch. The pulse lasted less than a nanosecond, and was followed by two more in rapid succession. Packer could smell the fumes of the composite fabric and the gel of the cav couch where the laser pulse had incinerated it.

He feared that whoever blasted his couch would now switch on the lights to view their handiwork. For a long agonizing moment Packer lay with his face to the floor, hoping against hope that the would-be assassin would leave.

Then he heard the quiet swish of the outer panel opening, and the intruder went away. A trembling Packer lay motionless and waited for someone to come and rescue him, praying that the killer would not return.

Time seemed to slow. Each minute dragged away painfully. Each second expanded to fill an eternity.

He waited.

At last Packer decided that the danger had passed. He stood warily and crept to the couch, fumbling for the light plate near the head. The light winked on and he stared down at the neat charred holes in the couch. Green gel from the support chambers bubbled out onto the orange fabric. The pulses had been calculated to burn through him; no doubt about that: three black rings in the couch—one where his head had been, one at his heart and one at his midsection—any one of them would have killed him.

He was still standing over the couch, acrid wisps of smoke stinging his nostrils, when he heard a voice behind him. He whirled around, ready to dive for the floor, then recognized Ramm standing there watching him.

"You look a little shook up, friend," said the Chief. "You okay?"

"Oh, it's you. Yeah, I'm all right. Someone tried to kill me."

"Tried to *what* ?" He punched in the access code and stepped through the door. "Are you joking?"

"I don't find *this* very funny," said Packer. He pointed down at the damaged couch.

Ramm let out a low whistle and turned to Packer apologetically. "Man, you're lucky to be alive. If you'd been asleep they would have drilled you."

"I wasn't asleep, thank God." He looked down at the three holes oozing gel from the depression of his body still outlined in the couch. He shivered. "I want out of here, Ramm. The game has changed. These guys, whoever they are, want to play rough. Next time I won't be so lucky, maybe."

Ramm raised a hand and stroked his jaw. "I don't know . . . "

"What do you mean you don't know? Look, this was supposed to be for my protection, remember? That's what you said. I wasn't protected very much, was I? I want out now!"

"Where will you go? Back to your quarters? To the lab? They'll be waiting for you."

Packer had not thought of that. He threw his hands out to Ramm and said, "What's going on here? This is getting crazy."

"You don't know the half of it. Come with me, we'll talk in my office."

Packer followed the security chief out of the cell block and into his private office. Ramm sat down on the edge of the desk and folded his arms across his chest. Packer sat down in one of the visitor's chairs and ran his hands through his red bush of hair.

"You want some coffee? Something to eat?"

"Thanks, maybe later." He waited for Ramm to begin.

"I found out a few things this afternoon that strike me as extremely odd. I think Kalnikov has disappeared—I can't seem to locate him anywhere. Williams is saying that due to Kalnikov's condition he was shipped out on the shuttle for medical assistance Earthside. I don't buy it. There's been one shuttle down in the past two days and no injured personnel aboard it according to the records."

"Then where is he? What's happened to him?"

"I don't know. I think he's still aboard here somewhere. They could have stashed him anywhere."

Packer got a sinking feeling in the pit of his stomach. He seemed to be riding a swift elevator down.

"Trouble is, it would take me a couple hundred man-hours to find him, and then the search would alert whoever it is that has him to move him somewhere else."

"What about the guy who tried to kill me a few minutes ago?"

"It's between shifts. My second-shift crew hasn't signed on yet. No one saw anything, I'm afraid."

"What kind of place do you run here?" Packer was quickly losing his temper. He had been cooped up in his cell for a day and a night and no one was on duty when the assassins struck.

Ramm dismissed his anger with a swipe of his hand. "I don't blame you for getting steamed. But you have to remember, we're not a police force—I mean, in a way we are, but this isn't a high-crime area. It isn't like a real city. Mostly we just make sure that people stay out of construction areas and watch the locks on the restaurant pantries after hours, that sort of thing.

"We weren't expecting a strike. You've got to consider that a place like Gotham isn't exactly equipped to handle an armed insurrection. It isn't in the blueprints. Nobody planned on that ever happening."

"Well," grumbled Packer, "maybe it's time that somebody started planning for it—if it isn't already too late."

CHAPTER TEN

THE CAMP of the bandits looked less like a camp and more like a gypsy village than anything Spence had ever seen. Tents of scrap cloth and tarp sewn together, draped over branches or supported with poles scavenged in the jungle, gave the place a wild, fanciful appearance. Small children scampered half-naked to see the odd-looking visitors. Old men sat around the ashes of the previous night's fire nodding and pointing and clacking toothless gums as the raiding party returned with the booty. Women came running to see what their men had brought home for them. Over all an air of whimsical gaiety prevailed.

It was hard for Spence to imagine that these peaceful, happy people made their living killing the unlucky and robbing the unwary. He had expected the outlaws' hideway to be a snake pit, dark and hateful, full of desperate men whose way of life made them vicious and unruly.

That these thieves had families that ran laughing to meet them amused him.

"Quite a picture," Spence whispered to Adjani as they moved down a wide avenue between tents and shelters made from empty cargo crates. Children ran along beside them giggling and pointing in the manner of excited children everywhere.

"Don't let it fool you, Spencer." Adjani spoke softly and peered with narrowed eyes at the leader of the bandits walking just ahead of them. "The cheerful highwayman is the more dangerous. Believe me, these men will not hesitate to disembowel us in front of their wives and children if it pleases them."

Spence thought Adjani was being melodramatic about their situation. But Gita, whose tongue had not stirred the whole of the trek into the jungle, rolled his eyes and quivered, saying, "Adjani knows of what he speaks, Spencer Reston. Listen to him. These men are cutthroats for all their easy ways."

"But you can't think they'd harm us now. We have nothing ot value."

"Don't you see? They have lived too long above the law; they have become secure, fearing nothing. Such men do not shrink from the worst deeds imaginable."

Gita nodded his agreement readily, so Spence said no more about it. Still, he found himself smiling at the children and gawking around the camp as if he were a tourist on holiday.

They had marched all night and rested only a few hours before striking off again. Now the sun stood high in the sky, filtering down through the leafy green canopy above. The prisoners were paraded through the camp and brought to the biggest tent and made to sit down under a large patchwork awning between two guards while the bandits proceeded to divide up the night's harvest of merchandise piled in the center of the settlement.

The shouting of the men and shrieking of the women was still in full chorus when the leader disengaged himself from the swarm around the goods and came to stand before them. The guards prodded the prisoners to their feet with their rifle muzzles.

The bandit leader, a huge hulk of a man with a spreading belly concealed beneath his flowing kaftan, eyed them with interest, and then spoke rapidly to Gita. Gita touched his forehead and bowed low. The leader pushed through them and went into his tent.

"His name is Watti and he wants us to follow him," explained Gita.

"After you," said Spence, and the three went into the leader's dwelling.

Though the interior was dark, the patchwork let in irregular splotches of light, decorating the inside with a speckled pattern that lifted and flowed as the tent breathed in the jungle breeze.

The *goonda* chief led them to a far corner and opened a flap in the side of the tent. Sunlight streamed in upon a bed of cushions on which a young boy rested so still that Spence thought at first he was dead.

Here was the reason they had been brought. The chief of the brigands wanted them to heal his son—that much at least needed no words. The look of the thief's face told as much as he gazed upon the boy's limp form. Likewise, his curt order to them left no doubt about their fate should their combined medical art fall short of curing the boy. A leisurely, painfully protracted death would commence immediately. That Spence also gathered without an interpreter.

Gita fell to his knees and began untying his linen sacks and rummaging through them. There were bags within bags, but he found one he wanted and opened it and drew out an old-fashioned stethoscope which he put on and immediately displayed his best doctorly manner, hovering over the boy and listening through the obsolete instrument.

Chief Watti seemed pleased and left them to their business.

"I hope we have enough medicine between us to do some good," remarked Spence when they were once again alone.

"It seems we have no choice," replied Adjani.

"His breathing is shallow and very light." Gita frowned. "He may be beyond help."

Adjani knelt over the patient and placed a hand on his forehead. "He's on fire! The boy is burning up with fever."

"What else do you have in your sack, Gita? Any drugs? Medicine?"

"Nothing much—novocaine, aspirin, a few antibiotics. I'm a dentist, remember."

"The antibiotics might be some help," said Adjani. "If we could only figure out what's wrong with him."

"We can try to get his temperature down in any case," said Spence. "Let's have the aspirin."

Gita reached his hand in and fished around and withdrew a small plastic bottle. "Here. Sixty tablets. Maybe enough, eh?"

"Let's give him some antibiotics, too, and a sponge bath and see if that will help." To Spence's amazed look Adjani replied, "Yes, antibiotics are still quite useful in this part of the world. Now then, Gita, go and tell Watti we need some water in a basin and clean cloths." Gita gave him a pleading look. "Yes, you. For all they know you're the only one that speaks Hindi. You'll be our spokesman."

Gita went out and came back in a few moments. They sat looking at the boy helplessly, desperately trying to recall the medical knowledge they possessed. Their lives depended upon such stray information now.

In a while a young woman in a yellow and orange sari entered the tent with a large bowl of water and several washcloths and towels. She spoke to Gita shyly and then withdrew a few paces to watch with folded hands.

"She is Watti's wife; the boy's mother, at least. I think Watti has more than one wife. She will get us anything we need."

Adjani moistened a cloth and proceeded to bathe the boy's fevered limbs. Spence took four of the aspirin tablets and crushed them while Adjani opened several blue and white capsules. "Get us some drinking water. And make sure it's clean," said Spence. Gita relayed the request to the woman who disappeared into the speckled shadows.

He took up a small cup and poured a swallow of the water into it and stirred in the powdered mixture. Adjani administered the medicine, lifting the boy's head and pouring it gently down his throat. Spence saw the boy's ribs poking out of his flesh and wondered how long it had been since he had eaten.

"We've got to get that fever down and get some food into him or we're sunk. He hasn't eaten anything in weeks, by the look of him."

"Very likely," said Adjani, and he went back to bathing the unconscious boy.

The day progressed with aching slowness. The three impromptu physicians took turns administering tepid baths and dosed their patient with aspirin at proper intervals. They dozed and checked the sick boy for signs of improvement and encouraged one another that they were doing the right things.

By evening the youngster seemed a little better, though it was hard to tell precisely. His temperature seemed to have fallen somewhat and he moaned slightly when Adjani started the baths again.

"Should we try to feed him?" wondered Spence.

"I don't know," said Adjani with a worried look. "I think tonight will tell."

"Meaning?"

"If he makes it through the night he'll get better. If not . . ."

"He's that bad, do you think?" Spence looked again at the prostrate form. The boy was pale and sunken-eyed; death did indeed seem to hover at his shoulder.

Gita rose from listening with his stethoscope. "I fear Adjani is right. His heartbeat is but a flutter. We may lose him."

"If we lose him we lose our ticket out of here." Spence turned and knelt over the boy as if to shake him awake and reason with him.

"Come on," said Adjani. "We'll take a walk if the guards will let us. I could use some fresh air."

They stepped from the tent and were met by the stern faces of the guards. Adjani motioned that they wanted to walk, and one of the guards nodded and pushed the other one to his feet to accompany the prisoners on their stroll.

The people of the bandit village eyed them curiously. Clearly, white men were a novelty to the younger ones, and a dark-skinned man dressed as a white man was perhaps equally unique. The pair drew long, unguarded stares wherever they went.

Neither spoke for a while. They just walked side by side among the crazy-quilt tents and listened to the raucous clatter of brilliant scarlet-and-yellow birds flitting among the treetops and swooping down from time to time in bold slashes of color.

"What are our chances, Adjani?" Spence broke the silence at last, saying what they both had on their minds.

"I don't know. It depends on the boy."

"What's he got—some kind of paratyphoid?"

"That's my guess. We'd need a lab set-up to know for sure. The point is we can't do much for him. The fever is in its third week, at least."

Spence was suddenly angry. "Why didn't they get help sooner? What's wrong with these people?"

"They are backward, ignorant. The same with poor people the world over. It is the way they have lived for centuries. They are not likely to change over the death of one small boy."

"On Gotham we would have had him cured and on his feet in less time than it takes his father to plunder a caravan. But here! What can we do? It isn't fair."

"Fair or not, this is the way it is—the way it always will be."

They had reached the extent of the village and the jungle stood before them a green wall. Their guard grunted and motioned them with the rifle to turn and start back.

The slanting rays of the afternoon light shone amber through the trees. The tops of the trees glinted gold among the green. Blue smoke from cooking fires began to thread into the air and the smells of strong spices scented their passage back through the bandit hideaway. The men, most of whom had slept all day, recovering from their night's work, stirred from their tents to gather in groups, talking loudly.

"Evil has many faces, does it not?" said Adjani, gazing around him. "This one is not particularly frightening. But it is evil nonetheless."

Just then a shout from the far end of the camp reached them. Spence saw Gita standing in front of the chief's tent waving to them and calling, "Come quickly! He speaks! Come!"

Spence and Adjani raced to the tent and found the boy, eyes hard and black in a face the color of old parchment, lolling his head from side to side moaning in weak delirium.

"Is he awake?" asked Spence. The boy's eyes, though open, had a dull-glazed shallow look.

"He is slipping into coma."

"We've got to do something," Spence said frantically. He fell to his knees beside the thin body, placing his hand on the frail chest. "The fever's worse." He looked at Gita and then Adjani with urgent expectation. "We've got to do something," he repeated.

"What would you have us do?" said Adjani.

"Anything is better than letting him die like this. Gita, get your pills."

"What are you going to do?"

"The only thing we can—megadose him with the antibiotics. He's dying before our eyes. At least this way he may have a chance."

Gita handed him an assortment of plastic bottles containing various drugs. Spence selected the antibiotics and emptied the contents of a handful of capsules into a small bowl.

"Gita, find the boy's mother," instructed Adjani. "Tell her to bring us honey or sugar water—anything sweet to drink. Lots of it. And hurry!"

"Don't die yet," whispered Spence as he worked. "Hang on, kid. Hang on."

Gita returned and handed Spence a vessel of liquid. Spence smelled it and said, "Smells like flowers; what is it?"

"Jasmine water. They drink it like tea. It is heavily sugared. Very sweet."

"Good, that's what we want." He poured some into a bowl with the crushed pills. "I'm no medic or I would have thought of this hours ago. The glucose will boost his metabolism. He's got to fight that fever."

The boy's mother entered and brought a jug of liquid which she handed to Spence. He smelled it and coughed, "Phew! What is that?"

Gita sniffed the jug and diffidently placed a tip of his little finger in the liquid and brought it to his tongue. "Mmm, it is puyati—nectar of the gods. Fermented palm sap. One develops a taste for it."

"Yeah? Well, we can't give him this."

"Why not? Undoubtly he drinks it already, and the alcohol might do him some good."

"You're quite a country doctor, Gita. But I have a better idea." Spence grabbed the basin Adjani was using to bathe the boy and dashed the water out of it. He poured it full again with the palm liquor.

"Now we have an alcohol bath. That ought to cool him off quicker."

Adjani nodded and dipped the cloth into the reeking brew. When he had finished he turned to Spence and took the cup from his hands, swishing the liquid around the rim several times. He lifted the boy's head and administered the medicine. Then he turned to the others.

"Well, that's done. Now we wait. We'll take turns watching him and bathing him round the clock."

Spence looked at the weak, pathetic figure wasted painfully thin by fever. Their lives hung by the slenderest of threads, as fine as the breath which raised the little chest slowly and regularly and all but imperceptibly. *Will any of us live to see another morning?* Spence wondered. *The next few hours would tell.*

CHAPTER ELEVEN

"WHAT ARE you doing here?" Ari had become aware of unseen eyes on her; she whirled around and met Hocking gazing at her with an unhealthy leer on his bony face. She had not heard him enter. Her father was asleep on one of the couches across the room and she thought of waking him, but decided not to.

"I have only come to see how my charges are getting along," Hocking said with oily civility. "Have you everything you need?"

"Let us go. You can't hope to gain anything by keeping us."

"Letting you go would be somewhat awkward at this point, I'm afraid. We've gone to an enormous amount of trouble to get you here. But maybe we can strike a bargain."

There was a slight whirring noise and the pneumochair slid closer. Hocking dropped his voice and his obsequious manner. "I want to talk to you. If you cooperate I might be able to help you. I have a plan."

"A plan for what?"

"For resolving this messy affair once and for all," whispered Hocking slyly. He glanced around as if to make certain no one overheard him.

"How do I know you'll live up to your part of the bargain?"

"You don't. But you'd be foolish to pass up any chance you might have to secure your freedom. I'll tell you something, Miss Zanderson. There are forces at work here that stagger the imagination—far beyond your comprehension. You are but an infinitesimal part of a design greater than men dare dream. That I am offering you a chance to save yourself should be enough for you."

As much as she distrusted the loathsome being before her, she wanted to believe there might be a way to influence him to release them.

"I don't know if I should."

"Listen, you little fool! Ortu wants you dead. You're a nuisance to him. But if you help me, I'll get you out of here safely. You have no choice . . . I won't ask again." Hocking glared at her fiercely. "Well?"

"All right. What do you want me to do?"

"Come with me. Now. And be quiet. Ortu has eyes all over the place."

Ari slipped after the floating chair as it flew along darkened corridors and down spiraling stone steps, deeper and deeper into the bowels of the palace. It was all she could do to keep pace with the egg gliding before her.

Finally they reached a large wooden door at the bottom of a flight of steps. Hocking paused before the door and it swung magically open before them, closing on them again once they had entered.

The room was large and dark, rank with the musty smell of age and silent as a tomb. There was a soft hum and a click, and instantly the room was washed in white light. Ari blinked and threw a hand to shield her eyes.

In a moment she lowered her arm and saw that they were in a room with stone walls at the very roots of the palace. The light came from two huge lamps set in the ceiling, but otherwise the room had no distinguishing features—save one: the enormous apparatus glinting coldy before them.

What it looked like, she could not describe. It seemed insectlike to her—as if it were a construction of nature rather than human engineering—but it had a strong, metallic appearance. The gleaming black thing stood on tall legs over a small platform with a sling chair on it. The chair she recognized as being a more or less common variety, but it was strangely out of place among the protruding knobs and convolutions of the sleek machine. Altogether, the thing had a vague, spidery appearance.

"What is it?" she asked. Her voice quavered, giving away her anxiety.

"This is merely a simple communication device—a sort of radio, you might say. It amplifies and projects brain waves. It won't bite you, my dear. I've used it myself many times. It's quite harmless, I assure you."

Ari was not assured. She liked her collaboration with the enemy less and less with every passing second.

"You're going to put me in that, aren't you?" she stated.

"I'm going to ask you to assist me, yes. That is, after all, why you came. Shall we begin?"

Hocking indicated that she was to take her place in the chair. Ari mounted the platform uncertainly and settled herself in the chair, perching on the edge of the fabric seat.

"You may as well make yourself comfortable," said Hocking as he went about readying the machine. "This will take some time."

"What are you going to do?"

Hocking could not resist a smirk at her weakness. Humans, he thought, were all alike: scared children in the presence of things too vast for their puny intellectual powers. "You will not feel a thing. There will be no sensation whatever. See? We are already beginning."

Hocking lied. There was an immediate sensation, and an unplesant one.

Ari suddenly felt dizzy, as if the room had shifted, and the feeling in her fingers—which she held clasped together in her lap—faded away. For a long moment she could not focus her eyes.

But the feeling diminished and she felt, rather than heard, a deep vibrant thrum moving up through the platform, through the chair, and into her very bones. She clamped her teeth shut to keep them from vibrating.

Two long pincerlike claws came down over her head; Ari closed her eyes so she would not have to look. When she opened them again she was bathed in a shimmering *blue* aura. It covered her like a gossamer gown.

The light in the room had dimmed and Hocking was nowhere to be seen. She sat motionless and gazed into the flowing light. It seemed a part of her, and she thought she had never seen anything so beautiful. It sparkled with unearthly radiance, flecked through with silver beams which burst like tiny comets as they played over her form.

She relaxed and centered her mind on the dancing light. As she did a numbness overtook her, starting at the base of her neck and working upward over her scalp. The feeling was unusual, but not unpleasant. She let it creep over her until it seemed that her head had become isolated from her body—there was no longer any connection between the two that she could feel. But at the same time this did not alarm her. She accepted it calmly and noted it somewhere in the back of her mind.

Ari's breathing slowed and she felt herself drifting. It reminded her of those last waking moments just before sleep overtook her—that delicious nether region between wakefulness and sleep when the body relaxed and the waking mind gave itself over to the subconscious.

In a moment, with eyes wide open, as if stargazing on a star-filled night, Ari began to dream.

She heard a voice nearby. It was the voice of her father and she was a little girl playing with her doll on the porch of an old house. The voice said, "Ari, where are you?"

"I'm here, Daddy," she replied. She looked around but her father was not there. She continued playing with the doll's frilly pink dress and heard again her father's call.

This time she rose from her play and looked out across a green lawn. The lawn was newly mown and smelled of cut grass. A light summer breeze blew clippings across the walk. Her father stood out on the grass and she saw him and waved to him.

"Come along, Ari. Follow me," he said. But he did not look at her. He seemed instead to look beyond her. This frightened Ari. She could not think why her father would not look at her.

"I'm coming, Daddy," she called as her short little legs scrambled down the porch steps.

Her father turned away and was walking quickly across the lawn in long strides toward a dark wood which grew near the house.

"Daddy!" the young girl cried. "Wait for me!"

The figure of her father reached the wood and stopped. He looked back and motioned her onward and then stepped in among the trees. Ari reached the place a moment later and stood outside, hesitant and frightened.

"Daddy, come out! I can't see you!" she shouted. Her tiny voice fell away among the trees.

No answer came from the dark wood. The afternoon sun stretched the shadow of the old house across the lawn and Ari drew away from it. She stepped lightly into the forest and was immediately immersed in deep blue shade and black shadow.

"This way, Ari," she heard her father say. The voice came from just ahead of her.

She ran forward, stumbled, picked herself up and ran on. She caught a fleeting glimpse of her father's back as he moved through the tangle of branches. "Wait!" she called. "I can't keep up!"

But the figure of her father moved on, never looking back.

Little Ari began to cry. The tears streamed down her face and she sat down on the ground and wailed.

"Why are you crying, Ari?" The voice was warm and gentle. The little frightened girl sensed in it a friendliness and understanding.

She turned and saw a tall man standing in the light of the fading afternoon sun, golden and serene. He was unlike any man she had ever seen; he seemed to exude peace and kindness. His large yellow eyes looked down on her with benevolence.

"My daddy left me," she sniffed, her fear dissolving. Here was someone who would help her. "I tried to follow him, but I got lost. I'm scared."

"Don't be afraid. I will help you. I am your friend." The figure reached out a hand and Ari took it, noticing with a child's curiosity that the hand had but three exceptionally long fingers. "Come with me."

Ari and the tall being turned and walked out of the wood and back onto the lawn toward the house. But as they neared the old structure it began to change. The walls melted and rearranged themselves, the roof slid away, the porch became a great courtyard—the house transformed itself into a palace of shimmering gold.

"Is this *your* house?" asked Ari. Her eyes sparkled at the scene.

"Yes," answered the being. "But now it is your house as well. You will live with me forever."

They drew nearer and entered the palace through a magnificent gate of scrolled silver. A group of people were waiting for them, and when these people saw Ari they all cheered and made sounds of welcome.

They moved across the courtyard; Ari heard beautiful music playing inside. She saw a wide gallery, lit from within by glittering lights, and heard laughter echoing through the palace. A wide bank of stairs led to the gallery and she ran to the foot of the stairs.

"Ari!" someone called. She looked up and saw her father surrounded by many others, standing on the stairs waiting for her.

"Daddy! You came back! Never leave me—promise?"

"Look who's here!" said her father. He raised his arm and stepped aside. At the same moment the people gathered around him parted and a beautiful woman dressed in white stepped forward.

The woman came down the steps holding out her arms for Ari. The little girl looked and at first did not know who the woman was. She looked again and saw that it was her mother.

"Mama!" Ari squealed.

Instantly she was swept up in her mother's arms and cradled to her breast. "Ari, my beautiful, beautiful child," murmured the woman. "I've missed you so much. I'll never leave you again."

Ari, overcome with happiness, pressed her head against her mother's neck and wept for joy. She heard the voice of the golden being saying, "Today your dreams have become real. You don't need them anymore. Give them to me and you can live here forever."

When Ari awoke she was back in the closed room with her father.

"Ari, I've been terribly worried about you. Where have you been? You were unconscious when they brought you in. Are you all right?"

She sat up and grabbed her throbbing head. "I'm okay—I think. Oww . . . my head hurts. I've been asleep."

"For nearly two hours. Where did they take you?"

Ari looked at her father. His words puzzled her. "Take me?" She dimly remembered Hocking coming for her and going somewhere dark and unpleasant, but nothing more. "I don't think they took me anywhere."

"Yes, they did. You were gone when I woke up. You should have told me where you were going. I was worried—you were gone so long."

"Was I?" She rubbed her head and closed her eyes. It made no sense. Nothing did, really. She had a vague picture of talking to someone and a warm, pleasant feeling associated with the picture. But who she had talked to, what they had said, anything at all about the meeting, she could not remember.

It was as if a piece of her mind, her memory, had been taken from her, wiped clean. She could not remember.

But the warm, pleasant feeling lingered and she smiled as it flowed over her like a gentle breath of air. "Wherever I was, it was the best place I have ever been," she said. "I feel like I was in paradise."

CHAPTER TWELVE

PACKER DISLIKED escaping from Chief Ramm—it made him feel like a low criminal. But he had no other alternative. He simply could not stand the thought of remaining in the cell another minute, waiting to be picked off like a rat in a basket. Whoever had tried to kill him would try again. He felt certain of that, and certain that this time they would succeed.

Probably last time they had been scared away by Ramm's coming back to the block; next time they would be more thorough. Ramm, for all his help, had demonstrated that he could not protect his prisoner. And though the security chief still maintained that the safest place for Packer was locked up in his protective cell, Packer disagreed. He had tried it Ramm's way, now he wanted to try it his way.

On his own he would be able to put some distance between himself and his assassins. So he had escaped, finding the opportunity when he was left alone outside the cell for a few moments while men from housekeeping installed a new couch in his cell. He simply had tapped in a new access code—one that required a single digit. Then he had taken a length of stiff wire from one of the housekeeper's tool carts and slipped it up the sleeve of his jumpsuit.

He waited for the end of the shift—the exact time when his first attack had come—and when he was certain no one was around he produced the wire and went to work on the access panel, bending the wire through the vent holes in the upper portion of the plastic portal.

The burly physicist had been rewarded with success a half hour later when the door slid open. He walked out of the cell block and through the security station like a cat on hot coals. But he had not been seen or challenged.

Now he hurried toward his own quarters in the HiEn section, changing levels and taking the tube tram partway and getting off two stops before his own to backtrack and see if he was being followed.

He reached the HiEn section and went directly to his quarters. While he took precautions against being followed, it never occurred to his trusting heart that his office and living mod would be watched. He entered with the flood of relief which all hunted creatures experience upon reaching the safety of their lairs. His relief proved short-lived.

As his hand moved toward the access plate a voice said, "Don't do that, my friend—if you want to live a little longer."

Packer froze in the darkness. He withdrew his hand and whirled around to face the unseen speaker. He heard a slight creak and a click, and a light struck him in the face.

He blinked and put up his hand. "Who is it?"

"What are you doing here?" his questioner demanded.

The voice was unmistakable. "Kalnikov?"

"Kalnikov—who else?"

Packer saw a hand reach out of the darkness and push the shade of the desk lamp down. The face of the big Russian leaned into the pool of light, grinning. "I am sorry, Olmstead. I had to make sure it was you."

"What are *you* doing here?"

The pilot shrugged. "I heard you were being held and I came to the only place they would not likely search—the room of one of their own prisoners."

"One of their prisoners—what do you mean? I was under protective custody. Voluntarily."

"Oh, I see. They gained your cooperation at a very cheap price, then."

"Kalnikov, what are you talking about?"

"Ramm and the others. How many others, I do not know yet. But they mean to take over Gotham."

"Ramm?"

Kalnikov nodded slightly. "Didn't you guess? They fooled you completely."

"I guess they did." Packer switched on the lights and crossed the room, collapsing in a chair. Kalnikov settled back at the desk and rested his long arms on the desktop. He looked boyish and bemused, a sly smile jerking the corners of his wide mouth.

"What's so funny, you Soviet sausage? We're both in big trouble."

"I was just thinking how surprised you looked just now. I'm glad it was me that met you rather than someone else."

"You scared me. I wasn't expecting a welcoming committee."

"Your trouble is that in your country you do not have a sufficient tradition of deception to make you naturally suspicious. It is very helpful in situations like this one. It allows you to view your position with a certain amount of objectivity."

"Well then, Comrade Skeptic, what does your naturally suspicious nature tell us we should do?"

"It tells me we should do what freedom fighters in my country have always done—go underground."

"Brilliant!" snorted Packer. "On a donut—even a big tin donut like this one—they'll find us sooner or later. There *is* no underground."

"My unbelieving friend, there is always an underground. You will be amazed at what we will find. Come now"—the Russian giant got to his feet—"gather up your things. From this moment on we are invisible."

Spence had never heard an authentic death rattle before. But when he heard it now, he had no doubt what it was: terrible and appalling, these were the last fighting gasps of a human life.

He had been sitting half-asleep beside the boy's sickbed, nodding through the third watch. The boy's mother crouched at the foot of the bed dozing fitfully. Adjani and Gita lay sound asleep in a far corner of the tent; Gita snored softly like a slumbering buffalo mired in his favorite wallow.

At first Spence thought that the rattle, like the gurgle of a broken water pipe, came from outside the tent nearby. He roused himself to look around. The sound came again and he stared in horror at the boy's blue-tinged body. The pale lips parted, the eyes sunken, head tipped back, the young face aged beyond its years by the illness and the glowing fire of fever; the eyelids snapped open and unseeing eyes burned out like black coals. The hideous sound bubbled forth from his young throat.

He watched in mute terror as death grappled hand-to-hand with life for the body of the youngster. Death was winning the contest.

Spence called out in the darkness to Gita and Adjani, fearing to leave the boy's side for an instant lest the inevitable happen. No sound came from his friends; they slept on.

Then, suddenly, the gasp was cut short and an expiring hiss escaped from between the boy's teeth. Spence stared down helplessly. That was it. He was gone. The boy's mother, now fully awake, her eyes wide with terror, sprang forward in a sudden rush of grief, clutching at her child's legs, burying her face in them. For a moment she lay there as though stricken dead herself; then she raised herself up and looked at Spence with eyes full of sorrow and reproach and rushed out of the tent.

Spence was alone with the body.

"No!" he cried. "You can't die!"

He grabbed the small, fragile body in his hands and shook it as an angry child would shake a rag doll. Then, thinking more clearly, he placed his mouth over the boy's nose and mouth and blew gently. He laid the body down and placed the heels of his hands over the boy's heart and gave a quick downward thrust. He blew into the open mouth again and alternated with quick blows to the chest.

"God, don't let this boy die!" Spence prayed, beating on the little chest with the heel of his hand. "Please, God, save him. Please!"

Spence was only partially conscious of the prayer, but he offered it over and over again as he worked, transforming the words into an urgent litany. Sweating and quivering at the same time, he worked like a robot gone berserk, performing his ritual over and over again and mumbling under his breath the plaintive prayer for God to spare the boy's life.

He labored this way for many minutes without response from the child. At last, muscles aching, sweat stinging his eyes, Spence collapsed light-headed over the still body and began to cry.

"God, in this stinking land of death is it too much to ask you to save one life? Where are you? Don't you care?" He sobbed, more out of anger and frustration than sorrow. "Where *are* you?"

It was no use. God did not intervene in his creation anymore—if he ever did. His eyes and ears were elsewhere, attending the birth or death of a galaxy perhaps, but not to be bothered with the passing of an insignificant *goonda* boy.

Spence sat up, drying his eyes. He looked sadly at the small body, pale and still in the lamplight. He groaned. "I could have believed in you, God. I almost did." He shook his head; a stirring of regret, as much for his own broken faith—so tentative and unformed—as for the death of the child, passed through him.

"I almost believed." He placed a hand on the boy's forehead and felt the warmth of the fever diminish as the body cooled.

It made no sense, this stupid waste. The sights of the last days flooded back on him. He saw a horde of stump-legged, hunchbacked beggars and starving children pressing gaunt faces toward him. He saw whitened corpses bobbing in the rancid river like so many thousand buoys. He saw the teeming darkness spreading over the city and knew this to be mankind's ancient enemy seeking to destroy the hapless victims cowering beneath its shadow.

"God! Why?" Spence pressed the heels of his hands into his eyes. "Why, why, why?"

The challenge went unanswered.

Spence looked at the young corpse lying so still and light upon the bed. It almost seemed that the slightest breeze would blow the small shell away like a leaf in the wind.

As if in answer to the mental image Spence felt a slight movement in the air and heard the rustle of the wind in the leaves outside the tent. He raised his head and listened to the night sounds. In the jungle all had become deathly still. Spence fancied he heard footsteps outside the tent, and then heard the bark of a camp dog.

The breeze stirred again, becoming stronger. He felt its coolness on his damp skin. The walls of the tent rippled under it; the lamp flickered and brightened.

And then everything became quiet. The wind stopped. The tent fell into flat folds again. The lamp flame stilled and dimmed.

The world seemed for a moment to hang balanced on the edge of a thin knife blade. One breath would send it toppling off on one side or the other. Spence held his breath to keep it balanced. He stared down at the dead boy.

In that moment eternities were born, time evaporated. Spence felt its barriers dissolve and flow away. He saw everything in crystalline clarity, hard-edged and in microscopic detail.

The dead boy's pale, almost translucent skin, the tiny black sweep of his eyelashes, the fine rounded curve of his nostrils, the delicate line of his thin, bloodless lips, the silken shaft of each black hair brushing his temples—all this and more Spence saw in a marvel of dumbstruck awe. Each object in his gaze had taken on a fierce, almost painful beauty. He was overwhelmed. He wanted to look away, to close his eyes to keep the sight from burning out his eyes, but dared not. He was held by a power stronger than his own and knew he could not escape it.

Then, as his eyes took in the terrible wonder of the dead boy's body, he saw a tiny flutter just inside the tender hollow of the throat. He heard a sound which seemed to thunder inside his brain, though it must have been barely audible. It was the long, shuddering whisper of breath being drawn into the nostrils and filling the lungs. It was the sound of life reentering the young boy's body.

The breath stopped—Spence wanted to gasp for air himself—and then it was released. The small chest sank. It seemed like an age before the chest rose again.

Slowly the breathing continued, becoming steadier, stronger and more regular. Spence's mind reeled as he saw color seeping back into the boy's cheeks and the pulse in the throat beating rhythmically.

He knew then that the boy would live and not die. The miracle was complete.

Spence threw himself on the frail body and hugged it to him. He placed a hand on the boy's forehead and felt the warmth of life returning. But the fever was gone.

When Spence raised himself up, dashing tears from his eyes once again, two dark eyes were watching him with curiosity. They blinked at him and then a little hand reached out for his. Spence grabbed it and held it tightly.

He was sitting there, looking into those bemused young eyes, clutching the small hand, when a commotion arose outside the tent. He heard voices, shouts, half-angry cries, and then suddenly the tent was filled with people.

Foremost among them was the *goonda* chief. Spence glanced around as the crowd tumbled in with a rush. By the expression on Chief Watti's face Spence knew the moment should have been his last—the man held a long dagger in his hand ready to strike. The mother of the boy crouched at his elbow biting the back of her hand. The others hung back—mostly women, already raising a lamentation for the dead boy, and other *goondas* with their rifles at the ready.

But the bandit leader took one look at his son, laying there with a feeble smile on his lips, holding the hand of his physician, and let out a whoop of jubilation. The dagger spun from his hand. His wife leaped to her son and cradled his thin figure to herself.

Spence stood slowly and looked around. Adjani and Gita, staring and blinking at the confusion around them, rose up and came to stand beside Spence.

"What happened?" said Gita, eyeing the rifle-toting *goondas* warily. These stared back at the prisoners and shook their heads incredulously.

"You wouldn't believe me," said Spence. "I scarcely believe it myself."

"Did we miss something?" asked Adjani.

Spence turned to regard the boy, now completely enveloped in the embrace of his father.

"No; nothing much."

CHAPTER THIRTEEN

ARI SAT on the small balcony of her room in the tower. The sunlight bathed her upturned face with its warm light and touched her golden hair, transforming it into spun sunbeams. She looked an angel wearing a mortal cloak, but dreaming of its celestial home.

Her thoughts were far from angelic. She had, in the days since Hocking first enlisted her aid, begun to fall into reverie and melancholy. Her father watched her withdraw into herself by degrees until she hardly spoke at all and sat daydreaming for hours at a time on the balcony.

When he ventured to move her from these fits of solitary introspection she would smile wistfully and say, "Oh, don't worry about me, Daddy. I was just thinking . . ." Though what she was thinking about she would never say. The elder Zanderson had begun to believe that she herself did not know.

He also believed, and rightly so, that it had to do with the visits Hocking paid her, and their trips to who knew where, to do who knew what. She did not speak to him of what went on, and increasingly she resented his continued asking about those secret sessions.

So he had become a silent worrier. He held his tongue, though it crushed him to see his daughter's spirit withering before his eyes. To fend off the growing sense of dread and doom he felt encircling them he had begun a course of conversation designed to keep her mind occupied and centered on the present.

But even his ebullient monologue failed to prevent the girl's odd moodiness. She would get up in the middle of a sentence and go out on the balcony to sit and stare out into the courtyard or, as she sat now, with her face toward the sun in an attitude of reverence.

His worse fears of a lifetime were taking flesh before his eyes: his daughter seemed to be slipping into the same strange malady that had claimed her mother. And that was almost too much to bear.

"Ari," he said gently, coming to stand beside her on the balcony. "What are you thinking about, dear?"

"Oh hi, Daddy. I didn't hear you come out."

"I asked what you are thinking about."

"Oh, nothing really. I don't know."

"It must be something. You've been out here a long time."

A sad smile played on her lips. "Have I? I'm sorry. I left you sitting alone again, didn't I? Oh, well . . . "

"Ari, look at me." The girl rolled large languid eyes toward him. "I don't want you to go with him when he comes."

"Who, Daddy?"

"Hocking. He's putting you under some kind of spell. He's stealing your mind."

"Nonsense!" She laughed, and the sound pattered down like light rain into the courtyard below. "Why would anyone want to do that? It's impossible besides."

"I'm not so sure anything is impossible anymore. But if he hasn't put you under a spell, you tell me what he *has* been doing. Where do you go? What do you do?"

"We don't go anywhere, really. A room, I think. We don't do anything. Honestly, I *have* to go . . . I am helping."

The last was added almost as an afterthought. Zanderson pounced on it like a hungry cat. "Helping? Who are you helping?"

Ari turned her eyes away and gazed out across the wall to the green hills beyond. "I'm . . . helping . . ." She could not say more.

"Ari! Look at me! Don't you see what's happneing to you? You don't even remember why you're doing it. You're *not* helping, Ari. You're being used. He's using your mind—you're becoming a . . . a vegetable!"

The outburst brought a wispy smile to Ari's lips. She raised her hand to her face and rubbed her cheek distractedly. "I do feel a little funny sometimes. It's so strange . . . " She turned away again. Her father brought her back, taking her shoulders and turning her around. "What is strange? What do you remember? Tell me!"

"It's so strange—I feel so sleepy inside, like my head is stuffed with cotton."

"Ari"—he took her hands and pressed them in his own—"promise me you won't go with him any more. You have to stop now before there's nothing left. Will you promise?"

"All right, Daddy. If you like."

"No, darling. It's not for me. It's for you—do it for your own sake. He's destroying you. Don't let him. Resist."

She looked at him vaguely; he wondered if she heard him at all. He decided to try a new approach to make her understand. "Remember when you said that we'd be rescued soon? I believe it now. I do."

"Rescued?"

"You said that Spence knew where we were and he'd come and free us. Well, I think you were right. I think he's coming now. He'll be here soon."

"Who's coming, Daddy?"

"Spence! That's what I'm telling you. Spence is coming."

Ari regarded her father with blank, uncomprehending eyes, as if he suddenly started speaking a foreign language. "I don't think I know who you're talking about."

"Spence! *Your* Spence—Dr. Reston. Don't you remember?"

"I don't know him," she replied slowly and turned away again, closing her beautiful blue eyes—now the color of shallow ice pools—and turning her face once more toward the sun. Her father staggered back into their room like a man stunned by a blow; he collapsed, dazed, on a bed of cushions. Then he raised clenched fists to his temples and began to weep.

The sun rose a fiery red gong above a green hillscape. Three tired travelers witnessed the sunrise with burning eyes. They had been marching through thick forest undergrowth al¹ night and were exhausted and hungry, not having eaten anything substantial for nearly two days—since being expelled from the *goonda* camp as sorcerers.

The spectacle of the red sun casting its bloodly glare over the thickly forested, steeply undulating hills brought but little cheer to the party. The relatively commonplace sight of the hard-beaten, rock-strewn, crumbling road did, however, improve their spirits somewhat.

"There it is!" shouted Gita. "I see it! Through those trees. There!"

The fat little man dashed through the thinning brush and rushed out onto the old highway. He fell on his knees and kissed its sun-baked surface in a show of heartfelt gratitude, like a primitive seafarer making a successful landfall. "At last, old toothless friend, we meet again," crowed Gita. Adjani and Spence, standing over him, watched with amusement. "I do not think I have ever seen a sight so wonderful or welcome," he continued, gazing ahead into the distance. "A road is a marvelous thing."

"It beats scratching through jungle, that's for sure," offered Spence. He, too, turned his eyes toward the north and saw the wall of mountains, purple and hazy in the distance, their faces still cloaked in night's gloom. "How far do you think it is?"

Adjani cocked his head and said, "We can't be sure, but I'd say Siliguri is still a hundred kilometers to the north and Darjeeling is half again as far."

"Yes, and all uphill from here," said Gita.

"Any chance of hitching a ride?"

"Very doubtful. Merchants are the only ones with vehicles. Our caravan undoubtedly turned back. Anyway, that was three days ago; even if they decided to go on they would be there by now."

Spence squinted his eyes into the distance. "Well, then we have no other choice. We walk."

Gita let out a small whimpering noise and said, "It seems the road and I are destined to become very good friends. But," he added on a more optimistic note, "I have always wanted to see the mountains."

They turned toward the mountains and began walking along the road, easily falling into stride. Spence noticed that the air seemed lighter, less dense and humid. He took it as a sign that they were beginning to climb ever so slightly up the grade toward the rarefied heights of the mountains. The freshness revived him somewhat, clearing his tired mind and inflating his sagging spirits.

With nothing but the rolling road before him he let his mind wander where it would.

As it had often in the gloomy hours when they traveled by night, the prospect of the impending clash with the Dream Thief intruded on his thoughts. What would happen when they reached their destination he did not know, and hardly dared guess. For now it was enough that some distance still lay between himself and his enemy. He felt in a way secure—although why this should be he could not say, since the Dream Thief had shown himself able to cross astronomical distances to touch those he wished to touch. No barrier seemed able to stop him. And where he was not physically present his underlings were.

Knowing what he knew, it seemed surpassingly strange to Spence that he should be pointing his feet toward the Dream Thief's secret home on a path of certain destruction. But that is exactly what he was doing. In the end he knew it was the only thing he could do.

Spence wondered if he were being drawn to his fate by the Dream Thief himself. It often appeared to be the case—he felt an impulse within him that did not come entirely from his own heart. Could the Dream Thief manipulate his thoughts?

And if so, how did he know *when* his thoughts were being manipulated? Which were his own and which belonged to the other?

He pondered these things, and he had pondered them often since leaving Calcutta. He was deep in thought when he felt a nudge at his elbow.

"You look lost, sahib." Adjani fell into step beside him, studying him.

"I was just thinking how foolish we are to be rushing like lemmings to our own destruction." He swiveled his head around and took in Adjani's reaction to these words and then turned again to his feet shuffling along. "You and Gita—you don't have to go. You could turn back. Gita should, at any rate; he has a family to think about."

"Yes, that's one way to look at it."

"Is their another way?"

"Of course. There is always another way."

"Let's hear it, then. It seems to me that we are three ill-equipped, insignificant, hardheaded do-gooders who haven't got the sense to get out of trouble when they have the chance. We're fools for thinking we can face up to the Dream Thief—whoever or whatever he is. It's sheer lunacy. How can we even dream we'd make a difference?"

"You know that the rise and fall of empires, the fates of whole nations, often hinge on the will of a single human being. One man of firm dedication can stand against an army.

"I don't know how this is going to end any more than you do. But I believe that the light that is in you and in me—in all of us—is greater than all the darkness in the universe. God is working in you, Spence; he has marked you for his own. And who can stand against God?"

Spence could think of no one offhand.

"Does that make you uncomfortable? To be chosen?"

"Sure it does. Anyway, why me?"

"That is precisely the question you cannot ask."

"I know. His ways are not our ways and all that."

"Precisely."

Spence continued walking. "I'm not buying it. What difference does it make if I believe in him or not? What possible difference could it make in the outcome? You believe, and look where it's got you. You're staggering down some God-forsaken road on a death march, for heaven's sake. And for what?"

"To a believer no place is God-forsaken."

The Indian continued. "You don't fool me, Reston. This protest is the last gasp of a dying agnostic. You're running swiflty away from God—right into his arms.

"But to answer your question, I'd say it makes every difference in the world what you believe. Belief is the sense organ of faith, as your eyes are the sense organ of sight. With sight you see the world, with faith you see God. Belief has the power to shape reality."

"Imagined reality. Your personal perception of reality."

"No, reality itself, as it is—cold, hard, factual reality."

Spence's scowl deepened over his face. He was in no mood for listening to a lecture on the philosophy of reality from Professor Rajwandhi, but it appeared he had no vote. The tack Adjani chose next, however, surprised him.

"Look at that mountain peak out there."

"Which one? I see several."

"The center one with the white cap. Do you see it?"

"Yes; I see it," Spence said flatly.

"Let's be scientific about it and call it the point of observation, the focal point. Now does it exist or doesn't it?"

"Of course it exists."

"Are you sure? Prove it—better still, show me the focal point. Can you pick it up? Smell it? Taste it? Does it take up space or have any dimensions?"

No answer.

"No, of course not. A focal point is not a physical thing at all and yet it exists. We can prove that it exists because of the things we can do with it. We can use it to gauge distance and height. We can direct radio waves to it to accomplish any number of things. In other words, the focal point exists because it produces effects we can perceive but cannot account for in any other way.

"If you were to stand on that mountaintop right at the focal point, I could view you with a telescope. But you would feel nothing at all while being observed. You would not in any way be able to detect the point of observation, and yet with it I could learn a great deal about you."

"Ah, but where does it go when I'm not thinking about it, or believing in it? It doesn't exist at all then."

"Precisely."

"Are you trying to tell me God is like that?"

"Not at all. I'm trying to tell you that belief shapes reality in unexpected ways. Your belief in the point of observation enables you to do things you couldn't do if you didn't believe in it. Get it?"

Spence scratched his head. His scowl was lifting, being replaced by a look of puzzlement. Adjani continued pushing home his point.

"Look at it like this: because you believe in the focal point you react to it in certain ways—it is real for you and it shapes the world as you see it. Believing in it even affects your behavior.

"If you looked through a telescope and saw a lion running toward you down the road, what would you do?"

"Climb a tree." Spence had become absorbed in Adjani's argument.

"Of course. You might do any number of things, but you would not say to yourself: 'the focal point does not exist, therefore the lion does not exist.'"

"Only a fool would react that way."

"Oh? Well, it might surprise you to know that is exactly how you've been reacting toward God."

"I don't see it that way."

"Explain it to me then, if you can." The remark drew no response from Spence. He glared ahead stubbornly. "Shall I explain it to you?"

"Go ahead—it's your nickel. You seem to have all the answers."

Adjani ignored the jab and went on as if he had not heard it. "How clear does it have to be for you? God is meeting you at every turn, Spence. Think about it. Back there in the camp you prayed for a little boy who died and he lived again. On Mars you yourself should have died and yet you survived—against all odds you survived. And what is more, a creature from an alien civilization awoke from a sleep of five thousand years to tell you himself about God. And you insist you cannot see it?" Adjani threw back his head and gave a little laugh. "What must he do to get through to you? What will it take before you believe? Must these stones rise up and shout?" He waved a hand over the rough, rocky path before them.

Although he posed as the antagonist in these discussions with Adjani, he actually agreed more than he admitted. Spence had reached the same conclusions the night the boy had been revived. It had affected him more deeply than he could express to another person. He had thought about very little else since that moment. He relived it constantly, still savoring the strangeness, the awful vividness of it.

Here was a reality that surpassed all previously known realities he had ever experienced. It was as if the source of all life had passed through him for one blinding instant. And in that moment he had seen himself and the world as he had never seen it before. The memory of it left him weak.

Perhaps that was why he was fighting so hard not to believe. Adjani was right—if he believed, it would change him. He was merely clinging to the last shreds of his tattered naturalistic world view. Giving it up was not easy, and not a thing done capriciously. Much of who he was, the person he knew himself to be, was wrapped up in that cold, concise, computer-generated view of the universe.

Adjani's question still rang in his ears. He turned to answer, not knowing what he would say, but feeling it in his heart. He opened his mouth to speak.

Suddenly, like a blast of hot wind which shrivels the tender leaves of grass, a wilting sensation passed through Spence. He tottered a few steps, threw down his bundle, and clutched his head. He turned and looked at Adjani, eyes wide and staring.

"Ari . . . Ari!" he cried and dropped unconscious to the ground.

CHAPTER FOURTEEN

WHEN SPENCE came to, Gita was holding his head between his pudgy hands, leaning over him. Adjani held a tin filled with water up to his mouth. "Here, drink this. Slowly. That's right."

Spence moved to sit up. His head throbbed wildly, but other than that he felt all right. "How long was I out?" He rubbed his head and rolled it around on his shoulders as if to see if it was still in good working order.

"Not long. A couple of minutes maybe."

"It is too hot to be traveling on foot in the daytime," said Gita. He had been saying that ever since they struck out on the road without stopping that morning. "I think we should rest."

"No, we go on," replied Spence firmly. "Maybe we'll find some transportation—Gaur is just ahead, didn't you say?"

"Sunstroke is nothing to sneer at, Spencer Reston." Gita's dark complexion had taken on a distinct ruddy tint. The extertion of their trip was telling on him.

"We should rest a while anyway. Gita is right. It is getting too hot to be tramping around in the middle of the day. We can move on at dusk."

Spence squinted up his eyes and gazed skyward. The white-hot ball of the sun seemed to strike down at them with a fury—perhaps it had been a touch of sunstroke which had felled him.

Perhaps. But there was something else, too. He remembered calling out for Ari when it had struck, and he still vaguely felt that she—or someone else—was trying to get in touch with him in some way.

He lowered his gaze to regard Gita and Adjani. Black spots swam before his eyes and he reeled unsteadily.

"Sunstroke," repeated Gita. "It is not good."

"We'd better rest, Spence. For a couple of hours at least."

Spence nodded and they moved up the road a few meters to a huge spreading banyan tree, there to recline in the shade among the snaking branches and hanging trunks.

He sipped some more water and sat for a while with his head in his hands. The landscape far to the north wavered like a projection on a fluttering screen as waves of heat rose up from the land. He had not noticed the heat before, but was acutely aware of it now.

Gita's bulbous blue-turbanned head found a rock to prop itself on and soon his snores filled the air with a sleepy sound. Flies buzzing among the interwoven limbs of the tree droned on, and Spence felt the strain and tension melt away.

He lay back against the cool bark of one of the tree's innumerable trunks and stretched his legs out before him. At once he felt more relaxed. He sat for a time listening to the snores and the flies and the occasional bird call and let sleep steal over him.

The sun was orange and already reaching toward the horizon when Spence woke up again. Gita still snored, and he could hear the slow regular rhythm of Adjani's breath rising and falling in the shade nearby. The flies still buzzed around their heads, and the birds still chattered in the upper boughs of the tree.

But there was something else, too. And that something else, whatever it was, had brought him out of his nap.

He listened, straining into the silence of the forest around them, not moving a muscle. It came again almost in answer to his search—a muffled snort and a low rustling sound as if something big was moving through the underbrush. The sound trailed off as he listened and it sounded further off than he remembered, though he could not be sure—he had first heard it in his sleep.

Spence got to his feet and stepped back out onto the road. He paused to listen again and then began walking along the roadside in the direction they had been traveling. His senses were pricked sharp and he had an unaccountable feeling of being directed to seek out the source of the sound which he could not explain. He glanced back toward the tree where Adjani and Gita still slept and then hurried away on his chase.

The road dipped just ahead into a narrow valley. As Spence reached the crown of the hill and started down into the valley he thought he saw something dart away into the brush at the side of the road. There was just a blur of movement as he swung his eyes to the spot and then the quiver of roadside branches where the thing had entered.

Although he did not know what it was that he followed, he strongly suspected that it was not human. He had ceased to think about the possibility of encountering another band of *goondas,* although the likelihood of meeting them on the road was just as great as before.

Closer, Spence slowed and crouched, moving with as much stealth as he could manage. The inner voice which had roused him said, "Go on! Quietly!" He obeyed.

He slid to the side of the road where the bushes grew thick and nearly impenetrable. He could hear the sound of leaves rustling and branches snapping. A hollow snuffling, like the wheeze of an expiring engine, came filtering through the brush, and then the noise stopped.

Spence did not move a hair. He remained half-crouched and half-standing, peering into the dense growth, and he had the uncanny sensation of being examined by someone or something unknown.

There was a muffled footfall. Slow and deliberate; moving toward him.

The bushes right before him shook their leaves gently and then he saw something long and thin moving out snakelike from the wall of hedge.

Instinctively he jumped back. The thing withdrew in the same instant.

But he had seen something, even as he jumped, that told him what he wanted to know—a small pink lip and two nostrils.

He stooped down and pulled up a handful of long grass by the roots and moved back out onto the road.

He lifted his voice and called out, "Simba! Come! Simba! Now!"

He waited and nothing happened, though he could sense the thing waiting for him. He repeated his odd summons, extending the grass in his hand.

Then came a soft snort and the bushes shook and parted, and out stepped a great gray elephant.

The beast advanced on Spence slowly, warily, trunk wavering, reaching out, scenting him. It stepped closer with ponderous grace and shook its huge head from side to side, ears flapping as it tried to make up its mind about him. Then it saw the grass he held, and the trunk swung down and nuzzled the offering.

Spence flattened his palm, and the elephant took the gift in with a facile movement of the tip of the flexible appendage and swung it up into its mouth.

"Nice Simba," said Spence softly. "Steady, girl. Nobody is going to hurt you." He continued speaking softly and reasuringly as he looked the creature over from a distance.

That the elephant was in distress he noticed at once, for as soon as it had stepped free of the surrounding brush he saw the empty howdah on its broad back. Clearly it had run away after becoming separated from its mahout.

Then he saw the reason—blood trickled down from the animal's shoulder and there was a ragged, raw piece missing from its ear. There was blood on the ear as well.

Goondas, thought Spence. They had attacked the driver and his passengers and the elephant had escaped. He did not know whether elephants were at all common in that part of India, but very little surprised him about the country anymore. He could as easily imagine a caravan of elephants as a convoy of clanking antique sedans.

The elephant, having accepted the peace offering from the nonaggressive human, decided to accept the man as well. It stepped closer; he remained rock still. The trunk swung out and began examining him thoroughly, poking at the pockets of his jumpsuit and snuffling at his neck and wrists.

He endured the scrutiny with dignity and self-control, marveling that a beast so large could move so deftly. He called it gently, raising his hand to caress its trunk, feeling the quivering warmth of the creature. "Simba, easy now. I'm your friend. I'm going to take care of you. Good girl. Good Simba."

The trunk curled around his hand and pressed its pink lip against his palm. He stroked the trunk and then stepped closer to pat the huge cheek. "Would you like to come home with me, huh? You would? All right, then. Follow me. Come along."

He stepped away from the animal and turned his back. He walked slowly and deliberately, restraining the impulse to stop and look back to see if the elephant were following. He wanted to act as if he expected the animal to obey him as it would obey its proper master.

Spence was rewarded when he felt a slight tug at his arm and looked down to see the tip of the trunk curl around his wrist. He patted the trunk and walked on.

When they reached the banyan tree the two stopped and Spence called out, "Wake up, guys! I found us some transportation."

Adjani was the first one on his feet. "Hey!" he shouted in amazement. "Where did you get that?" He advanced slowly and came to stand in front of the beast and a little apart from it, letting it get used to him.

"Careful, you'll hurt her feelings. This is Simba, and she's agreed to take us the rest of the way to Darjeeling."

Adjani wrinkled his face and peered at Spence askance. "You pretend to know this animal?"

"Not at all," admitted Spence. "I thought all elephants were named Simba. I found her just up the road. She's been hurt."

Gita, hearing the commotion, rose up slowly, rubbing his eyes. He took one look at the great creature and let out a shriek. "Save us!" he cried, throwing his hands in the air. But seeing that everything seemed to be in order, and that the elephant was munching proffered grass, not attacking Adjani, he got up and joined his friends.

"A real elephant!" he said proudly over and over as he looked at it from every angle. "I knew there were still some of these magnificent animals in the north country, but I never dreamed I'd see one."

"Are they so rare then?" wondered Spence.

"Oh, yes, very rare indeed. No one is allowed to own one but the high government officials. They are much protected and used as official vehicles by the regional governors—just as in the time of the Maharajahs. Better than a motor car."

"Well, this one wasn't protected enough," said Spence. "She's been shot. Go get your bundle of medicine and we'll see what we can do for her."

At this Gita threw up his hands once more. "Shot? Oh, merciful heaven! Who would shoot a governor's elephant? Who would do such a thing?"

"*Goondas* is my guess."

"If that's true," said Adjani, "we might find the rest of the party up the road at the scene of the ambush."

"I hadn't thought of that. Do you think any *goondas* are still around?"

"Not if they attacked a government carrier. They'd have hit and run pretty fast. They'd be far away from here by now. Reprisals in such instances are fairly swift and bloody."

Gita came back with his medical sack and laid it on the ground. "I don't have enough medicine to treat an elephant," he lamented.

"Don't worry; I don't think she's hurt very bad. Here, take a look yourself."

Spence pointed out the torn ear and the wound in the shoulder behind it. Gita probed the wound with his fingers while Adjani kept her busy with bunches of grass.

"The bullet did not enter the flesh," announced Doctor Gita after his inspection. "It was deflected off the hide, probably due to the angle of the shot and an inferior bullet—they often load them from used casings, you know. We will rub some sulfa into the wound and smear on some mud to keep the flies out of it and keep it from getting infected. In a few days she'll be beautiful again."

"Will she trust us to ride her, do you think?"

Gita's eyes grew round. "You intend to ride this animal?"

"Certainly. All the way to Darjeeling. You shouldn't act so surprised. I said we'd need some transportation and here it is."

Gita went away muttering to himself in an incomprehensible babble. Adjani laughed and Spence patted the animal on the jaw and looked into Simba's calm, blue-brown eye and said, "You'll have to help us, girl. This is our first time. Show us what to do when the time comes. All right?"

The elephant seemed to wink at him and encircled his neck with her trunk.

"Good girl. Good Simba. We're going to be all right."

Gita came back with a pile of mud on a large leaf. He sprinkled sulfa from a brown bottle into his hand and gently worked it into the wound in the elephant's side. That done, he smeared the mud over it as a bandage. "Well, we have done what we can."

"Then let's go."

"Do you know how to drive this thing?" asked Adjani.

"No, but it can't be too hard. I've seen it in old movies. Let's see." Spence walked to the head of the elephant and said, "Down, girl. Down, Simba."

Nothing happened.

"*Mehrbani se,* Simba," said Adjani.

The elephant lifted its trunk and nodded, sinking down on its knees laboriously.

"I thought you didn't know anything about elephants," said Spence.

"He doesn't," Gita quipped. "It just means *please* in Hindi."

Adjani smiled and spread his hands. "It worked, didn't it?"

"Well, who first?" asked Spence.

"It is your elephant, sahib. You go first." Adjani patted him on the shoulder.

"All right, cowards. I will. All you do is grab an ear and . . . " Spence stepped up on the elephant's knee and took hold of its right ear and swung himself up behind the head. "Nothing to it."

Adjani followed and climbed into the howdah. Then it was Gita's turn. He stood trembling on the ground. "Well, come on. You can't walk all the way with us and we can't leave you behind for the *goondas.* You might as well get it over with."

"It is easy for you, Spencer Reston. But I have a wife and five beautiful daughters. A man must think of his family."

"Come on, Gita, we're wasting time." Already the shadows of the forest were moving across the road and in among the trees, deepening in shades of blue.

Spence reached down his hand. "Come on; your people have been doing this for a million years at least."

Gita bit his lower lip and handed up his bundles. Then he clasped Spence's hand and scrambled up. He did not stop scrambling until he was in the howdah, clutching the sides.

"All aboard?" called Spence. "Here we go. What's the word, Adjani?"

"*Mehrbani se.*"

At the command the elephant rose up and began walking. Spence found that she was easily steered with a gentle kick behind the ear—with the right foot to turn right, with the left foot for left. A kick with both feet simultaneously made the elephant go faster.

Off they trundled, swaying like kings of old aboard their fabled mounts with tusks sheathed in gold. Spence found the ride exciting.

"This is what I call going in style!" he shouted over his shoulder to his passengers.

"Now do you believe?" Adjani yelled back.

"I'm beginning to," Spence said to himself. "I think I'm beginning to."

CHAPTER FIFTEEN

TOWARD MORNING Spence was awakened by the sound of thunder in the hills. As the sun came up, a leaden rain started leaking out of low murky clouds. The three stirred themselves and sat huddled under the banyan tree that had sheltered them through the night. They munched soft overripe mangoes and sweet pears Gita had bought for them in the last marketplace and waited for the rain to stop.

"It might go all day," remarked Gita sagely. "It often does this time of year. We are nearing the rainy season."

"If it doesn't stop soon we'll have to go on anyway," said Spence. He had begun feeling more and more uncomfortable about Ari—a feeling somehow connected with his fainting spell the day before. He had a strong sense of danger where she was concerned, and this sense made him impatient to reach her as soon as possible.

They waited half-an-hour more; Spence, leaning first against one of the trees' trunks and then another, was soon pacing like a caged bear. "It isn't going to stop," he announced, arriving at the end of his patience. "Let's go on."

Gita made a face like a man smelling rotten eggs. He heaved his round shoulders and shuffled to his feet. "Don't worry, Gita," remarked Adjani. "The bath will do us all good."

They stepped out into the sullen rain and untethered Simba, who also had been crushing the pulpy pears in her massive jaws. The elephant greeted her new masters with a rousing trumpet and examined each one and his pockets as she knelt and let them board her. Then they were off, heading northward, climbing slowly upward toward the mountains.

Spence saw the land through the hanging white mists and noted that it had changed a great deal since Calcutta. The jungle had become forest of a different type; the greens were deeper, tending more toward blue in the misty rain. Sown in among the lower trees he spotted tall pines shooting up out of the foliage around them and he could smell their scent in the air. Spence guessed they had risen several thousand feet in altitude already, though the climb had been so gradual as not to be noticed.

Nevertheless, he sensed a difference in the air—it seemed fresher and last night had been a little cooler than he remembered since coming to India.

They rode at a good pace for nearly an hour, each one cloaked in his own thoughts, like Gita wrapped in his turban, trying to keep out the rain which slowly seeped into everything anyway.

They came upon a small stream running across the road. Simba waded into it and then stopped and drank. She stood splashing her trunk in the water and blowing bubbles before squirting water into her mouth.

Spence let her have her fun; he did not know when they would be able to stop for a drink again. As the elephant stepped out of the stream he felt a quiver run through the animal like an electric shock and she froze instantly in mid-step, trunk reaching out, wavering as she sifted the air for a scent.

Up ahead the road wound sharply around a bend and was hidden behind a wall of forest. Spence could sense nothing that would make her react in such a way, but he knew better than to doubt an elephant's instinct.

"What is it? Why have we stopped?" asked Gita. His soggy turban dropped around his ears and eyebrows making him look like a waif wearing his father's clothes.

"Shhh!" hissed Spence. He gave a chop with his hand to cut off further discussion. He nudged Simba gently with his feet and she went slowly forward, with a ponderous, silent grace. He marveled at how smoothly and quietly the creature could move when she wanted to.

They crept toward the bend in the road.

Spence lay down on the elephant's head and peered ahead as far as he could as they came around the trees. He saw in the road a few objects of undetermined nature and then he looked down and saw something he recognized well: a severed human arm, thumb missing, lay directly in the middle of the road. Bloodless and pale, it had been washed clean by the rain. White bone gleamed painfully from the torn end, and the arm itself seemed to indicate a warning. *Halt!* it said. *Go no further!*

Lifting his eyes from the grizzly memento he saw the lions.

There were two of them—a male and a female, both wet and bedraggled by the rain. The big male was tearing at a carcass splayed in the center of the road while the female sat on her haunches waiting her turn to feed. The carcass had been worried beyond recognition—as had the others he now saw littering the area—but Spence, with a sudden sickness in his stomach, knew what they were. The shreds of clothing, the shoes and sandals, hat and gun told him all.

The lion, sensing the intruders for the first time, glared up defiantly and loosed a snarl that turned blood to water. Simba stood her ground, raising her trunk high overhead and in a tight curl. The lion growled more fiercely and then seized up the carcass with a snap of its jaws and dragged it off across the road into the forest. The tawny lioness followed with the miffed air of snubbed royalty.

"That was close," said Spence. He grimly looked around the scene of carnage. "I thought they were going to challenge us."

"Lions are cowards," remarked Gita, "though I was feeling none too brave myself. Still, not many will go against an elephant. We must be near Jaldapara."

"What's that?"

"Many, many years ago there was a great wildlife sanctuary called Jaldapara. I have heard that there are still lions there."

"Apparently they abound."

"This is what is left of the governor's party," observed Adjani. "I don't see anything to save. We'll have to report this to the authorities in Darjeeling."

"I wonder if there were any survivors." Spence urged the elephant onward, stopping only once to direct her to retrieve an official cap which had been worn by one the the governor's aides.

"The *goondas* probably did not leave any survivors," said Gita. "The only reason they allow the merchants to live is because they want them to go back and amass their goods so they can rob them another time.

"But this—" Words failed him. He shivered. "Merciful Father, protect us!"

They resumed their trek through the scene of ambush. Spence saw things lying in among the bushes on either side of the road, but he did not peer too intently lest he discover what they were. He had seen enough.

The next days were indistinguishable one from another—much as the towns and villages they passed through. They rose to swollen skies and rain soon after dawn. The rain continued until midday whereupon the sky cleared and the sun burned with vigor to turn the road and surrounding forest into a steamy, smothering welter.

The landscape changed little, offering only hills and more hills, some with spectacular gorges and deeply cleft valleys between, but after so many of these impressive sights, the travelers grew numb to such profligate magnificence. India, the Country of Too Many—too many people, too many languages, too many religions, too many customs, too many problems—had too many wonderful sights as well. The effect was to deaden, as all the rest deadened, too, in this strange land.

But as they began to ascend the final climb up to the high hills of Darjeeling, Spence noticed that the forest thinned and became scrubby. The trees were shorter and the hills more pronounced and steeper. Twice they crossed ancient suspension bridges whose cables had rusted—many had snapped and now dangled uselessly into the cataract below—and the missing steel plates formed open trapdoors to be cautiously avoided.

Once they met a dozen or so pilgrims, Buddhist priests, who were making a pilgrimage to Buddh-Gaya to the south. They wore bright yellow dhotis bedecked with garlands of white magra flowers that looked like little bells, and waved their prayer flags at the elephant as it passed, murmuring and chanting as they went along.

Not more than fifty meters away from where they passed the happy pilgrims, they encountered a beggar squatting in the road. Spence could see the man's leg outstretched beside him and he whined piteously as the elephant approached, flinching away from it, but making no move to scuttle out of its path. The wretch raised imploring eyes to the travelers, and Spence looked down as the elephant deftly stepped around the human lump in the road.

Then Spence saw the man's leg curled beside him in a grotesque and inhuman curve. He stopped Simba and slid down from his perch; Adjani and Gita quickly followed. The beggar, seeing this response, went into wild and fearful lamentations, afraid that the travelers would beat him and steal his pittance, yet wanting their help anyway.

"Oh," said Gita, looking at the man's leg. "It is not good at all. It is very far gone." He lifted the filthy, rain-soaked rag that covered the man's frame and Spence saw the hideous sight. The leg was a festering mass of green-black flesh, ulcerated and oozing pus and blood.

"What can we do for him?" asked Spence, turning away.

"Nothing," said Adjani. "He is beyond our ability to help. He's dying."

The cloudy eyes, the listlessness Spence beheld in the beggar's slack features confirmed Adjani's diagnosis. But he refused to accept the injustice of such a hopeless pronouncement. "We're going to help him," he said tersely. "If not to live, then we'll at least help him die like a human being."

Adjani gazed at his friend with wonder. "You are right, Spence. It is the least we can do."

Spence turned to view the chanting pilgrims as they hurried away, their song still hanging in the air. "Is your god deaf and blind?" he shouted after them, venting his outrage. "Doesn't he care? Is he even there at all?"

Spence picked the man up—he seemed to weigh nothing at all—he could feel his bones hard through their paper-thin covering of skin and rags. Adjani held the injured leg gently as they moved him to the side of the road. The beggar regarded them with scared, feverish eyes and whimpered with pain at being moved. "He has probably been sitting there for days," muttered Adjani. Spence looked at the place in the road where the man had sat. It was dry, and the footprints of the Buddhist priests in the mud passed mere inches away from where he had been.

Gita produced his medicine sack and began assembling some articles which might be of some help. He also brought the man a drink of water and some of their store of mangoes and pears. The man drank thirstily, but refused to eat a bite of the fresh fruit. He continued to watch them with mute suspicion as they exposed his leg and set about cleaning it.

The sight was almost more than Spence could stand, and the stink of it brought tears to his eyes. The foul limb had rotted away to nothing resembling a human appendage. Using a collapsible canvas bucket they found in Simba's howdah he fetched water from a nearby ditch running with clean rainwater. A few curious crows who had been watching the beggar from a distance now assembled on the branches of a nearby tree for a closer look.

Gita and Adjani delicately picked up the leg, which by the look of it had been crushed in an accident—perhaps when he had dived in front of an oncoming vehicle for some scrap of refuse someone had tossed to the ground. Spence began pouring the water over it, bathing it and washing away the filth and ooze.

This exertion started the blood flowing freely again over the gangrenous flesh and the gentle flooding of the water dissolved the decaying skin and muscle. Flesh and bones dropped from the leg as the water splashed down. The limb split and the stench of putrid flesh overcame Spence. The bucket dropped from his hand and he turned aside as the contents of his stomach came surging up.

Spence wiped his mouth on his sleeve and grimly picked up the bucket, but before he could begin again a crow from the tree above fluttered down and seized a small bone with a morsel of flesh still clinging to it. The bird snatched up its prize in its yellow beak and jumped back into the air and away.

"They're hungry, too," said Gita. "Do not blame them."

Spence, tears brimming in his eyes, raised the bucket and poured the rest of the water over the leg. They then tore up one of Gita's muslin sacks to use as a bandage; they wrapped what was left of the limb carefully and neatly in the dry cloth. They started to strip the sopping coverings from the beggar to clean him up, but he clutched at them so furiously that they let him keep his rags.

Gita offered more fruit, speaking softly in the man's tongue, explaining that they were not going to hurt him and did not expect to be paid for their kindness. The beggar gingerly accepted the fruit and opened his mouth, full of blackened, rotting teeth, to eat.

He took two or three mouthfuls and then lay back, still watching them as if he expected them to pounce on him at any moment. He closed his eyes and, with a long whimper and a violent shake of his bones, he died.

Spence could not understand why the beggar died so suddenly and so quietly. He looked at the still body in amazement, and then turned abruptly away.

"Spence, it's all right," said Adjani, coming close to him. "We did the right thing. We did what we could."

Spence shook his head sadly. "It was not enough."

Gita, standing over the body with outstretched arms, said, "See how he died, Spencer Reston? This one of the streets who in his life never knew a moment of compassion or concern knew both at the moment of death. He ate and drank and was bandaged and someone knew of his passing."

Spence looked at the body for a long time, trying to comprehend the life this discarded bit of human litter must have known. He could not—any more than he could imagine exchanging places with a jellyfish. The gulf between their respective worlds was just too great—light-years apart.

But Spence, in an effort of pure, selfless compassion, had tried.

They wrapped the body with the governor's flag which they found rolled in the howdah and carried it a few meters into the trees beside the road. They laid it in a hollow beneath a tree and with their hands covered it with rain-damp earth.

"Father," said Adjani as they stood over the grave, "receive one of your own."

They climbed silently back onto the elephant once more and rode on into Siliguri.

CHAPTER SIXTEEN

EVERY TIME August Zanderson looked at his daughter he saw the image of his insane wife. Ari had grown by degrees more listless and confused as the days passed and she continued to follow Hocking to their secret rendezvous. Each time she returned just a little more forgetful, a little more vague, a little less Ari.

She did not eat well and had grown pale and hollow-cheeked. She now slept a great deal, and even when awake seemed lost to the material world. It was as if the young woman was turning into a ghost before his eyes.

He had argued in vain for her to stop meeting Hocking, but he had no control over her. Every time Hocking came she was ready and waiting for him, though he came at odd times of the day and night.

Zanderson had threatened Hocking—also in vain—and had offered himself in his daughter's place. This had brought nothing but mocking laughter and derision. But seeing his daughter wither before his eyes made him determined not to let her go without a fight. He planned to confront Hocking next time he came. He had broken a chair leg and hidden it close to hand in case his point needed driving home with extra persuasion.

Now, as Ari slept like one of night's children, he paced before the door waiting for the summons he knew would come in time. When he heard the rattle of the bolt in the lock of the huge heavy wooden door, Zanderson squared his shoulders and took his place just inside the entrance.

Hocking swept into the room and at first did not see that his way was barred by the form of the director. But their eyes met and Hocking seemed taken aback somewhat, though he recovered instantly, saying, "Get out of my way. Get back."

"Ari's staying here, Hocking. Leave her alone."

"Get away, you fool! I'm warning you."

"And I'm telling you it's over. You're not taking her away from here any more. I won't let you."

Hocking's features sharpened at the challenge. "What will you do, Director? How will you stop me?"

"Don't force me to defend myself. I will." Zanderson's voice rose with anger. "I'm warning you. Get out of here and leave her alone."

"Stay out of this. You don't know what you're doing. I'm only trying to help you."

"Help me? Ha! Look at her!" Zanderson waved his hand wildly toward Ari's form. "She's been sleeping all day! She's exhausted. If this keeps up you'll kill her!"

Hocking glared at the man before him. His hand flattened on the tray of the pneumochair. "I'm telling you for the last time to get out of my way."

The director stepped slowly aside. Hocking moved forward to pass him and quick as a flash Zanderson's hand snaked out and snatched up the club. He swung it full force at Hocking's skull.

The move was not fast enough. Hocking's finger twitched on his knurled tray at the same instant and the improvised club bounced in the air bare centimeters from his head and fell away.

Stunned amazement blossomed on the director's face as he watched his well-aimed blow go awry. Hocking's eyes narrowed and his lips drew back in a snarl of rage. "How dare you assault me!" His voice crackled over the chair's audio system.

Zanderson, his determination evaporating, raised his weapon once more and brought it down. He felt the chair leg meet a resistant force which deflected it from its target. At the same moment he felt his fingers tingle and his hand grow numb. The club grew heavy and fell from his hand. The next thing the director knew he was on his knees, his hands clamped over his ears as a high-frequency sound burst through his brain. The sound drained all strength from his body and he toppled heavily to the floor.

"I would have expected better of you, Director. Imbecile! I should squash you like the insect you are." Hocking moved a finger on the tray and the director's eyes screwed shut with pain, and then he rolled on his side and lay still, eyes staring vacantly at the great vaulted ceiling above.

The white ovoid chair spun in the air and Hocking glanced up. Ari stood in front of him with a gentle, almost whimsical expression on her face. Her deep blue eyes seemed soft and unfocused. She looked like a little girl daydreaming.

Hocking noticed that though she must have seen what had happened, Ari seemed not at all disturbed by her father's demise. He quickly recovered himself. "Are you ready, Ariadne?"

"Yes," she said in a voice furred with sleep. "I'm ready. Take me to the dream machine."

"You know the way. You lead this time," said Hocking. "I'll follow."

Darjeeling was as different from Calcutta as sea from sewer. Fresh, clean, sparkling with quickened vitality, it perched on a steep crown of hill at an elevation that made the visitor light-headed. It was so far from the India Spence had thus far experienced that it might have been on another planet.

Surrounded by imperial mountains—twin-peaked Kanchenjunga the foremost of these kings—and purified by the thin, sun-drenched air, Darjeeling glimmered like a rare gem in Spence's eye. A vast shell of blazing blue sky spread over all like a silk canopy, and everywhere he looked tiny blue birds flitted from rooftop to street to rooftop.

The people of Darjeeling—Nepalese, Tibetans, Bhutias, Lepchas, and others of obscure origin—seemed sturdy and healthy and glowing with friendliness. Spence found the city nearly as intoxicating as the altitude, especially after the long string of lowland towns indistinguishable in their filth and misery.

"Darjeeling—jewel of the Himalayas!" crowed Gita. "I never hoped to see it."

They climbed the nearly vertical streets of the carefully terraced city, drawing long gapes and shouts from the colorful inhabitants, many of whom wore centuries-old tribal costumes of silk and feathers and ornamental silver jewelry. Children, seeing the elephant, scampered after them laughing and pointing. Their ascent through the lower portions of the city to the upper brought them and their unofficial procession to the seat of the government. Climbing short flights of steps and landings which seemed to go on without end, they at last came to the handsome golden-domed Raj Bhavan, the Governor's Palace.

Immaculate emerald grounds were enclosed within white brick walls sparkling in the sun with flecks of mica. Hand-pruned miniature trees lined the broad drive leading to the palace itself, a living relic of the British colonial era.

When the elephant arrived in the street before the palace, the guards at the iron gates took one look at the animal and the noisy crowd behind and ran to apprehend them with rifles lowered. They met them yammering and gesturing excitedly. Gita yammered back at them and kept pointing at the palace. After a quick consultation one of the guards ran away to fetch his captain.

While this was going on Spence looked around him as one in a daze. The mountains, so close they seemed within reach, towered up on every side so that wherever he looked he saw a new and striking vista. From this spot on Birch Hill, the government district, the rooftops of Darjeeling slanted away in descending ranks, giving the impression that one stood on the very roof of the world. The city's busy inhabitants went purposefully about their business with rolling exuberance and toothy smiles in their broad faces.

Spence was enchanted by all he saw and was content just to stare and drink it in.

"The governor will see you now." The words brought him out of his daydream. He turned around to see a short—all the people of this place were of small stature—but well-built man in a crisp green uniform standing before them. He smiled, showing a row of neat white teeth, but his snapping black eyes spoke of the turmoil their visit had plunged his staff into. "Follow me, please."

The scrolled iron gates creaked open and, with the captain at the elephant's head, they began moving up the tree-lined drive. At the wide palace steps they dismounted and were ushered in through two huge bronze doors. Spence heard a loud trumpet behind him, turned and saw Simba, trunk waving in the air, being led away in the care of two keepers with goads.

"Good-bye, old girl," said Spence. "And thanks for the ride."

"I had forgotten that we would have to give her up," said Adjani sadly. "I was growing fond of her."

Spence sighed and nodded.

The governor, by contrast with his subjects, was a tall man of princely bearing. Spence found it easy to imagine that he had somehow been transported back in time and sat in the presence of Indian royalty in the time of the Moghuls.

White marble gleamed at every turn, some of it covered with rich oriental carpets; potted palms sat in great beaten brass jars, and the almond-colored walls were hung with animal skins and carvings of jade and alabaster, ivory and teak. The ceiling, also carved with the intricate stylized designs of elephants, lions, and dancing maidens, glittered with gilt and was supported with large serpentine columns of green marble.

In one of the palace's many audience rooms they sat in an alcove formed by a screen that had been carved from thin slabs of yellow marble in the figure of thousands of intertwined roses. Red silk cush-

Dream Thief

ions on great rattan chairs made the travelers feel like members of
nobility as they sat sipping tea and conversing with the governor. A
hamal of the governor's serving staff hovered nearby with silver plates
of small nut cakes and sweetmeats.

"I am very distraught over the attack on my minister's party.
Nevertheless, I am pleased to have Ambooli, my elephant, returned and
to learn of this outrage against my authority. I am grateful to you for
this kindness. It shall be rewarded.

"Is there anything else which I may do to show my gratitude? You
have but to speak."

"Thank you, governor, but your hospitality has been proof
enough," replied Adjani.

"It is nothing. It would please me to know that while you remain in
Darjeeling you will make my home your own. We seldom receive such
auspicious guests, and I would enjoy the pleasure of your company." A
quick flick of his wrist with fingers extended sent the hamal scurrying
away. "You see? It has already been arranged."

"Governor—" began Spence.

"Please, enough of titles. To you I am simply Fazlul." His smile was
gracious, charming, and unaccountably reserved—as if he were playing
a game which required him to smile, but obviously felt it an imposition
upon his true feelings. Spence noticed that the governor's eyes kept
darting to the screens around them as if he expected at any moment to
leap up and surprise an eavesdropping assassin. On the whole, Fazlul
had about him an air of subtle, crafty meanness which he held in check
by diplomacy and refined manners.

Their host looked every inch the ruler of old capable of presenting
his guests with a fair daughter's hand, or sewing them up in goatskin
bags with wildcats—whichever fancy happened to strike him at the
moment.

"Yes, Fazlul," repeated Spence. "We have heard that there are ruins
of an old palace somewhere in the hills near here. Would there be someone who could direct us, do you think?"

"Oh, you are an archeologist? I thought so the moment I laid eyes
on you. Of course, you know that these hills hold many secrets. There
are many such sites which might interest you: palaces, temples, cave
tombs, shrines. This was once the center of the world, you know. And,
I would like to believe, it will be again.

"However, I will assign our state historian to confer with you and
advise you. He will provide you with a guide and I am sure will wish to
accompany you himself. As you will see, you shall all become very popular visitors. I hope your stay is a long one, because I think you will not
have time to accept every invitation which is sure to come your way.

"But tonight you will be my guests at a banquet which commemo-

rates the celebration of Naag Brasputi. It is a local festival. Very colorful. I am sure you will find it amusing."

The governor rose and placed his palms together and raised them
to his chin. "*Namastey,* gentlemen. Until tonight."

The three guests stood and bid the governor good day and watched
him walk away—shoulders high, back straight, and hands held close to
his sides as if wearing the crown and carrying the scepter of his office.

"I feel like I have just had an audience with the King of Siam," said
Spence.

"You are not far wrong," said Adjani. "His is an imperial line that
goes back centuries."

"He is a proud and ruthless man," remarked Gita. "Even in Calcutta we have heard stories about him. It would be better for us that he
did not esteem our company so highly."

CHAPTER SEVENTEEN

IF THE governor had contrived to impress his guests he could
not have succeeded more completely. They were called from their
rooms at dusk—after they had napped, bathed, and changed into new
muslin clothes—and were conducted to a great banquet hall which
opened at one end onto a vast lawn. People of all types—officials, ser-
vants, other guests, and dignitaries—were assembling in the hall, and
on the lawn a circus appeared to be swinging into action.

Walking out onto the broad green lawn in the fiery violet-and-
orange sunset which lit the mountain peaks around them with cool
flame, the three saw jugglers, fire-eaters, snake charmers, and acrobats.
A man hanging by his heels from a rope swung round and round on a
long pole, whirling as he went. Other performers walked tightropes,
and everywhere dancers displayed intricate and facile movements to
groups of applauding onlookers. Laughing youngsters threw flower
petals and splashed perfumed water on all the guests, and strains of
exotic music filled the air.

People from the city poured into the palace lawns and soon the
noise and revel reached the threshold of chaos, though a gay sort of
chaos.

Spence, Adjani, and Gita moved among the crowds and gawked

first at one strange sight—a man who drew wide acclaim by swallowing live snakes and then drawing them back out an inch at a time—and then at another—a man who pushed long steel needles through his cheeks and eyelids and the skin of his throat.

Spence found the festive atmosphere exciting and repulsive at the same time. He felt like a country rube who had come to town to see the freak show; it fascinated and amazed, but left a queasy feeling in the pit of his stomach. All of it was utterly beyond his experience, foreign and inexplicably odd. Nothing in his world of books and instruments hinted at the existence of this world he was seeing. He had nothing to compare it to.

Adjani hovered at Spence's shoulder, watching him with keen interest and explaining when he could what they were seeing and something of the significance behind it. Gita also supplied helpful explanations, but he was too caught up in the spectacle as a participant himself to count on as a guide. His round form could be seen darting here and there in the crush to join a dance or thrust into the forefront of an audience. He was soon decked in layers of flower garlands. His face shone with boyish enthusiasm; clearly, anyone would have thought that the entire show had been produced for his enjoyment alone.

As the first of the evening stars came out, adding their bright light to the color below, Spence and his companions were shepherded back into the banquet hall where they were seated at an enormous table at the open end overlooking the roistering scene of the celebration.

They and other dignitaries and ministers at the table were given bowls of rose water and hot, lemon-scented towels to freshen themselves from their exertion. Then hamals began circulating with trays of delicate iced cakes and other appetizers.

The governor appeared at a balcony just above the lawn in full view of his guests at the table and the festival crowd. A thunderous chorus of acclamation greeted his arrival. The guests at the table stood and were no less enthusiastic in their welcome than the populace on the lawn.

Fazlul, resplendent in gleaming white tunic and trousers, a long flowing white mantle edged in silver, and a white turban with a huge sparkling gemstone on his brow, raised his hands to the adoring revelers, and silence descended over them in a hush. He spoke a few words which Spence could not understand and then raised his hands once more and the celebration erupted into life. Spence guessed that their beloved leader had given his blessing to the occasion and commanded that the night be enjoyed to the full. Obviously, the order was immensely popular with all who heard it; they threw themselves into its execution in all haste.

The governor and his wife, a statuesque, dark-haired beauty

clothed in shimmering pale green, descended the broad staircase that joined the balcony with the terrace and moved among their honored guests. They stopped at each place and spoke with each guest briefly before moving on. Soon they were standing before Spence, Adjani, and Gita.

The three stood uncertainly as the governor announced to his wife, "These are the men I told you about who saved Ambooli. Gentlemen, my wife, Sarala."

With a smile of warmth and cheer the lovely lady raised her pressed palms together and inclined her head toward them. "Namastey, my friends. Thank you for saving Ambooli. She is, as you may have guessed, my husband's favorite. It was a regrettable tragedy, but we are glad that you have come to us. Please enjoy yourselves. I hope that I will have the pleasure of an audience with you alone very soon. News of the world comes so seldom to the mountains." She smiled again and Spence saw the hint of a wink. "And visitors even more rarely. We must sit down and have a long talk."

"The pleasure would be ours," replied Adjani smoothly. The governor nodded stiffly and moved away saying, "Enjoy the evening. It will be quite fantastic, I assure you."

"He was certainly restrained," whispered Spence to Adjani when Fazlul and Sarala had gone. "Did you notice he didn't look at us all the time his wife was speaking?"

"Yes, strange." Adjani shrugged. "Perhaps our stay here should be a short one. I would feel better if we weren't imposing on one so powerful."

"Is he so powerful, do you think? I don't know what to make of him."

Adjani shrugged again. "I'm sure we're making more of this than we should. I can think of no reason why we should come under his suspicion."

"Maybe not, but I have felt danger from him both times we met."

All at once a rattle and a clatter broke out just in front of the terrace. Musicians in costume with drums and tambalas and native flutes struck up an eerie, otherworldly music and a score of dancing girls came running.

"The floor show," said Spence.

"Dancing is a way of life in India. Everyone dances. And the various dances have special meanings. This is a festive dance, a dance of joy. The girls' costumes are handed down from mother to daughter over many generations. To dance well is to please the gods."

Though intricate, the steps and hand movements performed to the rhythm of the drums seemed to Spence to be more strutting and posing than dancing. But he drank in the sight of the lithe, supple bodies in their colorful red, green, and gold shifts with gold bodices and bare midriffs. Gold necklaces and earrings and noserings glittered in the light as the girls danced, slowly at first but with ever increasing tempo.

One dance was followed by another and another—sometimes with male dancers, sometimes with female, and sometimes mixed. Food on steaming platters arrived and Adjani supervised the filling of Spence's plates, providing a running commentary on what each dish was and its relative spiciness. Toddy flowed freely, and Spence drank the sweet-tasting liquor in great gulps, chasing the food with little regard for its potency.

In a short while he was gazing on all around him with glittering eyes and a beaming, if hazy disposition.

A troupe of actors took the improvised stage as the dishes were cleared away. Spence watched the incomprehensible drama—which seemed to him to center on the discovery of ants in one of the character's items of clothing—and slipped into melancholy. Perhaps it was a reaction to the strong drink or to the events of the past several days. At any rate he felt himself sliding deeper and deeper into a bleak and cheerless frame of mind, heightened by the noise and gaiety surging all around him.

Adjani noticed his friend's pensive demeanor and regarded him carefully. He was not surprised when—during a parade of floats in honor of Brasputi—Spence rudely got up from his chair and walked out onto the lawn without saying a word to anyone.

The other guests at the long table were already mingling among the celebrants once more, so no one noticed Spence's odd behavior. He moved into the throng dancing around a gigantic effigy of the green-skinned, six-armed Brasputi and was swept away in the flood of torch-bearing dancers.

He was not actually aware of his depressed emotional outlook. To him it merely seemed that he lost interest in the revel around him and sought a quiet corner to himself. He brushed past leering papier-mâché statues wearing garlands and grinning with lusty smirks on their green faces, and shook flower petals out of his hair as he moved through the jostling crowd.

He took no notice of these things, or of any of the other thousand sights before him. His eyes were turned inward, for he had begun to brood upon the object of his affection: Ari. She had not been entirely out of his mind for more than a minute at any time since they had parted company at the asylum near Boston. In all that had happened to him since, his uppermost thought had been of her.

That something very wrong was happening to her he felt in his heart. It seemed to come in waves, striking at odd moments—like the time on the road—as if he were being summoned. The feeling had come strong upon him as he sat over his dinner. He felt it like he felt an ache in his soul. She was in trouble and needed his help.

Now, as he moved across the lawn in blind retreat from the raucous festivities, he felt the pangs stronger than ever. He knew he was close to her—somewhere in these green hills she waited. He could feel her closeness as if she were beckoning to him across the distance in a silent call only his soul could hear.

He began to run, blindly, recklessly. He jogged across the lawn and found an open gate in the wall and ran out into the swarming streets of Darjeeling.

In his mind he heard a voice urging him on. *Run, find her! She needs you! Hurry! Every second counts! Run!*

And he obeyed.

The streets of the city were alive with the festival crowds moving their floats toward the Raj Bhavan. Later the images would be taken to the lake nearby and set ablaze and pushed out into the lake on their small barges while fireworks lit the night sky, symbolizing the victory of Naag Brasputi over his enemies. But now the parade was in full procession and the dancing, chanting townspeople vied for the favor of the governor in presenting the biggest or most richly adorned effigy.

Like a salmon running against the stream he fought the current of people moving toward the palace. One thought and one thought only drummed in his brain: *Find Ari. Find her before it's too late.*

He dodged here and there among the mobs and at last came upon a dark and quiet side street. He stood for a moment looking down its steep decline. *Go,* the voice said. *Hurry.* He went.

When he reached the bottom of the street he found himself on another level of the city, this one somewhat poorer and less well kept than the government section. The streets were narrower and the houses thrust up against one another and towered overhead. They were, for the most part, vacant, their inhabitants having joined the main celebration elsewhere in the city.

Spence listened to the sound of his own footsteps as he ran along, pausing only at intervals to find some new path. Without his knowing he was quickly moving out of Darjeeling proper toward Chaurastha, the city's ancient nucleus.

He did not notice that he crossed several bridges, nor did he hear the swift splash of the icy water below. These bridges marked the boundaries of Darjeeling. When he crossed them he moved into old Chaurastha—City of Dreams.

The streets fell away steeply in terraced flights, and steps flashed darkly beneath his feet; but he continued, driven by the urging he heard within him. He seemed directed toward a place he did not know but believed he would recognize when he found it. He let his legs carry him where they would.

The moon gleamed full overhead. In the city above he could hear the merrymaking of the multitudes, but here in the old city silence remained undisturbed. He could see the orange glow of thousands of torches in the sky, but here it was dark. He stopped to look around him and heard the rasp of his own breathing echoing among the dark walls and passages of the sacred city and the occasional bark of a dog.

He went more slowly, walking among the odd-shaped houses and shops in the deserted town, and came to a narrow old footbridge. He crossed it and found himself before a temple. The wide wooden gate was open, so he went in.

He moved like a shadow across the temple yard toward the small stupa in the center. The stupa was hive-shaped like all the others he had seen, but different. He entered the shrine and felt the cool breath of the evening on his face and neck as he slipped into the darkness.

The shrine was lit for the most part by moonlight falling through the hole in the center of the dome, but two torches burned before the deity's stone altar. Spence moved toward the altar.

It was a plain stone slab with words carved in it which he could not read. He stood gazing at it for some time, blinking in the flickering torchlight.

The feeling of having been directed to this place ran strong in him. He looked around and shook his head as one coming out of a dream in which he finds that his dream has come true.

How had he come to be here? Where were Adjani and Gita? Why had he come?

Spence passed a hand before his eyes. Had he blacked out again? No, he did remember certain things: running down darkened streets, pushing through crowds, garish idols grinning at him. It was all there, and yet it must have happened to someone else.

Along with the feeling of waking from a dream, overlaying all other sensations, was the unaccountable certainty that he had been here before; he would have sworn his life on it.

The shape of the stupa, its interior, the design of the altar, and the words carved upon it—they all seemed very familiar, and yet very strange. If he had been here before, he told himself, it must have been in another life, or on some other planet.

It *had* been on another planet: Mars! All at once it came flooding back on him, and Spence staggered under the weight of the memory. The stupa was an exact replica of the *krassil* he had visited in Tso, the ancient city of the vanished Martians.

He moved toward the idol standing in its niche behind the altar and raised his eyes. The stone gleamed with the oil libations that had been poured out upon it by the priests. But there was no mistaking the figure of the deity: Naag Brasputi, with his oddly elongated limbs and narrow body and huge, staring, all-seeing eyes was the very image of Kyr.

He let his eyes travel down the long arms to the wrist and the folded hands and saw what he knew he would see. Naag Brasputi had but three fingers.

Spence stumbled backwards and fell against something soft that clutched at him. He whirled around to see two eyes in a face floating in the darkness behind him. Spence cringed back and a voice spoke to him.

CHAPTER EIGHTEEN

"I HAD THE very devil of a time following you," Adjani said. "Bloodhounds couldn't have tracked you better."

"Adjani! It's you—what are you doing here?" Spence fell back and raised his hands to his head which had begun to throb like a tambourine in the hands of a firedancer. "Why did you slug me so hard?"

"I didn't slug you, but I should have. Running out of the governor's party like that . . . What were you thinking of?" Spence glanced up at his friend with a sickly, scared expression. Adjani saw it and knew what it meant. "Another blackout?"

"Not a blackout. It was different. It was like someone telling me what to do. I remember everything, but it's all sort of hazy . . ."

The details of his flight through the city came swimming back to his pulsing head. Lastly, he remembered his discovery.

"Adjani, look!" He made to turn around but had to grip the sides of the altar; flaming arrows of pain stabbed through his brain. "Do you see?" Spence pointed to the idol watching them smugly from its niche.

"I see. What is it? Old Naag Brasputi, I gather."

Spence grabbed Adjani's sleeve and shook it. "No! Look again!"

Adjani looked at the tall, thin image in gray stone more closely. He turned and said, "It is unusual, and very old, but—"

"It's Kyr! Or someone very much like him. It's a Martian, I swear it!"

"Are you sure? This isn't the toddy talking, or . . ."

"I'm positive. It's the very image of a Martian. Don't you see? It's all true. Here's the proof. One of their ships came here. They settled in these mountains.'"

Adjani, eyes narrowed and hand cupping his chin, stepped close to the idol and examined it carefully. "So this is what a Martian looks like. I will admit that it looks remarkably like your description of Kyr."

"Complete down to the three-fingered hands And look how tall he is. It certainly doesn't look like any of the other gods at all."

"And I know why. This one is very old. Carved long before the idols took on their classical, stylized form. After a while, the priests started making the gods appear more human."

"Man made god in his own image, is that it?"

"More or less. But this one is an example of what they must have looked like before that happened."

"Do you think this is the Dream Thief?"

"It's hard to say. Dream Thief is more a demon spirit. He takes many shapes." Adjani looked at the carving on the altar and ran his hands over it. "I can't read the writing here. It's a dialect I don't know."

"Gita might know it."

"Yes, he might. We'll bring him here tomorrow. Right now we had better get back to the celebration before we're missed."

They left the shrine and darted back across the temple yard. In the moonlight their shapes became those of spirits springing up out of the stones of the shrine and escaping into the night. They hurried back across the footbridge and through the old town. Upon reaching the ancient bazaar Spence stopped.

"Wait!" His voice was a stiff tense whisper. Adjani froze in his tracks. "Listen!"

Both men trained their senses into the darkness around them. Far away they could hear the sounds of the celebration still reverberating into the stillness; the salutes of fireworks rang like distant gunshots of *goondas* in the hills.

"I don't hear any—" Adjani began.

"Shh!" Spence cut him off.

Then he heard what had stopped him, though for a moment he did not know why. It was a mere rustling of leaves upon the paving stones, a whisper of a sound, like the echo of the day's traffic seeping back up out of the cracks that had absorbed it.

Adjani heard it too. "What is it?"

At first Spence did not know what to say. Then it came to him. It was a sound he had heard in a dream—the sound of death on rushing feet.

"Dogs! Come on!"

They ran down the narrow street between crumbling facades of the aged buildings. The moon shone between the buildings from above and he could see far down the street as if he were looking at a canyon whose ridges of stone rose in towering banks on either hand. Adjani ran at his side and they heard the muffled rush of the feet behind them.

Spence's lungs burned in his chest; he was not used to such exertion at high altitude yet. He ignored the pain and ran on through one street and then another. He threw a quick look over his shoulder and saw the glint of eyes in a churning black mass, formless in the shadows, sweeping ever nearer to them.

Then they were in a courtyard bounded on three sides by a high wall and open to the street. It was a marketplace; he smelled the sweet stench of rotting fruit and meat. The paving stones beneath his feet were slippery with filth; refuse piles formed dark mounds across the market square. A rat scuttling across the square stopped, raised up on his hind legs and sniffed the air, then jumped away and disappeared down a drain hole.

Adjani leaped to an empty stall and came back with two long objects. He thrust one of them into Spence's hand. "Here—just in case."

Spence looked at his hand and saw he had been given a heavy length of wood. He glanced from it to the street behind and saw the moonlight ripple on the backs of the dogs as on a swiftly running stream, glinting on the curved white slivers of their teeth.

"It's too late," said Spence. Even as he spoke he heard an enormous slavering growl as the dogs sprang into the deserted marketplace, pouring in through the narrow gate of the street and spreading over the stones in a flood toward them, jaws snapping, hackles raised, ears flattened to their angular heads. Just like in his dream.

Throw down your club, a voice said inside him. *Throw it down. It's over.*

"God, help us," cried Spence, shaking himself out of the numbing lethargy he felt stealing over him. It was as if a dream were trying to swallow him whole.

The dogs, more than two dozen of them, scattered across the marketplace, ringing them in. The pack leader, a huge black animal with a broad snout and long fangs, leapt forward with a throaty growl.

Spence raised his club and swung it down. The dog dodged aside and another jumped up from nearby. He swung at it, too. Adjani was already busy on his side.

The dogs ran around them barking and snarling and dashing in to slash at them with their teeth, as yet not daring to close in for the kill. They would try to wear down their prey first.

Spence and Adjani stood shoulder to shoulder fending off these feinting attacks with their clubs. How long they could hold out like this Spence could not say—already he felt the strength in his arms fading. The run through the streets had tired him.

The dogs edged closer and the black leader ran yapping around the pack, whipping his mongrel soldiers into a foaming frenzy, jumping on his hind legs and clacking his jaws in the air as he shook his head.

The dogs were all around them now, within striking distance. At any moment they would rush in. The first would fall with battered skulls, but the humans would not be able to get all of them. Spence could almost feel their teeth in his flesh, tearing and tearing.

"Stand back to back, said Adjani. "We can protect each other."

They moved to take up this position, and as if on signal the dogs charged them.

At the same instant Spence heard a flurry above them, a rustle in the air as of leather wings. Out of the corner of his eye he saw a strange shape descending. The dogs saw it too and a few of them turned to snap at it. He saw a flash of silver in the moonlight, and all at once the air vibrated with a sound that seemed to bore through him.

The foremost of the dogs fell to the ground as if they had been slain with a single unseen blow. They rolled, whining and biting themselves. He felt the air vibrate again, though he could not hear the sound; it was above the human threshold. This sent the rest of the animals yelping. Those felled by the sound lay as if beaten, breathing heavily, heads resting on the ground. The strange creature touched lightly down in the square a short distance away.

In the moonlight it was hard to make out a distinct shape, but Spence thought he saw a creature of about a meter or more in height with two locustlike wings on its back. Its lower legs were furred like a goat's, but it had the tail of a scorpion that curved up in a backward arch. Its arms were long and emaciated, its hands and fingers little more than sticks.

The thing held in its hands a shining silver ball; it was this object that had emitted the high-pitched tone that drove the dogs away.

Spence stood spellbound as the creature turned to regard him with a cold, alien stare. Its face, and this was by far the most frightening thing about it, bore an intelligent, distinctly human look. It gazed unblinking at him with pale green eyes that glowed in the moonlight and Spence, staring into those eerie, otherworldly eyes, suddenly understood that it was trying to communicate with him.

The idea filled him with such repulsion that he cringed. The urge to run out and smash the creature flooded through him. As if sensing his mood, the thing hopped back in uneasy, jerky movements and its wings rustled in the air like dry leaves on a dead tree and it flew away.

Spence followed it with his eyes until it disappeared over the rooftops. "Did you see that?" he asked, disbelief making his voice small and
uncertain.

"I saw it, but I don't believe it."

"Whatever it was, it tried to communicate with me." Spence turned
wide eyes to his friend, and a shudder passed through him. "Adjani, it
was a demon."

"A naga—a snake spirit. Here and now. We saw it."

Without another word the two ran from the square, lightly stepping over the panting bodies of stricken dogs. Once out of the marketplace they raced through empty streets back to the governor's palace.
Overhead, red and gold glittering starbursts lit their passage as fireworks blossomed in the sky.

They reached the palace walls out of breath and sweating, despite
the cool evening breeze coming down from the mountains. They moved
along the straggling knots of merrymakers still milling in the streets
around the palace, the greater number of celebrants having departed for
the lake to witness the burning barges. But several of the effigies had
been set on fire and were being paraded through the streets on long
poles to the chants of ecstatic worshipers.

They ducked in the still-open gate and proceeded across the close-
cropped lawn toward the terrace, threading among the throngs watching the fireworks.

A worried, hand-wringing Gita met them as they mounted the steps
of the terrace.

"You disappeared. I could not find you. There was trouble, yes?
Oh, I knew there would be."

"We're exhausted, Gita," said Adjani. "We'll go to our rooms."
Spence only nodded.

But as they turned to leave they were met by Fazlul, who seemed to
appear from nowhere. "You have had enough, my guests? So soon?"
He smiled warmly, but his eyes were dead in his face. "In any event, I
hope this evening's entertainment offered you a taste of the exotic and
perhaps an unusual diversion."

"We enjoyed it immensely, governor." Gita turned on his most
unctious, ingraciating manner. "It was a night to remember always.
I, of course, could go on all night, but alas!—my poor Western friends
are not accustomed to such strenuous celebrations. We beg your indulgence, for a night's sleep weighs heavy after our travels." Spence and
Adjani muttered suitable excuses for retiring, smiled, and nodded.

"Of course," replied Fazlul. "I am sure the exertions of your day are
telling on you now. Very well, you'll find your beds waiting. Good
night, gentlemen; and pleasant dreams."

"*Namastey,* governor," the three said in chorus. "Good night."

The governor moved away, the smile still on his lips. They watched him go and as soon as he was out of earshot, Spence turned to the others and whispered, "The sly devil knows what happened tonight, so help me! He knows!"

CHAPTER NINETEEN

THE SKY was pink long before the sun rose above Kanchenjunga to banish night from the city. But Spence had been up before sunrise. He had not slept much of the night, lying in bed thinking about the creature with the glowing green eyes. Finally, as the night lifted her dark veil and morning showed dull iron in the east, he rose and went to Adjani's room.

"We've got to get out of here," he said. Adjani was not asleep either.

"That's just what I was thinking. We should make some excuse and leave after breakfast."

"No, I mean right away. Now."

Adjani cocked his head to one side and looked at Spence closely. "Really? You expect some trouble?"

"I don't know. Maybe. I've been awake all night thinking about what happened—the dogs and that creature, the idol and everything. And Fazlul's knowing that we would go there." He paused. "Adjani, we weren't meant to return last night."

Adjani sat cross-legged in bed nodding gently, staring at a point just above Spence's head. Spence recognized his friend's manner of concentration and let him turn over the facts in his mind.

"Yes, perhaps you are right," Adjani said at last. "We will go. Get dressed; I'll fetch Gita. We'll leave at once."

Spence returned to his room and donned his newly cleaned and pressed jumpsuit and stuffed his feet into his boots. When he returned to Adjani's room a very sleepy Gita was rubbing his sleep-swollen eyes and scratching his belly as he finished dressing.

"To miss breakfast in this house would be a crime!" Gita lamented.

"I wonder if you would feel that way if it were your last breakfast on this earth?"

"So?" Gita's eyes grew round as grapefruits. "Then there *was* trouble last night. I knew it, though you never tell Gita anything. I must always find out for myself."

"Stop pouting and put your turban on," said Spence. "We didn't tell you because, well, because there was no time. We didn't want you to worry, and anyway, we weren't too sure about what happened last night ourselves."

"You think I wouldn't understand," said Gita dolefully, winding the long strip of thin blue muslin around his head.

"I don't think *I* understand," snapped Spence.

"We weren't keeping anything from you," explained Adjani. "We will tell you everything as soon as we are away from here. We must go now."

"I'm ready," Gita sniffed. "Let us fly if fly we must."

Spence crept to the door and opened it, looked both ways, and motioned for the others to follow. They stole down a long corridor and down the wide marble staircase to the great entrance hall of the palace. Not a sound could be heard in all the palace; not a soul was seen stirring in the gray morning half-light.

Moving as quickly and stealthily as burglars they crossed the cool marble hall, darting between the great green spiral pillars. Just as they reached the big bronze outer doors a voice, bold and clear and challenging in the silent hall, said, "Leaving so soon, my guests? I had hoped you would have deigned to stay a little longer."

The three froze and out from behind a pillar stepped Fazlul. He was accompanied by palace guards with old-style combat rifles which looked in excellent condition despite their age. The governor approached, wearing that same crafty smirk they had seen at their first meeting. "How ironic that you should choose to leave just as I was about to arrange a journey for you into the hills."

"We have done nothing, governor," said Adjani. "Let us go in peace."

"Oh, I have no intention of keeping you. None at all." He turned to Spence. "I believe you asked about seeing some of the local architecture —temples, palaces, and such. My instructions state that you shall have your wish."

Fazlul raised his hand and snapped his fingers and the guards stepped forward and took them by the arms. "Take them to Kalitiri. And make sure our visitors have a pleasant journey."

They were hustled out of the palace and into an antiquated troop carrier of a bygone era. The truck's engine coughed to life as they were bundled roughly in. Two guards sat at the end of the benches with them and two others inside the cab. They sputtered down the broad avenue to the gates.

Spence looked back at the palace and saw the governor standing on the steps watching after them. He felt betrayed and used—a dupe and a fool—and outraged by the sly ruler's easy way with them. He watched the tall white figure of Fazlul until they were out of the gate and past the walls where it gradually came to him that they were at any rate speeding on their way to meet the Dream Thief.

"I would have preferred our visit to be more of a surprise, but at least we won't have to walk," he mumbled to Adjani.

"For that we can be thankful. It would have been an arduous trip on foot. Who knows? Perhaps this is God's way of smoothing the path for us."

"In that case," said Spence, settling back for the trip, "I would hate to think what it would be like if it were rough."

Olmstead Packer tried to send a message to his wife and almost lost his life, and at the same time jeopardized all the carefully woven plans of the Gotham underground. Knowing that she was expecting to hear from him, and that she had probably been trying to reach him herself with news of her return to Gotham, he coded a message and sent it to her, little thinking that the mutineers might have put a bloodhound program into the system.

Chief Ramm's men were waiting for him as he stepped from the public booth on the Broadway axial.

"Are you Olmstead Packer?"

"Who?" Packer asked, feigning stupidity.

"Come with us, please. We'd like to ask you some questions." One of the men stepped forward and took his arm.

Since the axial was crowded with shift traffic, the guards had no doubt counted on the full cooperation of their prisoner—most people do not care to make a scene of their public disgrace. But Packer, having imposed upon the benefits of Ramm's protective custody once already, did not relish the thought of another stay. He shook off the guard's hand and yelled that he was being accosted. Immediately they were surrounded by curious onlookers.

The confused guards told the crowd to move along, and when they refused the guards got angry. Somebody said something and someone else yelled—all the while Packer was hollering that his rights were being violated—and when the guards went for their tasers Packer dived through the crowd and ran.

The security men followed him, but lost him in the crush around one of the radial tubes. A breathless Packer described the scene to a gravely nodding Kalnikov when he reached the safety of their hidden nest. Kalnikov then informed him that the guards had orders to kill.

"Are you certain?" Packer asked incredulously. His eyes showed white all around.

The big Russian chuckled mirthlessly. "We are both considered dangerous. We are marked men. You, my friend, will not be so stupid next time. You can tell your wife all about it when it is over. Until then—"

"Don't worry. There won't be any next time. I'm not that much of a fool to get caught in the same trap twice."

"You're learning, friend. Soon I'll make a real freedom fighter out of you." A big hand clapped the physicist on the back. "Did I ever tell you that my great-grandfather fought with Vyenkotrovitch in the War of the Commissars? He was one of the original Moscow Saboteurs. There was a real freedom fighter."

"You've mentioned him only about fifty times."

"Well, then, how about Grandfather Nikko and how he saved the President's life on the eve of the first election? Did I tell you that one?" Packer was not quick enough to pretend he had heard it. "No? Ahh, now *there's* a story."

Packer had grown used to Kalnikov's interminable stories, and was even beginning to enjoy them. They had, after all, a lot of time on their hands while waiting for this or that corridor to clear, or for one or another contact to appear with information. The two men had become very good friends and wily conspirators.

As Kalnikov warmed to his tale, Packer sat thinking of their future as fugitives. Their cramped hideout beneath the docking bay in the hydraulics service area had become a prison; Packer longed for the run of his lab again and vowed that he would never complain about his small office again.

"When are we getting out of here?"

"Eh? What's that?" Kalnikov was lost in his narrative.

"When is all this going to be over?"

"You are getting anxious, my friend."

"Who wouldn't be? I'm tired of all this sneaking around."

"Do not be impatient. We will find out more at the second shift meeting. I am expecting a report from our contact inside the director's office."

"We already have all these reports. They tell us nothing."

"I disagree. They tell us a great deal. They tell us that the mutineers are doing nothing. They are waiting. In the meantime they are trying to maintain the illusion that everything is running smoothly and normally. Though of course we know differently."

"We could disrupt that illusion."

"We could—and we will. But not yet. The time is not ripe."

"When?" moaned Packer. He did not have Kalnikov's disposition for waiting.

"Soon. Very soon. When the mutineers openly make their bid for taking control of the station—then we act. The citizens of Gotham will know which side to come in on. We will let the momentum of their own actions fuel their undoing."

"A lot of people could get hurt."

Kalnikov lifted his great shoulders. "Yes, some may be hurt. Freedom is a costly thing; it exacts a heavy toll always. But fewer will be hurt this way than if we acted too soon. We must not let the mutineers think there is any reason to act sooner than they wish to. Let their plans harden with certainty of success. Then when we arise to oppose them, they will have to abandon their plans and improvise. That is always a great disadvantage in struggles such as this."

"And in the meantime?"

"In the meantime there is always MIRA."

"Yes, always MIRA. But that is a long shot. We need proper equipment to even begin."

"The equipment is coming. It is coming. Trust me."

Packer sometimes feared that Kalnikov mouthed his revolutionary rhetoric the way a parrot mouthed saucy endearments—full of the bravado and dash, but utterly lacking in the ability to follow through. That the Russian pilot was a romantic dreamer he already knew; whether Kalnikov could back up what he so ardently espoused remained to be seen. Still, Packer had no better plan himself, so he clung to Kalnikov's ideas like a man dangling from a tightrope and prayed the drop wouldn't kill him.

CHAPTER TWENTY

"THERE'S NO question about it, Adjani. This *is* what we saw last night. It could not have been anything else." Spence turned the charm over in his hands, studying it closely. "But it doesn't do justice to the genuine article by half."

"You saw a naga spirit, Spencer Reston? I cannot believe it— though a great many unbelievable things seem to be happening to me of late. Do *you* also say you saw this creature?" He looked at Adjani with a half-skeptical, half-awed expression.

"I saw it, Gita. And I agree, it is undoubtedly what this charm represents. But Spence is right, the creature far surpasses this trinket for strangeness."

They were huddled together in the shade of the troop carrier while the governor's palace guards ate a leisurely midday meal. The thin mountain air was cool on their faces, the sun was hot and they were grateful for a brief respite from the back-breaking ride over the wretched road.

"And not only that," Spence continued. "We found a temple with an image of the Dream Thief. The *real* Dream Thief!"

"Undoubtedly it was Brasputi—the ruler of the Rsis and Vidyadharas. You will find his image all over Darjeeling."

"This one was in the old section."

"And it looked just like a Martian."

"I wish I could have seen it, in that case."

"Don't worry, Gita, we're all going to see the real live Brasputi very soon."

"What are we going to do?" moaned Gita. "To be delivered into our enemies' hands like chickens for the plucking . . . ahh!" His round face convulsed in an expression of deepest grief for their impending plight.

"We're not there yet," soothed Adjani.

"Far from it," said Spence. "I have something up my sleeve here I've never told you about—either of you." He reached into a zippered pocket of his jumpsuit and pulled out a small flattened shell-like disk. He held it in his hand and felt its strange power quicken to his touch.

"What is it?"

"It's called a *bneri*—it's some sort of signaling device. Kyr gave it to me. He said that if I ever needed him I was to take this and hold it while thinking about him, and he would know I was in trouble and he'd come to help."

"Let me see it," said Adjani. "A psychoactive instrument. Fascinating. Why didn't you show me this sooner?"

"I don't know. Maybe there's still a part of me that thinks I'm going to wake up and find this has all been one grand absurd dream. But this —this tangible object reminds me it's real—too horribly real. I don't like to dwell on it."

"Try it," said Gita excitedly. "Oh, please try it now."

Spence looked at the disk in his hand and felt its warmth filling his palm. He closed his eyes and began to concentrate, but before he could even frame a single thought he felt it snatched from him. His eyes flew open and he stared into the barrel of a rifle.

One of the guards, watching them closely, had come up while they were talking. He held the *bneri* in his hand and turned it over, frowning.

"Gita, tell him it is nothing—a shell. Ask him to give it back, please." Spence smiled at the guard as he spoke, but his voice was taut as drawn wire.

Gita rapidly conveyed the message to the guard. He looked at the object and at Spence and then took the device and flung it into the brush at the side of the road. The last Spence saw of his valuable gift, it was skimming through the bush-tops down the side of the mountain.

"No!" he cried, jumping up.

The soldier shoved him back with the butt of his rifle and Spence fell against the side of the truck. The leader of the guards called his men to him and there was a short secretive conference.

"I don't like the look of this," said Gita. "What are they planning?"

Spence, horrified, ignored the comment and stared at the place where he had last seen their only hope sailing away and moaned, "Well, that's that. We're in it now." He turned to his friends. "I'm sorry. I never should have gotten you mixed up in any of this. It's my fault."

"Spence, for the last time stop apologizing. Do you have such a monumental ego that you believe this to be all your doing? This is just one more battle in the age-old struggle between the powers of light and darkness."

Spence could take no comfort from this speech. He still thought of his trouble as *his trouble;* the thought that it might indeed have some larger significance did not console him at all.

The truck rumbled up a winding mountain track and rounded a curve cut in the side of the mountain. A tiny village swung into view.

"There it is," said Adjani. "Rangpo—that is where the seminary of Ari's grandfather is located. You can see the walls of the old monastery just off over there. See them?"

Despite his black mood, Spence looked eagerly at the village. It was much as he had imagined it. "Why a seminary in such a small, backward place? Why not Darjeeling?"

"Who knows? Perhaps Rangpo was more receptive to Christianity. It is often the way of God to choose the least among us to do his will."

It did not make sense to Spence, but he was learning that little about God made sense in the normal, rational way. "It isn't much of a place."

Just then Gita, who had been gazing at the scenery, looked up and said with a shout, "What was that? Did you see it?"

"See what?" Spence looked in the direction Gita's wiggling finger pointed—behind them and skyward. He saw nothing.

"It was a flash of light. Very bright. Just there."

"Lightning, most likely," replied Spence, watching the gray clouds flowing down from the mountains. The sun had become a dim, hazy, dirty yellow ball without much warmth or light. "Looks like it's going to rain."

"It was like no lightning I ever saw," Gita maintained, though he offered no other explanation.

All three searched the sky from the back of the open truck, but saw nothing out of the ordinary. They settled back as the truck bumped along the steep, rutted road. They passed through Ranpgo, barely slowing down, and reached the mountain road when the truck slowed and then stopped.

"Why are we stopping?" asked Gita, jumping up as the truck rolled to a halt.

Spence looked around. They were hemmed in on every side by tall trees and brush; he could neither see the mountain ahead nor the town behind. One of the guards came around the side of the truck and motioned them out with his rifle.

"Do as he says," said Adjani. "I don't think this was in the plan."

"What are they doing?" whined Gita. 'Oh, something is very wrong!"

"Quiet!" snapped Spence. "Keep your wits about you! Adjani, ask him what's going on."

Adjani spoke to the guard who seemed to be in charge and received no answer. Two of the guards hung back, as if fearing what was about to happen.

The three prisoners were shoved to the side of the road and the leader cried, "Halt!" He raised his rifle. The other guards stood close by, but did nothing. Their faces were pale and their eyes were afraid.

"They mean to kill us!" said Spence. He glanced at Adjani. "Tell them we'll pay them to let us go. Talk to them!"

Adjani raised his hands and called to the soldiers. Spence could not understand what he said, but it seemed to have little effect on the men—they still stood indecisively hanging back, waiting for the deed to be over. The leader gave a curt reply.

"It's no use," said Adjani. "He says he has his orders."

"Then let's run for it!"

But it was too late. The leader of the guards spoke a stern order to his men, and they reluctantly raised their guns and aimed at the prisoners.

"God, have mercy!" cried Gita, covering his face with his hands.

"Run!" screamed Spence.

He heard a sound and realized that it was the click of a trigger. He saw the glint of sunlight on the steel barrel of the gun and looked into the black bore, from which issued a tiny projectile. He threw himself to the ground and rolled toward the shelter of the trees behind them. Then he heard the report of the rifle exploding into the silence, shaking the leaves on the trees and sending birds into flight.

Spence glanced back, even as he rolled, and saw an amazing thing. The bullet cleared the barrel of the gun and drifted toward him leisurely. It moved with aching slowness, and appeared to lose power and sink back to earth. The missile tumbled end over end and dropped in a lazy arc to land before him in the road in a little puff of dust. It lay there gleaming and spent.

A look of wonder appeared on the faces of the guards. They glanced at one another nervously.

"Look!" yelled Adjani. He pointed ahead of them up the road.

There stood a tall, thin figure clothed in a radiant blue, skintight garment, his arm outstretched, holding a long glowing rod. Behind this figure stood a squat, roundish, bell-shaped object that shimmered as if through waves of heat.

The soldiers, too, saw the figure. They drew back. One of them fired his rifle and all watched his bullet sink feebly into the dirt at his feet. At this the soldier threw down his gun and backed away. The others turned and fled with him, leaving only the leader who mumbled something under his breath and then turned and ran after his men.

Spence was on his feet running toward the strange figure. Adjani and Gita came on more cautiously behind him.

When they reached their friend they found him embracing an extremely tall humanoid who gazed at them with great round amber eyes.

"Kyr!" shouted Spence, almost beside himself with relief. "You came! You saved our lives!"

Adjani's jaw dropped and Gita rubbed his eyes.

"Adjani, Gita . . ." said Spence turning to the astonished men. "Kyr, these are my friends."

The Martian regarded them with a long, unblinking gaze as if reading their thoughts. "Men of Earth," he said at last, "I am happy to meet you." With that he slowly extended his long, three-fingered hand.

CHAPTER TWENTY-ONE

"I SHOULD melt your flesh where you sit! I should blast your shriveled body to atoms! How dare you defy me!" The ancient eyes flashed fire and the voice croaked with murderous rage.

Hocking, for once, appeared at a loss for words. "I . . . I did not defy you, Ortu. Th-there must be some mistake."

"There is a mistake and you made it when you gave heed to your own overreaching ambition. You will pay for this error, but first I want to know if you have any notion at all of what you have done. Do you have the slightest idea what you have ruined with your trifling, puny efforts? No answer?"

Hocking had never seen his master so angry. He thought it best to keep his mouth shut and weather the blast if he could.

"No? Well then, I will tell you," Ortu spat. He raised himself up and sat on his cushions erect and commanding, though he had not moved from his place. His hairless head gleamed like a polished knob; the hanging folds of skin around his neck jerked with every venomous word. The gleaming circlet across his forehead glowed hotly, and the great yellow eyes, burning out of their enormous sockets, undimmed by age, pierced the object of their focus like laser beams. Hocking shrank even deeper into the yielding cushions of the pneumochair.

"Your meddling has jeopardized the work of a thousand years. Centuries of cultural and social conditioning have brought us to the precise moment of maximum vulnerability. The *tanti* is at last attuned to the exact mental frequency of the collective human mind. Mankind trembles on the threshold of our new world order, and does not even guess what is about to happen. Like dogs they await the coming of a master to lead them."

"How has anything changed, Ortu? It is still as it was. Nothing has been lost."

"Silence! A great deal has been lost! I thought you were smarter than others of your kind. Use that miserable brain of yours, then— think what you have done!"

Try as he might Hocking could not think what had gone wrong. He did not even know exactly how Ortu had found out about his plan to eliminate Spencer Reston.

"Does your tongue fail you? Well it might, since you do not fathom even the tiniest fraction of the whole.

"The *tanti* is ready, is it not? It has been tested relentlessly for many years." Ortu sank back into himself, and glared dully at Hocking. "Its power has been increased a billion-fold."

"Correct." Hocking's mouth was dry and he croaked.

"With the *tanti* we possess the ability to control the universal sub-conscious and thereby control the behavior of every human being on earth. With it we can literally rule the world."

"Control a man's dreams and you control his mind," said Hocking. He had heard the maxim often enough.

"And yet, in the final calibration experiment what happens? Un-expectedly, we discover a man capable of resisting complete domination. How is this possible?" Ortu crossed his long thin arms across his narrow chest. "Answer me!"

"I don't know," snapped Hocking. "Obviously, if I knew it would not have happened."

"Well said. But do you not even now perceive your error? Did it never occur to you that where one man resists there may lie the secret of all men's resistance? That is why I wanted him brought here—to learn the secret of his ability to withstand control. Instead, you seek to eliminate him, to destroy him. If you had succeeded we would never know."

"You saved him, didn't you?" Hocking fought down the twinge of fear that coursed through him as he remembered his unsuccessful attempts to kill Reston. "I fail to see how I have seriously harmed our plans, let alone damaged our overall contingencies."

"Then allow me to illumine you, oh *wise* one," mocked Ortu. Hocking colored under the scorn. "Reston has contacted a member of my race—"

"Impossible! It is beyond current physics . . ."

"It is *not* impossible. I have just said it has happened. It is a fact. He did not travel to distant galaxies, no. He has awakened one of the Guardians and has summoned him here."

"I don't believe it!"

"You will believe it. Long ago when we on Ovs migrated we left behind in each city one of our own to guard all that we left behind against the day when others would come, that the knowledge gained should be wisely used and our treasures respected."

"Reston could not have discovered this—no one on Earth believes Martians exist, much less Martian cities."

"You, who believe nothing—how do you know what men believe in their innermost hearts? And why do you keep telling me these things are not possible when indeed they have happened?

"Men believe that their salvation will come from the stars, from benevolent beings who will show them the way. *That* is what men believe today. Have I not spent hundreds of years nurturing that belief? Creating wonders in the sky, strange and unexplained events on the ground? All to prepare the way for this final stage, for the willingness of humankind to accept a savior from beyond their world.

"It has all been part of the social and mental conditioning. Men speak of UFOs and watch the sky by night for a sign that their space brothers are coming. And why? Because I have willed it so. I, Ortu, have programmed it to be so."

"How can one man, even a very stubborn man like Reston, change that?"

Ortu sighed. "Because within him is the force to withstand, and to undo all I have done. And the Guardian who is with him now will not allow our work to continue—he will see it stopped."

"Why?"

"Because he must. It is his life-sworn duty."

"Then they must all be destroyed," said Hocking, for the first time speaking with anything approaching hope. "I was right after all."

Ortu's head began weaving back and forth. "You still do not understand. Perhaps you are unable to comprehend what I have been telling you."

"I understand that if our work is in danger we must take any steps necessary to eliminate that danger. We must stop them."

"How do you propose to do that?" Ortu scowled.

Thinking fast, he said, "Your disciples could do it. Send them out to destroy our enemies."

"You have left us no choice. I will summon them." Ortu's head sank. For once he seemed to wear the full weight of his years. His voice sank into a rasping whisper. "Go now."

Hocking swept out of the swirling, cloud-choked chamber and found Pundi lurking in the hallway nearby. "Bring his disciples at once!" he ordered. The servant hurried off on pattering feet to retrieve the chest of gopherwood containing the six teak boxes.

Gita, whose wide round eyes never for a moment left the alien, kept hopping up and down in a kind of ecstatic dance, first on one foot and then on the other. He was beside himself, almost literally. And though he did not enter into the conversation with the others, he did not miss a word.

Spence and Adjani were endeavoring to explain their present situation to Kyr, who listened intently. It was a marvel to Gita that the Martian could speak so well; Spence had explained the being's remarkable facility, but that did not diminish Gita's sense of wonder that the first words he heard from the mouth of an extra-terrestrial were in plain English.

Spence explained, "We have very good reason to believe that one of your own—an Ovsian—came to Earth during the time of the Great Migration. He has lived for thousands of years somewhere in these mountains—a place called Kalitiri. The soldiers in the truck were supposed to be taking us to him but . . . they evidently changed their minds."

Kyr pondered this information; his eyes narrowed and he looked away toward the mountains. "If one of my race is here, he will be found. He must be convinced to return to Ovs. It is forbidden to interfere with an alien culture."

"Unfortunately that appears to be just what he has been doing here," said Adjani. "We think he is somehow connected with Spence's blackouts and the dreams; that is, he is responsible for them. On at least one occasion what Spence had dreamed has come true."

"The *tanti*—dream maker," said Kyr. "It is a device—a transmitter capable of influencing brain functions and inducing mental imagery. It was used on Ovs as a medical instrument for treating those suffering from acute mental disorders."

"I'm afraid it has been put to a very different use here on Earth," replied Adjani.

"Then the *tanti* must be destroyed; those who would use it must be stopped."

"Our thoughts exactly." Spence glanced around at the late afternoon sky. "But it will be getting dark soon. Perhaps we should find shelter before nightfall—at least, before the soldiers work up enough nerve to come back."

"Come with me," said Kyr. "We will use my vehicle." A long arm swept up to indicate the still-glowing object sitting in the center of the dirt road.

"A flying saucer," said Gita. "I'm going to ride in a flying saucer!"

"*Vimana*," said Kyr. "It is called a *vimana*."

"Sky car! He is right!" exclaimed Gita. "The word is exactly the same in our language."

"Why not?" chuckled Spence. "No doubt that's where it came from in the first place."

"Then it is really true! And the myths of my people . . . " Gita began and stopped, stricken with the implications of this revelation.

"Are myths just the same," finished Adjani. "Though with a grain of truth behind them."

"A *mountain* of truth, sahib," said Gita, shaking his head. "When I said before that I believed your story, I never *dreamed* . . . To think they have been worshiping Martians all these years! It staggers the mind!"

Spence listened to this exchange and smiled. As they started toward the *vimana* he said, "Kyr, how did you know to come here?"

"Your *bneri* summoned me."

"No, it was taken from me before I could use it. One of the soldiers grabbed it just as I was about to send you the signal."

"I received the signal and I answered it."

"But how? How could you have come so quickly? Only a few minutes passed before you arrived. Does your spacecraft travel so fast?"

"I do not know what you mean, Earthfriend. I was aware of your presence on this road. I watched the truck from before your entry into the village when you were stopped on the road."

Now Spence was completely confused. "That can't be—I had not tried to signal yet. You would have had to receive my summons before I sent it!" He shook his head and looked to Adjani for help.

"Just when *did* you receive the signal?" asked Adjani.

"Your question has no meaning. I cannot answer." The Martian shrugged his narrow shoulders in a human display of ignorance.

"No meaning? Are you saying that time is irrelevant to the working of the *bneri*?"

"It works outside of time, as thought is outside of time. Therefore you cannot ask 'when' of it."

"I don't get it at all," muttered Spence. "Do you?"

"I think so," said Adjani. "Prayer often works the same way. We sometimes see that the seeds of the answer to our prayer have been sown before we even knew to pray. This is possible because God is not confined to time as we are. Past, present, future—he moves through each as he will."

Kyr made a low whistling sound, and translated it for them. "This God you speak of. He is the All-Being—the Source."

"Yes," replied Adjani. "You know him? You worship him?"

"Worship?"

"It means to revere, to hold worthy, to adore, to praise and love."

Kyr shrugged again. "This, I believe, is implied in living before him. We know him and feel his presence with us at all times."

"It isn't that way on Earth," said Adjani. "Men must choose to know him and worship him of their free will."

"It is the same with us. But who would choose not to know him?" Kyr gave Spence a quick, ironic look.

"You'd be surprised," said Spence.

"I told you once that I would find a way to explain the ways of the All-Being to you. But I see now that there is a barrier between us which I cannot cross. It was placed there by Dal Elna, who made you different from us. My explanations would not satisfy you."

"I believe you, Kyr. For an Earthman, nothing will do unless he finds the All-Being by himself, in his own way."

Just then Gita, who had been silent during this exchange broke in with, "Look! The townspeople from Rangpo are coming. They have seen your *vimana*. We must hurry away now or we may be here all night."

"We will talk of these things at greater length when time is not important. Now we have work to do," said Kyr. He turned and headed toward his craft. At his approach a red line appeared at the top of the object and slid down along the side, slicing it in two. A brilliant light flooded over them as the two halves parted to receive them. Spence, Adjani, and Gita stepped hesitantly into the light and followed Kyr into the craft.

The people of Rangpo saw four figures disappear inside a red beam of light and then a loud whirring sound filled the air as the unidentified flying object grew suddenly bright orange and then flashed over their heads in an instant, moving over the town toward the mountains to vanish in the clouds.

CHAPTER TWENTY-TWO

THE GENTLE evening closed around them like a soft and loving hand. The cool air brightened the fire as it crackled under Gita's deft fingers. The deep blue shadows darkened in the forest of green bamboo and the rustlings of monkeys and birds in the trees quieted. Kyr's spacecraft rested a few meters away in a clearing; it gave off a dim bluish glimmer now, its systems shut down for the present.

Gita hovered near the tall alien's shoulder—shyly, nervously, like a schoolboy in the presence of a high dignitary, a schoolboy who did not dream of contributing to the conversation of the adults, yet desired above anything to remain within the charmed circle of their words.

Adjani had not stopped asking questions since they entered the *vimana.* Ideas between the two were exchanged at such a rapid rate it made the head buzz to think of it. Spence lay back and smiled with a kind of dreamy indulgence as if to say: He is my friend, after all, but I gladly share him with you. It was enough for him to sit basking in the warm friendship of the group, a thing he had not grown overly used to in the course of his stoic life.

He reclined and let the high words and ideas roll over him like the warm breakers on a sunlit beach, rising to a swell and then lapping over him, filling him with happiness and good cheer. It seemed he had been waiting for many years for this special time.

There in the clearing on the mountainside, before the rustic campfire, Spence felt the approach of something he had longed for all his adult life. It was a thing that went by various names, depending upon his frame of mind at the time he felt the longing. Most often he called it *certainty,* and what he meant by that was the assurance of something absolute and unchangeable in a universe of change.

As a scientist he had long ago given up ever trying to find that immutable absolute; the only law of the universe he knew that could be counted on was change. Hot things lost their heat; cold things grew colder; solid objects became vapor and vice versa; speeding particles slowed; orbits decayed, matter decayed, flesh decayed. Entropy reigned. Nothing remained changeless and unchangeable.

That the immutable absolute he sought might be the Divine Being had never occurred to him. But it came to him now; what is more, he felt a distinct presence drawing inexorably closer. For some reason—perhaps because he was in India—he imagined it in the shape of a great tiger. He felt as if he was being stalked by the fiery ferocious creature; the hair at the base of his skull prickled. A chill wavered along his spine.

Then Kyr stood in the firelight, towering over the group huddled in the yellow circle of light. The conversation had stopped. All Spence heard was the snap of the fire and the evening sounds of the forest.

Kyr looked at each of them in turn, gazing with his great piercing eyes. What he was thinking could not be guessed—the look seemed filled with an emotion beyond Spence's stock catalog of responses.

Kyr began speaking slowly, quietly. "In my world of long ago it was our custom when meeting one another after a long absence, or when leaving for a time, to share a special meal, the *Essila*. On the evening of our first meeting, before we face what may soon overtake us, I would like to share it with you, my new friends."

With that Kyr went to his spacecraft and entered it, returning a moment later carrying a globe in each hand. These he sat down near the edge of the circle of light and settled his large frame beside them. The Earthmen crept closer.

Kyr took one of the globes and raised it. "In our leaving and arriving we are one. When apart and when together we are one. In the many there is One."

Spence recognized that last phrase as one Kyr had once used in referring to the All-Being.

The globe in Kyr's hands opened from a center seam and the top hemisphere parted to reveal the contents of the interior: a kind of whitish, fluffy, diaphanous substance that looked very much like clouds.

"A body is made of many cells, yet it is one body. A life is made of many days, and yet it is one life. Each man's body and each man's life is a reflection of the One who gave it. In the many there is One."

Kyr held his long hands before the fire and his eyes closed. His voice became almost a chant. Spence knew that if Kyr had been speaking his own tongue the litany would be a song. What Kyr must have been doing to translate it bordered on the miraculous.

"If we mount to the stars, Dal Elna is there. If we descend to the dust of death, Dal Elna is there. Dal Elna is in all things: the stars, the dust, the stones, the fire. Yet these things do not contain Dal Elna. In the many there is One.

"Stars are born and stars die, and Dal Elna knows their passing. In the deeps of space Dal Elna's ways are known. On created worlds and worlds yet to be created Dal Elna's name is sung. Dal Elna calls forth light out of the darkness and sets the planets in their orbits. Nothing exists that does not exist in Dal Elna. In the many there is One.

"Before time began, Dal Elna was. When time is gone, Dal Elna will remain. Soon time will cease and the curtains of our minds will be parted and we will see Dal Elna. All living souls will know Dal Elna. In the many there is One."

Kyr lowered his hands and raised the bowl and offered it to each of the men sitting near him. Spence reached his hand in and took some of the wispy stuff; it tore away in a long shred, pink in the firelight.

Then Kyr took some and set the bowl aside, saying, "To eat of the *Essila* is to mingle souls, to know another as you are known. Therefore, let no one eat of it who does not love the other."

Spence looked at each of the others. He had not put it into words before but yes, he did love Adjani and Gita. They had risked their lives to follow him, to help him, and he loved them for it. He could think of no other friends he trusted more.

Kyr seemed to be waiting while each made up his own mind and then, seeing that all were of one accord, he said, "Taste the sweetness of your love for each other. In the many there is One."

Kyr raised his fingers to his lips and the others followed his example, their eyes shining in the dancing light.

Spence felt the *Essila* melt as it touched his tongue and suddenly his mouth was full of the sweetest tasting substance he could have imagined—a sweetness beyond simple description. But it did not cloy or sicken in its sweetness, though it overwhelmed all other senses.

He swallowed and felt a spreading warmth surge through his midsection, tingling even to his extremities. He suddenly felt a closeness, a warmth he had never felt among others before. He looked across at Adjani and the slim Indian seemed to shine, his face glowing with a kind of subtle radiance.

He glanced at Gita and saw a wide grin of undiluted happiness gleaming on his round face. Two big teardrops slid slowly down his cheeks as he looked from one to the other of those around him.

Spence felt his own heart swell inside him until he thought it must burst. He felt himself higher, nobler, and more true than he had ever know himself to be in his life. He, too, felt radiant, absolutely glowing with kindness and compassion.

Part of this he knew to be emanating from the others as much as from himself. It was true; their very hearts and souls were mingling like rare and precious oils, each one increasing the worth of the other, yet losing nothing of its own value.

Spence felt himself lifted out of himself and he knew each of his friends as he knew himself. In that moment he knew their weaknesses and failings, yet loved them in spite of any shortcomings, forgiving them, as he forgave them in himself.

There was another presence he could not describe; it was utterly foreign to his frame of human reference, though it shared many of the same basic essences. This presence inside him he knew to be Kyr, and he loved the Martian for his utter, alien uniqueness and his freely flowing compassion.

He drank in these impressions and savored them, treasured them, cherished them. He wanted the moment to last forever and to have that incredible, unutterable sweetness on his tongue.

But Kyr raised the second globe and it opened before him. He took the upper part of the globe and handed it to Adjani, and then handed one to Gita, and in turn to Spence. Spence saw that there were several of these bowls nestled inside one another and Kyr withdrew one for himself. Then he poured from the lower half of the globe a liquid that sparkled in the firelight.

When each bowl had been filled with the liquid Kyr raised his own bowl and began to speak once more. "All rivers run to the sea; all roads reach their destination. In every beginning lies the seed of the end. But in Dal Elna there is only Beginning. In the many there is One."

Kyr brought the bowl to his lips and drank. Spence and the others followed his example.

The strange liquid had no taste that Spence could describe—not sweet, at least not as sweet as the first substance had been, but not bitter either. It touched his lips with a tingle like a mild current of electricity applied to his skin.

He rolled the effervescent drink on his tongue and felt as if he had tasted cool fire—the stuff seemed almost alive. He swallowed it and felt its playful sting all the way down. He drank again, more deeply this time and let the cool fire dance on his tongue. The effect made him want to laugh out loud or burst into song. He felt the inner fire seeping into his veins, quickening his heart. Suddenly he was more alert, more conscious than ever in his life.

He looked through new eyes at the world, and what a world he saw! Though it was night and dark he could see the tall slender ranks of bamboo all around, saw the firelight dancing on their thin shafts. He saw narrow, tapering shapes of the leaves with the delicate saw-toothed edge individually and precisely drawn and duplicated. Each was a thing of exquisite, inexplicable beauty.

Above the leaping flames of the fire he saw an insect. In his heightened vision it became suspended in motion, moving in slow, graceful sweeps as its tiny, transparent wings beat the air. He could see the glitter of light scatter across its multi-celled eyes, and the iridescent gleam of its carapace. He saw its legs dangling as fine threads beneath its sectioned body and the gentle curl of its antennae along its back.

Raising his eyes he saw the heavens, at first dark, now almost bursting with the light of countless stars—each star shining with clear, crystalline light, hard-edged and fine with beams piercing as needles.

Everywhere he looked he saw some new wonder, some commonplace revealed in a way he had never seen it before. The ordinary had been transformed into the extraordinary, the normal into the supernormal.

His friends still sat in the same positions as before, but he saw them wholly changed. He saw not their outward appearance only, but now he saw their inner selves unmasked. And each was larger, more fair and strong in every way. They sat wrapped in shimmering auras of gold and violet, as if clothed in living fire. In their faces he glimpsed unfathomable tenderness, and something he could only call wisdom burned out from their eyes, but a wisdom purer and finer than any born of Earth.

Spence looked at Kyr and saw not the elongated Martian but a creature not unlike himself and the others, resembling them and yet slightly different in subtle ways he could not name.

And where before Spence had felt radiant, he felt now as if he were throwing off sparks. He caught fleeting glimpses of the colored rays as they streamed from him to blend with the light of the others.

Spence felt full to overflowing with the joyous, scintillating, reverberating love he felt for his friends. He felt the power of their love for him and for one another, and it was a mingling of deep strong water which flowed out in all directions from the center, like a fountain or a spring with an endless source.

But he sensed another subtle yet still distinct presence too. This presence interwove all the others and even his own, to hold them and to overlay them at the same time without losing its own distinction. In that heightened awareness he sent out the fingers of his mind to examine this presence. He extended his mind toward it and tentatively touched it. Instantly his mind recoiled, staggered as if by a blazing bolt of lightning.

He knew then that he had touched the Source itself.

He felt dizzy and intoxicated, completely shattered by that single brief encounter. Then his mind began to fill with thoughts strange and wonderful and terrifying in their clarity and force.

He saw galaxies swinging in the frozen deeps of space, flung like pebbles on an endless beach; he heard the roar of silence drowned by the music of the galactic movement. The song of the stars—all heaven was filled with it!

He saw worlds upon worlds springing into existence before nameless suns. On each world life leaped up, sprung from the voice that had awakened it. Plants of every variety, animals of every description, human creatures as different as could be imagined, yet all possessing the divine inner spark that was the immutable stamp of the Maker.

He saw his own world as one minute fleck against the darkness, and knew that his life, and the lives of every man who had ever lived, was but a single faltering step in the Great Dance of Heaven.

The Dance flowed and ebbed according to the will of the Maker, and all moved with him as he moved. There was not a solitary figure in the Dance that was not in his plan—from the seemingly random shuttling of atoms colliding with one another through the limitless reaches of empty night, to the aimless scrabblings of an insect in the dust, to the directionless meandering of a river of molten iron on a world no human eye would ever see—all was embraced, upheld, encompassed by the Great Dance.

In the many there is One. At last Spence understood.

One Dance, but it took all space and time to describe it. One life, but it took all living things to define it. One mind, but it took all thought to know it. And still it could not be described, defined or known in its entirety. He knew why Kyr and his kind called it the All-Being, for it transcended all that it touched even as it stooped to create it.

And though it spawned a billion worlds, gave voice to a trillion celestial lights, directed the course of a quintillion lives, the All-Being was One: inseparable, indivisible, indissoluble, immutable. All-Wise, All-Merciful, All-Holy, All-Knowing. Infinite and eternal . . .

The rest went spinning by Spence in a dizzying flood of thoughts and feelings and images of power and grandeur untold. He was left gasping and breathless by his single fleeting contact with the God he had long denied, but could deny no longer.

Spence bowed down before the Presence in all humility and surrender, acknowledging it as the first spontaneous act of worship he had ever performed. As he did so he knew that it knew him as a friend and that he had nothing to fear from it now or ever. He felt loads of guilt and shame roll away from him and he heard a voice inside his mind say, "Hear me, son of dust. Why have you run so long and so hard? What were you trying to escape? Your running is over. Enter into my rest."

"Yes, yes, yes," Spence heard his heart reply. "Please tell me how."

"Trust me. Look for me, and then follow."

Spence felt a rushing tide rise within himself flowing out toward the Presence, but still he knew the choice to be his alone. One word would halt the surge and stay it, or it would be released to flow forever without end.

"Yes," said Spence. "I will follow. Lead on."

CHAPTER TWENTY-THREE

RAMM STRODE purposefully into the room where his men were assembled and waiting. The talk in the room died as the chief of security glared coolly around him.

"All right," he said. "This won't take long. I have just received orders to proceed to phase two of Operation Clean Sweep. Therefore, the escapees must be apprehended at once. Squad leaders, you are to double your efforts. I want every sector double-checked. Work around the clock if you have to. I want them found *now!*—before they have a chance to stir up any trouble. Got it?"

There was a grumble of assent. "What are you waiting for? Move out!" said Ramm. The security force rose at once and proceeded to file out of the briefing room. In the guardroom beyond he could hear the squad leaders calling their groups together and organizing for a renewed search. He glanced around the empty room and then left by a side door.

When he arrived at AdSec he pushed his way past the receptionist and went directly into the director's office. Wermeyer's puzzled face glanced up from the wafer screen he had been gazing into.

"Well?" the former assistant asked, leaning back in his boss's chair.

"We haven't caught them yet, but we will. It's only a matter of time. After all, they can't go far."

"Yes, well . . . see that you take care of it."

"I can handle it, don't worry. How are things going on your end?"

"Running like clockwork. I was just looking over the projections for the completion of construction on the engine installation. We're right on schedule. Hocking thinks of everything."

"Let's hope so."

Wermeyer gave him a quick questioning look. "What's that supposed to mean?"

"Nothing. I'm just a little nervous about this, you know. Taking over an entire space station . . . I mean, it's never been done."

"Relax and do your job and everything will go as planned. Did you get your orders?"

"Right. Phase two is in operation; I've already told my men. Any word when the machine will arrive?"

"Not yet. Hocking said to stand by. That's what we're doing."

"How about the new master program?"

"Ready and waiting. MIRA won't know what hit her. All communication and operation functions will be under our control as soon as we are given the word. If anyone has any thoughts about signaling for help there won't be a thing they can do about it. As for resistance—"

"I'll handle any resistance. I don't expect there will be much. It's awful cold and lonely out there . . ." He nodded past Wermeyer toward the huge observation bubble and the stars glowing brightly beyond.

"Yes, well, let's hope it won't come to that."

Ramm turned to leave. Before he reached the door he stopped and said, "Let me know the minute Hocking checks in. We'll want to secure the docking bay in case Packer and his pilot friend have any ideas."

"You let *me* know the minute you find them," returned Wermeyer tartly. "This has gone on long enough."

How long the vision lasted, Spence did not know. When he came to himself again the fire had died down to glowing embers and the moon had lowered in the treetops. Crickets chirped their trilling nightsong and the breeze down from the mountain slopes had freshened to a chill.

Gita lay curled near the remains of the campfire sound asleep, his turban resting on his outstretched arm. Adjani sat with his knees drawn up, head nodding on his chest. Kyr, his long thin legs crossed and his long arms wrapped around his narrow chest, sat gazing into the glowing coals which reflected in his great yellow eyes.

The effects of the *Essila* still tingled in Spence's limbs and pulsed in his brain; he still tasted a trace of sweetness on his lips. But the mingled rush of thoughts and emotions, of shared essences and spirits was gone.

"It is over," said Spence quietly. The Martian turned his head to regard him intently.

"Yes, Earthbrother. All that remains is to thank the One who gave us the *Essila* that we might know each other more perfectly."

"I will thank him the rest of my days," said Spence. The memory of all that had taken place still burned within him, and he knew he would carry it with him always. "Does it always have such power?"

"Sometimes more than others. The first time is the most overwhelming, but each time is different . . ." Kyr ran out of words to explain and fell silent. Spence understood that it was not a thing discussed and analyzed, only experienced and accepted. He wondered if the others had undergone the same thing he had.

The wind shifted then and Spence heard a sound that tripped a warning in his mind. "Did you hear that?"

The alien cocked his head to one side. The nightsong continued to ripple through the forest undisturbed. "I hear a great many things—all of which are new to me," replied Kyr at length.

"Perhaps it was nothing but the wind—" began Spence, but he heard the sound again, this time more distinctly: a faint whirring buzz like the rustle of dead leaves on a tree. He knew what it was; he had heard it before. "No! Not again!" he shouted, leaping up.

He stared up at the sky through the opening in the trees overhead and saw the outline of several black shapes sliding over them as the sound of those vibrating wings reached them with a dry hiss.

"We've got to get out of here!" cried Spence. "The Dream Thief has found us!"

"What is it? What's happened?" Adjani sprang up at once.

"The demon is back—the Dream Thief's demon. I think there's more than one this time . . . Let's get out of here!"

Spence turned to rouse Gita, but Kyr scooped him up in one effortless motion and began striding off into the clearing toward the spacecraft.

Spence and Adjani hurried after him through the tall grass, glancing skyward as the sound of the dreadful buzzing increased.

They reached the vehicle as the first of Ortu's disciples swooped down. A voice in Spence's head said, *Stop! Don't run!*

Spence stopped and turned to see a creature touching down a few meters away. It looked at him with glowing green eyes and he saw its horrid, manlike face grimacing in the moonlight. It had huge membraned wings like a bat's attached to a human-looking torso that sprouted four arms. The lower half of the body resembled a serpent's— the thing looked exactly like the small charm Adjani had found.

Immediately another dark form came down behind it and another just off to one side. All stared at him malevolently with their hideous luminous eyes.

"Get in quickly!" Spence felt a touch on his shoulder and felt himself jerked around. "Spence!" Adjani cried. "Move!"

Adjani appeared before him, shouting at him, it seemed, from a great distance. He felt himself drawn toward the gruesome creatures with the glowing eyes. He wheeled around and started walking toward them; he could feel a will outside his own directing his steps.

"What am I doing?" he wondered.

Come here, directed the voices.

"Spence!" shrieked Adjani. "Come back!"

Spence stopped and shook his head. He was almost upon the wicked creatures when he felt himself lifted off the ground and carried bodily back toward the waiting *vimana,* now glowing bright red-orange. He twisted in the steely grasp and saw Kyr looking over his shoulder at the demons.

They had almost reached the spacecraft when he saw a glimmer out of the corner of his eye. One of the demons held a glittering thing in his hands which he aimed at them. In the same instant a mighty sound ripped through him—a sound which seemed to melt his bones and turn his bowels to jelly. Kyr stumbled and fell and Spence in his grasp was thrown to the ground.

Before he could think or move he felt icy fingers on him. He saw a thin, stick-fingered hand reach out for him, and the cold touch of those hideous hands on his flesh sent ripples of revulsion through him. Spence struggled weakly, but his will had abandoned him and he could not break the grasp. At the same moment he sensed his consciousness leaving him. Dark clouds seemed to gather before his eyes and it was as if his skull was being opened and his brain plucked from its cavity. He was powerless to stop it.

He teetered on the edge of consciousness and saw Kyr laying next to him, eyes open and staring up at the star-spattered sky. Then a grotesque face was peering into his own and Spence looked into the cold green eyes of one of the creatures. In its hands it held a silver sphere which it lowered toward him. Spence sensed that when the sphere touched his head he would be completely under their control.

The sphere came nearer, bare centimeters away from him now. He squirmed on the ground, but the effort was futile and absurd. He lay still and closed his eyes.

Even as he did so a piercing ruby light flashed out and struck the sphere; the object shattered in the creature's grasp, and disintegrated.

He was released from the spell. He jumped to his feet and tore the clutching hands of the awful creature from him, lashing out at it with his feet.

He heard a shout and saw Adjani rushing up beside him with a long rod in his hand—the thing flashed in the moonlight and Spence recognized it as the weapon Kyr had used to save them on the road earlier that afternoon. The air smelled of scorched metal and Spence's head throbbed with a booming ache. His ears roared with the sound of a distant ocean. But he was free.

Adjani took the end of the object in his hands and swung into the foremost of the creatures. They all lurched away out of range, and Adjani grabbed Spence by the sleeve of his jumpsuit and pulled him back toward the spacecraft.

"Wait! Kyr is hurt," said Spence. "We've got to get him on board. Gita! Lend a hand! Hurry!"

They bent over the alien's body and lifted it, slinging it between them as they made for the ship. Spence heard the air buzz above his head and saw one of the demons dart past him. Two more stood between them and the Martian spacecraft. "They've got us cut off!"

The airborne naga swooped at them from above. Adjani spun and raised the rod in his hand and once more the ruby beam split the night. The shot hit the monster in the chest as it swung down toward them, grotesque hands outstretched and grasping. There was a bright flash and Spence saw the being jerked back through the air as if it had been yanked by an attached wire. An agonizing scream gurgled from its inhuman throat and the thing fell to earth. But to everyone's surprise, the creature climbed back onto its legs and rejoined the others.

"We can't stay here. We've got to run for it." Spence looked at the still-unconscious body of the alien at his feet. "I'll carry him. You cover our retreat. Let's go!"

Gita, his whole frame shaking with fright, helped lift the stricken Kyr onto Spence's shoulders while Adjani kept the naga demons at bay, brandishing the rod. The jolt to the first demon seemed to have made them cautious, but they had regrouped and were closing in.

"Gita, you lead the way. We're right behind you. There!" shouted Spence, shoving Gita ahead toward the forest. "Get going!"

The demons saw what was happening and began shrieking in rage. They leapt into the air to pursue the chase.

Spence, with Kyr slung across his shoulders, stumbled on as fast as he could, slamming now and again into branches and trunks of trees as they gained the forest. Adjani stayed at his elbow, steadying him and guiding him through the thick tangle. Occasionally he turned to loose a shot at the beings darting after them.

They ran on a downward course that grew steeper as they went along. To Spence it seemed that they had traveled for hours, but it must have been only a few minutes before his lungs began to burn and his legs tired. But he kept moving.

The forest began to thin out and the undergrowth became sparse. He imagined he saw lights through the trees ahead. "I think I see something!" cried Gita. "Yes! It is the village! Rangpo is ahead."

"Can you make it?" asked Adjani. "Let me take him."

"No, I can make it. Let's keep going." Spence allowed himself a quick backward look. "Where are they?"

"They're right behind. But they seem to be keeping their distance."

"They're afraid of your weapon there—"

"Or they're waiting for us to run out into the open."

"I hadn't thought of that." The thought made Spence's heart sink once more.

The way became steeper and rocky. Spence fell several times over rocks and landed on his knees. Each time Adjani hauled him to his feet and they hurried on. Then they were standing at the edge of the forest looking down at the village on the hillside below. They could hear the obscene buzzing of the demons' wings growing louder and more ominous as the creatures closed in.

Spence, his heart pounding wildly, his breath coming hard, leaned heavily on Gita's arm. "Well, it's now or never. Let's go!"

Gita muttered a prayer and dashed out from the shelter of the trees; Spence followed on his heels. Instantly there was a shriek above as one of the creatures streaked down upon them. "Down!" cried Adjani. Spence threw himself to the ground and heard a raking claw whisper by his head. He glanced up just in time to see Adjani running toward him.

"Look out!" he shouted. But it was too late.

Adjani, watching the sky behind, did not see the fallen tree trunk lying directly in his path and went down hard. The weapon in his hand was thrown out and sailed through the air to land midway between them. Adjani squirmed back onto his feet and dived for the alien weapon. There was a whir in the air and a dark shape swooped down and snatched the instrument away.

Spence, helpless under Kyr's weight, watched all this happen. "Oh, no!" he groaned.

"Look here!" exclaimed Gita. "The Lord be praised!"

Spence swiveled his head in the direction of Gita's voice and saw smooth high stone walls shining faintly in the moonlight. Adjani was instantly beside him lifting Kyr. They slung the Martian between them and made for the wall.

"This way! Hurry! The seminary! Run quickly!"

They reached the wall and ran alongside it, looking for an opening to duck inside. Gita disappeared around a corner and they heard his voice call back to them, "Here is a gate! Hurry, my friends! A gate!"

When they caught up with him he was hammering on the gate with his bare hands. A single lamp burned in a lantern over the entrance. They huddled in the pool of light, as if it might offer some protection against the terrors of the night.

Spence leaned Kyr against the archway. A moan came from the alien's throat. "I think he's coming out of it. Can you see them?"

Adjani, eyes to the sky, replied, "No, but I'm sure they're out there. Strange, I don't think they followed us. I don't know why."

"I don't *care* why, just as long as they leave us alone."

"I hear someone coming," said Gita, still pounding on the wooden gate with his hands.

In a moment they heard a voice from behind the door speaking rapid Hindi. Gita answered and then said, "Please, open up! We need help!"

There was a grating sound as of a bolt being drawn back and then the door creaked open and a face appeared in the crack.

"Who disturbs our rest at this late hour?" Black eyes glittering in the light glanced quickly at each of them in turn.

"Please, sir. We seek refuge behind your walls. Our friend is hurt. May we come in?"

There was a slight hesitation and then the door was thrown open wide, revealing a small man with a smooth bald head which gleamed in the moonlight. "You are welcome, friends. How can I help you?"

As soon as Kyr was moved inside Adjani whirled to the door and shut it, throwing the bolt. Their host narrowed his eyes and looked sharply at his guests.

Spence saw the look and said, "We mean you no harm, sir. We won't trouble you further."

"I am Devi, dean of the seminary. I was just on my way to my quarters when I heard you knocking on the gate. Are you in trouble?"

"We were traveling on the road earlier," said Adjani. "We camped in the forest."

"Wild animals found us and pursued us," said Gita, his eyes big with fright. "We came here, Your Eminence."

Devi laughed. "You have had a time of it, yes; I can see that. Now about your friend." He bent to examine the Martian.

Spence quickly turned to hide the alien's features. "He'll be all right. He fell. We had to carry him. I think he's coming out of it."

Devi nodded. "I won't pry. Your secrets are safe with me. Wild animals have been known to wander nearby in these forests, though it has been a long time since anyone saw a lion or tiger. But we'll let that keep for now." He smiled and Spence saw his bald head bob. "Now you'll want to lie down and rest, I think."

"We don't want to put you to any trouble, sir," said Adjani.

"Oh, no trouble. I am only sorry I do not have beds to offer you; they are all full. But follow me—I will find something."

He turned and led them across the courtyard toward the main building of the complex. Their steps echoed faintly on the stone walk. They moved cautiously, peering into the sky for the dreaded shapes. But the sky was clear and bright and the moon fair. Not a sign of the demons could be seen.

CHAPTER TWENTY-FOUR

KALNIKOV lowered himself carefully through the man-sized hole in the lower deck beneath the docking bay staging area. The hole was made for more standard-sized spacemen, not Russian giants, and Kalnikov was a husky giant at that, so he had to squeeze his shoulders through carefully in order to keep from getting stuck. Once through, he dropped down a short ladder and made his way through a junction tube to the maintenance room that he and Packer had made their home, war room, and base of operations for the coming revolution.

He entered the room, filled with cylinders and hydraulic hoses and the electronic servo boxes which operated them. Packer sat hunched over a small console at a tiny table in the cramped room, his face green in the reflected light from the screen he stared into.

"How goes it, friend? Progress?"

"Hmph. It's enough that you give me obsolete tools to work with—you expect progress, too?"

"You are getting to be a very disagreeable fellow, Packer. But I don't mind," the Russian said cheerily. Packer looked away from the screen at his companion and noticed a definite change in the man's appearance—he seemed buoyant, full of smiles and winks.

"Have you been drinking?"

"No, I have news."

"What is it?"

"First you must tell me how you are coming on your little project there."

Packer frowned. In the last several days—or was it weeks?—he had not stirred out of their prison. For most of that time he had been sitting before the small screen staring at green phosphorescent blips and scrambled letters and numbers. MIRA was a tough old girl to crack, and he had only the tools of a fourth-form schoolboy to do it with.

They had decided to risk tapping MIRA's data bank to monitor the flow of information between the administration and security offices—between Wermeyer and Ramm. To do that they needed a terminal and a hook-in that would not be noticed when engaged. Kalnikov had scrounged an old manual keyboard model from a dusty corner somewhere and put Packer to work. He had been working constantly ever since.

"I am becoming permanently hunchbacked," said Packer. "That's how I'm coming. As for the project, well, who knows? Tomorrow or maybe the next day. It's too early to tell. MIRA's got a thick shell, tough as armor. And there's only so much this kiddie computer can do." He paused and dismissed the machine with a wave of his hand, and then continued.

"But I've organized fifteen of my best third-year men into teams. We've split the program into five parts and each team is working on a portion of the key. Right now, I'm merely trying to juice up our system here to handle the sneak feed once we're on line."

"Then we are in?"

"Not yet. Soon though. I've been able to worm in using the auto-hydraulic servo connect lines and I've reversed a couple of them without anyone noticing so far. There may be a red light blinking somewhere that someone may notice, but we'll have to chance it. There's still a way to go yet."

"When?" asked Kalnikov, crossing his great arms across his wide chest.

"Like I said, soon—tomorrow or the next day. Maybe longer. The problem is that the best program engineers in the world put in state-of-the-art worm traps. Sliding into the data core means outsmarting the traps and that's next to impossible. It would probably be easier to put your ear to the keyhole and listen that way."

The Russian was unimpressed. "It can be done. Anything one man can do another can undo."

"Thanks for the encouragement."

"But it must be done by tonight."

"What? Now wait a minute—" Packer leaped from his seat and sent his chair crashing backwards to the floor.

"Restrain yourself, please. We need to be on line by tonight. I have received word through the network that messages have been received this morning."

"Messages from who?"

"It is all in code. We don't know. But the effect has been to increase the effort to find us and to expose the network."

"Oh, great."

"Time is growing short. Something is about to happen and they want us safely out of the way before it does. We need all the advance warning we can get. We must get into MIRA's datafiles and read those signals—and any more that come through."

"They're really upset, huh?" Packer raised his eyes upward.

"They are even sniffing out the ventilation systems—they say there is a chemical leak from sanitation and traces of cyanide were found in the air. It is just an excuse, of course, so people will not become alarmed."

"Then it's only a matter of time before they flush us out of here."

"I am taking care of that. I am in contact with my second-in-command. He is with us. He will either disrupt the search of the docking bay, or he will obstruct it in some way. We don't need to worry yet. Anyway, he will be able to warn us. But about tonight . . ."

Packer sighed. "I'll do what I can. We're all exhausted. We've been working at this round the clock."

"Do your best, comrade. Soon your work will be rewarded." Kalnikov turned to leave.

"It's coming down soon, isn't it? How long do we have?"

"Within the next forty-eight hours, perhaps sooner. Take heart, my friend. Soon you will be a free man again." The big pilot stomped off humming a vaguely martial melody.

"Yes," muttered Packer, "one way or another I'll be a free man." Then he returned to his keyboard and tapped in an exhortation to his team of code-cracking worm masters and asked for a progress report. That done, he settled himself back to work once more.

August Zanderson stood in the dark. Evening had deepened around him as he waited, motionless, like a stone image of a man awaiting the summons that would call it to life.

Nearby he heard the gentle rise and fall of Ari's breathing, sounding like the shallow wash of sea upon the sand heard from afar. Upon returning from her last encounter with Hocking drowsy and incoherent, she had lapsed into a deathlike sleep. Her father had stood over her watching until darkness removed her from his sight. Now he listened to her breathing, clenching and unclenching his fists while alternately cursing and praying for her recovery.

After a while he became aware of voices in the courtyard below. The hushed sounds drifted up through the open balcony doorway. Stirring himself he stepped woodenly onto the balcony to peer into the darkened space below. He heard the rush of feet hurrying away to some other part of the palace and then all was still again.

He turned to go back to his sentinel's post near his daughter and as he did so he glimpsed, black against a lighter sky, the passing of several large, ill-defined shapes winging over the palace toward the lower slopes.

A feeling of dread accompanied the passing of the eerie shapes. Zanderson shivered involuntarily and moved back inside.

"All we want is a bed for the night," said Spence. "We'll be gone in the morning."

"Please, you may stay as long as you wish. Until you are rested and your friend is able to travel again, do not even think of leaving. You are safe here and most welcome. We are a poor seminary, and our students are poor, but we are rich in the Spirit and a great wealth of grace is ours. What we have we will share with you gladly."

Spence was about to protest, but Adjani cut him off saying, "We are most honored, Dean Devi. Of course, we will stay as long as is necessary. Your hospitality is most welcome."

Devi's smile was warm and pleased. He turned to the door of the chapel and opened it and led them in. It was dark and warm inside and smelled slightly musty with age—like an old library or museum, thought Spence. The scent was not disagreeable at all; rather it made him feel secure, as if he had stepped into a safe harborage well out of reach of the world's blasts and alarms. This, then, was what the ancients meant by *sanctuary*. Here on this holy ground nothing could harm him. He was safe and at peace.

At once he felt the weight of care roll off his shoulders.

He looked around at the high-vaulted ceilings, barely outlined in the soft light of candles burning in great iron holders in the front of the sanctuary.

"Yes, this place is very old, and most holy." Devi spoke in hushed tones.

As he spoke, Spence became aware of the presence of others in the chapel. He had thought they were alone, but realized, as his eyes became accustomed to the dim light, that there were several figures silently bent over something at the front of the chapel. "Are we disturbing something?" He indicated the figures.

"Not at all. Let us make your friend comfortable and I will tell you about them." He nodded toward the figures outlined in candlelight.

Kyr had recovered enough to move under his own power, but still seemed not to know where he was or what was happening to him. Adjani, who had been supporting him, laid him down in a nearby pew, propped his head on a cushion and spread the blanket over him which Devi had provided. Gita lay down at the other end of the pew and both were soon sleeping peacefully.

"I think he's going to be all right," whispered Adjani as he joined Devi and Spence. Both Spence and Adjani had been careful to keep Kyr in the shadows as much as possible so as not to alarm their host with the alien's presence—it would have been very difficult to explain, after all. With him now resting safely in the pew both men breathed a sigh of relief. Their secret was safe a little while longer.

Devi motioned them away to a place where they could talk more freely without disturbing the sleeping men. Spence looked at the kneeling figures; he could see them clearly now, bowed over the image of a cross set in white stones in a mosaic on the floor.

"They are the Friends of Intercession," said Devi. "They are observing their office of prayer."

"Friends of Intercession? A holy order?"

"Yes, but not the way you mean. It is a society, but anyone may join. We are all members here at the seminary. It was given its modern name by a professor we had here many years ago—an American like yourself. He had a daughter, a little girl, who was taken ill and nearly died, I believe. They held a prayer vigil for many weeks and she eventually recovered. He attributed her deliverance to our intercession and gave us the name, though that, as I say, was before my time."

"They've been praying ever since?"

"Oh, yes, and before—long before. The practice goes back many centuries. I told you this place was very old. Tradition has it that it is founded on the exact spot of the first Christian church in India. This chapel rests on the foundations of that first church. St. Timothy himself is said to have visited this place, it is that old. The apostles spread the new faith to the ends of the Earth in accordance with the Lord's Great Commission. Their seed found fertile soil here and took root.

"From the beginning this has been a place of prayer. We observe this most venerable and holy rite in our turn as the others did in theirs. It stretches back through time in an unbroken chain, spanning the years, joining us to the very first believers."

As Devi spoke, the door to the chapel opened and a lone figure slipped in and took its place at the front of the sanctuary, replacing one of the members of the little group who then got up and left just as quietly.

"So it goes on," observed Devi. "Sometimes in large groups, or small; sometimes a lone student or faculty member kneeling silently. They come to pray and stay until someone else comes to take their place. The chain stretches on—forged a link at a time."

Spence was overwhelmed by the enduring devotion of the society. He had never heard of such a thing, and could scarcely comprehend such selfless pity. The quiet, fierce discipline of the Friends of Intercession left him almost speechless. "What do they pray for?" he asked, embarrassed at once by the crudeness of his question.

"They pray for whatever the Spirit lays upon their hearts. But always for love, wisdom, and the strength to do God's will, and also for his presence to be manifest in the world. We pray that the Lord will come in glory, and for the Father to deliver all men from the evil one. As the name suggests, we intercede for all mankind before the Throne of Light."

They talked a little longer and then Devi left them to their rest. Spence crawled into his berth in a nearby pew, one thought uppermost in his mind: it *must* have been Ari's mother. That sick child whose illness had galvanized the seminary into organizing the society that continued its vigil of prayer even to this day. Indeed, who else could it have been? Had she paid some price with her broken life? Had her suffering purchased some measure of grace that he now could draw on in his time of need? Even as he held the thought he remembered One whose sacrifice had paid an ultimate price for all of them.

Strange, the economy of heaven, thought Spence. He had the undeniable feeling that somehow, beyond mortal reckoning, an order, a fine symmetry reigned that counted him and the mad Caroline Zanderson in its balance, and linked them in its accounting together with the all-but-forgotten seminary with its humble students kneeling obediently in endless prayer. Against what? The Dream Thief? Perhaps unknowingly, but also against the greater darkness of evil that gathered over the face of the Earth, the vast unreason that threatened always to extinguish the light, but could not.

And why not? Because a tiny society, together with all the other small and seemingly insignificant ones the world over, held fast to the flame, keeping it safe within the strong fortress of its devotion—even in the midst of the enemy's own camp.

Strange, the economy of heaven.

They left early the next morning before anyone else was astir. No one, not even the three kneeling over the inlaid cross at the front of the sanctuary, saw them go. Kyr appeared to have fully recovered from the aftereffects of the sonic blast that had stunned him. He walked across the seminary courtyard in the silver light of dawn easily and swiftly with Gita, a short pudgy shadow, by his side.

Spence lifted the wooden latch, pushed open the gate, and stepped out to face the world once more. He felt rested and calm, as if he had been given some deep assurance that his restless groping in the darkness was not in vain. He sensed within him the tiny pricking sensation that quickened the heart and keened the senses, that told of a new awareness of purpose. The night spent in the seminary had been a healing interlude, a blessed convalescence that he badly needed.

Without speaking they retraced their hurried steps of the night before, working back to the place where they had camped. By the time the sun had risen in the treetops they were standing once more at the site of their campfire, now cold ashes in a blackened ring. There was silence all around as they stared across the nearby forest clearing. Kyr's spacecraft was gone.

CHAPTER TWENTY-FIVE

HOCKING SWEPT noiselessly into the murky chamber. Clouds of incense rolled before him and scuttled away as he passed. Ortu sat immobile on his platform of cushions, head upon his chest, long arms resting on his knees. It was the same energy-preserving position Hocking had always seen him in as long as he could remember. The ancient Martian rarely moved.

But the old head rose as Hocking drew nearer. "What is it?" demanded Ortu. "What do you want? I have not summoned you."

"I saw the naga return. What news did they bring?"

There was an edge to his underling's voice that Ortu had not heard before. He glared back at Hocking and said, "I will tell you when I choose."

"You will tell me now," said Hocking evenly.

The great yellow eyes flared open and focused intently on the object before them. "You dare to question me?"

"I am tired of playing the obedient servant, Ortu. From now on we will act as equals—"

"Equals! Never!"

"As equals, Ortu. I have suffered your caprices long enough. For years I have waited in your shadow, but no more."

"Get out of here, you fool. Remove yourself from my sight. You are drunk on your own dreams of power. I alone say what will be and when." The *kastak* flared and subsided into a steady purple glow.

"Not any more, Ortu. I have dreams of power, yes, and ambitions of my own that you know nothing about. Some of them I have already begun to put into action, while you sit by and do nothing."

"Oh? What are these puny plans, wise one?"

"Tell me what happened—what did the naga find?"

"They escaped."

"How? What happened?"

"What difference does it make? They escaped . . ."

"And the Guardian?"

"And the Guardian with them. They are on the way here now."

"Then we must be ready for them when they arrive."

Ortu sank back into himself. "Do what you will, we are no match for a Guardian . . . I am too old."

"Ortu!" cried Hocking. "Listen to me! I need you! If we are to crush them I need your power!"

The Martian withdrew further into his normal trancelike state. "You cannot defeat them . . . it is too late. We have failed . . ."

"No!" screamed Hocking. The pneumochair swung closer to the rigid figure before him. Ortu did not move. Hocking glanced at the lowered head of his master and saw the circlet, the *kastak,* now throbbing irregularly. His own thin hand, shaking slightly, reached out toward it. In an instant the source of Ortu's power was in his grasp.

Ortu's eyes snapped open. "What?" he gasped. A startled expression appeared on his face.

"Give it to me!"

"No!" Ortu drew back his head, but Hocking's skeletal fingers held tight. He felt Ortu tugging away and was amazed at how weak his master was. With a quick snap he jerked the circlet and the *kastak* was his. "With this I am in control!" He held the *kastak* before Ortu's stricken face. "The power is mine!"

"Give it back!" cried Ortu. "You can't know what it means."

"I know enough to save us, if you won't."

"No—I—I need it . . ."

"It is mine now, Ortu."

The alien made a lunge toward Hocking to snatch the band out of his hands. A finger twitched on Hocking's tray and Ortu was flung back against his cushions in a heap.

"I am in control now, Ortu. *I* say what will be."

Ortu did not move from where he lay; his eyes watched Hocking dully. "Give it back to me," he pleaded. "I will die without it."

"Then die!" Hocking backed away from the squirming alien. "You are no longer any use to me, Ortu. I have endured you long enough."

"Ahh!" Ortu raised a hand and rolled weakly forward as if to prevent Hocking's retreat. But he lacked the strength to rise and so lay quivering as if chills assailed his frail body.

Hocking left the room and did not look back. Already he was framing a plan in his mind. He would let them come to him and then destroy them all—except Reston. Reston too would be crushed, but first that stubborn will of his must be broken completely. Before he was finished with him, Reston would beg for death and would die with Hocking's name on his lips.

Hocking's features contorted in a leer of pleasure at the image of Spencer Reston groveling before him, pleading for release. And he would give it, oh, yes, he would give it.

On foot the travelers pushed through sparsely forested hills upward, higher and higher toward Kalitiri. The way was well known and well marked. They could see the mountain itself, serene and majestic, trailing white wisps of clouds from its slopes, standing before them remote and aloof from the world of men.

They climbed through terraced fields of millet and rice, cut in the sides of the hills like the wide stair steps of giants. They passed the hillfolk working the fields with their buffalo or repairing the breaks where rain had carved out gullies in the terraces and washed the soil away. Others, burdened like pack animals, hauled firewood from the forests above the villages. Over all hung an air of quiet industry which seemed peaceful and good.

The peasants, with their baskets of woven twigs, went about their work pausing only to glance at the three newcomers and their tall companion in silence, or to hail them with a wave and a shout as they passed. Spence, watching the toil around him, began to feel as if he had been there before—some time ago. It was the same sense of *deja vu* pricked before at various times along the way. He felt he really did recognize the place. But this time the scene carried with it none of the strange panic that used to seize him in his dreams.

Of course. That was it! His dreams!—he had been here in his dreams. Spence stopped and looked around as if he were lost in a place that nevertheless seemed extraordinarily familiar. These hills were the hills he had seen in his dreams, and these were the ragged peasants who labored so hard to pull the stones from the ground and haul them away. It was as if he had stepped back inside his own dream; for a moment the world was frozen and unreal. The feeling passed and everything around him took on its normal appearance. The strange flashback receded, leaving behind only a residue of mild disorientation which he shook off.

"What is it, Spence? Are you okay?" Adjani was beside him with a look of concern wrinkling his brow.

Spence forced a smile and said, "It's nothing. I seem to think I remembered this place for a moment. It was in one of my dreams."

"And?"

"And nothing—really, it's all right. It just kind of gave me a funny feeling." He laughed. "Maybe somebody's trying to tell me something."

Adjani only nodded and said, "Come on, but let me know if you have any more flashbacks. This may be dangerous territory for you."

Spence had not considered that he might be especially vulnerable the nearer he got to the Dream Thief. The idea made him feel that every step closer to Kalitiri drove another nail into his coffin. It unnerved him, making him feel small and weak.

At last they reached the place where the gorge separated the mountain from the winding mountain pathway. The palace was still some distance away, but could be seen, its dark walls showing between the trees that had grown up high around it.

"There it is," said Gita, pointing. "And here we are." He looked at his friends with an anxious expression. "What are we going to do? There is no bridge."

Gita was right. At the place where the bridge had been, all that remained were two huge posts dangling great fibrous ropes swinging in the winds that raced through the chasm.

"What *are* we going to do?" echoed Spence. "Is there another bridge?"

Gita shook his head slowly. "No, sahib. It is not likely. These hill-people use the same pathways for generations. The only time they make new ones is when a landslide carries away an old one. It is certain that this is the only way. That the bridge has fallen away shows what little use the people have for this path. Kalitiri is not a place they care to go."

Kyr looked into the deep gorge. "Compared to the rift valleys of Ovs, it is nothing."

"You aren't suggesting we try to climb down there and back up the other side, are you?" Spence was incredulous. He gazed down into the dizzying depths to the swirling water below and then back up the sheer, jagged rock face of the other side. The gap was a good twenty or thirty meters across. "Without a good rope, I wouldn't dare try it."

Gita rolled his eyes in mute terror at the thought and threw up his hands. Adjani looked from one to the other of the group. "Well, there's only one way to find out, I suppose. We can buy some rope from the villagers. Perhaps they'll even help get us across."

Spence swallowed hard. "Kyr and I will stay here. You and Gita go and see what you can find. We'll scout out the best place to climb and meet you back here."

Gita left with Adjani, protesting that it was no use, that he would not mind being left behind in the least, that climbing always made him sick to his stomach. His protests diminished as he and Adjani returned back along the winding path and were soon out of sight.

Spence stood looking at the patch of forest which for the most part hid the palace from view—all but the gleaming hemisphere of the domed stupa in the center and the spike of the thin tower beside it. Nothing stirred that he could see. The place looked overgrown and deserted, a habitation of monkeys and parrots—the same fate suffered by ruins the world over.

But he also sensed a power in that place which exerted a hold on him. He could feel it drawing him, its pull almost a palpable force. Was it outright foolishness to presume that they could accomplish anything by going there—the four of them, weaponless and very much at disadvantage? Was this a fool's errand? Was it part of the Dream Thief's plan from the beginning?

As if reading Spence's dark thoughts, Kyr turned to him and said, "Do not allow despair to eat at your heart, Earthfriend."

"I'm afraid, Kyr. What can we do against him?"

"Do not be afraid. Dal Elna has not brought us this far only to fail."

"I'm not so sure. Why did he let any of this happen in the first place?"

"Why? That no one can know—the answer is beyond our highest thoughts."

"We have no weapons. Nothing to fight with."

"We are far from helpless. You had nothing when you were lost on Ovs, yet you survived; more, you increased in strength and wisdom."

"That was different."

"How was it different?" Kyr looked at him intently with his great yellow eyes. Spence had no answer and so turned away. He began walking along the edge of the precipice in search of a likely spot to descend. He tried to shrug off the feeling of deep foreboding that had begun to swarm over him—as if the close proximity of the palace and its occupant increased his sense of helplessness and dread. But the oppression would not be shaken off. If anything, its grip on Spence was tightening. The fact that Ari also was held in its grasp—a thought which was never far from his mind—made it that much more potent.

After searching along both sides of the pathway for some distance, they found no better place to make a crossing than the spot where the bridge used to be. So they returned to wait for Adjani and Gita to come back.

They did not have long to wait. No sooner had they settled themselves beside the old bridge post than they heard a commotion coming up the hillside. Soon Gita's blue knob was seen bobbing toward them with Adjani's slim form beside him. But behind them marched what appeared to be the entire population of Rangpo and surrounding countryside. All were babbling at once and shouting, as if they were on their way to a major sporting event, which they were; they were coming to see the foreigners cheat death on the rocks. Bets were laid and wagers had already been made on the improbable outcome of success.

Spence looked aghast as Adjani and Gita came strolling up. He glanced quickly at Kyr—there was no way to hide him now, no way to disguise his alien appearance.

"Sorry," said Adjani. "We tried to discourage them, but . . ." He gestured to the crowd around him, who had fallen strangely silent in Kyr's presence. "They had to come. We're stuck with them, I'm afraid."

Black eyes sparkled, whispers buzzed through the throng as the villagers beheld the alien. Kyr gazed back at them calmly and the awestruck hillfolk became reverently quiet, apparently believing themselves to be in the presence of a god, or at least a very powerful spirit of some order unknown to them. They watched in wonder as he stood and came forward to take the ropes they carried.

Gita turned to the crowd and said something quickly. "I told them not to be afraid, that he is our friend, and theirs."

Kyr took a coil of handwoven hemp rope and slung it over his shoulder.

"Kyr, what are you doing?" said Spence.

"Watch and you will see." He stepped to the edge of the gorge and lowered himself over.

"Wait!" said Adjani. "Let us tie a safety rope around you."

Gita closed his eyes. "Oh, merciful heaven!"

"There is no need. This is one skill all on Ovs possess from the time they are very young. It is a game."

With that he threw himself over the edge, much to the chagrin of the onlookers. The crowd rushed forward, most expecting to see his tumbling body smash against the stones. Instead they saw the strange being lightly skittering down the face of the chasm, as deftly as a spider, his long arms and legs spread wide, gripping the rock in impossible handholds. Down and down he went, as easily as a man descending a staircase.

Spence and all the rest marveled at Kyr's swift, sure movements. In no time the Martian reached the bottom of the chasm and began propelling himself across the surface of the thrashing cataract. Like some kind of great gangly waterbug the alien skipped across the churning waves in a manner that defied description. Once across, he raised his head to regard his audience crowded over the edge of the precipice, and then reached up and started climbing the opposite face as swiftly as any lizard scaling his favorite sunning rock.

Then he was standing across from them, weaving his head from side to side, smirking as if to say, *It's easy, just do what I did.*

"Well done!" cried Adjani. And immediately the crowd went wild with shouts and cheers. Spence just shook his head in disbelief and grinned.

Kyr proceeded to tie one end of the rope to one of the bridgeposts on the other side of the gorge. He then heaved the coil back across to the other side. It took several attempts, but they finally caught it and made it fast to the opposite bridgepost. The villagers then took over.

Another rope was passed across and tied to the second bridgepost. They then had two parallel lines stretched taut across the chasm. Spence didn't see how that could possibly help them, but he kept quiet and let the men from the region work. He and Gita sat down on a rock nearby and watched the new bridge take shape.

The sun was a murky yellow ball low in the sky when the third rope was tied off. This one was actually made up of four separate lines braided together and slung between the first two. There were workers on both sides of the gorge now, a group having shimmied over on the first lines, pulling themselves across hand over hand with their legs entwining the rope.

Next, more ropes were woven from the two upper strands to the bottom one to form a vee-shaped trough. And though the work went quickly enough, Spence was acutely conscious of the passing of time—the day was almost gone. Night came on quickly in the high hills. Once the sun had slipped behind the curtain of mountains darkness crawled across the high places and valleys, though the sky might stay light for hours.

The sun's last rays were already shining on the peaks, turning their snowy caps into golden crowns, and Spence felt the night chill seeping into the air when the new bridge was finished. And even though he had witnessed its construction from the first moment to the last, the rope bridge still appeared a thing of miraculous invention, as if it had suddenly appeared and spun itself across the void like a magical spider web.

"Well, who's first?" asked Adjani.

Spence looked at him for a moment, not quite understanding the meaning of his question. Then it struck him—it was time to cross. "Oh, uh—you go first, Adjani. You have more experience in these things."

"Me?" He looked around. The hillpeople, watching them eagerly, smiled and pointed at him.

"You see, Adjani? They want you to be first to inaugurate the new bridge. You don't want to disappoint them."

Adjani took a deep breath and said, "I suppose not. All right, here goes." He fixed his gaze on the bridge and stepped up to it, clutching the parallel ropes, one in either hand. A cheer went up from the crowd. "I feel like a tightrope walker in a circus!" he called back over his shoulder, and with a look of deep concentration on his face he began to walk across, placing one foot carefully in front of the other, gripping the sides and not stopping until he was on the other side, beaming back at his friends. "Come on! It's easy!" he called.

"Gita, you're next," said Spence. "Let's go."

"But, sahib! I—"

"Don't worry, I'll be right behind you. Just do what Adjani did. You won't have any trouble." He led the sputtering Gita to the bridge and placed his hands on the lines.

Gita gulped and gaped and stared into the darkening depths of the chasm below.

"Don't look down, Gita. Keep your eyes on the other side. Watch Adjani; he'll help you."

Gita, his face ashen and his hands trembling, put one hesitant foot on the footline and tested its strength. He carefully positioned his weight on the rope and then moved out a centimeter at a time.

"Keep coming," hollered Adjani from the opposite side. "Don't stop and don't look down."

Gita inched his way across in agonizing slowness, swaying violently from side to side with each step. He reached the middle and then stopped, afraid to go any farther.

"Don't stop!" cried Spence. "Go on, you can do it. You're doing fine. Just keep moving."

"Dear God in heaven!" cried Gita, helplessly.

"Come on, Gita. You can do it," coaxed Adjani.

But Gita, eyes shut tight, hands clamped on the swaying rope, could not move.

"Don't panic," said Spence. "You're doing fine. Stay calm. I'm coming to get you."

Without a second thought, Spence stepped on the footline and began working his way out to where Gita remained frozen in the center of the bridge. He kept up a reassuring banter as he went, and Adjani offered soothing words from the other side.

"We're going to make it, Gita. Just stay calm. Don't make any sudden moves."

The bridge swayed and bounced as Spence moved out. The breeze whistled in the rocks below and the ropes creaked with the combined weight of the two men. It was then that Spence knew Gita's fear to be real, for he felt it too. He swallowed hard and willed himself to go on.

Gita was right ahead of him. He had stopped in the center of the bridge, and his weight made the angle of descent somewhat sharper for Spence. This, combined with the natural tendency of the bridge to swing and bounce, made the footing even more hazardous.

"Gita, I'm right behind you. I'm coming up on you now; don't move."

Spence did not want to frighten him further by surprising him. He could see Gita's hands like claws clutching the handlines, his knuckles white.

"I'm here, Gita. Now, we're going to move together," soothed Spence when he came within two paces. A sound like a sob drifted back to him from the Indian's throat. Spence realized it was the beginning of the Lord's Prayer repeated rapidly over and over. "I want you to start moving again, Gita. Ready? Move when I tell you. We'll go together. Left hand first. Okay. Move."

Gita slid his hand along the rope and took a step.

"Good. That's it. Now the right."

They moved a few more steps together and then Spence stopped to help steady the bouncing bridge. Gita went on and reached the other side. There was a burst of acclaim as Gita's feet touched solid ground once more.

Spence made to follow Gita, but was watching Gita's reception rather than attending to his feet. He lifted his foot, the bridge swung, and Spence, his eyes still on the scene before him, felt the awful sensation of treading out into empty air.

Unbalanced, the bridge pitched further, and Spence felt his other foot slip off the footlines. His right hand lost its grasp and scratched for a hold. He saw the darkness below him and heard the rush of the river below. it all seemed to come flying up toward him to pull him down and swallow him. He heard someone yell his name.

Even as it was happening Spence knew that it had happened once before. In a dream. The thin line between his dream and the terrible reality that now engulfed him blurred in that instant and melted together. That he would fall, he knew. Knew it with rock-solid certainty. He would be crushed on the rocks below and his body swept away in the river. It was all foretold in the dream.

The world spun around him. The sky above, the bridge, his friends, the villagers, the greedy darkness below—all revolved in kaleidoscopic fashion. He felt his grip on the handline slipping and a fuzzy confusion passed over him. He shook his head to clear it and cried out for help. The echo of his own voice range sharply in his ears and died away in peals of laughter.

His fingers, burning with pain, slackened and he felt the rope twist in his hands as it slipped away.

CHAPTER TWENTY-SIX

"I DON'T like it. It's getting too dangerous." Packer stood with his arms folded across his chest and his back to his listener. His red hair, uncombed for many days, stood out in all directions like a shaken red mop. His normally fresh jumpsuit was rumpled and sweat-stained, and his face, gray with fatigue, bristled with long red stubble.

"What would you have us do about it, friend? It is dangerous, yes.

We are not playing a child's game." Kalnikov slumped back round-shouldered in his chair and frowned at the ceiling. He, too, showed the strain of the passing days.

"We could try to get him out," suggested Packer.

"Too risky. Besides, just the attempt would tell them they have captured an important prisoner. It would also tell them that we have a good network of spies reporting their every move. In cases like this, unfortunately, it is better to wait and do nothing. We must not endanger the network.

"Just leave him? It's my chief assistant we're talking about, you know; head of our glorious network."

"All the more reason to remain calm. He must not be made to appear at all valuable. Otherwise, they will think they are in a position to bargain with us. They must never think that! They must remain uncertain on that score. We must keep them guessing. Silence is better. And it is better for Jones, too. You will see."

Packer ran his hands through his hair and sat down with a flop in a chair opposite the Russian pilot. A deep frown creased his unhappy face. "I suppose you're right. But I still hate it!"

"I know. It is most unfortunate. But there is yet hope. We do not know what he may have told them. He may have convinced them he knows nothing of our whereabouts. And unless they are very desperate, they will have to believe him. I don't imagine even Ramm is bold enough to begin arresting people wholesale. The mutineers must still maintain *some* semblance of order—at least for a little longer. So, perhaps they will release Jones, eh?"

Packer nodded slowly. Kalnikov continued. "Now, then, how are we coming on the break-in?"

"MIRA's shields tumbled a few hours ago."

"That's good news! Yes? Fantastic! That is something to cheer about at least."

"Well, yes and no. Without getting too technical, let's just say we're only sixty percent home. There's still a long way to go. MIRA's a tricky gal. She's state of the art and her data blanks are all biochip components. They're a lot tougher to manipulate at arm's length. More complex. We can roam around inside her circuits and sample bits and pieces of stuff we run across, but that way it would take years to find what we're looking for. And there's a good chance that we'd stumble over an internal tripwire of some kind and give ourselves away—they'd know they had a worm. They'd start shuffling the stuff around and we'd never find it. We need to know where the information we want is stored, and we also have to find which lines they're using for communication. In short, we need a master key to the system layout. A road map. We're working on it now."

"Well, keep working on it. Let me know as soon as we have something." Kalnikov got up and brushed the bags out of his uniform. "I've got to go and pick up the last shift report from my second-in-command."

"There is one thing, though," Packer called after him. "We could order a shutdown of certain on-board systems throughout Gotham."

"Oh? How would we do that?"

"It's simple. We merely introduce false information into the matrix —say splice in a signal for a faulty blower fan or something. MIRA would shut down the ventilator in order to check it out, or she'd signal someone to go fix it. Anyway, it would be shut down while all that was taking place. It might be useful."

"Oh, yes," Kalnikov smiled broadly. "You never know what might be useful."

Ramm paced back and forth in front of the director's desk. Wermeyer sat watching him, drumming his fingers on the wooden desktop.

"It's not good. I have to let him go soon; I can't keep him indefinitely—we haven't charged him with anything. People are asking questions."

"Well then, charge him. Think up something. If we let him loose now he'll know we don't have a clue where they are. And if he *is* in contact with the others, they'll know it, too."

"Any word from Hocking?"

"For the third time—no, not yet! Relax, will you? Getting nervous won't help. Everything's going as planned. The takeover is right on schedule."

Ramm shook his head and glared at Wermeyer. "I won't relax until this place is buttoned down tight. Right now there are too many variables. Too much can go wrong."

"You're a worrier, Ramm. I've already told you, nothing can go wrong. Why don't you stay here and have a drink with me? You look as if you could use one."

"No, thanks. I'm still on duty," replied Ramm coldly. He turned to walk out of the room. "Still, I wonder what can be keeping Hocking. He was supposed to have been here by now."

Wermeyer only shrugged and turned away. Ramm was a worrier— a good soldier, but a worrier and a stickler for detail. But soon it would all be over and then the station would be theirs. And after that? Well, who could tell? Anything was possible. Anything at all.

Spence felt the rope twist in his grip as his fingers let go. He saw it slide sideways. His hand clawed the air. It seemed that he hung motionless for a fraction of a second before sinking backward into the chasm. He heard the screams of horrified onlookers and recognized his own name among unintelligible shouts.

He twisted in the air even as he fell and managed to snag a piece of the side-webbing of the bridge. With one hand he caught the length of rope and held on. Then, blood pounding in his temples so hard that he could hardly see, he managed to get his other hand on the rope and haul himself back up a few centimeters.

The rope was a weak lifeline; it served only to prolong the agony. For as he clung to the rope, kicking his feet to maintain his grasp, the strand snapped and he plummeted into the chasm below—to the renewed shrieks of those watching on the banks above.

Spence saw the darkness rushing up toward him and the gray-brown rock face slipping past him only an arm's length away.

Then something struck him. At first he thought he must have collided with a rock jutting out from the stone wall. There was a tearing sound—as if he had snagged his clothing on the rocks. In the same instant he felt a sharp pain between his shoulderblades. He caught and spun, arms and legs jerking uselessly. His head snapped forward, driving his chin into his chest.

He was dangling in mid-air. He turned his head to see what had saved him and looked up into Kyr's two huge eyes. The blow Spence felt between his shoulderblades was Kyr's lightning-fast grab at his clothing. The Martian now held him with one hand, clinging precariously to some near-invisible handhold with the other.

Moments later they were clambering over the edge of the precipice, eager hands pulling them to safty. Adjani gripped Spence's arm very hard and pulled him away from the edge.

Kyr bent over him and asked, "Are you injured?"

"No. Dizzy. I'll be fine."

"I am sorry if I hurt you, Earthfriend. Your gravity does not allow me to move with ease. I fear I struck you too hard."

Spence only shook his head.

"I never saw anything like it!" cried Gita. "I never saw anyone move so fast in my whole entire lifetime. Great merciful heavens!"

Spence turned to the chasm. "My dream almost came true just then. Thank God it didn't. And thank *you*, Kyr. I owe you my life."

"I am glad to serve you, Earthfriend. I sensed you were in difficulty."

"Look at that!" shouted Gita behind them. "Our audience is leaving. Show's over!"

They turned to see the villagers filing silently away, heading back to their homes as darkness closed on the mountains.

"I don't blame them," said Spence. He nodded toward Kalitiri, seen as a dark, impenetrable mass over them, now indistinguishable from the mountain around it. "We go to beard the lion in his den. I'm sure they don't want any part of it. But I wonder how they knew?"

"They are a very superstitious people, these hill-dwellers," said Gita. "They do not like to wander these mountains in the dark. Only tragedy can come of it. When the sun goes down, they light their fires against the night and squat in their home until morning."

The last of the hillpeople were gone now, padding softly away in the twilight. They had gone quietly so as not to arouse the slowly awakening spirits of the hills.

"What do we do now?" wondered Spence out loud. "Any ideas?"

"Yes," said Adjani, "I've been thinking about it all day."

"And?"

"And I think it's time we had a council of war."

CHAPTER TWENTY-SEVEN

THE IDEA was ludicrous. Plain silly, it seemed to Spence. The four of them were going to try to break into the Dream Thief's stronghold bare-handed—with not so much as a bludgeon to swing between them—and what? Reason with him? Talk him into putting aside his evil schemes? This one who, through the mysterious *tanti*, wielded power over men's minds, could direct their very thoughts according to his will—they dared to approach him?

It made no sense. It was not logical. Their chance of success, Spence reckoned, was nil. But what could they do? Something had to be done; someone had to try. It had fallen to these four; there was no one else.

So Spence turned his eyes away from the dark, imposing shape of the palace. "Shall we go over it again? Just to be sure we all know what to do?"

They had been over it several times, but once more would not hurt, and it gave them something to do while they waited for the moon to rise above the rim of hills to the east. Spence could already see a slice of the moon showing; it would not be long now.

"Right," said Adjani. "We all watch each other and go quietly. Spence and I will go first; Gita and Kyr follow. We don't know if the gates are guarded, but it looks pretty quiet from here. We haven't seen anybody moving. Probably they're not expecting anything."

Of course they're expecting us! Spence shouted inwardly. *They know we're here. They've been waiting for this as much as we have!* But he said nothing and nodded as Adjani continued.

"Once we're inside, we try to find Director Zanderson and Ari. Then we look for the machine—Kyr will know what to look for. Okay? Remember, we have the element of surprise on our side. If we aren't seen, we just might pull it off without a hitch."

There was much that was not said. They all knew it, but nodded their agreement just the same. Of the four, only Kyr seemed not to have any reservations about what they were about to attempt.

Adjani looked around him. The moon had risen and was pouring her liquid light all around. The palace, with its leafy camouflage, shone traced in silver. "It's time. Let's go," he said and stepped from their hiding place onto the rocky, overgrown path leading to the gates.

Spence followed him and they crept toward the massive walls, which appeared to grow still more massive and impenetrable as they neared. The waiting had only served to make their task more hopeless in their own eyes, and the Dream Thief more terrible.

It was with an overpowering sense of dread and doom that Spence stole toward the huge wooden gates.

Not a branch moved, not the slightest breath of a breeze ruffled the leaves. The ruin appeared a dead and abandoned relic, a shrine to an earthly deity long departed. Perhaps it was true; perhaps the Dream Thief did not exist after all. Or perhaps he had gone.

Even as he thought these things, Spence knew they were not true. He had been drawn to this place by forces greater than his own volition. Whether by the Dream Thief or some other, it did not matter. He was here. Very well; come what may he would see it through.

"Listen!" whispered Adjani. "What's that?"

Spence had been so self-absorbed he had not noticed any sound at all. "I don't—"

"Shh! Listen!"

There came a sound like laughter, or singing heard from very far away—as if from a boat far out across the water. The sound came to them and then drifted away, just the barest hint of tinkling voices; almost nothing at all. Then all was silent again.

Adjani and Spence looked at each other, shrugged and continued toward the gates.

Spence could now see the individual beams that made up the gates. He could see the great iron bands which bound them. The dark walls arching over them rose higher and, though smooth, Spence saw where a person might find adequate hand and foothold for climbing.

They had almost reached the entrance when there came a scratching noise from behind the gates, and suddenly this gave way to a great creaking groan as the huge gates swung open.

Spence froze in his tracks. Adjani crouched down. There was a buzzing sound in the air above them that made Spence's stomach tighten and his heart leap. It was a now-familiar sound, and one that filled him with despair.

Then he saw them: three pair of luminous green eyes just inside the gates. Three more dark shades passed just overhead. He glanced around to see the forms of three naga demons touching lightly down behind them.

Then all the creatures began advancing at once, drawing the circle tighter around them. Spence and Adjani stepped close together. The creatures inside the gates moved into the moonlight and Spence saw that the one in the center carried a large silver orb—the same object he had seen before, that had stunned the dogs, and later had knocked out Kyr.

The malevolent creatures came closer. Spence looked back and saw that Kyr and Gita had not moved from their hiding place. The creatures appeared unaware of their presence; perhaps Kyr and Gita would remain unnoticed and could help them in some way.

The beings came nearer, surrounding them completely now. There was nowhere to run, and running was ineffective anyhow—one blast from the silver orb and it was all over. Spence felt waves of helplessness and horror rise in him and subside. The creatures were within a few paces, ringing them in completely.

Spence looked into their glowing green eyes. Thoughts came into his head, thoughts which he knew were not his own. Inner voices spoke to him. *Come with us,* they said. *You will not be harmed. Come.*

Spence raised clenched fists to his head as if to drive the alien thoughts out. *No!* he shouted inside. *I will not!*

But his feet were already moving toward the gate—the demons were taking them inside. He opened his mouth to speak, but could not make his tongue move. He stared around in mute terror. *God, help us! Save us!*

They shuffled past the opened gates and under the arch. Spence felt some will other than his own directing his steps now. And though he fought it, still he moved on. He was powerless to stop himself from doing what he did not want to do. He was under complete domination to a force greater than the force of his own will.

Then, once again, from out of nowhere the sound of singing reached his ears: closer this time and more distinct. But it was not singing, it was the sound of many voices, excited voices, clamoring all at once, coming closer.

The force that grasped him slackened and he turned to glance behind him. A long line of bright lights were swinging through the night toward them. For a moment he could not think what they were, but the voices came from these lights that floated swiftly nearer.

Torches! He grabbed Adjani by the arm and swung him around, pointing to where the torches massed together at the head and trailed off in single file behind. All at once it hit him. He found his voice in the same instant. "The villagers!"

The naga demons hesitated momentarily. Spence felt their hold on him withdraw as their attention shifted to this new development. The creature with the orb stepped forward, his wings half-fanned out from his repulsive body. He raised the orb just as the first of the torchbearers came running up.

Spence saw their faces in the light; the blades of makeshift weapons flashed in their hands—hoes and machetes and other implements. They rushed forward toward the creatures and then halted in confusion as the demon with the orb scuttled forward and raised the object over his head.

Spence threw himself headlong at the creature and knocked the sphere away. He landed with a thump that knocked the air from his lungs and saw the silver object roll to the side.

There was a great cry and the peasants came rushing in. He felt icy hands on him and saw two creatures clutching at him, lifting him to carry him off. He yelled and was immediately surrounded by villagers bearing clubs and machetes. Then he was being hauled to his feet and he looked up to see Kyr bending over him.

"I'm all right. I'm fine," he said, standing.

"Come on!" cried Adjani, right behind.

The peasants swarmed around them, pushing through the gates. The night was filled with light and noise—it was like a river flooding into a dry valley. Here and there the current eddied. Spence saw knots of men pummeling the earth; hoes and shovels rose and fell, and he knew that the demons would trouble them no more.

"They came back," he said in disbelief.

"They came back, indeed!" shouted Gita. His round face split into a wide grin. "God be praised! They came back to help us—and also to share in the treasure they believe we will find inside."

"Then I hope they get some!" said Spence. "But right now we'd better find what we're after."

Adjani was already leading them across the ancient courtyard. The echo of excited voices and the reflection of torchlight on stone came back to them from every corner. They ran to the nearest and largest structure and entered through a wide entrance into the main corridor.

The press of bodies carried them along together. The excitement seemed to shoot through them all like sparks. They came to a smaller corridor that opened off the main one. Spence stopped and turned. A single door closed off the further end a few meters away. Spence walked toward the door.

CHAPTER TWENTY-EIGHT

THE SOUNDS of the rout receded in the corridors behind him as the villagers swept on. He heard shouts from other parts of the palace, but here it was dark once more and quiet. He stood looking at the door and knew what awaited him on the other side: the Dream Thief, old Naag Brasputi, the fearful ruler of men's minds.

Spence found it strange that he should feel so calm at this moment; he had no fear, no terror, not even any alarm that he should be so close to the monster's own chamber. It was as if, once resigned to facing the thing before him, it held no more terror for him. Its power over him was broken. And yet he knew that could not be the entire explanation; there had to be something more.

He heard a rustle beside him and someone moved. "Yes, he is here," said Kyr, raising his hands before the door. "I feel his presence . . . " He paused and added, "but the life force is growing weaker."

Spence reached out and pushed the door. It swung open easily and he stepped through the low stone archway and into a large room reeking of incense and hung in a brown cloudy haze. Large stone vases lined the walls of the room and candles burned in clusters all around. At a further end on a stone dais amid a sea of bright-colored cushions slumped the old Martian all alone.

The ancient head came up slowly, feebly. The great yellow eyes opened and regarded them with cool contempt. The wattled throat trembled and the mouth opened. "So, here you are at last, Guardian."

Kyr stepped forward slowly. "Who are you?" He spoke so that Spence could understand him.

"I have worn many names in the time of my life. Which would you like to know? Brasputi—that is how I am known to many. Dream Thief, some call me, I am told. Ortu was my name when I walked

among my own kind." He tilted his head up to regard the imposing
form of Kyr. "It is strange seeing one of my race after so long."

"Ortu," Kyr breathed, his head weaving back and forth. "Why?"

Words unspoken passed between the two aliens. Ortu accepted the
authority of Kyr, for his gaze slid away. He said, "I will tell you." His
eyes closed and his head sank back to his chest and as if in a trance, he
began to speak:

"We sought the far stars and I led many bright ships to homes
under different suns. But always there burned in my mind the beauty of
this world and its people. It seemed to me favored of all the worlds I
had seen. When the *vimana* under my command malfunctioned we
could search no more and I led my colony back here. We came to this
place, then little inhabited. We lived here in peace for many long years,
But we established no colony—the radiation that damaged our *vimana*
also damaged our bodies and we could no longer reproduce our own
kind.

"In time our people died, some through the strange diseases of this
world, some through age, some were killed by the primitive Earthmen
we tried to help. I alone was left of all who had come. And here I
remain."

"You know it is forbidden to interfere with the Earthmen. You,
Ortu, argued it before the Council. You were the one who showed us
the way of courage."

Ortu was silent for a long time. His body trembled and he seemed
to be disintegrating before their eyes. When he spoke again, his voice
had changed, lapsing into the whistling lilt of Martian speech, though
the words were still Earth words. "We were doomed. My colony would
never flourish, never achieve the bright vision I had worked so hard to
make reality. We were *dying . . .* "

Again a long silence. And then his voice came again, still more
strained, with Martian and Earth speech freely mixed together.

"To die unsung by the Sons of Ovs . . . *helith vsi jvan* . . . tried to
help, to teach them, but *renni ospri* . . . so primitive. It took so long, so
long . . . *bvur elchor shri.* I wanted to teach them. I waited years, but
progress was too slow. I burned for them.

"One by one the bright ones died . . . *rsis Atrı, Pulastya, Kratu,
Vasistha, Pulaha, Marici, Angiras . . .*" The words were familiar to
Spence, who remembered that these were the names of the gods of
Indian folklore Adjani's father had told them about. These had been
Ortu's comrades, now long dead, but still remembered and strangely
revered in India's fantastic legends.

As Spence had suspected, the coming of the Martians had given
birth to one of the most widespread. enduring religions of mankind.

Hinduism was founded upon a primitive misunderstanding, a mistake of cosmic proportions.

Spence stared at the ancient Martian as the wavering voice went on.

"The errors, the needless slaughter, the *sengri*. We tried to teach them . . . we loved them, but they would not understand." At this the crinkled eyelids snapped open once more and the yellow eyes glared out defiantly. "Is it any wonder I learned in time to hate them? Their world was perfect, and yet they were bent on destroying it!"

"You had no right!" shouted Spence. Ortu's head swung wobbily toward him.

"*Benasthani risto!* No right? I took it on myself. I had the *kastak*—the power. The only way to keep them from destroying this world and themselves was to bring them under my rule, and for this I have labored centuries of your time." Ortu shrugged and seemed to grow weary of talking. His head fell forward on his sunken chest and he closed his eyes once more.

"I don't believe you," said Spence. He quivered inside with rage at what had been done to him by the twisted and perverted creature before him.

"I had power," muttered Ortu. "With the *tanti* I planted ideas, dreams in men's minds bringing them ever closer to the time when I would reveal myself as their ruler. But it is over now . . ."

The hairless head rolled on the shoulders and the terribly thin, wasted limbs fell feebly aside. The body teetered momentarily and then toppled forward onto the cushions on its side. It jerked once convulsively and then lay still.

"No!" shouted Spence, rushing forward. He wanted to pound the life back into that obscene body and make it talk to him, to tell him why the things he had been made to suffer had been done to him. He felt cheated and used and violated.

"He is dead." Spence felt cool hands on him as he stood seething over the body of the Dream Thief.

"But how?"

"He was very old and sick. The seeds of his destruction were sown long ago. Only the power of the *kastak* kept him alive. Now, he has joined the bright ones. It is over."

"No. It isn't over." Spence looked around the room quickly, coming to himself. "Where's Hocking? We've got to find him before . . ."

Just then they heard a stifled gasp and turned to see a slightly bowed figure standing in the doorway. It was Pundi, the old manservant, with his hand over his mouth, eyes wide with amazement.

Spence went over to him and grabbed him by the arm before he could run away. The servant's face had gone white and he stared at the body of his master laying so still on the cushions.

"Where are the others?"

"Is . . . my master . . . ?" Pundi turned his wide eyes on Spence and Kyr in turn. His expression was one of fear and relief mingled in equal proportions.

"Yes, he is dead," said Spence. "Tell us where the others are. Where's Ari and her father?" he demanded, shaking the servant's arm.

At that moment Adjani and Gita appeared in the doorway. They looked at the body of the dead Martian, and then Adjani announced, "We can't find them—Ari, her father, Hocking. We've been all over this part of the palace."

"Where are they?" Spence shouted at the servant who still gazed at his fallen master. The man mumbled something unintelligible.

"He says that his master's *vimana* has been made ready," replied Gita.

"Quick!" said Spence, pushing the bewildered Pundi before him. "Take us to them! Hurry!"

Kyr stooped over the ancient body of the Dream Thief, folding its limbs and arranging it carefully. "Go," he said. "I will join you."

Spence, Gita, and Adjani left the chamber pushing Pundi ahead of them. As they entered the corridor they heard a low rumble which shook the foundations of the palace to its mountain roots.

"What was that?" exclaimed Spence. He and Adjani looked at each other.

"It sounded like a blast."

"It was the *vimana* of my master, no doubt," said Pundi.

They dashed through the passageway and out into the courtyard. Over stones thick with moss they ran and stopped to stand looking at a brightly blazing orange star that burned up into the heavens, diminishing rapidly.

White smoke still billowed from the ruins of the collapsed central dome, which for centuries had sheltered the vehicle.

"Hocking!" said Spence.

When they burst into the tower keep they found August Zanderson sitting with his head in his hands moaning and whimpering.

"Director, what happened?" said Adjani rushing to his side.

A quick look around the room confirmed Spence's worst fears: Ari was gone. He knew, even before her father told them, that Hocking had taken her with him to make good his escape.

"Where's he taking her?" asked Spence, dark fire flashing from his eyes.

"I can't be sure, but I think he intended to go back to Gotham. He said something about the station being ready to receive them—he had

two others with him. There may have been more." His face, at first
hopeful and expectant, now fell as the impact of what he said hit him
afresh. "She's gone. We can't catch them now—it'll be days before we
can get a shuttle up. Oh," he moaned, running his hand through his
hair. The man was vastly changed since Spence had last seen him. He
looked gaunt and haggard; a straggly, speckled beard of coarse stubble
lined his jaw. His eyes were red-rimmed and deeply pouched.

"We'll catch them," said Spence.

"We'd better hurry," said Adjani. "They have a good head start."

CHAPTER TWENTY-NINE

THEIR PLAN failed miserably. Hocking reached the station
first and was ready for them. A brief scuffle in the docking bay—
resulting in taser darting all around for the would-be rescuers—put a
swift end to the rescue attempt.

Spence came to laying facedown in a cell, groggily shaking off the
effects of the taser dart and wondering what had happened. They had
counted on Director Zanderson's sudden forceful appearance to throw
the mutineers into panic, thereby giving them time to marshall the help
they needed from Gotham's alarmed populace.

But they never had a chance to sound the alarm. Chief Ramm and
his men had been waiting for them the moment they stepped from the
craft. It was all masterfully calculated.

Looking at it now Spence wondered why they had thought it could
have turned out any differently. They acted foolishly and had been
easily outsmarted by Hocking. How could it have been otherwise?
Their every move had been foreseen.

Now he was alone in a cell in the security section, feeling as if
someone had clubbed him and then used him for a pidg bird. He felt
weak and mushy inside, his limbs trembled with the neurological aftereffects of the taser jolt, his mouth tasted of blood, and his nose
throbbed from taking the full force of his headfirst dive into the floorplates when the dart hit him.

With a groan he rolled into a sitting position and saw a small pud-
dle of dried blood where his face had pressed against the floor. He
hesitantly touched a finger to his nose and found it painfully swollen,
but probably not broken. It had bled freely all over his jumpsuit.

On hands and knees he dragged himself to the small vestibule set in the wall. He ran water in the tiny sink and splashed it on his face, washing the blood from his cheek and neck. He rinsed out his mouth, spit, and then glanced at himself in the mirror.

The forlorn image he saw staring back at him did not greatly cheer him. Nor did his prospects for the immediate future.

What would they do with him? And the others? Then he remembered Ari. Hot black rage flowed up like molten lava within him. Where was she? What had they done to her?

His rage burned out in futile ravings and exhausted itself in hurling him against the clear plastic door to his cell. He slid once more to the floor to sit with his back against the door, panting, crying tears of anger and frustration, grinding his fists against the floor.

The wave of temper left him and he lay dejectedly against the door. It was then that he smelled something burning.

The smell of melting plastic filled the cell within seconds, throwing him into a fit of coughing. He lay down on the floor to keep from suffocating on the fumes. Smoke from a spot in the center of the floor began to rise, forming a thick black cloud on the ceiling of the cell. He watched the column of smoke, fascinated and appalled at the same time. *What the devil is going on?* he wondered.

He did not have long to find out.

There appeared in the center of the cell first a blackened circle, and then the area dipped and sank as if the floor at that spot was melting—which it was.

Black fumes rose from the floor trailing black, snaky wisps. Spence feared he would be suffocated very soon; the pocket of clear air diminished rapidly as the cloud pressed down from the ceiling.

He waited, holding his breath.

Even as he began choking on the fumes he heard the sound of tearing fabric and then, through the smoke-dark haze, saw a head pop through the hole which had formed in the floor.

The head, wearing goggles and a breathing apparatus, looked around the room and then saw him. A hand appeared and motioned him closer.

Tears streaming down his face, Spence wormed his way over to the edge, squirming on his stomach. The floor beneath him was hot like a griddle.

A mask was thrust into his hand and he blindly fumbled to put it on and drew the oxygen deep into his burning lungs. He was handed a pair of thick gloves and motioned down into the opening in the floor.

With the gloves on he gripped the still-smouldering sides of the aperture and lowered himself through. He felt hands on him, steadying his descent so that he would not touch the hot metal rim of the hole

Once below the floor he cast aside the gloves, tore off the mask, and jumped from the platform that had been erected directly beneath his cell.

"Packer! What are you doing here?"

"We must apologize for not meeting you at the gate earlier." A thickly-Russian accented voice sounded behind him. "We were unavoidably detained."

"Kalnikov! You, too?"

"Are you all right, Reston?" Packer, his mask dangling from his neck, pounded him on the back. "It sure is good to see you."

"I didn't expect this, I—"

"Don't thank us yet. We're not out of the woods by a long shot."

"Where are the others?"

Kalnikov raised his eyes and pointed upward.

"Still captive?"

"We're working on getting them out now. We've been very busy these last few hours. I'll have to tell you all about it—"

"Some other time," said Kalnikov. "Please, comrades. We must get away from here at once."

With that the Russian stooped and lifted a bulky cylindrical apparatus to which was attached hoses and a sharp nozzle. "This is our latest invention. No space station should be without one."

"I'm convinced," remarked Spence. They all hurried off along the maintenance catwalk crowded with conduits and pipes and vents of various sizes.

"What's below all this?" asked Spence.

"Commissary kitchens," replied Packer.

"Where are we going?"

"You'll see."

They walked until they came to a ragged-edged opening that had been cut in a huge conduit. "This is our golden highway," said Packer. "It's a vent shaft that runs the whole circumference. We've had to make a few alterations in design, but it serves its purpose."

They stepped inside where a small electric maintenance cart was waiting for them. "Kalnikov will take you to command central. I'll wait here for the others. They should be coming along any time now. I want to make sure nothing goes wrong."

Spence got in the cart and they were off; the single headlight threw its beam into the darkness of the round, seamless tunnel. After a journey which he guessed was at least a quarter of the way around the station they halted and got out and went into another tube with a ladder inside it. They climbed down the ladder to the next level and continued their way, finally arriving at a tiny room littered with tools and materials and scattered pieces of various machines.

"What happened here? Explosion in the spare parts bin?"

"We have not, for obvious reasons, been able to call housekeeping to properly furnish our little nest. We thought you would desire freedom over pleasant surroundings."

"I'm not complaining, believe me. It looks great. Small, but great."

"We thought you'd like it."

"What happens now?"

"That we will have to see about. Our first objective was to get you prisoners free. Nothing has been decided beyond that."

"Have they taken over then?"

"No—not yet. Not officially, anyway. There has been no announcement, no overt actions. For most citizens everything continues as normal."

"Most?"

Kalnikov smiled proudly. "There is a small but efficient cadre of enlightened individuals." He favored Spence with one of his bone-rattling back slaps. "Welcome to the underground, Dr. Reston!"

Within the hour the little room under the docking bay was crowded with people talking excitedly and loudly.

Adjani had joined them first, followed by Gita and Director Zanderson. "Where's Kyr?" Spence asked. The cadets who had brought the last of the prisoners just shook their heads.

"You got someone else with you?" asked Packer.

"Yes," said Spence. "A . . . uh, friend."

Packer regarded Spence suspiciously, but did not press for details. "Then they've taken him somewhere else." He turned to his cadets. "All right, you shuttle jumpers, clear out. Keep your eyes open and watch your exits, and scramble your trail. We can't be too careful. Now get going; I'll be in contact as soon as we figure out what to do next."

The cadets, grinning with high spirits at the adventure they were on, left silently and swiftly. "Now then," said Kalnikov. "To business."

"Right," agreed Packer, looking at Spence and Adjani. "But first I think you two have some explaining to do."

They all sat down at a conference table that had been hastily set up in the cramped service area. Kalnikov took the head chair and Packer sat at his right hand. Spence, Adjani, Gita, and Zanderson filled in around the table. Director Zanderson, when an offer was made to allow him to resume command of the station, replied, "As long as those maniacs are in power, I have nothing to control. I'm not a guerrilla fighter, gentlemen. Please, let's not stand on false ceremony. You, Kalnikov and Packer, are in charge—we'll keep it that way."

"We accept your recommendation, Director," said Kalnikov.

"Now I would like one of you to tell us exactly what we're up against. We have been working at somewhat of a disadvantage up to now."

All eyes turned toward Spence and Adjani, and they began to relate all they knew of the Dream Thief and his plans of world domination. The others sat spellbound as the incredible tale unfolded.

". . . Dream Thief is dead," Spence concluded. "We saw him die. Apparently, Hocking has usurped power from his master and is now bent on carrying out his own schemes here aboard the station."

"That makes sense," agreed Kalnikov at length. "We suspected the rebels on Gotham were receiving orders from someone on Earth. We had no idea who it was. Who is this Hocking?"

"A madman."

"And a twisted genius," added Adjani. "He will stop at nothing to achieve his aims, and he has in his possession a machine to make those aims a reality."

"What sort of machine?" asked Packer.

"It's called a *tanti*. Most simply described, it is a consciousness-altering device once used in psychiatric medicine," explained Spence. To Packer and Kalnikov he added, "You won't have heard of it. In fact, Adjani and I have never actually seen it, but it exists and it is somewhere here on Gotham."

"And we believe," continued Adjani, "that it has been modified into a machine capable of broadcasting to entire sections of the globe, or to the whole world through the use of satellites. That is why this station is so important to Hocking. It gives him a permanent base of operation beyond reach of the world's powers."

Packer rubbed his chin and frowned. "Granting what you say is true, preposterous as it sounds, what exactly does this machine, this *tanti* thing—what does it do?"

"I suspect," began Spence, choosing his words carefully, "that it interacts in some way with electrical impulses in the brain. It stimulates certain cortical bodies—those normally associated with subconscious activity, for example—and imprints its own predesignated pattern of wave impulses."

"In other words?"

"In other words it shapes thought, induces dreams, manipulates the mind itself."

"Mind control," said Kalnikov.

"Precisely," replied Adjani. "Spence here can vouch for its effectiveness. We almost lost him to it."

The others regarded Spence carefully, as if trying to detect any sudden changes in him. Spence smiled grimly. "On a purely personal basis I can say that the effects are devastating. What will happen when the *tanti* is loosed upon the Earth . . . well, consider a world where half the population is driven to end its insanity in tortured self-destruction and the survivors become mindless drones serving a warped master."

The room was silent. Director Zanderson, his voice steady but tense, spoke next. "It's up to us, gentlemen. Hocking is to be stopped at once and that machine destroyed. Every moment he is allowed to continue his schemes, we are that much closer to universal chaos."

Kalnikov put his hands flat on the table. "The pieces are fitting together, yes? We will now entertain ideas for stopping this monster and his nightmare-making machine." He looked around the table at the tight ring of intense faces. "What are your suggestions, comrades?"

Hours later, the plan that was finally hammered together lacked several key elements toward making it completely foolproof. But whatever it lacked was more than made up in bare-faced audacity.

CHAPTER THIRTY

"WHY WASN'T it ready? I gave orders for everything to be ready on my arrival!" Hocking's pneumochair buzzed ominously across the floor. Ramm, Wermeyer, Tickler, and several others watched him silently, unwilling to upset him further.

"You failed—that is, we failed to anticipate your coming so soon. We were waiting for your signal. We had only a few hours' notice— there wasn't enough time," explained Wermeyer.

Hocking frowned. "My plans were, shall we say, compromised. It won't happen again! But nothing has changed. Get your men on it at once. I want the platform completed and the machine installed and ready for operation as soon as possible. Do you hear?"

"I already have men on it—they should be finished within the hour," said Wermeyer.

"Excellent! And the engines?"

"Ready for testing—also within the hour."

"That's better! See what you can do when you follow instructions and stop whining? Very well, we will begin projection as soon as the *tanti* is calibrated to our new orbit."

There was a slight commotion in the antechamber and one of Ramm's security men came white-faced into the room. He went straight to his chief and handed him a note. Ramm glanced at the note and his hand trembled.

Hocking's eyes narrowed. "What is it?"

"The prisoners—Reston and the others . . ." He looked to Wermeyer for support. "They've escaped."

"You idiots! You bumbling idiots!" Hocking exploded. "I'll have you—"

"We're on their trail now. They will be apprehended," Ramm was quick to add.

Hocking appeared ready to pursue the subject further, but then abruptly changed his mind. He looked at each of his crew in turn as if weighing their fates individually. The others watched and waited nervously, aware that some decision hung in the balance.

"It won't matter," Hocking said finally, so softly that some had trouble hearing. An awkward jerk of the head dismissed them. "You can go now." The floating chair showed its back.

There was the swish of an opening portal and the group filed out. Hocking turned and saw Ramm still standing there. "Well? What is it?"

"I, uh, nothing." His nerve failed him at the last second. "I was just wondering why Reston is so important to you."

Hocking's features tightened in a mocking sneer. "He is *not* important to me!"

"Then why do you want him so bad?" Ramm knew he was on shaky ground. "I mean, why don't you just let me kill him and be done with him once and for all?"

Hocking squirmed in his chair and grimaced. "Oh, I will kill him. Eventually." He went on, speaking more to himself than to Ramm. "But first he must be made to suffer as I have suffered. He must bow to *me!* He must acknowledge my superiority! Yes, yes. He must curse his weakness . . ." He glanced up and shot an angry look to the security chief. "You're dismissed."

Ramm dipped his head and left without another word. Time was running out. The prisoners had to be recaptured. He joined Wermeyer who was waiting for him in the next room.

"Well? What did you expect?"

"I don't know," Ramm said angrily. "What did he mean—'It won't matter'?"

Wermeyer shrugged. "Who can tell? Obviously it isn't important. He's got some scheme, that's all. I suggest you find the prisoners before anything happens."

"Getting worried, Wermeyer?"

"It's *you* I'm worried about. You know how he gets." He jerked his head toward the room they had just left and its occupant within. "I'm beginning to wonder why I ever let you talk me into this."

"You've got the director of this station locked in your cell and you're starting to second-guess your involvement?"

"Had. I *had* the director locked up."

"Just get him back and it'll be smooth sailing from here on, I promise you."

"It seems to me you promise too much." With that Ramm marched off. Wermeyer watched him go and then hurried away to check on the mounting of the *tanti* and the alignment of the newly installed engines; both projects were now in their final stages. Soon the station would be pushed from its orbit to travel wherever they willed. He could not help smiling to himself: everything was going according to plan.

Wearing the green jumpsuits of housekeepers—which Packer's cadets had filched from the laundry—Gotham's loyal defenders stood stiffly, glancing at their digitons and avoiding one another's eyes. "It's almost time," said Packer. "Want to go over it again?"

"No need," replied Zanderson. "We all know what to do." He looked at Spence. "Got the drug?"

"The encephamine is ready." He looked at Kalnikov and Packer and said, "I've made up the three vials. There isn't much, but dropped into the venting system it should be enough to sleep the entire station for two, maybe three minutes. It's potent stuff."

Kalnikov held up his arm. "I'm marking 16:43 . . . ready . . . mark!"

Spence looked at his digiton. "Right." The affirmation was echoed around the circle.

"Well," Packer took a deep breath, "this is it. Let's go."

"God go with us," said Zanderson.

Spence looked at Adjani standing next to him. "Once more into the fray, eh?" Adjani smiled and nodded. He opened his mouth to speak and then hesitated. "What is it? Forget something?"

Adjani's eyes went hard; his features tensed. "Adjani!" Spence touched his shoulder and felt the muscles rigid. His eyes darted to the others—they were stopped in their tracks, too.

Then he heard it, the high-pitched, prickling sound—the sound of his nightmares. His mind squirmed as a curtain of darkness descended around him. "Hocking!" he gasped. "The *tanti!*" He felt his fists ball up and grind themselves into his eyesockets. He screamed, a painful pinched cry issued from his throat, and he slumped to the floor.

A leaf fell, swirling from a great height. It twisted and spun and rode eddies in the air as it slid down and down, spinning and spinnning. Spence watched it with fascination and saw that the leaf was really a face—tissue-thin and nearly transparent, with holes for eyes, nostrils and mouth. It was, in fact, his face.

This thin skin had been torn from him and released, set free on the wind to float where it would. Spence watched it fly, hoping that someone would catch his face and return it to him. He saw a sea of hands spring up, reaching for the tumbling face, waving, straining to snag it.

And then it was in the hands of someone he could not see. The hands held the fluttering object gently and carried it toward him. He could only make out the outstretched hands holding the semitransparent tissue between them. The person with his face stopped in front of him and held it up to him. He took it and put it on.

Instantly he could see more clearly. Before him a beautiful young woman with golden hair and eyes of china blue smiled prettily and said, "That's much better." She held out her arms toward him and he stepped hesitantly toward her. As his arms closed about the girl, she faded from view and he was left standing alone once more.

"Ari!" he shouted. He heard the echo of her laughter receding from him and then silence. "Ari!" He started running toward the place where he last heard the sound.

"I've got to find her," Spence whispered. "I've got to find Ari!" He struggled up groggily, like an exhausted diver spending the last of his strength stroking toward the surface. He could feel the pull of the *tanti*, like the pull of the strong undercurrent on a diver. Part of him longed to give in and let the current take him, to float peacefully into oblivion, into the gentle darkness. *Give in,* the current insinuated. *Don't fight me anymore. Give in.*

"No!" Spence shouted. His voice boomed at him from a distance. "I won't give in!"

Then, like the diver who feels his lungs must burst, but gives one last kick and feels his head break the surface as cold, clean air streams into his burning lungs, Spence with sheer strength of will forced his consciousness to return. Objects around him became clear and distinct once more. His vision sharpened and the awful dizziness left him. He was free.

He stood blinking, not daring to believe, but it was true: he was free. He had moved from the secret hiding place of the underground— that much he knew; he had some vague recollection of having run or walked through endless tunnels. As he looked around him now he saw that he was standing on one of the main axials near a junction tube. All around him lay the motionless bodies of Gotham's inhabitants felled by the first projection from the *tanti*. It was as if some monstrous carnage had taken place and the dead lay sprawled. Eyes staring, unblinking. Unseeing. Unknowing.

The sight sickened him and he turned to run along the axial, dodging the bodies in his path. *Hocking is insane,* Spence thought. *He has turned his terrible machine on the station! But of course that is exactly what he would do—subdue the station first, bring it under his control.* Why hadn't they thought of that? They were too busy worrying about what it would do on Earth to think about what the *tanti* would do to Gotham.

But Spence had survived the first pulse—as he had survived all the others. He wondered if he could resist the next one when it came; and come it would, soon. He had to find Hocking and somehow shut off the machine—before there was no one left to resist.

But *he* was the only one who could resist, the only one who stood between Hocking and his evil ambitions. That realization brought with it a keen vision. His senses sharpened; reality divided and rolled away on either hand. Darkness stood on one side and light on the other. He saw clearly the path before him. He squared his shoulders and put his feet on the path.

Spence arrived at his lab, rapped in his code and the door slid open. He bolted across the threshold. There on the floor before him lay the prostrate form of Kurt Millen. A quick look in the control booth found Tickler asleep in Spence's chair. "The rats always return to the nest," he muttered. He viewed the destruction of his office—files and disks were scattered all over the room. "I wonder what they were doing with all this?"

He reached out and grabbed Tickler's shoulder and gave it a rough shake. "Tickler! Can you hear me? Wake up! Tickler!" Spence frowned; *Hocking didn't even spare his own,* he thought.

A moan passed the man's lips. Spence shook him again. "Where's your boss? Hocking—where is he?"

"Umph . . . " said Tickler.

"Come on, old weasel. Where is Hocking! Tell me and I'll leave you alone."

"Ahhh . . . I . . ." Tickler's head rocked forward on the console.

"Tickler, listen to me!" Spence bent close to the sleeping man's ear. "I am trying to find Hocking. You're the only one who knows where he is—that makes you very important."

"I . . . am . . . important . . . " he muttered.

Spence smiled darkly. "That's right, you are important. Now tell me where he is."

Tickler sighed dreamily. "No . . . one . . . knows . . . "

"If you tell me, I'll make sure everyone knows you were the one who told. You'll be famous."

"Famous . . . important," whispered Tickler.

"Yes, now where is he?" He jostled the man again. *Hurry! Before its too late!* he cried inwardly. Outwardly, he forced himself to remain calm. "You can tell me, Tickler. It's important."

"Hocking . . . " He started, but did not finish.

"Yes! He's hiding. Where?"

"Hiding in the . . . cylinder . . . always in the cylinder."

The cylinder! Where's that? Spence gave his former assistant another jolt. "The cylinder, Tickler—I don't know where it is."

But Tickler did not respond. He was sinking deeper into his mindless sleep. Spence was losing him.

"Where's this cylinder? Tell me now or you'll never be famous!"

"'s in the stars . . . " said Tickler and he sank at once beyond Spence's reach.

"In the stars?" Spence wondered aloud. "I'm no better off than before."

Think, he told himself. *Stay calm and think. Where can you see stars from the station? Any observation bubble, of course. Then that's not it. Where else? Outside, then.*

Spence turned and ran back through the lab with the helpless, hopeless feeling that time was running out.

Ari lay in a deathlike slumber on a low couch. The soft light pooling around her made her already pale features seem still more spectral. He hair lay limp and dull in streaming disarray, falling over the side of the couch almost to the floor.

She did not move when a thin whirring sound, like the buzzing of a mechanical insect, came near her. She did not attend to the voice that addressed her.

"Ariadne," the breathless voice sighed. "Ariadne, my love."

A thin, skeletal hand reached out and touched her cheek, withdrawing from the unnatural chill of that soft flesh as from a prick of a needle.

Then the trembling hand stroked her white throat and lingered over the outline of her breast and came to rest upon her cold hands clasped over her stomach. A jerking finger traced the fine bones of her hand and wrist which showed through the ashen skin.

"Oh, Ariadne . . . " The voice was a quivering sigh that pinched off like a sob. "Soon I will awaken you and we will be together. My lovely, my Ariadne. Soon you will be mine."

The shaking hand moved to stroke her hair, brushing the temples slightly. "I am so sorry, my dear. So sorry. I did not want to harm you. But you will understand—in time you will understand. You will love me as I love you, my pretty. As I love you. In time you will see the vision that I see, you will share my dreams.

"It's all for you that I have done this. Yes, that's it. All for you. For us, my dear. I had to show them. They think they have spoiled my plans. But I will show them all what fools they are. My superior intelligence will shame them. And you will love me, my dear one. Oh yes, you will. You will, you will."

Hocking withdrew his hand and it fell back onto the tray of the pnuemochair. His eyes glittered hard in his skull and he licked his thin lips with the tip of his tongue. He could not bring himself to tear his eyes away from her. It was as if her beauty held him in a trance; it was the flame that had drawn this grotesque creature to her.

In his perverted way, Hocking loved her. The nearness of the young woman during the long sessions in Ortu's palace had gone to his heart. Seeing her fearlessly face her task for the sake of her beloved stirred him strangely, and he began to imagine that it was for him that she sacrificed herself. He imagined also that she had grown to love him as he loved her, though he had never so much as breathed of his feelings for her.

At last he turned away and the chair whisked itself to another part of the room and another couch. He paused here, too, and his glance sharpened once more to his normal arrogance. He began speaking in low, menacing tones.

"You should not have come, alien. There is nothing but death for you. I will destroy you in the end. I must. You cannot be allowed to live on here, and where we are going there is no place for you. But for a little while you are still valuable to me."

The great elongated form lay still.

Hocking turned away from the inert Martian and went back to gazing at his bank of vidscreens which showed various scenes of Gotham's citizenry sleeping between the pulses of the *tanti* projections. "This, my children, is but a taste. Soon you will be completely in my power." He looked at the chronometer, counting down the time to the next pulse. "Very soon."

CHAPTER THIRTY-ONE

SPENCE WALKED to the end of the docking bay to a maintenance platform and then stood poised for a moment before jumping off. He jumped awkwardly, kicking in his minithruster a fraction of a second too late. He failed to escape GM's artifical gravity as gracefully as he had planned. He banged his leg on the edge of the platform as he came back down; then the thruster on his back took over and lifted him away.

Once free he maneuvered himself deftly, turing to draw away from the station backwards. He floated along the surface of the gigantic torus, as the station spun slowly beneath him. Above, some distance away, hung the great circular radio antenna with its long snout. He rose toward it, scanning the station as it passed beneath him.

Spence felt the thrill of space walking, but tried to supress it and center his mind on the more urgent task at hand. Still, he could not help stealing glances at the infinite star-spangled face of the deep and at the quarter-crescent of blue-green Earth rising beyond the further horizon of the station.

A cylinder, he thought. *Where is this cylinder?* He scanned the rotating station for anything that looked even vaguely cylindrical. He punched his thruster and drew further away from GM's horizon. Then he saw it—lit by the brilliant white and yellow work lights of the construction crews. *The new telescope housing. It looks like a cylinder.*

Spence scanned the construction site and saw pieces of long metal girders floating in space, and large duralum sheets in stacks near the central tower. Tiny workmen—in special suits that made them look like miniature spaceships—floated motionless nearby.

Hiding in plain sight, he thought. An image flashed to mind of Hocking, a venemous spider, bloated by hate and an insatiable lust for power, sitting in the darkness of his foul lair, spinning his treacherous webs. The image revolted him. And now he was about to enter that spider's presence.

He flew over the construction site and down to the telescope housing. When he came near enough, he jabbed a button on his forearm panel and the magnets in his boots gripped as his feet touched the metal grid of the trafficway. He tilted forward precariously; he had not judged his angle of descent precisely and his forward momentum carried him past vertical. He fell to his knees and banged his helmet on the trafficway. *Steady now,* he told himself. *Stay calm.* He picked himself up carefully and noticed a magnetic wrench laying on the grid.

He picked up the wrench and moved toward the housing. It was a huge cylinder-shaped appendage rising from its cradle on the surface of the torus. When finished, it would be completely detached to allow full and undisturbed viewing of any point in the heavens. But now it was anchored securely to the station. There was a walkway leading toward it and a light above the entrance.

So this is where you've been hiding all along, he thought. *Well, Hocking—I've found you. Now what?*

He pushed the access plate at the entrance. Nothing happened. He had expected as much, since it was undoubtedly coded and he didn't know the key. But he took the wrench and swung it with as much force as he could into the plate. The mechanism shattered and tiny pieces of plastic flew away in all directions. He smashed the wrench into the circuitry again; there was a bright flash and the portal slid open.

Spence entered the tiny airlock and went on through. He closed the inner door and then tried the outer. To his surprise it closed, and he heard the hiss of air filling the chamber. When the light changed from red to green he took off his helmet and struggled out of his suit.

The inner door slid open automatically and he crossed the small anteroom to the lift tube. He walked forward on wooden legs and stepped in. His stomach tightened and his heart beat fast. He could feel sweat on his back and under his arms. An unsteady finger reached out and touched the lift button.

At the sound of the lift tube sighing up from below, Hocking turned away from the console; an expression of concern flickered across his wasted features. The lift stopped and the panel slid aside and Reston stepped out.

"You!" gasped Hocking. His eyes showed momentary surprise which was covered instantly.

"It's over, Hocking." Spence glared at his enemy steadily. "Your little game is finished."

"Liar!" spat Hocking. "Look for yourself—" He pointed to a bank of vidscreens showing the work of the *tanti*—the whole station was a morgue of still bodies held in suspended animation. The Dream Thief's terrible machine had done its work well.

"Give it up," said Spence.

"Ha!" Hocking whirled back to him. "You have plagued me from the beginning—you and that stubborn will of yours. You may pride yourself on your accomplishment, Reston. You resisted when no one else could—anyone else would have succumbed long ago. But not you."

"You're stalling."

"Silence! Ortu was right about you. You are dangerous. But it's different now. *I* wear the *kastak.*" He nodded slightly and the narrow band gleamed on his forehead. "You see, this time you will not escape."

"Where are they, Hocking? What have you done with Ari and Kyr?"

"You fool!" Hocking drew nearer. "Save your breath; you will need it. I mean to crush you like an insect."

"Where's Ari?" Spence demanded. He noticed Hocking's eyes shift toward a partition across the room. He went to it and pushed it aside. Ari was lying on a cav couch. The sight of her stunned Spence. He turned with fists clenched at his side. "If you've hurt her, so help me—"

"You can do nothing!" Hocking's chair rose higher in the air and came closer. Spence waited, not knowing yet what he would do.

Hocking leered down at him. "I am your master, Reston. Say it."

"Never!"

"Say it!" roared Hocking. His face was now very near Spence's. Spence stared steadily back at his enemy but refused to speak.

"Say it!" cried Hocking and as he did so the *kastak* flashed. There was a cracking sound and a bolt leapt from the pneumochair and struck Spence in the chest.

He felt that jolt pass through him and his whole frame was shaken as by an electrical charge. He flew backwards several meters through the air and landed on his back.

"Now we'll see who has won!" crowed Hocking.

The pneumochair slid closer. Spence, his vision blurred by tears of pain, squirmed and got up on his knees. He braced himself.

Out of the corner of his eyes he saw the flash. Instantaneously the charge struck him again and slammed him to the floor. He rolled to his side and turned his face toward the lift tube, half-expecting to see Adjani dashing to his aid. But on one would come. He was alone.

A sick feeling spread through the pit of his stomach. Spence knew that he was going to die. He heard Hocking's demented laughter pinging around the room's metallic walls. Hocking had conquered after all.

The thought stirred anger in him. *My God!* he thought. *After all I've been through! To die at this madman's hands! God, help me!* He pushed himself up on his limbs and knees.

A third blast jerked his limbs out from under him and his head struck the floor. Fiery yellow balls of pain exploded before his eyes and he saw Hocking's face in them, taunting him, mocking him.

"Say it!" Hocking screamed. "Say it and you will die quickly."

"No!" Spence shouted. He rolled himself up on all fours.

Another bolt hit him and he felt a weakness in his arms and legs. His breathing was becoming labored. The repeated blasts were draining vital energy and clouding his mind with pain. He felt his strength ebbing. *The tanti,* he thought. If he could get to the control and disable it, there might be a chance.

Slowly, straining every nerve and fiber, he rose, placing his hands on his knees. He raised his head and looked at Hocking who bobbed nearer, his face twisted into a grotesque mask of hate.

"You can't kill me, Hocking." The words came slowly and with difficulty. His tomentor loomed nearer. "And you can't make me bow to you."

"No? In a few moments you will beg for death. You *will* acknowledge me!" Hocking tilted his head back and laughed; his head shook wobbily on his thin neck.

Spence heard again the cracking sound and instantly another bolt struck him. It staggered him back a few paces, but he did not go down. Though he might die, he would not allow himself to go down again.

Hocking propelled himself closer, coming in range to deliver the killing blow. The *kastak* shone like a beacon on his head. Spence let him come.

Now he could hear Hocking's breathing. It seemed to fill the whole room. He moved toward the console. The crackling sound was building again. Hocking drew closer. Spence tottered forward slowly with his head down.

Spence did not look at him but continued on.

"Stop!" cried Hocking. "You'll never live to reach those controls."

Just as Hocking closed on him Spence jerked his head up and looked to the side. "Ari!" he cried.

Hocking awkwardly turned his head toward the couch where the young woman lay. She was there, asleep as before; she had not moved.

"You won't—" he began, but was cut off as Spence leaped toward him, snatching at the thin tangle of wires that emerged from the base of his skull. "Ahhk!" he screamed.

Hocking squirmed and the chair dodged to the side. Spence grabbed the wires and hung with all his might.

There was a tremendous snap. Spence's arm was wrenched from his shoulder; he felt it leave the socket.

He looked and saw he held a handful of loose wires.

In the same instant Hocking's chair crashed to the floor and its occupant was tossed out like a rag doll as its circuits sputtered and fused, sending gray smoke and sparks into the air. Hocking rocked on the floor helplessly, emaciated limbs splayed—a pathetic puppet without strings. The *kastak* slipped from his head and rolled across the floor out of reach. He jerked and twitched and then lay still, moaning, eyelids fluttering.

Spence, grasping his arm at the shoulder, stood over the crumpled figure for a moment and then turned away. It was over, but he felt no joy at winning.

He went to Ari's couch. The awful stillness of her body made the breath catch in his throat.

"She is not dead." Spence swiveled to see Kyr standing over Hocking's body behind him. "But this one is." A long hand indicated the skeletal body. A small pool of blood was spreading beneath Hocking's skull. He stopped to pick up the *kastak* at his feet. It still pulsed with its strange power.

"Kyr, you're all right." Spence sank down beside the couch.

The Martian bent his long frame over Ari's bed. He studied her face for a moment and then touched the rim of the *kastak* to her forehead. "You have released me from the hold of that one. I will release her from the sleep of the Dream Thief."

Kyr closed his eyes and a deep thrumming sound filled the room. Spence sensed a warming flow of energy moving around him. It lasted only a moment and then Kyr stopped. There was a long sigh. Kyr removed the band, but Ari's features still bore the deathlike traces of her sleep.

Spence blinked back hot tears. He clutched one of her cold hands to him as his mouth seemed to fill with bitter ashes. "Oh, Ari," he cried. "Ari!"

He felt Kyr's hand on him. "Let your tears be of joy, Earthfriend. The Dream Thief's power is broken."

Spence raised his head slowly, hesitantly, and found himself looking into the loveliest blue eyes he had ever seen.

CHAPTER THIRTY-TWO

THE PARTY bubbled around him like a pot beginning to boil. Spence stood to one side with his arm in a sling, nursing a glass of apricot-colored champagne, watching the bubbles rise and burst as knots of guests crowded this or the other hero and the stories were told and retold to ever-eager listeners. Of all the figures in the drama of the moment only Spence remained aloof and alone, as much by choice as by chance.

The party had been Director Zanderson's idea—a way to reward in part the loyalty of the faithful and to thank his rescuers. After a lavish dinner the long tables had been removed and what the director called an "intimate" reception commenced, which seemed to include the whole of the station's population.

Kyr, of course, was the main attraction. Every eye in the room strayed constantly in his direction. Even Spence found himself from time to time watching the Martian, towering head and shoulders over the throng pressed around him. The room sparkled with energy, as if high-voltage live wires were pumping electricity into the air. Spence could almost guess what the headlines would read like back on Earth.

Kalnikov, sporting a bandaged wrist, and Packer, his left eye blackened by a blow he had received in the tangle with Ramm and his men, wore their wounds like badges of courage as they held forth to a mixed audience of MIRA technicians and third-year men and others of the sort who were mesmerized by the intricacies of the computer-cracking caper. Adjani was besieged by a crowd who hung on his every word and murmured amazement as they plied him with questions concerning the adventure.

Gita, whose natural innocence and charm made him an immediate celebrity among the Gothamites, kept a large coterie of well-wishers laughing with tales of adventures real and imagined, all told in his inimitable fashion.

August Zanderson, in top form, directed what amounted to a roving press conference as he visited each group in turn to extol in ringing platitudes the bravery and fortitude of all concerned.

Spence had heard the stories, too. The quick-thinking Ramm and his men, combing the air shafts, searching out the loyalists' hideout, were hit along with everyone else by the *tanti*'s pulse. Upon recovery they continued the search, stumbling into the hideout, still dazed. Luckily, most of the loyalists had awakened by the time Ramm reached them. A quick combat ensued in which several cadets got darted by sluggish security men, and in which Kalnikov distinguished himself as a pugilist of the first magnitude—laying out Ramm and three of the more obstinate of his men in as many swipes of his great fists. Packer, too, used his fists to good account, and the remaining rebels offered no further resistance.

Dr. Williams, alone and confused, barricaded himself in his office where he was collected in due course, surrendering peacefully in exchange for consideration in the prosecution of his case by GM attorneys.

Zanderson and Gita recaptured AdSec, having little difficulty subduing the sleeping Wermeyer. The director was back at the helm by the time the effects of the *tanti* had worn off—much to the chagrin of his former assistant. The director had then gone on the air, broadcasting over the loudspeaker system of Gotham, to reassure a groggy and bewildered populace. After the initial shock, the space station had slowly gone back to business.

It was all over, but the retelling.

Spence sighed and glanced around. He had not seen Ari but for a brief moment before dinner. He craned his neck, hoping to catch a glimpse of her—last seen, she had been surrounded by a flock of her friends and a gaggle of doe-eyed young functionaries from the AdSec pool.

"Looking for someone?"

"Tell you the truth, I was looking for *you.*" Spence looked into his glass.

"How sweet."

"I . . . uh, guess you're glad to be back . . ." *Imbecile!* he shrieked inwardly. *Tell her!*

Ari smiled, but the light in her eyes dimmed somewhat. "Yes, I am glad to be back. Aren't you?"

"Oh, sure . . . I guess." Spence looked away. How could he tell her all the things he wanted to say? It was not the time or the place—it was all wrong. Something had changed between them and that fact loomed like a dark cloud over both of them. "That's great about your mother."

"Yes, isn't it? The doctors say there's a better-than-even chance she'll get better. Daddy even talked to her this morning. She's certainly undergone a dramatic improvement—almost overnight. I'm so happy. I . . ." She let her voice trail off and then said softly, "Spencer, have I done something to hurt you?"

The question stung him. "No!" He looked up quickly. "What makes you say that?"

She shrugged and tilted her head to one side. "You do—the way you're treating me. Avoiding me all day, and now tonight . . ."

"The way *I'm* treating you—"

"You have to admit you haven't been very friendly since we've been back."

Spence colored and looked away. How could she blame him for the coolness she felt—it was her doing, not his. He struggled for a reply, but was saved by Adjani's sudden appearance.

"There you two are! I was hoping I'd get to see you tonight. I was finally able to break away." He indicated the swarm with his hand. "It's quite a get-together, isn't it?" He noticed the look on Spence's face. "But you don't look like you're enjoying it exactly."

Oblivious to the tender feelings he might have been trampling on, Adjani blundered ahead. "Ari, did Spence tell you his news?"

"No, he hasn't." Her voice was a little stiff.

"Too modest, I guess." Spence wondered himself what it was that Adjani had in mind—there were several things he had been comtemplating but none of them were at all decided.

Adjani finally sensed that he had walked into a touchy situation and endeavored to remove himself forthwith. "Excuse me, I promised Packer a word. I'm sorry I interrupted."

Adjani left and a painful silence descended behind him. Spence felt the urge to walk away, but fought it and stayed, realizing Ari must have felt the same way.

"What are your plans, Spence?"

"I don't know, not really. I only know I can't continue my work here."

That was a surprise. "Oh?" Her face remained calm, apparently unconcerned.

He looked at her, trying desperately to recapture some of the intimacy they had once shared. "It's no use anymore," he said; he might have been pronouncing judgment on the state of their relationship. Her eyes slid away from his. He hurried to correct the impression he had given. "I mean, it doesn't matter anymore. Something changed for me out there, Ari. There's so much to be done . . . I just couldn't be happy in research again. Not after what I've seen."

"Oh."

"You can see that, can't you?"

"I guess so. We've all been through a lot."

Spence shook his head. "I didn't mean it that way. *I've* been changed, Ari." He fumbled for the words. "God called me—for the first time in my life I feel like I've been called to something higher than my own ambitions."

"That's wonderful, Spence." Ari forced a smile. "I mean that. I'm glad for you."

It was all wrong. Nothing was coming out like he hoped it would. The distance between them yawned wider by the second. There seemed to be no way to bridge it.

"What will you do?" Ari's voice was tentative.

Spence shrugged. "I think I should wait for a while before I decide anything."

"I see."

"I can't see getting into anything too hastily."

"Of course."

She was not making it any easier on him. Spence took a deep breath and crashed ahead.

"I thought about going home for a few weeks. I'd like to see my family . . . there's a lot of loose ends I'd like to tie up, a lot of lost time to make up for . . ."

He looked at her and she turned away, but Spence thought her chin quivered and the light glinted liquidly in her eye.

"Actually, I was kind of wondering if you'd go with me."

There, I've said it at last.

She looked back at him and all at once her manner changed. Spence felt a warmth of feeling rush over him.

"Oh, Spence, really?"

"Sure, that is . . . I mean, there are some people I want you to meet. My family." For a moment they stood before one another; Spence felt the room shift slightly and then Ari was in his arms and his face was buried in her hair. The world seemed fresh once more and, peculiarly, lemon-scented.

"Now *that's* more like it!" The reunited couple turned and met Adjani and Kyr gazing at them. "I was wondering how long it would take for you two to get reacquainted," Adjani said.

Spence was aware that every eye in the room was now on him. He did not care.

"Adjani and I have been talking," said Kyr. "There is something I must say to you in the presence of your friends." The Martian drew himself up to make his announcement. "I have decided that it is time to give the gifts of my people to the people of Earth."

"Spence," Adjani chimed in, "he wants you to lead the team that will organize and catalog the treasures of Mars!"

Spence did not respond; he could think of nothing to say.

"Did you hear me? Nothing in the last ten thousand years compares with this!" Adjani quickly perceived the source of Spence's hesitation.

"I know you want to do something about all the disease and poverty—you want to help those people you saw down there. Your eyes were opened to a world you never knew existed, and you have some vague notion of going back with food and bandages. But isn't it possible that God is putting in your hands the means of doing that on a far grander scale than you could ever dream of doing on your own? Think of it! As head of the discovery team you could choose how the gifts of Kyr's people could be best implemented on Earth."

True to his calling, Adjani the Spark Plug had made the connection. It was several moments before Spence could speak. A lump the size of a potato had formed in his throat. He felt Ari slip her arm through his and give it a squeeze.

"It is what I want," said Kyr. "You have proven to me that the men of Earth can be trusted. Ortu's wrongs must be redressed; his actions have left a heavy debt of suffering that must be repaid. It is time to give what has been saved for you. Dal Elna put this into my mind."

"You honor me highly," said Spence. "Of course I will accept. But only under the condition that Adjani shares the responsibility with me and you, Kyr, remain with us to teach us and lend wisdom to our decisions."

The Martian nodded. Adjani, fairly dancing with joy, cried, "Excellent! We will begin at once!"

"Not so fast! You two can begin at once. I have some personal business to attend to first." He looked at Ari. "Don't we?"

Just then Packer and Kalnikov came up with Gita in his blue turban bobbing between them. Director Zanderson followed close behind, beaming like a cherub.

"Gentlemen, and lady," he said formally with a nod and a wink to his daughter. "Dr. Sundar Gita has agreed to remain with us for a while and take a refresher—tuition and instruments courtesy of GM, of course. And who knows, he may get to like it here and stay on. We're bringing up his wife and daughters on the next available shuttle."

"Please, you are too kind. I am, however, much needed at home." He grinned. "Though my wife and children would never let me pass up the opportunity to let them come and see this place. It is a dream come true."

"Welcome aboard!" they all said in unison.

Director Zanderson glanced around the group. "By the way, I want to congratulate . . . That's funny—I could have sworn Spence and Ari were just standing here."

The garden seemed cool after the stuffy warmth of the party. The station was tilted away from the sun and the solar shields were open to the light of a spray of stars. Crickets trilled their evening song among the leaves and a fountain pattered gently nearby. The moist, perfume-laden air lay still and dark. They had exhausted themselves in talking and now Spence and Ari wandered aimlessly in green solitude, their steps lit by small lanterns set in among the foliage along the pathways.

"We'd better be getting back," said Spence after a while. "Before they send out a search party."

"Mmm," sighed Ari, raising her head from where it rested lightly on his shoulder. "I feel as if I'm in a dream. It's a shame it has to end." She turned to face him, looping her arms around his waist.

"It doesn't have to end," he said, pulling her closer to him. "The dream is just beginning."